THE
GOD TATTOO

Also by Tom Lloyd from Gollancz:

The Stormcaller
The Twilight Herald
The Grave Thief
The Ragged Man
The Dusk Watchman

Moon's Artifice

THE
GOD TATTOO

UNTOLD TALES FROM THE TWILIGHT REIGN

Tom Lloyd

Copyright © Tom Lloyd-Williams 2013
All rights reserved

An older version of 'Beast in Velvet' was first published in
the collection *Enchanted Realms II* in 2002.

'Afraid of the Dark' was first published in the e-zine
Twilight Times in 2003.

The right of Tom Lloyd-Williams to be identified as the author
of this work has been asserted by him in accordance with the
Copyright, Designs and Patents Act 1988.

First published in Great Britain in 2013 by Gollancz
An imprint of the Orion Publishing Group
Orion House, 5 Upper St Martin's Lane, London WC2H 9EA
An Hachette UK Company

This edition published in Great Britain in 2014 by Gollancz

1 3 5 7 9 10 8 6 4 2

A CIP catalogue record for this book is available
from the British Library

ISBN 978 0 575 13127 9

Typeset by Input Data Services Ltd, Bridgwater, Somerset

Printed and bound by CPI Group (UK) Ltd, Croydon, CR0 4YY

The Orion Publishing Group's policy is to use papers
that are natural, renewable and recyclable products
and made from wood grown in sustainable forests. The
logging and manufacturing processes are expected to conform
to the environmental regulations of the country of origin.

www.tomlloyd.co.uk
www.orionbooks.co.uk
www.gollancz.co.uk

For Fiona, and Pickle

CONTENTS

INTRODUCTION

The Twilight Reign was never intended to be about one person –
not even a group of people. For better or worse in literary terms,
I didn't just want to do a series that followed Isak's story. He
was the fulcrum about which history turned and changed, but
that would be meaningless without the events themselves taking
centre stage. Stories are about people first and foremost; I've
written that often enough in critiques of manuscripts, yet in part
I've ignored my own advice. The Twilight Reign is about people
and events; each shaped by the other and inextricably bound
together.

   Most of these stories touch upon the plot of the Twilight Reign
and at very least they're part of the world the story exists in,
with many of the characters and locations also appearing in the
novels somewhere. Some are only referred to or had died prior to
events, but when a series is on a scale such as this one there are
countless stories surrounding and leading up to the overarching
plot – I've just picked a few.

   Several, like 'Velere's Fell' or 'A Man from Thistledell', influ-
enced the course of the novels rather than the other way round,
being stories I'd just wanted to get out of my head at the time.
Only later did they reveal themselves as significant to the greater
plot, but that's part of the pleasure to be found in writing a series
like this. Others, like 'A Man Collecting Spirits', were aspects I
wanted to pursue further, and some just happened because my
mind is a rather dark and random place.

   You won't find many major characters from the series here,
but during world-changing events it's not just a few people who're
touched by them so I wanted to show some of the broader picture.

I guess it's no real surprise that before *Stormcaller* had evolved into its final incarnation, three of the longest stories in this collection were already written – despite the longest concerning events at the end of *Ragged Man*. There are at least half-a-dozen ideas that I just can't get right on the page yet, so they haven't made it into the collection. One day I might have the luxury of finishing stories such as 'Dead Man's Gold', or one of the most important to the series; the ill-fated expedition when Morghien met Rojak and Cordein Malich. Until then however they'll just have to exist only in obscure references only I'll be able to spot.

Don't see this collection as required reading for fans of the novels – it isn't. But nor is it, I believe, an attempt to squeeze extra profit out of the world of the Twilight Reign; that would have probably been the prequel trilogy covering the Great War several fans have asked for. Just for the record, it would be quite interesting to see that trilogy, I suppose, but most people know how it ends and several years of my life dedicated to writing something I'd find 'quite interesting' ... well, I doubt I'll ever be convinced.

As it is, this collection shows a flavour of my (Twilight Reign-related) thoughts over the twelve-odd years I've worked on the series. They've always been a part of the story I wanted to tell, but I didn't ever really expect them to see the light of day. Whether or not you've read the series, I hope those thoughts will prove entertaining.

A BEAST IN VELVET

Some men know in their bones what law they serve, what fibre or faith determines their actions. Others are a product of circumstance; hammered into shape by the life they lead or the family they were born to. As a child I was a lawless brat – I've always held it was my profession that moulded me and few would dispute it. As an old man, consigned by a game leg to watching the Land as it passes me by, I realise the truth is more elusive than that. A single moment is sometimes enough to break such bonds.

For those who do not live in this glorious whore of a city, I was a captain in the City Watch of Narkang; that sprawling miasma of humanity forged into a nation by one man's iron will. Over the years of his reign I witnessed a rate of change and growth perhaps unequalled throughout history, moulding the city-state of my birth into the capital of a nation to rival any in the Land.

For a man of the Watch, this meant ancient enemies now lived side by side; gangs of immigrants and locals waging silent wars of conquest and survival. Gold flowed into the city and caught every man, woman and child in its deceitful grasp; birthing a thousand new crimes unheard of when I was a boy.

Without the divine mandates handed to the Seven Tribes we had only ourselves, our faith in our ruler and no more. Our laws were the product of fine minds, not scripture, while the very imposition of the law on Narkang was a yoke the people chafed under.

Growing up in the lawless time before the conquest, I gave myself body and soul to this new order for reasons more than idealism. Narkang had changed. Narkang had become better for all the simmering tensions it contained, far from the city of violence and corruption it had once been. I spent many a faithful year in the service of truth and the law, but then a day came when my world changed – the day I discovered truth was not the holy absolute I had once trusted it to be.

By the time of the following events I had found myself content with life as never before. A wife, two daughters and a son gave me a happy home, while a collection of promotions and unfortunate demotions had seen me to my most comfortable post; fifty officers and a modest diocese under my command. The politics of the city I happily left to those better suited to it, and in turn I was rarely bothered by that treacherous world. It was in this capacity that I awoke one crisp autumn morning, head fogged with wine and wife growling like a she-bear at the exuberant youth who'd barged his way past the maid who answered the kitchen door.

Crimes within my district are normally under my sole authority, but this morning I was dragged from my bed to find my horse already saddled and myself well behind events. An undiplomatic order, relayed verbatim by that dear foolish boy serving as my assistant, told me that my superiors were waiting upon my arrival.

The traders of the Kingsroad all recognised my uneasy style of gallop and called bawdy encouragement as I passed. Arriving at a whorehouse close to the docks it was instantly obvious that something dismal was afoot.

The building was as any other in those days; young, untreated wood made with as much haste as skill. Though newly-built and in the flower of its youth, the building seemed to sag under the weight of its existence and the grime of the area. My men lingered silently outside under an oppressive fog of gloom, as thick in the air as opium-smoke. By contrast my journey had been through that invigorating crispness one only finds in autumn, so their manner was all the more unexpected.

I clattered to a halt and was immediately struck by a sense of guilt at violating the quiet. When Count Antern exited the

4

building to greet me, even he seemed to wince at the sou
his own voice. As adviser to the king and member of the
Council, Antern was far my superior, but one I had met frequently in the course of city business. The Commander of the
Watch reported to him in effect so Antern's presence at the
scene of a crime was an ill omen, one compounded by the silk
handkerchief he held to his mouth and the grip he had on his
rapier hilt.

My relationship with the count was reserved. He had the atti-
tudes and ideals that came with a long pedigree, but an intelligence worthy of respect. For his part I was a commoner no
different in status to his manservant. To his credit Antern didn't
dismiss me as worthless or a fool as many of his peers did, but
we would never be friends and it was a fact neither of us needed
to acknowledge.

Today he was as affected by the atmosphere of this place as
the rest. He gave me only a distracted nod before gesturing me
inside. A yellow lace curtain that bore the establishment's ill-
reputed name hung over the door. I pushed it aside and entered
an opulent common room of lounging chairs and sofas surrounded by brightly coloured drapes. On the walls was a host of
paintings. In the light of day and this strange mood, the images
looked ridiculous and grossly crude.

The corrupting stench of opium rushed up to greet me, laced
with the scents of fire-spices and rich tobacco. Two young ladies
sat weeping gently with my sergeant looming over them. His
expression was grave and he stood so close I wondered for a
moment whether the girls were suspects or in need of protection.
Both were wrapped in yellow shawls patterned by songbirds –
the mark of the house – but aside from those they wore only
plain shifts. Without the powder and paint of their trade I was
struck by their plain and childlike faces. My daughter was older
than both and the thought of her working in such a place sent a
cold chill through me.

I caught my sergeant's eye, but that place had even got to my
grizzled deputy. He kept his silence as I was ushered up a thin
stairway off to the left.

'Word is out about this already,' commented the count wearily.

'Only the two who found them are still here, the others ran for the nearest tavern.'

'Just what has happened?'

Trepidation had banished the last vestiges of sleep's peace and I turned to look Antern in the face. He waved me on, nudging my elbow to direct me up the stairs.

'Best you see yourself.'

The closest to a warning of what awaited me was a puddle of vomit just outside the doorway to the highest room. When I raised an eyebrow at Antern I saw no trace of embarrassment on his ashen face, he merely indicated that I enter.

When I had finished bringing up my hurried breakfast, my sergeant appeared at the top of the stair. For a man who had fought on a score of battlefields, even he was reticent about re-entering that room. I shall refrain from describing it. Suffice to say that when the door had been broken down, it was clear that no simple drunk did this. I could hardly believe any man capable of such a thing.

'Do you recognise those symbols on the wall?' The count spoke to me through his handkerchief and I quickly followed his example. The stench of torn bowels was nearly overwhelming.

On the wall above the bed was some semblance of writing and a variety of arcane shapes, bloody lines painted in haste. Not anything a simple thief-taker could understand, but I noted them down all the same. The script had an arcane styling, grouped into four distinct sections and centred about a cross within a circle.

I stepped closer, observing that the centre symbol had not merely been painted on as the rest appeared. The killer had employed some sharp tool to scratch lines into the wood, numerous short straight cuts that combined to form the whole symbol. This design had then been carefully smeared with the life-blood of these fallen women. The implement had cut deep into the wood, but left a wide path. I compared it to the edge of my dagger. No knife produced such a mark.

'Three glasses.'

My sergeant indicated the table below the window with the stump of his left wrist. His practised eye drank in each inconsequential detail as he moved about the room, careful not to disturb anything. He paused over a platter of food and inspected it carefully before crouching to inspect the large stain on the rug below.

'This ain't blood here – it's wine,' he said, sniffing the dried red mark.

'But that is,' I replied, pointing to the congealed mess in one of the glasses.

'So we have a murderer who threw away his wine to fill the glass with blood. A person who tore these girls apart and left with the door secured from the inside. Damn.'

I opened the window. There was blood on the outside too, smeared above the lintel and towards the roof. It wasn't a climb I'd have liked to attempt.

The room was a scene beyond anything I had ever imagined. Scarred into my memory, the horror was to plague me in the dark corners of night for years to come. The week that followed the discovery was spent in a tiring and thankless hunt for clues or witnesses – to the profit only of stern notes from my commander and the City Council. Meanwhile terror had gripped my ward and a name haunted the streets as it did my dreams.

Vampire.

Sunset on the following Prayerday found me on the balcony of the watch-house. Beside me stood my assistant, the innocent fourth son of a suzerain who was to be groomed for the office of Commander of the Watch. Brandt was good company for a man prone to melancholy. A light-hearted and spirited youth, he had served me well for two seasons by then and remained undaunted by the horror of the monster we sought. At the tender age of fourteen winters Brandt still had a lot to learn, but already had developed the unswerving loyalty that made many love him. It is a cruel irony that this devotion to duty would be the very reason he died, when over the years he had become one of the finest young men I had ever known.

My heart broke as I heard of his foolish bravery on the walls of the White Palace. So many times I had told the eager youth to leave battle to his soldier brothers, but he had stood back to back with the Lord Isak against that final ferocious breach. It is said he saved the entire city that day; certainly the king himself gave thanks at Brandt's funeral and his ashes still occupy pride of place at the temple of Nartis. His heroism, and I call it nothing less, was the inspiration of my greatest fury; the democratic decision of Brandt's watchmen to seek glory with their king on the field at Moorview. Perhaps his example went even further than that. They also suffered terrible injury, but emerged in glory.

At the time, slate roofs were still infrequent in this burgeoning part of the city. Though Narkang is now famed for its purple slate, it was predominately thatch that bore a gilt edge for those precious minutes before the ghost hour. Wrapped warm against the breeze, we could see much of this side of the city and almost the entirety of our district. What we thought we might see amid the gloaming I am unsure, but there Brandt and I stood – waiting for our questions to be answered.

From that balcony I could smell the sea's salt and spices roasting in the market. I stood with my elbows upon the wooden rail, staring out into the reddening sky while Brandt rested his chin and scrutinised those below. He was a fine mimic and constantly studied the manners of others, taking great pleasure from his unseen vantage even as the shadows obscured his view. When the whistles started to call a second act of tragedy, he and I were among the first to hear the piercing calls of my officers.

'Do you think it's happened again?' he asked me, a tremor of anxiety in his young voice.

The calls were clipped and repeated – a crime discovered and help required rather than officer in danger. The difference between the two was speed. The latter brought your comrades riding as though the creatures of the Dark Place were close behind, while in the second they would canter, eyes scanning for anyone hurrying away.

'Gods, I hope not,' murmured I, with a thought to going home. The scents on the breeze had reminded me of the dinner that would welcome me there.

'If it has, what will you say to the commander?'

'What I said last time, I suppose. I'm a thief-taker. Not a priest, not a mage, not a soldier. I understand the minds of men. Who can say how a monster thinks?'

Brandt strained his eyes in the fading light to place where he thought the choir of whistles was coming from.

'It is rather close to the whorehouse,' he ventured.

'Sure?' I asked, a cloak of doom settling about my shoulders.

The boy turned his hazel eyes up to meet my gaze and nodded. 'It's close.' His ears were sharper than my own and the evening was clear. 'Nearer to us I'd guess, but close.'

With a sigh I returned to the cramped corner that served as my office, retrieving my sword, cloak and gloves before descending to the stable.

'Well, Captain, what do you make of that?'

I looked at my trusted sergeant, a gruff war veteran not much prone to displays of emotion. Now his face was thunderous, his one great fist clenched so tight the effort caused his whole body to tremble. When I peered into the room my sentiments echoed his.

'I don't think I'll be wanting my supper no more. Gods, what a mess. If it weren't for the symbols I'd say this was a whole new problem.'

The room was a ruin. What had probably been a family meal was now utter devastation. Whatever had been in here had torn the furniture apart in addition to, what according to the neighbours, had once been a family of four. Those same neighbours had refused to investigate the tumult emanating from these rooms, the top floor of a building that contained three other families.

Such was the thrall fear and rumour had over the district, they had barred the doors and sat in prayer through the chaos. This had happened late at night, yet none had dared investigate and only much later gone to fetch the Watch. No doubt donations to the temples would again rise once word got out, something that was likely to be soon with the crowd gathering.

'Tell me what happened,' called Count Antern, as his

bodyguards battered a path for himself and another man I didn't recognise.

I was unsurprised to see Antern there so soon, he was said to be the king's spy master after all. No doubt half the guard were in his pay. With a glance at his companion – a slender individual wearing expensively tailored clothes and an eye-patch, the shadow of his wide-brimmed hat extending down to the small point of a beard common among the city's duellists – I began to tell what I knew.

'A family now. The same creature, I assume. More of those symbols, but this time it looks like a bear went berserk in there. Only clue's a scrap of velvet snagged on a chair. You had word of those symbols yet?'

Antern had promised to enlist one of the king's wizards to decipher the bloody writing, but no word had been forthcoming, much to my annoyance.

'A bear you say?' purred the other man, cutting Antern's attempted reply short. 'I've never seen one that could write before, might be a valuable creature. Still, I suppose that explains why it's able to dress in velvet.'

My temper almost got the better of me, but Antern came to my rescue and got there first.

'This is, ah, Nimer. A man of special qualities, the king feels. He is here to assist the investigation – you will extend him every courtesy.'

Only then did I notice the golden clasp that held Nimer's cloak and marked him as a servant of the king. Unassuming in size, but a contrast against the black silk and velvet of his doublet, the bee device was the personal emblem of the king. It declared him as a bad focus for my ire for only clerks of the council and King's Men wore the bee emblem.

From the way his hand lounged on the hilt of his longsword, I could tell which Nimer was. Clerks tended to do little that endangered their eyes, while King's Men were not expected to grow old, let alone emerge from their service unscathed.

'Very well,' was the best reply I could muster.

'Now then, Captain, what is your best guess?' Nimer asked in a clear, aristocratic tone. He was perhaps not quite as young as I had first thought, the small beard and clipped moustache belonging to a younger generation, but still I felt old by the way he looked at me.

'With the last one, a vampire. With the two sets of symbols, a sacrifice for summoning daemons. With the mess and noise he made here, no fucking idea. I don't think the symbols are even the same, 'cept for that cross in the centre.'

Nimer gave a strange little smile and tapped his cheek with one finger in exaggerated thought. After a few seconds he looked up and stepped through the wrecked doorway, into the despoiled kitchen. Curiosity was all I saw on his face at a scene army veterans found sickening. I tried not to wonder what were these 'special qualities' Antern had spoken of.

'Interestingly enough I'm informed the symbols are most commonly used in the banishing of daemons, not summoning as you had quite logically surmised. As for the cross, it looks to be an elven core rune.'

'Meaning?'

He looked up at me with the look a spider might give to a fly that had spoken out of turn.

'Runic systems are not my forte, but leave the matter with me. If it proves to be important I shall rush to inform you. Now, don't let us keep you from your duties.'

And that was my first meeting with the man called Nimer. A man with special qualities. A man who had answers to the strangest questions, and asked even stranger ones. A man whose mind seemed to be able to shrug off all concerns and mould itself to any bent or problem he required at the time.

I have no doubt that in another life Nimer could have been an actor without peer, but his stage was a greater one. I saw him most days after that, we even ate together once or twice. I found myself truly liking the man – for all that not once did I come close to understanding his brilliantly reflective mind. Some days he deferred to me and acted as my young assistant would, on others he adopted a regal authority that I obeyed without thought. The only consistent feature of the man was the remarkable colour of his one good eye, a pale blue glow that both bewitched and chilled.

One conversation we had during that time remains perfectly clear in my mind. Nimer had arrived at the watch-house one afternoon about a week after our first meeting. He claimed to have been just passing and called in to collect a copy of a statement. Having secured the papers he required, Nimer looked me straight in the eye and asked a most curious question.

'When I was younger I knew a man who claimed to be a native of no single place. Having lived in this city from an early age, he nevertheless claimed lineage from four separate states, and called each one home. When I asked him why, do you know what he said?'

I could think of no suitable answer and merely stared in puzzlement. Nimer's face blossomed to life for a moment and he gave me an affectionate pat on the shoulder before turning to leave. As he approached the door, his cool mocking voice called out.

'He said, that way, no matter how successful he was in life, he would always have a cause to fight for.'

That was not the only time he bemused me, nor the only time I suspected I did not understand the full implication of his words, but it stayed in my memory as my lasting impression. That was Nimer's way; to bewilder and puzzle those about him, and keep any answers he might have close, but always it was clear that he would have not bothered to perplex someone he lacked respect for. In themselves, I saw his games of condescension as a mark of respect and felt glad he was not my enemy.

The fact that he was a well travelled, highly educated Narkang native – possessing a face I didn't recognise despite glimpses of the familiar – deepened my suspicions that he was an assassin of the king's, perhaps separate even from his elite agents, the Brotherhood. A killer of breeding who possessed a ruthlessness none of the vermin on my streets could hope to match. It was an aspect I could never quite reconcile with the countenance he shrouded himself in, but I think I could have been a friend to the man I got to know over that time.

Over the next few weeks, two more attacks occurred; connected to the others by a variety of strange symbols, scripts and the rune. Nimer spoke sparingly of them, his one eye glittering to tell me he withheld as much as he was revealed. Instead he would expound upon irrelevant points of scholarly antiquity. He was well aware such tomes of research were not available to me and took some obscure amusement in the fact.

I say obscure because he held no notions of class that I ever heard, only those of intellect. While I could not match him there either, Nimer still gave a measure of respect for what I did possess. I did my best to ignore those clues that were beyond my scope and hoped ultimately they would prove unimportant. My belief was that if I caught this fiend, evidence would probably be either in abundance, or unnecessary.

With ten bodies on our consciences we had come no closer to stopping the horror, and the pressure was mounting on all sides. Panic reigned on our streets and riots brewed, with vigilantes already responsible for the deaths of four more men. There was also the more subtle anger over our failures, in the eyes of my friends and family as well as city officials, although of course Nimer exhibited no sign of the weight I felt bearing down. To add to our problems the last two victims were a scion of some eastern suzerainty and the son of a marshal. Obviously they had been seeking the glory of catching whatever beast we hunted, but they had instead been deprived of their heads.

Powerful families now bayed for blood with the commoners, only louder and with pointed words. Count Antern had taken it upon himself to berate me daily for our lack of progress in the name of the king, but in Nimer's company he was far more restrained – a disquieting observation considering Antern's position in the government.

The royal assassin, as I now termed him privately, had advanced a theory that for the latest two attacks, the third being the slaying of two beggars in the next district, the symbols and invocations were growing more extreme. His reasons for this were either continued failure, or a ritual to culminate later. Neither theory gave us much cheer but we had very little else.

Nimer's time with a prominent mage had proved as equally fruitful as my own surveillance and draconian hours for my officers. The rituals were impossible to decipher. 'A mess of complexity' was how the mage had described them. The consensus among his select colleagues was that an ancient and forbidden text was involved, one beyond their experience.

As for my efforts: glory hunters, the morbidly curious and a variety of religious fanatics had actually swelled the numbers walking the streets of my district. How to watch for suspicious behaviour in that collection? They suspected each other and fought, incited mobs and, on two occasions, managed to fall from rooftop vantages. Blood ran freely across the city and the frenzy of fear continued to build – while through it all, Nimer sauntered with a cold, distant interest and my officers feared to tread.

The first snows of the season arrived after another ineffective week, to find me again on the watch-house balcony, staring out over the city in late afternoon and praying for a clue. In truth I knew I was praying for another death. That tells a sad tale of desperation, but desperate we certainly were.

As I watched the soft flakes drifting slowly past my face, the morbid depths of my soul tried to see how many of the murder sites were visible from where I stood. From my high vantage I easily picked out the sharp peak of the whorehouse, and the chimney marking where that poor tailor's family had been butchered. The other two were hidden from my sight; resting on a lower plane and hidden by buildings since they had occurred in alleys that faced away from my chilly sight.

It was an almost casual observance that reminded me both the first two scenes bore windows that looked in that same opposite direction. A cold prickle of realisation and dread accompanied the thought. For a moment I felt light-headed, as though the breeze had swept up my soul and lifted it into the air before I grasped the rail and steadied myself. Still my knees trembled as I pictured what type of man would have an opposite view to myself.

In the distance I could see only one building of sufficient elevation; one point to see each and every mark that featured on my map downstairs. I knew there could be no coincidence – whatever skill or instinct had earned me my position over men of family connections, it strained at the bit now. I was in a saddle within twenty seconds, bellowing incoherent orders to a bewildered sergeant and galloping off so fast they had neither a clue where I was headed, nor the time to pursue.

I reached the city offices in record time, knowing I would feel the full fury from the Watch's master of horse, but determined to retain the frame of mind that had produced my revelation. The building then housed all of the administration needed to run the city and support the Public Assembly, which presided from the famous domed chamber at the heart of this place.

Of all the city's high officials, only the Commander of the Watch was not based there and the bustle and swarm around the wide stone stairway was typically chaotic. A statue of our king wearing armour and a flamboyant hat, atop a rearing war-horse, stood at the centre of the courtyard, the few yards surrounding that bronze sculpture the only part of this gravel arena that was deserted. Coaches stood on hand for the important people, an odd assortment of citizens scuttled around in all directions and I added to the problem by walking up to the huge stone stairway with my head nearly turned around on my shoulders.

Uncaring of who I collided with I barged my way up, head craned to look out at my city over the courtyard wall and unheeding of cries and curses flying my way. To my intense irritation I found my view blocked by the pocked face of a soldier of the Kingsguard at the summit of these steps, who earned a tap around the cheek for his impertinence.

In the ensuing struggle with a pair of guards who had no better way to fill their day's duty, it was none other than Nimer who pulled them off me, his bee device sufficient to halt their interest in damaging me further.

'I hope you hold greater respect among your own men,' he declared with a thin laugh. 'And what brings you here? Have you any news?'

I looked deep into that inscrutable gaze for a moment while I regained my breath and was struck by a most disagreeable, but palpable, sense of suspicion.

'Ah, no. It was another matter. I've been neglecting my other duties and found a task I'd forgotten, so I wasn't in the mood for bored guards.'

Nimer, as I have already mentioned, was master of his own demeanour, but I hope it is not mere vanity when I say he accepted my words with no further question.

'Can I offer you a drink before you go about business?' he asked, guiding me inside to the high corridor that ran down the side of this whole building.

To my left was the city, visible through a row of eight immense windows. The lead lining of the panes was inlaid with gold leaf so that, as one looked out, the view was framed in rich border. To the right was a blank wall of the great chamber covered with enormous tapestries. I felt unaccountably revolted by the opulence of the place all of a sudden and turned to the view instead. Hands on the sill, I looked out to where I could just make out the tower of my guardhouse in the distance.

'This is where you work?'

'On occasion. I have an office down this hall,' Nimer said, joining me at the window.

'Do you still notice the view these days?'

I gestured towards the scene framed in gold. My hand was trembling at that point so I ended up pointing more with a fist than a finger as I strove to control my emotions. Without making it obvious I raised myself up a little on my toes, to better appreciate the view of a man one or two inches taller than I.

Nimer frowned. 'What a curious question.'

'But do you?'

'I suppose not,' he said with a shrug, 'when one is accustomed to the sight there is little need to take in the panorama daily. Are you sure you're all right? Your colour's decidedly odd all of a sudden.'

'Oh yes, just tired. I can see the watch-house from here – all I can think about is crawling under my desk to sleep for the rest of the shift. How about you? Now that you're looking, what draws your eye?'

The cold blue of his eye seemed to glitter in the light. It reminded me of when he had mimicked my voice and manner for the benefit of my men, but now bereft of humour. Another wave of nausea gripped me, but I was too far gone to stop now and forced myself to look him straight in the eye.

'Well, let me see,' he said, peering past me through the increasing gloom of dusk. 'Ah yes, the tavern on the far side of the Queen's Square. If I could choose I'd soon find myself there with a jug of wine and a girl. Unfortunately, my working day appears to only be beginning. We're due for another unfortunate occurrence, likely you'll be sending for me later unless some humble watchman gets lucky.'

I took one further look at the city and affected a weary nod to the prospect before turning back to face the King's Man. That drink sounded decidedly less attractive in his company, no matter that I could almost taste the brandy he usually carried in a hip flask. I muttered some excuse about waiting outside for the Commander of the Watch and he made no question of it, also eager to be elsewhere.

My legs carried me back to the guardhouse in a dazed meandering, the horse I had ridden there walking patiently by my side. A sickening whirl of emotion and confusion filled my head, with one image burned into my memory for ever.

Five locations, all sitting on a golden line that this admirable and terrifying man passed each and every day. Four places of horror, and one tavern as yet unscarred by events.

The evening passed slowly for my impatient spirit. The only man I confided my thoughts to was my trusted sergeant. He agreed that Nimer seemed to have been laying down a challenge – to pit me against his aristocratic talents. An array of faces he'd come to know these past few weeks would merely drive him away. I was also unwilling to risk my men by setting them against a killer of such breeding.

My sergeant was an old soldier who knew how to stay alive, while the rest were good watchmen who had never dealt with sober, trained swordsmen. Their job was to pacify and arrest rather than kill, and Nimer would give no second chances. As for myself I confess I failed to think; through arrogance or rage I cannot say but as many would have called it idiocy as gallantry.

We made our way to a private house overlooking the square, the only reputable corner of my district. We arrived well into the ghost hour when the lamplighters had already passed. Three of the four crimes had taken place deep in the night and it was unlikely he would have rushed now. I felt certain such a man would spring surprises only once his game had started.

As we waited I found plenty of time to think about these killings and the motives behind them – trying to piece together the meagre scraps Nimer had teased me with as he supposedly reported the conclusions of others. My head was pounding by the time our generous host – a man whose friendship I had earned two years previously by bringing a nobleman to justice – arrived with a cupped candle and his cook bearing sustenance.

His anxious face, tight with anger, reminded me of my purpose and I forced myself to focus on the task at hand rather than vague questions. The house afforded us an excellent view of proceedings and we spent a long while scrutinising faces, clothes and gaits for any sign of our foe. There were none for several hours, but the Queen's Square was well lit and the choices relatively few given the recent events.

As the tavern was emptying of all but a few regular drinkers and my eyes were wilting, a furtive figure in a long hooded cloak crossed the cobbled square. His path took him past the tavern and to the adjoining building – my instincts blazed at the very sight of him. The figure bore little resemblance to Nimer at this distance, but I knew to expect a disguise and had already assumed the tavern would only have been a starting clue. Clutching at my comrade's arm in wordless excitement I indicated the doorway and rose to leave. We both carried short-swords suitable for fighting in corridors or the cramped, overhung alleys of this city, while I hoped pistol-bows would even the balance between us. Though neither of us were strangers to weapons, I feared meeting any King's Man in a fair fight.

I was a man of the Watch, trained to make my eyes my greatest tools so it had not gone unnoticed that for all his silks and velvet gloves, Nimer wore a proper soldier's blade at his hip rather than some duelling accessory. Though obviously a beautiful weapon and finished with all finery, it was no fop's toy but a heavy length of steel as cold as his stare. I was resolved to use my small crossbow to wound or arrest him. Once he was winged I might have time to think about what came next, or it might give me a fighting chance at least.

We slipped out through the servant's entrance of our hide and made our way through the shadows until we had reached the adjoining building. Despite this being my district I knew almost nothing of the place and had never seen the door even open. Some said it was a gentleman's club but even the best of those tended to witness duels and other foolishness that attracted the Watch's attention, this one had seen nothing of the sort and even its name was a mystery to me. It was a large building of three storeys that extended a long way back with a recessed and reinforced front door. Whatever breed of gentlemen constituted the members, they didn't encourage visitors.

The door was ajar when I reached it. I entered cautiously, one hand on the iron-ring knocker to keep it silent, and found myself in some sort of reception area. A desk faced the doorway, unmanned, while a luxurious scarlet sofa stood up against the right-hand wall and a wide staircase led up to the first floor. There a single painting on the wall, a romanticised scene of a coastal village, but no mirrors or other adornments; just expensive oak panelling and a polished parquet floor. It did indeed seem to be some sort of private club, but a wealthier one than to be expected in my district. I knew for certain it was not one for any of the district's main trades, no dock guild or anything of the sort, but far from the richer parts of the city where the elite passed their days.

Feeling a pang of concern for whoever normally manned the desk, I wasted no time in heading for a pair of oak doors at the foot of the staircase, recessed slightly so as to be concealed from the entrance. With my bow at the ready I crept inside, easing the door open with my sword-tip and one boot advanced to catch it being slammed back. Inside, the impression of luxury was continued; a large welcoming fire and lamps illuminating an orderly reading room, but deserted.

With no signs of disorder or violence there, I abandoned the room and headed past the staircase to the more unassuming passageway at the end of the hall, one that looked like a servants' entrance to me. It was dark, but faint light flickered from around the corner at the far end. It outlined three doorways down the right-hand wall, most likely storerooms and all latched. I crept down the passage, keeping clear of each doorway and walking as silently as I could. At the corner I eased around it, pistol-bow first, to see a half-closed doorway four yards off.

Through the gap I saw my quarry, or rather a long cloak that looked like the one I was after. As I reached the door I realised it was a kitchen as the smell of fried onions and garlic wafted out, but there was also a scuffling sound like boots brushing a stone floor. With his back to me his long cloak obscured whatever he was doing, but just as I pushed the door open he put his arm out to shake it free of the cloak. In his hand was a blood-stained dagger.

I shouted for him to stop, but no sooner than the sound had left my throat he bolted – not even pausing to look around as someone taken unawares might but darting away with sudden, surprising speed. I fired as he disappeared through a doorway on the far wall, out of surprise as much as anything, but in my haste I missed. He vanished around the corner in the next heartbeat, leaving a twitching man splayed over a long table, his exposed chest pin-cushioned with half-a-dozen ornate daggers. I felt a red mist descend over my eyes and raced to pursue the monster, charging after him into a corridor lit only by the moon shining through a far window.

Catching my shin on a low table that stood just around the corner, it was fury rather than athleticism that saw me upright to the other end – a mad violent scrabble where I careened from one wall to the other before reaching the window. My foe was already halfway out by then so I leaped blindly, grabbing at anything I could.

Fingers closing around the hem of his trailing cloak, I crashed in a heap below the window. I hauled back as best I could, body braced against the wall, and felt a great lurch as the man was wrenched back against the wall. My fingers sang with pain as I took his full weight, but a moment later the clasp popped open. The cloak billowed up in the moonlight like a vengeful ghost while a crash and clatter came from the alley below. A few moments later my sergeant pounded up the corridor behind, hauling me up but I hardly noticed. In my eyes the cloak hung on the air by a taunting breeze as I dragged it towards me to grip the top end – the silvery moonlight shining down onto one the broken clasp there. The broken clasp in the shape of a bee with wings outstretched. The king's bee device; worn by all in his employ.

With a roar of anger I threw myself through the window without a thought to safety. I fell heavily, a six-foot drop on the other side, but rage eclipsed the pain in my knees as I saw a door bang shut across a small courtyard. A woman shrieked from within the room and when I staggered to the doorway she pointed with mute terror to the right-hand choice on the far side of her kitchen. This brought me to a storeroom and a brief glimpse of my prey as he half-emerged – turning as I entered and dragging the door shut after him.

I gave a wordless bellow of triumph. He had to have run himself into a corner, most likely down in a wine cellar. There'd be no exit there and he'd retraced his steps too slowly. I stopped a moment to catch my breath and cock the pistol-bow I somehow had managed to retain. My short-sword I had dropped somewhere so I drew my nightstick instead. It was a poor alternative, but better than a dagger and capable of cracking the thickest of skulls.

Forgetting to wait for my sergeant I wrenched the door open. No sooner had light crept through the breach than a curved blade lashed out, but I was ready for it and deflected it into the doorframe. With the knife trapped I launched myself forward and put the boot in, in the finest traditions of the Narkang Watch.

With a strangled squawk the man crumpled over my steel-capped toe and clattered backwards. For good measure I punched him in the side of the head and smashed him back down the short flight of steps again. He hit the dusty floor hard and collapsed in a heap.

Taking no chances I fired the fresh bolt into his thigh – just in case he thought me stupid enough to have never seen a man play dead before. I was rewarded by a scream of pain and the man scrabbled at the floor, crawling weakly towards the back of the cellar in a pathetic effort to escape. I didn't follow him yet, the cellar was a small one and contained no hiding places so I was happy to let the sick bastard fear the worst. My fury turned cold and quiet as I sat on the steps, reloading my bow before fetching a lamp from the storeroom. He squirmed face-down on the cellar floor, sobbing and howling in a puddle of what wasn't just blood. The more he wept the greater my contempt became – he was nothing but a coward who couldn't stand a tiny measure of the brutality he'd meted out.

Anticipating this moment all evening, I'd expected better. The measure of a man is how he acts when he's down and beaten, but this wretch was worse than a cowardly child. As I watched him wriggle through the dirt the disgust welled up inside me so powerfully I raised the bow again; bending to temptation before oaths I had sworn years before returned to haunt me. The lamp illuminated the cellar with a fair glow and my eye was inexorably drawn to the wooden pillars that supported the low roof. In the lamplight, the pillars with their diagonal supports and my black mood, I was reminded of a gallows and that was enough to stay my hand.

'Now hear me you piece of shit,' I struggled to say, my throat thick with rage until I took a few more breaths. 'I got eight more bolts here. If you don't explain a few things right now I'll get some more practice in – then maybe go fetch one o' your knives till you start talking.'

My hand trembled at the horrors the man had inflicted, as well as the cruel disdain of his affected concern. The bile rose in my throat and I tasted blood on my lips as I bit down in an effort to stop myself pulling the trigger. Evil was the only word I could muster and nothing in my years of these streets could compete with the scenes this man had left in his wake. I needed a reason, sane or not, for the indiscriminate violence he had inflicted. My hatred demanded that, demanded I know the full pathetic and contemptible reasons that had led him to do what he'd done. After years of seeing the worst of what folk could do to each other, I still wanted to believe there might be a reason behind all this madness. The alternative frightened me, it still does.

He said nothing and simply lay in a broken, wretched heap as I moved closer. I felt the revulsion tighten my finger as it did my throat. My vision darkened, my rage becoming a fierce pain behind my eyes and when the moment cleared I saw his body jerk in mortal agony.

For an instant I was sure I had fired. Then my senses returned and I spun around. The bow was smashed from my hand, bolt unspent but now forgotten. I didn't even attempt to raise my stick as a gleam appeared at my throat.

'Dear fellow, that expression is most unbecoming.'

'But you— I ...' I stammered, unable to connect my thoughts to words of any form.

'But you thought that was me?' Nimer cocked his head, sword never leaving my throat. 'I'm hurt; depravity is not among my "special talents" and if it were, you would have not caught me so easily. That man is a clerk to the City Council, just one of many and unremarkable in almost every way. Oh my friend, hundreds pass that window each day, but you only had a mind for me. Perhaps I should be touched you keep me so close to your thoughts.'

He wore a wide-brimmed hat that gave his face a sinister shade, but it was nothing compared to the sudden, unnerving smile he gave me. His cold, executioner's expression blossomed into some mad, cruel humour and my skin chilled at the sight.

'You killed him,' I managed to gasp. 'Why? You killed my damned prisoner! Why?' My anger returned and at last I found some strength again. 'You executed him before he even stood trial! For all that horror he gets a quick, clean death? He deserved to hear the whole city curse his name before he went to the headsman, the king's justice—'

'The king's justice has been done,' Nimer said sharply, cutting me off, 'and there will be no word of his identity ever revealed, do I make myself clear?'

'What? How dare you dictate my job to me? The Watch is the king's justice, not some sanctioned assassin ...'

'Oh my dear Captain,' came his cool, mocking voice. 'I'm most appreciative of your help in this, and let me assure you your efforts will not go unrewarded,' he said, holding up a hand to ward off my protestations, 'but for a man of such insight you are extraordinarily naive.'

To my look of bewilderment he merely laughed and sat back on the steps, sword resting against the wall within easy reach. He pulled a silver cigar case from an inside pocket and selected one, then offered the case to me. Defeated and baffled, I took one of the slender cigars, all thoughts of violence evaporating from my mind.

I numbly permitted Nimer to take the lamp and light both cigars from the flame. He puffed ponderously at his, the satisfied air of a man whose onerous task was now complete, while I stared and tried to form coherent thoughts.

'If you want this kept quiet, why are we enjoying a cigar while the crowds assemble?' I asked, sinking down onto an oak casket. 'Someone must have heard that woman scream, or she's gone to fetch help. For that matter, where's my sergeant?'

Nimer waved his cigar dismissively, leaning back with the poise of a man utterly at ease. 'Oh, Coran will keep people away, I left him back there somewhere.'

'Coran? The king's bodyguard?'

He smiled as if to a child. Offering the silver case once more, but closed this time, he showed me the engraved emblem and initials. A bee with initials inscribed on the wings. Emin Thonal – King of Narkang.

My throat closed dry. I stared first at the case, then him, then the corpse – all in a drunken haze as the world lurched treacherously beneath me. Nimer nodded at the look on my face and removed his hat, pulling off the eye patch to reveal a healthy eye as cold and arresting as its twin. He scratched at the thin beard and moustache.

'Strange how a few tweaks to one's appearance can make all the difference, especially to people who've only ever seen you at a distance. I was a little concerned I might be too old to wear a silly little beard like this, but I suppose no one is likely to mock a King's Man for affectations of youth.'

'This has happened before, hasn't it?'

'Oh yes. Not so dramatically I'll grant you, but my city grows so quickly and chaotically it is by far the best place for madmen to hide. People are missed less often and neighbours rarely know whom they live next to. And that is precisely why these murders were not the deed of some public servant but a vampire. One you caught and killed all alone.'

'I, I don't understand.'

'Very well, I shall explain. I am building a nation and it grows at a rate I can barely control,' he smiled frostily, 'despite my special talents. We do not have the luxury of a common heritage, only our own endeavour and unity. We cannot afford to wonder whether a killer walks amongst us, to live in fear of our own kind, not when we have enemies out there who would exploit such a thing. The city is one step from revolt each and every day; this you know only too well. But when plagued by vampires, werewolves, daemons and the like, we know our enemy.

'Such creatures are rare in these parts, most of the time nothing more than a story to keep the little ones in hand. But they are not the only monsters in this Land and it's those that are indistinguishable from men you meet every day that are truly terrifying. A vampire is a banner to the population, as the Gods or the tribes of man are. You can see my busy bee waving from half the flagpoles in the city, but it is my enemies that fly the most important banner.'

'What madness was this?'

'How to define madness?' his voice hardened suddenly. 'The man believed he was possessed by demons, that they drove his actions. His research into demonology was extensive, if pursued with a less-than-scholarly instinct. Perhaps he was correct, perhaps not. Best that point be down-played.'

'And the runes?'

King Emin hesitated, looking thoughtful for a moment before continuing.

'Unimportant. The reference was an obscure one to a false demon cult that once had great power, but is now extinct. It crops up in several of the more deranged works, but has failed the test of time and research. Again, that is something you will not speak of again.'

'And what if I won't keep quiet?'

'Then I will have sorely misjudged you. This clerk will be

remembered as a spy, from Tor Salan or the Circle City perhaps, it doesn't matter. His memory will be reviled as you wished, just not quite for the reasons you've witnessed. What does matter is that truth is a weapon. Your job is not just to uphold the law, but also to protect this irrational and dangerous population from itself. My people's own imagination can cause them more hurt than they, or even you, could appreciate. You saw that when the vigilantes started to beat people to death. Folk need few enough reasons to panic and whenever that happens, someone gets hurt.'

He reached out a hand. 'So, are you with me?'

I stared numbly at the offer, knowing I was defeated. And for my sins I took it and all it implied; realising it was the truth I sought, as perverse a reason as that may seem. I had spent my life hunting transgressors, driven to put a name and reason to every crime. To illuminate the darkness for those who needed protection in my own small way.

Now I saw the truth from a king's sight – how he protects his realm, how he needs his own truth in the void he inhabits. Cloudy and shifting, there was a light to be found there, but sometimes uncovering it would only ever be a disservice to the people I served.

That has been my life ever since. Now, as I feel Death's hounds draw ever closer, I am prepared to kneel at my Last Judgement and hear His words – content in my choice for the sake of others.

It took a killer called Nimer to show me who I was. Many years later I thanked him for it. He merely smiled in that way of his.

THE GOD TATTOO

Daken's stomach growled, long and angry.

'Piss on this nation o' cowards,' he muttered, 'so fast to surrender there's no pay for an honest man.'

'Tole you we should've joined the other side,' added his nasal-voiced companion.

Daken glared at the man trailing him and gave the reins of the horse he was leading an irritated twitch.

'An' I told you, Yanal, to shut the fuck up about that.'

The smaller mercenary shrank from the look and pulled his coat tighter around his body. He shivered and greasy trails of unkempt hair fell over his face like a veil. Underneath that was a streak of mud across Yanal's face, pasting his hair down onto his forehead. He'd tripped a few hours back, trying to keep up with the pace Daken had set, and ended up lying flat on the muddy road.

That had been Daken's only laugh of the day, and the past few as well. Yanal was getting worried; he could see a familiar set to the big man's jaw and knew it boded badly for the next person to piss him off. They'd not been comrades for long, only a few months, but any fool could tell a penniless and hungry white-eye was a dangerous beast.

Not as tall as many of his kind, Daken had a build to rival a Chetse warrior and the similarity didn't end there. The white-eye's arms, as thick as Yanal's legs, were covered in tattoos – hardly the stylised scars of the Agoste field, where Chetse veterans put recruits through gruelling tests, but displaying a variety of styles. Yanal guessed many were charms and wards Daken had collected over decades of soldiering – making bargains and trading favours with any witch or hedge wizard he met.

They walked on, Yanal keeping well back so Daken had time to calm. He didn't have a horse of his own, had sold it weeks ago when it looked like Canar Thrit was going to requisition every horse it could. Bastards hadn't done it in the end, but the rumour had meant he got sod all for the worm-ridden creature.

There was a light dusting of snow on the empty fields on one side of the road, nothing much but enough to make Yanal fervently hope they found some decent shelter for the night. The sky was clear and there was precious little breeze; no biting wind thank the gods, but a frost for sure after nightfall. A tangle of hedgerows skirted ash trees and young oaks away to their left, barely enough to keep the worst of the chill wind off but as much as they'd managed the last two nights.

'Sun's on the way down,' Daken commented from up ahead. 'We better start lookin' for somewhere to sleep.'

'Aye,' Yanal said miserably, trying not to stare enviously at the white-eye's thick sheepskin coat. His own was nothing like as warm. 'Last of our food then.'

'Should've learned to use that bloody sling better then,' Daken replied sourly. He looked back. 'And don't you start looking at my horse that way.'

'I weren't,' Yanal said sulkily, 'you made it clear enough last night.'

'Good …' Daken took a breath as though to continue but stopped dead, jerking on his horse's reins to bring it up. 'Well, looks like it's your lucky night, I won't have to eat you either.'

Yanal flinched at the thought as Daken pointed ahead, down the road. He was as savage a fighter as any man Yanal had ever met and it was hard to put much beyond the axe-wielding madman.

'What is it?' he asked hoarsely.

'Someone up ahead.'

Daken was perfectly still now, weight on the balls of his feet like a hound poised to spring. Yanal moved up beside him and looked to where the white-eye pointed. He couldn't make out much, just a dark shape that had to be another traveller two hundred yards down the road.

'They seen us?'

Daken shook his head. 'Don't look like it.'

Without taking his eyes off the other traveller he reached for the axe he'd stowed on the saddle. Plundered from a recently deceased cavalryman who'd been cheating at cards, it was a long-handled affair with a crescent blade on one side and a small clenched-fist hammer on the reverse. Daken tossed Yanal the reins and slipped off the road.

'Ride up and keep 'im talking – I'll circle around and catch up when he's not looking.'

Yanal nodded, eyes flitting to his spear and short sword, also bound to the saddle. 'Bastard better have some food.'

'Won't help him either way,' Daken said softly, the dangerous edge restored to his voice. He slipped off into the undergrowth and quickly the sound of his footsteps faded to nothing.

'Aye, true enough,' Yanal said and hauled himself awkwardly into the saddle.

A lone traveller was just asking for trouble and they could meet a lot worse than Daken. A white-eye only enjoyed killing in battle when he was worked into a frenzy; out here it'd be clean and swift. He nudged the horse into a brisk walk and started to catch the figure ahead.

Daken heard hooves on the dirt road and cursed mentally, there were no voices accompanying them despite the order he'd given Yanal. He'd wanted their victim to be chatting away, not listening for danger. Now that wasn't happening Daken couldn't tell what was going on. This would be a short-lived robbery if their victim was walking with a cocked crossbow, but he was fast running out of options.

He glanced behind him. The ground was pretty open, a few bushes to hide behind but none as thick as the ancient hawthorn he was presently behind. Once they passed that he'd have precious little cover if he was going to hide.

Fuck it, he thought and tightened his grip on his axe.

The hooves came closer, so close they had to be just a yard or two behind the hedge. With a snarl he pushed himself up off the ground and sprinted around the hedge towards the two figures on the road. Their horses shied and turned, forcing both travellers to grab their reigns and lose a precious second as Daken closed. Yanal was on the near side but dropped a pace back as Daken came. His companion was a tall man in a long patchwork cloak, each coloured patch edged in metal and set with what looked like glinting glass charms.

Suddenly the image changed and Yanal became the further man, then the air seemed to waver before Daken's eyes and the two figures winked out of existence, swapping places once, then twice. Daken staggered, confused by the strange happenings, and looked from one figure to the next. Just as he focused on one they swapped again and he saw it was an illusion, each one backed by a black silhouette in the instant the images swapped. He kept going for the right-hand figure, now the man in the cloak, and the man reached an open hand towards him.

Daken charged.

A searing flash of light whipped across his eyes and the charms of protection glowed warm on his skin – then he reached the man and punched the top edge of his axe into his ribs. The man folded inwards under the blow, legs collapsing as one final burst of magic sparkled the air and dissipated. The air went still again, the gloom of evening returning as Daken blinked down at the figure doubled-over at his feet. He scowled; it was Yanal.

Bugger.

He turned, bringing the axe up and around as he moved. The tall man stepped back with unnatural speed and the weapon caught nothing, but before Daken could close the gap an explosion of white light burst before his eyes. Desperately shielding his face, Daken fell back and ended up crouched on the road; axe abandoned and hands over his eyes as knives of pain scraped his skull.

'Are you quite finished?'

Daken cursed and growled with fury, but even as he fought back the pain he knew he could see little beyond the stars bursting darkly before his eyes.

'I'm gonna fuckin' kill you,' the white-eye gasped, reaching blindly for his axe.

'Like you have your friend?' the mage said, amused, as a moan of pain came from behind Daken.

'Yanal?'

'Ah Gods!' the man gasped weakly, 'you ...'

Wincing, Daken shook the daze from his head and looked at his companion as best he could. Yanal was sprawled on his side, curled around his chest where Daken had struck him and whimpering. The blow had been a heavy one; even without a sharp peak on the axe-blade he would have snapped a few of the man's ribs on impact.

'Your friend will die,' the mage declared, taking a step closer to Daken, 'unless you do exactly as I say.'

Dakan finally found his axe and used it to push himself to his feet, but as he wobbled on treacherous legs something struck him on the chest and knocked him back.

'Are you listening?' the mage said. He stood over Daken with a strange greenish light playing around his head. When he pushed back the hood of his cloak, Daken blearily made out the thin, imperious face of a middle-aged man staring down at him like he was a beetle flipped on its back.

'Never liked 'im anyway,' Daken said drunkenly. 'Still gonna fuckin' kill you.'

The mage sighed. Through the haze Daken saw he had strange yellow eyes that made him look something other than human.

'Very well, if you're too stupid to play to the niceties, what's the betting something in the packs on that horse is yours?'

Daken rolled onto his front and managed to manoeuvre himself until he was up on one knee, trying to make sense of what was going on.

'What's it to you?' he said eventually.

The mage crouched down to his eye level, close enough for Daken to reach out and grab his throat, but the sight of yellow lightning crackling over the man's skin overrode thirst of retribution. 'Fancy having the hounds of Jaishen catch your scent?'

'You gonna to set some dogs on me?'

The mage smiled like a snake, his teeth unnaturally neat and white in the last light of evening. 'Jaishen is the lowest depths of Ghenna. You will need more than a juicy steak to distract them once they have your trail.'

Daken thought about it a moment. He was a savage man, but

the look in the mage's eyes chilled even him. 'You mentioned niceties?' he croaked.

'So I did. I can save your friend's life and not damn you to an eternity in the Dark Place – so long as you do me a little favour.'

He grunted and heaved himself up. He moved reluctantly, feeling suddenly like an old man with the weight of the Land on his back. 'Okay, who do you want me to kill?'

'Quite the opposite,' the mage said with cold delight, 'I want you to be a knight in shining armour, to save a lady in distress. Who knows? Perhaps it will suit you better than highway robbery – mark a new chapter in your life.'

'Oh sure,' Daken said, 'White-eye merc turns hero; they sing that one all the time.'

He slung his axe through a loop behind his shoulders and tried to dust himself down, still a little unsteady. With an effort he matched the stranger's unblinking gaze, noticing only then how the mage was significantly taller than he, a rarity in these parts.

'So where's the silly bitch who got herself kidnapped then?'

Daken moved silently through the neat lines of trees, a dagger ready in his hands. At the end of the row he paused and crouched, keeping to the shadows as he surveyed his next move. The estate seemed quiet for the moment, but there was no easy path in as far as he could see. Like most white-eyes Daken wasn't a man who played well with others, but right now he wanted some backup. His kind could usually count on attracting mercenaries who knew their business, men who could take orders and didn't panic in a fight. Ex-soldiers tended to know the value of a leader as strong and fast as only white-eyes were, just as they knew what happened when you argued with one.

Fucking damsel in distress eh? he thought, as a sense of unease grew in his belly. *Still, everything he told me so far has been true. Let's hope that continues.*

The estate was a remote one, grand but belonging to another age. The perimeter wall surrounding the main grounds was newer than the house within and more appropriate to the border wars of the last few decades, but still it was old with long stretches of brambles growing up it and the nearest part fallen in. They were further north than Canar Thrit and the recent fighting had never reached these parts. No doubt the occupants hadn't bothered with anything so costly as repairs, knowing it would be over one way or the other before any soldiers reached here.

The orchard ran almost up to the fallen stretch of wall, stopping no more than twenty yards short. It was open ground, but they didn't seem to have anyone there guarding the way, to Daken's amazement. It seemed to bear out what the mage had told him; that they were guarding against a magical incursion, but still he was suspicious.

He settled down to watch and listen for patrols, content enough in his sheepskin coat that a half-hour passed easily. Twice he saw faces on the walls, with a main lookout on the topmost part of the house watching the road and open ground to the west. The house itself was split into two parts, a grand three-storey block set imposingly on an outcrop and a smaller L-shaped north wing beyond.

Most of the windows were dark, just a single pair of shutters in the north wing that were edged with light and two more in the main building. Around the wall however were torches set into brackets or driven into the earth itself, burning brightly below painted symbols on the stone. He didn't recognise the symbols, but guessed they were wards of some sort – how they would stop a mage from walking through Daken didn't know, but he just had to hope they wouldn't prove a barrier to him.

Time to move.

He crept forward to the very edge of the orchard's cover. The greater moon, Alterr, wasn't particularly bright tonight, but he didn't want to linger in the open in case the guards were a decent shot. He took a deep breath and ran for the broken line of wall between the two furthest-apart torches. No warning voices cried out and soon he was at the foot of a pile of rubble that someone had clearly made a half-arsed attempt at piling back up again.

Clearly it would fall with a gentle push, but Daken didn't want to risk the noise. He found a stable part to hold onto and vaulted the pile, trotting forward until he was again in shadow – this time in the lee of a rose bush that hadn't been pruned for a few seasons. Before he could move again he heard the creak of a door open on his right. He turned to see a man in a studded jerkin at the open doorway of a stone outbuilding set against the inside of the wall. Not waiting to be discovered, Daken charged.

He covered the ground in a few swift steps, lunging forward with his dagger before the guard had properly seen the danger. It pierced the man's jerkin with barely a scrape of metal, the force of the blow enough to throw him back through the open doorway.

'What—?'

From nowhere a second face appeared on his left, a soldier reaching for his sword even as he stared down at his fallen comrade. In one movement Daken slammed an elbow into the man's arm to stop him drawing and grabbed him by the neck. He jerked the man forward and smashed his forehead into his nose, feeling the bone crunch under the impact. The blow drove the man backwards, sword forgotten and lungs still filling to cry out as Daken stabbed him in the armpit. A second blow finished him off but then the first guard began to huff and wheeze in panic. Dakan stamped behind him and felt his boot come down on the man's chest – not enough to kill him but it winded him and bought the white-eye enough time to open his throat.

He stopped, forcing himself to be still as he listened over the hammer of his heart for sounds of alarm. There was nothing, no shouts or clatter of feet.

'Good start,' he muttered, dragging the first man's legs inside the doorway and closing it a moment while he thought. Both were a lot smaller than he and dark-haired – there was no point in attempting subterfuge when he was a broad, shaven-headed white-eye.

'How about a bit of distraction instead?'

He looked around the outbuilding. It was pretty much empty, just a table and chairs with the light of a small fire to illuminate it – clearly they were using it as a guardroom, which meant more would likely be here soon. With his dagger he levered a log from the fire and rolled it out of the grate. He looked around and spotted some sacks in the corner so he kicked it over to them and, once they were alight, took one and hung it over a rafter for good measure. The thatch would catch happily enough, even on a cold night, and in a few minutes he'd have enough of a distraction to follow the mage's instructions.

Daken reached for the door latch and stopped, suddenly noticing something odd about the two dead soldiers in the burgeoning light. Each one had strange flowing tattoos on his face, running from his cheeks and down his neck to disappear underneath his jerkin. The lines didn't seem to be writing of any kind, nor any sort of God's device. When he went to the other body he saw they weren't an exact match but the style was the same for certain.

'Good,' he muttered with a wolfish grin, 'I was getting suspicious that fucking mage had told me everything. Whatever this is least I know what I'm lookin' out for. Better than findin' out what he didn't tell me as it kills me.' He looked up at the burning roof. 'Time to move.'

Peering out of the doorway he saw the grounds were still deserted. What in Ghenna's name was going on here he couldn't tell, but the mage had said his damsel in distress would be occupying most of their attention. What that meant the mage hadn't said, but it had been clear most of them would be inside, with her. Daken had guessed they were up to some sort of ritual using her as a sacrifice and hadn't been corrected, so most likely he was running out of time.

'Right, find the house shrine,' he muttered, remembering what details the mage had given him.

When he'd scouted all round the house he'd noticed a pair of thin, double-height windows flanking the house's main entrance. While they weren't the only grand windows in the building to contain glass, they were dramatic and west-facing. The first light of dawn would stream through them and most likely reach the length of the imposing hallway. It would be an arresting sight for any pious fools droning through the morning devotionals, most likely they would be there.

He skirted the back of the main building, keeping to the shadows. The Hunter's Moon, Kasi, was behind the building, sinking fast to the horizon but Daken guessed he still had a while before midnight. If there was a ritual to be done in darkness, most likely they'd do it as Kasi went down and the darker half of the night began. There were several doors in view, but he didn't bother trying any of them. Instead he went to the corner where the two distinct buildings were joined and assessed the stonework there.

There was a lead-lined gully where the roof of the lower building met the side of the larger, a pipe leading down from that to a water butt. Using the gully as a low point to aim for, the pipe and stonework around one of the windows proved enough to allow him to scale the side. Before long he was crouched in the gully, working the numbness from his complaining fingers as he gauged the next stretch.

Above was a protruding balcony built into the stone, too far away to reach from where he was, but the roof of the lower building sloped sharply up to his left. He gingerly walked up the tiled roof, wincing as two cracked under his weight, until he was level with the balcony's wrought-iron rail. Freeing his axe, he reached as far forward as he could with it, assessing the distance he had to jump. The axe was well short of the balcony, another four feet he guessed. Considering how much run-up he'd have, Daken wasn't confident of making the jump.

Bugger, what else is there? He looked at the axe in his hand, then up at the iron rail around the balcony. If he could maybe hook it on one of the iron bars, he'd be able to pull himself up. It wouldn't be easy, but white-eyes were unnaturally strong and he knew he had it in him, no matter how heavy he was. Daken picked his way halfway down again and looked up at his proposed route.

If I fall, that's going to make enough noise to get them all out here, he realised as he set himself.

As quietly as he could he ran five feet down the roof to get up some speed, then launched himself forward at the wall ahead and kicked up off it. Reaching as high as he could, Daken slid the axe head through the bars and twisted as soon as it was through.

Gravity dragged him down hard, even with both hands tight around the axe handle it was almost wrenched from his grip. A sharp pain briefly flared in the wrist that took the brunt of his weight, but he refused to release his grip and a moment later he was just dangling above the rain-gully, legs swinging freely. With a grunt he raised himself to shift one hand above the next, then hauled as hard as he could to pull himself close enough to the balcony to grab its edge.

He hung another moment until the swing of his body under him slowed again, then shifted one bar closer to the wall to set his boot against the stone to use it for support. Within a minute he was crouched on the balcony and unhooking his axe from the bars of the rail, ready to enter the house itself. He tried the door that led off the balcony and was unsurprised to find it bolted, but nearby was a shuttered window with a simple latch that his knife could work open without difficulty.

This high off the ground, the window was big enough for even Daken to crawl though. He checked he couldn't hear anyone coming to investigate then eased himself through and shut the window behind. In the darkness of an empty room Daken grinned. The hardest part was over; now he was inside their defences and undetected. The main part of the manor house was oblong and Daken stood at one end of that. If the hallway was as grand as he suspected it would also contain the main staircase, but in a house this large there would be servant stairs too.

He went to the door ahead of him and tried to see through the keyhole. The corridor beyond it was dark enough that he couldn't make anything out. When he inspected the other door he saw it didn't have a lock, just a simple latch. Clearly this was a disused suite of rooms, all connected to each other. He stowed his axe and drew his dagger again, easing the door open with the weapon ready. There was no one in the other room but it did have a few pieces of furniture, a large bed and looming wardrobe, all draped in dust-sheets. The next room was similar to the first except it didn't have an exit onto the corridor, just a musty garde-robe in the back corner, so Daken returned to the second and waited at the door, listening for a long while before he opened it.

He found himself on a bare stone corridor that led off to the left and met another from which a faint light shone, while on the right it turned a tight corner a few yards away. He followed it that way and was rewarded with a narrow doorway covered by a long drape that led to a cramped servants' stair. He walked slowly up to the third floor, his only illumination the moonlight that crept through a slit window halfway up.

There he found a similar corridor and stalked along it until it met the central landing. Somewhere down that he could hear the tap of footsteps walking slowly towards him. A single pair; walking with the measured pace of a guard doing a circuit inside their perimeter.

He transferred his knife to his left hand, pressing his back against the wall that hid him. His practised ear told him when the footsteps were just at the corner, two steps beyond the point where the anxiety of adrenalin screamed for him to strike. He was reaching just as the figure came within one pace – dragging himself around the corner as he brought the knife up. The guard flinched at Daken's sudden appearance, but had no time for anything else before the knife-blade was at his throat, its edge pressed hard enough to break the skin.

'Move or cry out and you're dead,' Daken whispered, his other hand around the guard's which in turn clasped his sword hilt.

The guard was an average-looking man who could have been anything to Daken's eyes. He was middle-aged and clean-shaven; not as battered or unkempt as most mercenaries but clearly no raw recruit either. After an initial moment of panic in the man's eyes he grasped the situation with the clarity of someone who'd felt Death's hand on his shoulder and recognised Daken wasn't exaggerating.

He didn't nod of course, standing perfectly still without replying but Daken could see he understood easily enough. Keeping the knife at the man's throat he turned around him and put a hand to his back, pushing him towards one of the doorways off the corridor. The man realised what he was being asked to do and walked without complaint into the room.

'Do what I say and there's no need to kill you. Now, lose the sword belt.'

The man perceptibly sagged with relief that he wasn't going to have his throat cut in the next few moments and fumbled to obey – taking care not to drop his sword and make any undue noise or do anything else that might annoy the white-eye with a knife at his throat. Daken took hold of the back of the belt and pulled it away from the guard's unresisting grip.

'Good. Now I'll be tying you up soon enough, but first tell me where she is.'

The guard made a puzzled sound. 'Her?' A moment later Daken heard him gasp. 'The mirror? You've come to free her?'

The white-eye sensed the change in his prisoner immediately; body tense, lungs filling. Without thinking he wrenched back with his dagger, cutting deep into the guard's throat as he moved back. The man turned half around, hands rising as though to reach for Daken, but the movement was never completed as a spray of blood followed the knife and he crumpled to his knees. Daken took another step back and caught the dead man by the arm, easing him down while trying to avoid the worst of the blood flowing out over the wooden floorboards.

'Man wanted to live,' he commented dispassionately, 'until he heard what I wanted. Wasn't expectin' that.'

He dragged the body away from the door and considered his next move. Even loyal guards were rarely eager to sacrifice themselves in the faint hope of warning their master, and what did a mirror have to do with all this?

'Startin' to feel screwed over by my employer,' Daken said softly, a grin once more creeping across his face. He sheathed the knife and pulled his axe out.

'Now we're on familiar ground. So there's a mirror involved in this ritual – most likely they're usin' it as some sort o' gateway. That and a blood sacrifice. Fucking daemon-worshippers; always eager with a virgin and sacrificial knife.'

He returned to the main passageway and cautiously headed down it. At the far end there was a solid balustrade beyond which a large wrought-iron chandelier hung. Only half its candles were burning but they were enough to cast adequate light around a central space that seemed to extend from ground level right up to the roof. Over the carved balustrade came sharp voices, several men talking over each other until a fist was thumped on a table and Daken heard a voice clearly.

'Put the damn fire out, we can argue about who set it later!'

Daken's grin widened a fraction as he heard feet scurry to

obey. Unable to see any more guards on this level he crept forward and hid behind the balustrade as he decided his next move. He'd marked the stairways leading down to the first floor already, off to the left above where he guessed the shrine was. Flush against the back wall they came down from the sides to meet in the middle, the positioning making it clear they opened out to meet the lower stair at the second floor.

Almost on hands and knees he crept to the end of the balustrade and looked around the thick pillar at the corner. The way was clear to where the staircases met so he edged down the steps to the next corner, keeping hidden behind the balustrade with his axe at the ready.

'Do you think it's him, sir?' a man said from the hallway below, younger than the first.

'I don't know,' the other said with a sigh, 'but we've warded this estate with everything Parain knows and double-checked it all – I don't see how he could have got past all three layers of wardings.'

'Could it be her?'

'Don't be stupid, man! She's bound securely right there, go and check for yourself if you don't believe me.'

That seemed to spark fresh panic in the younger man. 'No! No, of course, sir – I know Parain has done his job.'

Two voices speaking frankly, Daken thought, tightening his grip on his axe handle. *Sounds like that's as clear as I'm likely to get.*

Without waiting he straightened and jumped the short flight to a square half-landing, finding himself with staircases on each side leading down. In the hall ahead were two armed men dressed like campaigning knights, staring astonished up at him as he came. A third was at the foot of the right staircase, foot poised to ascend but similarly taken by surprise.

Daken kept on straight, one hand on the balustrade as he vaulted it to control his fall. As his feet left the landing time seemed to slow, Daken seeing the older, aristocratic-looking man reaching for his sword as the other recoiled from the shock. Then he caught sight of a fourth almost directly below and the Land speeded up again.

Twisting in the air, Daken managed to bring one knee up as

he dropped. He crashed into the soldier's shoulder and knocked him aside into one side of the archway below the balustrade. The man collapsed to the floor, but Daken caught himself on the other jamb, ending up in a crouch as he absorbed the shock of a ten-foot drop. Not bothering to turn towards the danger he drove forward, axe ready to catch any blow but none came. Three quick paces took him to an altar decked out in all sorts of arcane objects – charms, wreaths of half-a-dozen plants, all surrounded by painted symbols on every available flat surface. In the centre of it all stood a mirror, Daken guessed by the shape, covered with an altar-cloth bearing Death's symbol.

'No one move or I break the mirror!' he bellowed, chancing a look behind him.

There were open archways on either side of the altar too, three ways they could come at him and he wouldn't be able to cover them all. He kept moving, looking left and right with the axe held out before the mirror.

'Stay your weapons!' the old man roared as his companion started forward. 'All of you – hold!'

Once he was sure they were going to keep to his order, the man composed himself with remarkable speed and addressed Daken directly. 'Stranger, don't do anything rash – breaking the mirror would be as dangerous to you as the rest of us.'

'Don't you be so sure o' that,' Daken said, still moving warily, 'folk say I'm mad; ain't one for takin' the safest path.'

'Fair enough,' the old man said placatingly, before his tone suddenly turned sharp. 'Takkar, back off now! Get back, do nothing without my order or I'll kill you myself!'

Through the archway ahead of him, Daken saw a man's shadow on the flagstones and put the edge of his axe to the covered mirror. As commanded, the man edged away again and Daken watched his progress by the way the old man turned his head. Satisfied the man was far enough away he relaxed a touch, but was quick to cut the old man off before he could speak again.

'You keep 'em back – now I got a mission here, so bring me the girl and I'll go.'

The old man cocked his head. 'Girl?'

'Aye, the one you've got prisoner.'

Both men exchanged looks, the older raising an eyebrow at his companion then giving a short bark of laughter. 'Tell me, stranger, who sent you on this mission?'

'Someone I met in the pub,' Daken growled, his grip on his axe tightening at the man's amusement. 'Now enough out o' you, where's the girl?'

'Ah, well – here with us, I suppose.'

The older man took a pace forward, making a show of keeping his hands raised and away from his weapons. Daken could see there was still a trace of laughter in his eyes, however concerned he was about the threat to the mirror.

'Let me explain; my name is Marshal Sallin, my companions and I belong to an order of knights ...'

'Do I look like I want a fucking history lesson?' Daken snapped, his white-eye soul starting to snarl at Sallin's laughter. 'You've got five seconds to stop giving me bullshit or the mirror goes.'

'That's what I'm trying to tell you,' Sallin said hurriedly, 'she's in the mirror!'

Daken glanced back at it then checked his flanks again. The archways were empty – the only explanation was that he was stalling for time.

'Look! Look for yourself.'

Sallin gestured toward the mirror and pointedly took a pace back to allow Daken time to do as he suggested. The white-eye hesitated a moment then jerked the altar-cloth off the mirror, revealing a large, flawless piece of glass surrounded by a thick gilt frame.

'Well?' he demanded. In the mirror he could see himself and little else. He angled it to see behind him and the knights hadn't moved from their positions.

'She's there,' Sallin assured him.

Daken was about to turn away when, in the reflection, a head peeked around the archway between him and the two knights. He whirled around and saw nothing, but in the reflection the head hadn't moved. It was hard to make out in the weak light, but he could see it was indeed a girl, in the first flourishes of beauty. Her dark hair hung loose about her shoulders and her dress seemed to be composed of dozens of coloured scarves all woven together.

'Well bugger me sideways,' Daken breathed.

'So you see,' Sallin announced, 'this is no simple kidnapping – nor are we the villains of this piece. Now, if you would be so kind, please take your axe away from the mirror and let us be about our task.'

'Eh? Why? I was sent here to free the bitch, not worry about what happens to you after.'

He took hold of the top of the mirror and lifted it off the altar, but when he tried to carry it away from the altar it was as though a steel-cord was attached to the back. Try as he might he couldn't drag the mirror more than a yard from the altar, despite his prodigious strength.

'Look up,' said the younger knight, smirking.

Daken did so and discovered symbols painted onto the top of the altar room, a magical ward of some sort.

'That's right; you're not taking her anywhere.'

Daken paused, the familiar growl of anger in his stomach intensifying. 'Fine,' he said eventually, 'if that's how you want it – fuck the lot o' you.'

He set the mirror on the ground, leaning against the altar, and straightened up. The older man relaxed visibly, but then Daken swung his axe down through the centre of the mirror and shattered it.

'No!' both knights cried together, but the mirror had imploded under the blow and a thousand shards of glass dropped to the floor. 'What have you done, you fool?'

'Freed her,' Daken said simply, his turn to smirk now. 'That was my job, remember?'

'But?' The older man drew his sword and turned in a circle, as though expecting an attack from behind. 'Where is she?'

Daken moved forward, clear of the archways and the men backed off. He saw four in the hall and more lingering in a doorway ahead. Each one had their weapons drawn now but none seemed to be focused on him.

'What's happened?' howled someone from down the corridor behind the newcomers. 'What have you done?'

'The mirror's been broken,' Sallin said briskly, sounding now like a commander giving orders. 'What does it mean, Parain?'

The man, clearly a mage, forced his way out past the soldiers and into the hall. 'Mean? It means she's bloody free!' He pointed at Daken. 'Who in Ghenna's name is that?'

'Someone who don't like bein' pointed at,' Daken snarled.

'Never mind him,' Sallin demanded, sounded increasingly worried now, 'define "free" – she's not here with us, why hasn't she appeared.'

Parain looked around wildly for a moment then composed himself. 'I, ah, the wardings, that's why. Nothing can incarnate within the grounds, her spirit is here but she'll be without form and vulnerable still.' He brightened. 'We can still do the ceremony! If we can trap her again, that is – we need to find where her spirit's gone.'

'Where could it go? Another mirror? I've not seen many here.'

'Or into a person, she could possess their body still.'

Sallin turned slowly towards Daken. 'But we've all been warded against her touch. She only has one option there.'

'What the fuck are you all on about?'

Sallin started to chuckle. 'Take off your coat!'

'What?'

'Take your coat off,' Sallin repeated, unbuttoning his own tunic and pulling his shirt up. Underneath were more strange blue tattoos, markings on his skin like those on the men Daken had killed earlier.

With one hand he did as Sallin suggested, unbuttoning his coat and lifting the segment-mail shirt underneath. A blue light was playing over his skin, tracing a strange path he couldn't feel. As he watched the light began to intensify and then he felt it, sharp and hot enough to make the white-eye hiss with discomfort.

Parain laughed abruptly, a high nervous giggle that broke off as soon as Daken glowered at him. His darkening mood didn't stop Sallin from joining in to the laughter however and Daken's nostrils started to fill with the hot smell of rage.

'You came to save her!' Sallin explained, beckoning forward

his men. 'Unfortunately for you, we're the only ones who can save you from her!'

The old man started towards him, sword raised. 'The mirror didn't matter for our ceremony – it was only the vessel to be broken when we banished her from the Land! Some damn-fool white-eye will do just as well, I assure you.'

Daken moved without replying, his axe flashing through the air to chop through the nearest man's sword arm. On the backswing he turned and buried the weapon into the next, barrelling on to batter another aside and find himself within reach of Sallin.

With the deftness of his kind the white-eye brought his axe around to catch Sallin's rapier with it, hooking the thin weapon and twisting it out of the way. Always moving he dragged the old man closer to him and smashed his forehead into the knight's nose, feeling the crunch and spurt of blood on impact.

He turned and tossed the wailing knight towards the next attacker, bowling that one over while he freed his axe again. The rest hung back a moment, spreading out around the hall – seven, eight of them, all looking nervous but all armed.

A scratching sensation like a cat's claws began to work at his chest and stomach, but Daken ignored it. The laughter echoed in his ears, Sallin's and a girl's mingling to further enrage the blood-crazed white-eye. One of the knights advanced a cautious step and something snapped inside Daken. The white-eye howled and charged.

Outside, at the broken stretch of wall where one torch was burning low, faint sparks of blue light began to prickle the night air. In response, on the other side of the warding, the darkness seemed to fold inward upon itself and from the boiling mass of night a figure stepped forward. His yellow eyes flashed as a cruel smile crossed his face. Taller now, his skin was smooth and pale – unnatural and timeless under the weak moonlight.

'Litania, my little trickster,' the God said softly. 'Did the nasty men mistreat you?'

A girlish laugh broke the night air. 'I think they're paying for it now, Father. And all I wanted to do was play; these mortals have a poor sense of humour.'

'Yet you've marked the white-eye? His kind are unlikely to change that opinion.'

'Oh Father,' Litania trilled, 'but I like this one and I've always wanted a pet. Can I keep it? Please?'

THE MARSHAL'S REFLECTION

The case I present to you now is not one I was involved in myself. Rather, I hardly touched upon events and did nothing myself, but it remains an undeniable curiosity. The pertinence I leave to your fancy.

I had been retired several years when, one morning, my son-in-law arrived at my door in perplexed mood. The city was enjoying the last few weeks of a fine and gentle summer as it eased its way into autumn. The season had been peaceful and balmy, free from scandal and mystery for a change. That summer, to place it in the reader's mind, was the last-but-two before the shadow of war came to Narkang. Not long enough for me to forget the vital details, but I fully admit the words are my own rendering.

As Brandt was admitted to the veranda I noticed immediately the state he was in. Normally meticulous in his appearance, Brandt's hair was unkempt, his clothes dirty and crumpled, while his eyes betrayed a lack of sleep.

'My boy, whatever is the matter?' I exclaimed upon seeing him this way. 'Come sit down. Danc, fetch some wine and food.'

While my manservant bustled out I directed Brandt – by then Commander Brandt Toquin of the City Watch – to a seat, and prised the bundle of papers from his grip to set them down on a table.

'Sir ...' he began, in his distraction slipping back into the routine of my assistant that began when he was but fourteen winters.

'Ah Brandt, enough of that! You forget your station's higher than mine ever was. Take a moment to breath there. I'm in no rush, and I expect this case will wait another minute.'

He looked up and nodded. Straightening his jacket and smoothing back his hair restored some of the composure that characterised the man in my eyes. I settled myself back into my chair and started things off as I saw them, affording him time to get his thoughts in order.

'So let me guess the facts I can. There has been a death, possibly more than one since single deaths are generally simpler. You've hardly slept so I assume the victim held office, rank or title – title being the most likely. You look like you're being harried by your superiors and that won't happen often to a brother of Suzerain Toquin. Lastly, you've a puzzle that requires a different direction, so this was no jealous lover or assassination.'

Brandt smiled and nodded, helping himself to the rosehip tea I'd been drinking before speaking.

'I'd be impressed if that one-handed crony of yours hadn't been at the watch-house yesterday. But you're right; there is something I need a twisted mind for.'

At that I joined his smile. His superiors on the City Council had often commented that my company over his formative years had produced rather less of the tractable public servant some had once hoped for. During one well-publicised argument with the Council, my influence had been described as that of a 'twisted mind'.

'We have two dead, early two nights past. A marshal named Tirelir Calath and his wife, who happens to be niece to Count Antern. You can imagine that the Watch is rather anxious to find more answers than we have currently.'

I sat back with a sigh, my world feeling a little darker and colder. I had scant love for Count Antern, but a great deal of respect. His niece was an attractive and gracious woman as far as I could remember. The two were recently married and children expected soon; a union born purely of love and one I had found a joy to behold on the single occasion I had seen the couple together.

'I know little of the marshal, other than his family is from Inchets. They're wealthy, but I don't believe Marshal Calath is a man of politics or trade – a man with less conflict in his life would be hard to find.'

48

It was, in part, a lie. I had met the marshal on numerous occasions, though only ever in passing. We were both members of a private gentleman's club, one that Calath used only infrequently and such time as he did spend there was passed in the extensive library. I knew some of his activities, many of the club members being academics who gossip worse than watchmen, but nothing that seemed applicable to murder.

'Well we can find no evidence of a suitor for the Lady Calath – Lady Meranna – no evidence of very much, to tell the truth. At present we don't even know how the killer entered the house. There is something I think you'll recognise, but perhaps you should read these reports first.'

As he spoke, Brandt reached over and gave the papers sitting on my side table a sharp tap. Scratching the stubble on my chin I picked up the first of the stained pages that harked back to my days of servitude for the city. It was a constant source of private amusement and public embarrassment that our records were always in a bad state. Food, drink, sweat, blood; we had presented to the court evidence with a whole range of trappings and clearly things had not changed much since my dismissal.

'That one is the murder report,' said Brandt, indicating the ink-spattered page I had taken. 'The others are in order underneath so you might want to read it last.'

As directed, I slipped the sheet to the back of the pile and peered at the one revealed. Noticing the effort this required, Brandt took the reports from my unresisting hand and declared he would read them aloud. I was happy to accede since Danc was standing at the door with razor and towel in hand and a maid had appeared with some breakfast for Brandt. I relaxed while the world progressed about me.

'Firstly some background information about the marshal,' Brandt began after a reviving swallow of wine, 'furnished by your good friend the count. Marshal Calath was well thought of by those who knew him; a man of intellect and scholarship, whose leg was malformed and twisted from a difficult birth. It is said that he was a shy child who became bookish because he could not join in with the other children, but quickly he came to love the pursuits when he realised he could excel and leave others his age in his wake.

'Calath became prominent as a historian before turning his hand to theology and the ... ah, unnatural aspects of the Land most particularly. The stranger worlds of necromancy, daemonology, cults, local Aspects, these things appear to have been particularly fascinating to a crippled youth. When Calath's father realised just how intelligent his son was he employed the best tutors in the city, but the younger Calath outstripped their teachings by his twentieth winter.

'This, ah, episode, took place some three months ago, a minor matter perhaps but telling to what happened more recently perhaps. It seems the marshal had been taken ill after working late, some sort of fit the doctor believed. Ah, here it is ...

'"I was summoned to the house of Marshal Calath in the early hours of the morning by a stablehand. Upon reaching the house I perceived a gloom upon the place. The servants spoke in low anxious voices and glanced nervously about themselves. When I questioned one I was informed several had heard distant, whispering laughter echo through the house; so evil and portentous in tone that they feared to investigate. A terrible cry had followed not long after a second instance of laughter – they believed that to be the marshal's voice crying out with such horror that they were spurred to action.

"Outside his chamber they found the lady of the house desperately attempting to open the door, but unable to turn the handle. The housekeeper had her set of keys so these they tried, but discovered it was not locked – rather secured from within.

"The stablehand and coachman were fetched and together they put their shoulders to the door. The task was not easily accomplished, but with the urgings of Lady Calath they succeeded, doing considerable damage to the door and frame in the process. Once admitted they discovered a scene of complete disorder. Papers were scattered over the floor and the long mirror that stood in the centre of the room had shattered. The marshal himself was slumped unconscious on the floor. He appeared unharmed, but they could not rouse him and I was called.

"What they could not explain when I arrived was how the door was secured. There was no sort of bar or bolt to fasten it – only the lock that the housekeeper swears was open and inspection of the damage bore the assessment out – and nothing had been dragged to block the passage of the door inwards.

"The presumption was that the marshal fell at the door and prevented its opening. When I made a cursory examination however I could find no bruising or other injury one would have expected, considering the force required to damage the door as they had. The nature of his injury was mysterious. I could find no wound save cuts to his knuckles where he had apparently broken the mirror. His breathing was shallow and laboured, his pulse weak but constant with no sign of fever. I tried to rouse him with smelling salts but he was caught in a state deeper than some mere faint.

"The marshal's condition appeared to be stable. I concluded he would only benefit from rest and instructed his lady wife to massage his head to encourage the flow of blood. I could only presume his injury was one born of the imagination, something I knew to be powerful for I had on more than one occasion been privileged to hear the ghost stories of his own devising.

As the first rays of dawn touched his bed the marshal began to stir. Evidently he had been greatly disquieted by his experience, but I knew my place well enough not to intrude on a wife's work. As soon as I was sure he was well enough, I took my leave."'

'Well, what more?' I asked, taking advantage of the fact that Danc's blade was currently not at my throat.

'That's all the good doctor says in his statement. He didn't dawdle in the house and paid no attention to what the marshal said as he was roused. We have to rely on the testimony of the manservant, one Imah Veser, for the next part, but I found him to have little imagination and a distinct fondness for his master so I believe it's faithfully told.'

'Good, but wait. I believe you need the attentions of this razor more than I. Danc can read the next passage while you become presentable for my wife.'

Brandt acceded to this, knowing that my wife's fondly sharp tongue would delight in his appearance. He took the mirror and blade offered by my man with a smile, propping the mirror against a vase and touching it slightly to the left in search of the best light. As a nobleman he had grown up with people to do such things for him – as a watchman he preferred to wield himself any blade at his throat.

Danc made his way around the table and took the seat I had indicated to him, much accustomed to reading and writing on my behalf now that age and past injuries make the two difficult.

'"My master awoke with a pale and shaken appearance, but the presence of Lady Calath seemed to calm him and he relaxed under her touch. While I attended him and helped him dress, my lady gently questioned him on what had happened. He seemed unwilling to speak freely in my presence, which I found strange if you don't mind me observing. I've been with him for years now, since long before he married, and believe myself trusted entirely regarding all of his business and personal affairs. What he did say was confusing. I think his dreams must have been unpleasant since he spoke of taking fright at his reflection. I overhead something of 'a face in the mirror that was not his own', which made me think that he had seen a face at the window though I cannot see how an intruder could have scaled the wall."'

'That's true,' interjected Brandt with a flourish of the razor. 'We investigated the entire building after the murder. It would have taken a man with unnatural skill to climb the blank face and peer in. The servants also remembered the drapes being closed and the window fastened on the night of the murder, despite the warm evening.'

This information imparted, Danc took up matters once more.

'"For the next few days the master of the house lay abed, recovering. Lady Calath gave instructions for the other two looking glasses in the building to be covered – such was my master's dread of a reoccurrence. He gave no explanation for the laughter other than blanching at his wife's mention of it, which prevented further discussion of the matter. Once his health – always a somewhat tentative circumstance in my experience – was restored, life returned to normal and we spoke of the incident no more. The door was repaired before the master left his bed and the frame of the mirror removed to the attic where it remains now".'

At that break in the proceeding my wife entered to greet her son-in-law. The interlude during this murky affair gave me the chance to reflect upon what I had heard thus far. I am not a man who can leap to the correct conclusion in a fit of inspiration. Years of practice mean a slow repetition of the facts in my mind might lead me to the same destination as my more illustrious friends, but it is a far longer process. Unfortunately I found myself only able to note that any clue to the marshal's illness died with his wife, but it was too early to pursue that grim path.

Having made her pleasantries my wife discreetly excused herself, once she had secured the promise of a family meal that night. With the nervous smile of a man who worked irregular hours at the best of times, Brandt watched her retreat and continued.

'I, ah ... Ah yes. When pressed, the manservant did give us two further pieces of information, though only with great reluctance.'

'For what reason?'

'None selfish,' replied Brandt after a moment's consideration. 'Firstly, he is extremely loyal and they do cast a strange light upon the household. Secondly, he showed little regard for either source and only mentioned them out of diligence and my insistence. The first was the account of a chambermaid – who didn't strike me as quite the fool Veser believes – of an incident that by itself one would dismiss. The other I have only Veser's retelling as my source, for he heard it from a visiting cousin of the marshal, one Darayen Crin, who has since returned to his holdings in the north.'

'Well, enlighten me all the same,' I said eagerly. I must confess that when the enigma is not my responsibility, I enjoy a mystery immensely. Reclining there, with this story unfolding before me, was an excellent way of passing a morning allocated by my wife to financial affairs.

'Very well. The cousin had visited Marshal and Lady Calath a few weeks after that original fit, for want of a better word. He is related to the marshal through his mother, younger sister of the previous marshal. There was a difference in age between them, but according to the manservant this only resulted in an air of levity surrounding all three.'

'The lady enjoyed this cousin's company? We sure he's not

returned to the city in secret? She was several winters younger than her husband if I recall.'

My suspicions had now been raised, but before I could get over-excited Brandt dismissed the notion.

'The manservant assures me the lady treated this cousin as a foolish younger brother. While Veser is a man to protect his master's honour, if his feelings about Lady Calath were feigned he's a better actor than any agent of the king's. I have confirmed that the cousin is well married, with an heir born two summers past.'

'You still possess an overly naive view of the human nature, my boy.'

Brandt's grin told me what he thought of that suggestion. 'Perhaps, old man, but the cousin's a merchant by trade and led his wagon train back to Inchets. Any absence would be hard to hide and Count Antern has sent someone to check up.'

My son-in-law cleared his throat pointedly. 'Anyhow, if you can control your suspicions for five minutes, I'll tell you what the cousin reportedly said.'

I gestured for him to continue, which Brandt did with a ceremonious shuffling of papers as though daring me to interrupt and jump to another conclusion again.

'When Master Crin first arrived at the house, the marshal had spent the morning abed. He explained it as nothing grave; merely a headache that he wanted to clear, so as to enjoy the company of his guest. Crin had arrived early and since they were close he visited the marshal immediately. They spoke greetings for a minute and then Veser arrived to attend his master.

'After he had retired from the room, Crin took the manservant aside and asked whether he had noticed anything unusual. Veser replied no, but Crin had been insistent that when he first arrived, the marshal's face and arms were covered with long red marks. He described the marks as scratches that had just failed to break the skin, raised welts that had faded as they talked. The marshal seemed unaware of the marks and nothing was said, but his cousin expressed concern over his constitution again before departing one week later.'

'Curious, but minor. Read me the statement given by the maid,

I want to hear what Veser was so happy to dismiss.'

Brandt took first some tea to clear his throat, then returned to the papers and scanned his eyes over the sheet for a moment. 'Actually, this should fit in later, but I'll read it now. The reason will become apparent.

'"It happened three weeks back, well, the first thing did. That man who came to the door was a few days after, but his shadow came first so that's where I'll start. I was cleaning the dining room as usual when the marshal came in looking vexed. I stepped into the window bay to keep out of his way and watched him take a box from the corner cabinet and open it on the table. I didn't see what he was looking at, but I did see his shadow on the table. I don't know how, but as I watched it the shadow began to ripple, like it was a reflection on water or something.

"At first I thought it was the heat, but it just got stronger and then moved all of its own. I swear it did; the marshal never moved, but his shadow reached out a hand to me and it had claws on the ends of its fingers! I couldn't take that no more and I screamed. I'm sorry but it was going to touch me! As soon as I screamed and the marshal turned, the shadow went back and I ran for the kitchen."'

Brandt finished abruptly and fixed his gaze upon me. With his hair in some semblance of order, Brandt's dark eyes were arresting and bright with intelligence. Despite his slightly dishevelled air he looked a nobleman once more. I felt a swell of pride that such a fine man waited for my opinion, not to mention was father to my only grandchild, before reminding myself of the task at hand.

'And the man who came to the door?'

Brandt hesitated a moment and then raised the page once more. 'I'm not entirely sure what to make of this, but certainly it's odd enough:

'"Three days after that a strange man came to the door late at night. It was past midnight when I was woken by a knocking on the kitchen door. I thought it was one of the kitchen boys at first, so I opened the small window in the door to tell him Master Veser had locked up and retired. But it wasn't anyone I knew, I've never seen anyone who looked like that.

55

He had long black hair, loose over his shoulders, and the prettiest face I've ever seen on a man.

"I know that's a strange thing to say, but he weren't so much handsome as pretty like a girl, like the mistress was. He was stood close up to the door, waiting for me to open the window. He asked for the master so I said he'd have to wait while I fetched Master Veser. His voice was strange; high like a woman's but it was certainly a man – he sounded like he was almost singing the words to me.

"He was dressed like some sort of minstrel and had the same air of confidence that type perform with. If you'll forgive the thought, it reminded me of when I saw the king when I served at a ball – he commanded the room with just a look while the whole Land turned around him. His smile worried me though, the minstrel's I mean. Made me think of a cat, I didn't see his teeth but something about him made him look like he was about to bite. After a moment he stepped back and told me to give the master a message instead and not disturb the whole house. He said his name was Rowshak, or something like that ..."'

'Rojak,' I interrupted with a cold feeling in my stomach. 'I've heard the name mentioned at my club. Can't remember what about, but it's foreign, Embere I believe.'

'Rojak then. Anyway;

'"he said, 'tell your master, he's been prying where he shouldn't and he owes me a debt already. He'll see me next time I come.'

"Then he just turned around and left. When I told Master Veser the next day, he took me straight to the marshal. I told him how it happened, but he didn't say anything. He just looked ready to be sick, and locked himself up in his study the rest o' the day.

"The minstrel never came back in the end. If it weren't for the master's reaction I'd have thought he'd come to the wrong house. I did smell something like peach brandy when I opened the window and wondered if he'd been drunk – though no drunk I ever saw looked so focused as that. Can't for the life o' me think how the master might know him though; to owe him money or anything of the sort. He never gambled or did anything illegal. He was as good a man as any I ever met, kind to us all and the Lady Calath too. To mix with a rogue like that, I just can't imagine it.'"

I was quiet a long while.

'It's too much of a coincidence for the man to have found the wrong house,' I admitted at last, my fervour for the mystery now waned. 'However, the marshal makes a strange candidate for blackmail, the more likely coincidence could be that a man from his past came to collect on an old debt from a wilder youth – hearing Calath was settled and respectable there might be more to collect.'

On another day I might have felt this was a prank to be played on retired watchmen with not enough to occupy their days, but I knew that was not the case. I could not admit it to Brandt, but I knew the name Rojak – had heard mention of a minstrel cruel and utterly without morals from men who moved in more dangerous circles than I – and did not envy him the involvement.

'I can find no real political interests at all,' Brandt said in agreement, apparently accepting my plausible assessment, 'nothing that would require corrupt dealings and his personal life seems to be one of sleepy contentment. Marshal Calath appears in all respects to have been a man of learning who lived on a stable income and well within his means. From what I know of his research the only illegal works would be useless to him, but a nobleman's reputation can be a fragile thing.'

'Useless in what way?'

'Well, there are no legal limitations on access to historical or academic works, certainly not to a man so highly respected as Marshal Calath. The only works that are banned are the dangerous magical tomes and I'm told they're just books unless you have the ability to use them. To you or I they are nothing but words on paper, no matter how knowledgeable one might be.' At my expression he added, 'I went to the College of Magic and spoke to the Archmage. He explained all of this, and checked that none of the books we found were banned even to mages.'

'That tells us nothing, bar the fact that the killer might have found what he was looking for. Still, I assume you would be more animated if Calath had been capable of magic so perhaps we should be looking elsewhere.'

For the next account Brandt took position by the empty

fireplace, leaning easily on the mantelpiece with a rather more relaxed air about him.

'We have now a report taken yesterday from a shopkeeper on the Springs Road, a man named Gorters. It refers to an incident that took place just over a month after the marshal's first fit. The manservant, Veser, tells me that this instance – of which he was unaware until I asked him – preceded a dramatic tumble in both spirits and health of Marshal Calath.

'"Marshal and Lady Calath had entered the shop with something of a celebratory air, so Gorters was careful to state at the outset. Though the marshal's leg seemed to be affording him a little discomfort it didn't appear to have affected his mood a shred as they went about looking for a present for the lady. The shop is one that sells fine gifts; ornaments and furniture of the highest quality I'm told, but with people like my brother and his family passing most of the year in Narkang these days, I'm sure trade remains good."'

Brandt and I shared a smile there. His brother, Suzerain Toquin, was a proud and extravagant man whose wealth had increased dramatically as Narkang prospered. The brothers lived very different lives nowadays and I knew Brandt was more comfortable as a part of my family than his own.

'"The shopkeeper guessed from their demeanour that she was expecting a child – though when we questioned the servants there none claimed to know of it so we must assume Gorters was wrong – but they would take no suggestion from him and were content to browse.

"When the marshal expressed dissatisfaction with the wares on display, the shopkeeper directed him to the back room where some of his most recent arrivals were stored. Accordingly, the marshal entered this room, leaving his wife admiring a cabinet of trinkets with Gorters.

"Only a minute had gone past when the heard a cry of dismay, a yelp like a frightened dog so the shopkeeper described it, but Lady Calath rushed through as if it were a matter of life and death and Gorters followed. When they entered they discovered the marshal facing a massive ornate mirror; one Gorters had bought from an auctioned estate only a week previously. It was of an old style; unremarkable in form or

58

provenance but of a sort recently popular with the merchants of the city apparently.

"The marshal stood with his back to the door, hands gripping the frame of the mirror and shoulders trembling. His wife rushed to his side, but Gorters said he could not bring himself to enter the room. While Lady Calath tried in vain to drag her husband away from the mirror, crying out his name in a terrified voice, Gorters caught sight of the marshal's reflection. The man was quite willing to express his cowardice in this matter, rather surprisingly I felt, but the man was adamant about what he saw.

"In the mirror he could see the marshal's face clearly, or rather, in his own words; 'it was the face of Marshal Calath, but distorted into something awful. His features were twisted, his eyes filled with shadows racing like clouds on the wind, lip curled in purest hatred.'

"Whatever Gorters truly saw, it shocked and horrified him enough to ignore Lady Calath's repeated calls for his assistance. As he stood there, transfixed by that 'daemonic visage' he heard a voice, a voice he claims came from the mirror rather than the marshal himself.'"

'Well, his fear got the better of him then, this is clearly another symptom of Calath's illness,' I said, unable to keep my opinions to myself. 'At this point I don't believe in any supernatural explanation. I may not understand the workings of lunacy, but I've heard enough of it to believe our marshal had become a truly ill man.'

Brandt looked at me with what I term his professional expression; one he normally reserved for overeager young watchmen. It was only my advanced years that reminded me not to apologise, even if I kept quiet thereon.

'"The voice was distant; echoing and faint, but still it burned into my memory and I'll never forget that moment. It said 'no escape from the shadows.' In response the marshal spoke, a single word in the voice of a man near dead with terror: Azaer. I don't know what it means but he spoke clear enough and it seemed to shock Lady Calath as much as I – more, for she seemed to recognise it and went white at its meaning."

'And that is the real reason I came to speak to you,' Brandt said in a subdued voice. 'As much as I value your experience, I'll win no friends by consulting with you on a case such as this – not with the reputation they painted you with. But I remember that case not long after I came to work for you – when you killed a vampire, or at least that's what the whole city said. Years later, when I married Liese, you told me the truth about that, how it was a madman who thought he was possessed by a daemon called Azaer.'

Brandt had a grave expression on his face, but what I wondered most was how much was he resting on this case. That celebrated victory over a 'vampire' changed my life and Brandt knew this all too well. It set me upon a path other than that of a simple watchman. Was he hoping that for a similar turn of fortunes, an avenue into high office that had been denied to him by three elder brothers?

He raised the parchment without waiting for me to find a response and cleared his voice.

'"*Before anything more could occur the marshal wrenched his hands off the frame of the mirror and drew a dagger from his belt. Because of his leg he had never been trained to use a blade and wore none, but carried a dagger that had been a gift from his father instead of the more traditional blade. The marshal raised the weapon in both hands above his head, struggling as though either his own body resisted or it were the weight of a grown man he lifted. Only then did Gorters find his courage, his fear of that monstrous face in the mirror eclipsed by his fear for Lady Calath's life now a weapon was drawn.*

"He dragged her away from her husband, but the marshal seemed not to even notice her absence. It took all his strength to face down whatever he saw in the mirror before he stabbed the dagger down into the mirror itself – right into that twisted face, so Gorters tells. The moment ended, Calath slumped to one knee and would have collapsed entirely, knife abandoned on the floor, had his wife not run to gather him. Gorters particularly noticed the marshal heaving for breath, gasping like a man who had just run a race across the city".'

'Indeed, or perhaps more fittingly, fought a battle – with whatever daemon inhabits his soul.'

'Daemon?' questioned Brandt.

'Daemon of the spirit,' I corrected. 'This man was not possessed, nor haunted I'll wager. Calath is – was – learned, and learned in the supernatural. That means he may well have come across the Azaer cult in his studies.'

'But what was that? I can find no trace of any such cult in any library or history.'

'And nor will you,' I said firmly. 'I doubt you'd be allowed to enter the sorts of collections that contain such a reference unless your brother was the one to make the request. They would only be found in the king's private collection and other closed libraries, but that's of little matter. The Azaer cult has been dead for years; knowledge of it is restricted because about a decade back a necromancer tried to revive it. Though the order was long dead the name still carries weight among men of power, most especially those who are trained in magical arts. There's an irrational fear they carry from the old wives' tales taught to novices at such places. Once you get them to acknowledge the truth of the Azaer cult, I'm told they do admit the foolishness of their fears, but it's a fear that lingers in the bones and defies explanation or exorcism.'

'So this is a dead end?' asked Brandt with a most disappointed tone. I am afraid that under my tutelage he must have contracted a love of the mysterious, one I should have discouraged. Few of us can profitably spend too long considering the stranger side of this Land and even fewer remember to consider the inherent dangers. Even with the example of my own disgrace, Brandt remained fascinated by things that went beyond everyday life.

'I'm afraid so,' I confirmed. 'There's no way this extinct cult could have caused any deaths, excepting the foolish or mad enacting deeds in the cult's name. A friend of mine wrote a work on the subject once, "The Origins and Place in History of the Azaer Cult" I believe. He'd seen the hurt caused by rumour and ignorance so he sought to consign it to history – demonstrate how there had never been a daemon called Azaer and those who acted in its name were merely the credulous or the criminal.'

'Damn,' Brandt said with abrupt finality. He gave the sheaf of papers one last look then dropped them lightly on a table and turned his back on them.

'Well then, I'll not bother you with the other accounts here. They're merely the same events recorded from the memories of others involved.' He then gave me a curious look. A sparkle of mischievous cunning I felt, one that made me wonder what foolishness I had just uttered. 'I shall therefore proceed straight to the murder report, wherein lies the mystery.'

Brandt took a moment to stretch his limbs, quite aware of the torment he was now causing. Walking over to the window he stared out at the gardens below, the faint smile on his face at my expense since I doubted the gardener at work was a sufficiently enjoyable sight. Brandt was a tall lad and at that moment I was struck by the realisation of how he towered over me. Despite my advancing years I still thought of Brandt as the awkward youth who had once scurried around the watch-house and blushed whenever he saw my daughter – not least because I had delighted in passing on her intentions to marry him as soon as she announced them.

Liese had been a mature girl of sixteen at the time, he a bumbling youth of fourteen. The difference in their station had been entirely overcast by the embarrassed awe he held my daughter in. It was hard to remember that this tall and powerful man was that same boy, now possessing a sharp mind and political aspirations.

'To begin with I shall set the scene,' he started suddenly, rounding on me with a smile on his face, but his eyes grave. 'As I have told you, the marshal and lady were found together, dead. We are not entirely sure what they were doing, but they were in his chamber with the door locked from the inside. They had brought out the only other large mirror they owned in the house ...'

'Wait, what was the condition of the marshal in the days before?' I asked in a professional capacity. If the man was touched by madness then his demeanour in the preceding days would have been crucial to shedding light on the deaths. If a man was to spiral down towards murder and suicide, there would surely be worsening signs in the days and weeks prior.

'His manservant insists that both the marshal and lady were in excellent spirits. They had spent many hours reading and writing together in his study and it was as if the fruits of this endeavour had restored their strength. They ate well, both taking a healthier colour due to restful sleep and many hours in their garden.

'Anyway, the scene,' he reminded me. 'On the marshal's desk was a book that dealt with exorcism and they had inscribed various symbols to this accompaniment on the wooden floor, having rolled back the rugs. Various historical works were scattered on the desk, all pertaining to Calath's usual studies according to Count Antern.

'The most significant addition to the room, aside from the mirror – which betrays a certain courage considering their experiences – was an amulet that was hung from the mirror's frame itself. It appeared that they had secured its loan from a friend of the Antern family, a priest of the temple of Larat who, among other things, had tutored Marshal Calath in his more arcane research. The amulet was a charm against hostile magics. All I can conclude from it is that they were taking a scientific approach to the matter ...'

'And attempting to rule out malevolent curses or spells cast by any unknown enemy,' I finished for him. 'A commendable effort, and I suppose one that will aid us later on since it can be tested by some authority in the city for validity.'

'Indeed,' said Brandt, sounding slightly put out that I had jumped in. 'I've already done so; as far as can be determined the amulet is not a fraud, but was not required that evening. Apparently it would have broken had malign magic been done against Calath, or at least broken before anything so fatal could have taken place.

'The windows of his study were fastened securely; in fact they had been nailed in by the stablehand that morning. An iron grille set into the brickwork protected the chimney flue, we cannot determine any possible point of entry that would leave no trace, nor alert the servants below who had remained in the building. As a last measure the same priest of Larat had consecrated the room, supposedly sealing it against intrusion by malign spirits.'

'So, we have a room that must, as far as I can tell, contain the killer. Continue.'

'The servants had received strict instructions not to intrude.

They did not until it became clear the next morning that the marshal and lady had not left the room at all during the night. They broke the door down to discover their bodies lying on the floor; the marshal before the mirror, the Lady Calath a little way closer to the door, but evidently she had made that distance crawling weakly. The blood trail is quite distinct – that she made it even a few feet while losing so much blood attests to a remarkable strength of will.

'The room was untouched, but there was a hole in the mirror – whatever had made that hole had smashed through the glass with enough force to shower them in shards. One such piece had torn the throat of the Lady Calath and remained lodged in the wound, the others caused a dozen minor wounds to each.

'The marshal had died where he had stood. Some weapon or implement had been driven through his chest, crushing the bones that stood in its way before ripping at his heart and rending it to pieces. That is all they found and nothing was touched before I arrived.'

He hesitated. 'And there is our problem. Our only explanation is that Marshal Calath in some fit of madness murdered his own wife for no reason, then managed to rip out his own heart using just shards of a mirror.'

Brandt stopped, seeing the effect his words had had on me. I bowed my head in prayer as I pictured the pale, waifish figure of Marshal Calath – my watchman's mind making it all too easy to see him broken and dead on the floor. It was an even more shocking image when my thoughts turned to the joyful and gracious lady I had seen from afar on several occasions; pain where once there was only sweetness and cheer. Sitting down opposite me once more, Brandt maintained his silence while the awful scene played before both our eyes; a whirl of sickness and horror filling my head.

Danc, perceiving the quiet from the room that he had left mere minutes before, took this quiet to be a natural break in proceedings and hurried in. He faltered somewhat when taking in my ashen features, wracked with confusion for a murder I could not explain no matter what my experience had boasted when Brandt arrived.

Handing Commander Brandt an envelope with a muttered apology, Danc retired hurriedly and closed the door behind him. Brandt took one look at the seal and glanced up with increased concern etched on his youthful features.

'It's from the king. The courier must have been directed here from my office.'

'Well open it, what does he say?'

Drawing a knife from his belt, Brandt slid it under the seal and removed the expensive vellum that bore the crest of the king. As Brandt flashed the page toward me, I saw it was in the king's own ornate script. The letter had not been sent by a palace functionary but King Emin himself.

Brandt cleared his through. 'It reads:

'"*Commander, The matter concerning the death of Marshal and Lady Calath is closed. The thief who broke in and committed this deed has been apprehended and justice served. You are to be commended for your efforts and I trust fanciful theories pertaining to this matter will be discouraged.*"

'I ...' Brandt looked up with a bewildered and pained expression, one I recognised only too well from my past.

Rising, I took the papers from where Brandt had left them and dropped them into the empty fireplace. I had no intention of actually setting them alight, but the look in Brandt's eyes showed I had secured the desired reaction of resigned agreement.

'This isn't the first time, trust me. The concerns of the king are not ours. Not justice, not the facts that detail each movement and action, not whatever you think of as truth. Truth is, to him, merely a weapon; a tool to use for whatever—'

He raised a hand to cut my feeble speech short. With an effort that seemed to add twenty years to him, Brandt lifted himself from his seat and made his way to the door.

'I've heard enough of your stories to know what you mean – and seen the king greet you personally, which tells me enough of their validity. You've been more of a father to me than my true sire. If you've lived with it and keep a respect for yourself then so can I.'

He paused and stood a little taller before he continued. 'Then so must I. I've always trusted your guiding hand when I couldn't see the way myself. I hope you'll explain to me one day, but until then I'll follow.'

He reached the door and then turned with a curious expression on his face. 'Tell me one thing though. With the circles you run in now, who was it that wrote the book – the book that disproved the existence of the Azaer cult?'

I gave him a weak smile, no humour in it but a trace of pride in the instincts he'd learned at my side.

'A friend.'

A MAN COLLECTING SPIRITS

Morghien looked up at the man staring at him from the next table. A blacksmith's brawn, a mule's face and a pig farmer's smell – this wasn't encouraging. Ever since Morghien had sat down with his beer and taken that first blessed mouthful, mule-face had been glaring at him. It was late afternoon and the village tavern had a half-dozen patrons, but only this one was giving him the evil eye.

Grey-haired and old enough to be unsure of when his prime had been, Morghien cut a nondescript figure at the best of times. The life of a restless wanderer did little for a man's appearance and his face bore the marks of two lifetimes, neither of which had been a whole lot of fun. It wasn't often he felt over-dressed in a tavern, but his soon-to-be adversary wasn't even wearing boots. Everything below the man's knee was caked in pale, crusting mud and his shirt was torn in several places.

The farmer had clearly been working all day rather than drinking and Morghien guessed it had been the summer sun that turned the farmer's mood rather than beer. Lady Midday's whispers normally made a man faint or heave his guts, but Morghien had seen enough of the Land's strangeness to rule nothing out.

Gods, he can't be sizing me up, can he? Morghien wondered with a sinking feeling. *I look older than his father, what sort of shit-brained hick could think he needs to prove himself against me?*

Morghien gave the man a wide, friendly grin. It didn't seem to improve matters. The farmer's hand tightened into a fist and he didn't take his eyes off Morghien even as he drained his own beer.

There he goes. So much for a quiet drink.

'Bit early isn't it?' Morghien called, quiet enough that only the folk nearest him paid any attention.

'You talkin' to me?'

Morghien blinked. 'My apologies – I assumed looking straight at you when I spoke would've been clue enough.'

'You tryin' to be smart?'

'Doubt your reaction's going to be much different either way,' Morghien muttered under his breath. 'Yes, I'm talking to you; you've been glaring at me since I came in. Now I might have pissed off folk up and down this fair Land, but I don't reckon we've met before, so don't you think it's a bit early for the *"we don't like strangers in these here parts"* crap?'

'For an old bastard you got a big mouth on ya,' the farmer growled, pushing himself to his feet. Turned out he looked bigger standing than hunched over a beer. 'Strangers in these parts we don't mind, but troublemakers get thrown out on their arses and I reckon I know which you is.'

Morghien rolled his eyes, fighting the urge to let the man talk his way into trouble. He could frighten off the brainless mule easily enough, but he really didn't need the trouble of a public display. Old he might have been, but Morghien had a few tricks lurking in the dark corners of his mind – tricks even his friends in the Narkang Brotherhood wouldn't choose to tangle with.

All around him the room had fallen silent, tense and twitching like rabbits waiting to run. He took a moment to inspect the faces watching him from elsewhere in the tavern, determined not to rush into a confrontation for a change. Most of the onlookers seemed apprehensive at what the farmer was looking to start, but not all. A small woman sat at the end of the bar with a thin-faced man and they both simply watched the scene unfold.

Dispassionate, iron-grey eyes watched him while the woman idly played knotted black threads through her fingers. Morghien had noticed her as soon as he'd arrived and done the right thing when he had, bought the witch a drink as a mark of respect before retreating to a table of his own. The man – her husband or something approximating it – had long dark hair, a thin beard and hollow cheeks, but the piercing eyes of a crow. He was at least curious and watched Morghien with a strange intensity, while the witch hadn't decided to pay him much attention.

'Is this how strangers are greeted in these parts?' Morghien asked the room in general, his eyes on the witch. 'When you first came here, Mistress, were they so friendly?'

The witch took a sip of beer and considered the question. 'Not so much,' she said finally, prompting the man beside her to smile. 'But you know respect sometimes has to be earned, sometimes taught.'

The farmer glanced between Morghien and the witch, unwilling to back down, but not so stupid as to go against the witch's wishes.

'I'm a bit old for teaching anyone about respect,' Morghien said.

He glanced down as surreptitiously as he could at the axe that hung from a loop on his pack. He wasn't sure he could reach it in time, which was a shame. It would be enough of a threat to make an unarmed man back off, while the dagger at his belt was more likely to get him killed than anything else. Every man wore a knife, certainly in parts such as these. Lady Midday might not be a spirit one feared, but there were plenty of others around that would do more than whisper at you.

'Who says you'll be doin' the teachin'?' the farmer snapped, trying to regain the initiative.

'Oh I think you'd learn somethin' any road,' the witch drawled. 'Might be a good lesson too. Or you could show our new friend here that you're a real man and buy him a beer instead. Brawling's for little boys after all, drinking's for men I'm told.'

The farmer pursed his lips, then gave a sharp nod and sat back down. He didn't look happy with the outcome, but the witch's tone had been clear enough; the fun was over. With an approving nod the witch touched the hand of the man beside her and he slipped behind the bar. When two beers had been poured the witch herself brought them over, sitting at Morghien's table as she did so.

Her grey hair was seamed with black. Looking closely, Morghien realised she wasn't as old as he'd assumed – a good ten years younger than he himself appeared – but the eyes were cold and knowing. This close he knew for sure she wasn't just a medicine woman, a soul like that ruled the village, not served it.

Morghien accepted the beer and raised it in a toast to the farmer. The man gave a gruff grunt and looked away, but Morghien saw his shoulders relax a little and guessed the gesture had had the desired effect.

'So stranger, why are you in these parts?' the witch asked with a deliberate lack of edge to her tone.

Without meaning to, Morghien glanced out the window. The shadows were long over the dirt path leading up to the tavern, the ghost hour wasn't yet upon the Land.

'Can't a man be just passing through?'

The witch gave a knowing smile. 'Could be, but we're not on the way to much here – and anyways, you ain't a normal sort o' stranger.'

Morghien gave a snort. 'Coming from a witch with a husband?' he said softly, looking over at the thin man who'd returned to his seat at the bar.

The man's deep-set eyes and narrow beard made him look something rather more sinister than a tavern-owner, but he placidly endured Morghien's attention and raised his drink in toast without comment.

'Can you see me bein' welcome at temple even for my own marriage?' the witch asked levelly.

'Perhaps not,' he conceded, 'but when it looks like a dog and barks like a dog ...'

'It's a bloody dog,' the witch finished, 'and oddity that you are, call me bitch and see how welcome you feel then.'

Morghien grinned. Getting under the skin of others was something of a speciality of his. Often it still resulted in adding to his collection of scars, but folk became sloppy when they were annoyed and sometimes they let slip things they shouldn't. In his line of business that was usually worth a little trouble.

Without warning, the witch reached out and touched two fingers to the back of Morghien's hand. He snatched it away, but was too late to stop her sensing something and the witch's annoyance was replaced with curiosity.

'Didn't your mother ever tell you that was rude?'

'Sometimes rude isn't the worst outcome.' She leaned forward and peered into his eyes. 'There's a whole mess of somethin' inside you and that tells me I should know your business here before you get a friendly welcome.'

Morghien hesitated. Having expected a threatening tone of voice, it wasn't what he'd got at all.

Hah, I've spent too much time with soldiers, always trying to piss the highest. Witches don't need to bother there.

'Ghost hour's coming,' he commented, sipping his beer.

The witch's eyes narrowed, then he saw a small spark in those grey eyes. 'The watcher in the willows? Oh wonderful, some idiot with a handful of power thinks he can come and save us.'

He didn't rise to the bait. 'I'm surprised you haven't tried yourself.'

'Some of us have more sense than power; you don't know what you're playin' with here.'

'Trust me; I'm not looking for a fight with anything or anyone.'

'Then leave it be,' the witch hissed, 'no one round here walks the river-path 'cept when the sun's out – I made sure of that and I don't intend to let you stir up any more trouble than we already have.'

'Then tell me more than I've already heard,' Morghien insisted, 'because I intend to head that way as soon as I'm finished.'

The witch watched him like a cat for a long while, trying to read his whiskery face. He understood her concerns and gave her time to think. If what he'd heard was true, a careless hand could bring horror down upon the village, but Morghien knew she'd not have seen anyone like him in these parts.

My own particular sort of fool, I am, but I know my limits.

'I'm not here to play the hero,' he said after a while, 'I know when a risk isn't worth taking.'

She glanced outside. The sky was starting to darken to a deep, cloudless blue. A pair of pigeons hopped from branch to branch in a large oak just outside the tavern, from which was hung half a hundred long strips of colourful material. A week past, at the midsummer festival, the villagers would have hung offerings to the spirits of the forest from those dyed lengths. Morghien had inspected them before coming in; only the birds had touched the offerings, the local spirits had kept well clear.

'Drink up,' she said in a resigned voice. 'I'll tell you on the way.'

'You see the line of willows?' the witch said, pointing ahead. 'Walk that way and it'll speak to you.'

Morghien nodded. There were half-a-dozen or more ancient hanging willows a hundred paces down-river; silent but for the sound of their tendrils dipping into the water under the urging of a gentle breeze. Anyone walking along this side of the river would have to pass underneath them and walk within the enclosed space below. He could barely see through the thick green fronds; the sun had only recently sunk below the horizon but the river bank was uncommonly gloomy.

'You'll not leave without giving somethin' up,' she warned.

Morghien held up a silver coin that, despite the grime on it, glittered bright in the gloaming. 'Not what it wants, but it'll do.'

'Don't you anger it now.'

'Oh I intend to do more than that,' he said softly, still staring into the darkness under the willows but seeing nothing. 'Something of a speciality o' mine, that is.'

'Then do it right,' the witch said with finality. 'I'll be watchin' too.'

She plonked herself down on the riverbank with the ceremony of a little girl, arranging her skirts around her while gently slapping the bare soles of her feet on the water's surface. Once comfortable she pulled out a tobacco pouch and stuffed a pipe with a dark brown wad. She pressed it down hard before leaving her thumb in the bowl for a while, then withdrew it hurriedly as the tobacco began to smoulder. She sucked hard on the pipe, waiting for it to be fully lit before washing her thumb in the river.

'Go on then,' the witch said, waving Morghien forward. 'Don't let me hold you up.'

He stared a moment longer, realising the pipe had been a small demonstration for him – *I have some power myself; make sure you can top that before going any further.*

'You're a nag, woman,' he replied with a smile and walked away, heading for the willows.

Despite the summer evening, he couldn't hear any birds or animals in the area. Only the river's quiet burble broke the silence; no swallows came to drink during their evening hunt and he saw no nesting ducks in the rushes. There was only the heavy blue-grey of dusk settled over the surrounding trees and an uneasy silence.

Before he reached the willows, Morghien stopped and looked into the water. He could see the bottom clear enough, it was not deep.

'Come closer, stranger,' came a voice as elusive and whispery as the wind, 'come close so I may see the gentle lines of your face.'

Morghien suppressed a smile. If the watcher in the willows thought him just some village simpleton, so much the better.

He took a tentative step closer. The curtain of hanging willow branches was thick enough for him to be unable to make out much, all he could see was a dark, hunched shape wrapped in a long piece of cloth like a blanket.

'Take pity on me, good traveller,' the figure softly pleaded, 'for I am blind and helpless.'

Morghien edged to a few paces short of the willow branches. The other figure was just within, close enough to part what divided them.

'Are you hurt, friend?' he asked in a halting voice. *It appears that sounding nervous comes more easily than I'd realised.*

'Blind I am, lost I am,' the other moaned. 'Waylaid by thugs, taunted and beaten. They took my belongings and tossed them in the river, laughing like jackals. I am so cold, so hungry. I have been alone here for days – will you help me, good sir?'

'What help do you need?' Morghian asked, knowing the answer already.

The one behind the curtain reached out an imploring hand. It was pale and withered, age-spotted and filthy. Morghien got a better look at the watcher in the willows now; a frail old man with a ragged dark blanket wrapped around his body and over his head, one hand holding it in place at his sagging throat. His eyes were screwed up tight, his mouth hanging slightly open to reveal a blackened tongue and the broken stubs of teeth.

'My possessions they threw away, my purse they took and emptied into the river. For cruelty's sake, not theft. A dozen silver coins I had in that purse, earnings to last my family through the winter.' The old man was pleading now, his voice hoarse and rasping.

'In the river here?'

'Not far from here,' the old man insisted, 'I did not dare stray far from the spot in case I could not find it again. I have been here for three days, praying the blessed Gods would send someone to my aid.'

Praying? That's a nice touch, said the part of Morghien that was a much practised liar. 'Certainly I'll help you!' he said with zeal.

'Do we have a bargain?'

'We do! The chains I will drag up Ghain's slope will be plentiful enough, I'm sure. Let's hope the Mercies are watching this evening.'

The old man bowed his head as though giving thanks for Morghien's words. The wanderer saw his cracked lips twitch at the mention of Ghain, the mountainside of purgatory that led to Ghenna.

'The Mercies see all,' he intoned, 'they will reward you, as will I when my silver coins are in my hand.'

Morghien slipped his pack from his back and set it at the river's edge, within easy reach. The water was chilly after the day's warmth when he stepped down into the river. Glancing upstream he saw the witch still sitting where he'd left her, puffing on her pipe and watching everything that went on.

He waded out into the centre of the river, the water reaching only up to his groin but flowing at a brisk pace. As he looked around at the water he could feel the old man watching with hungry intent. When Morghien turned back he saw the man kneeling on the bank, carefully within the trailing curtain of willow.

'Somewhere about here?' he called brightly. 'Shall I start looking here?'

'Yes, yes,' the old man called urgently, 'they must be near there!'

Morghien noisily splashed around him for a while, turning in a circle while a tiny trail of white mist bled into the water below him.

Dear me, like a toddler in the bath, he thought, careful to keep the smile that provoked out of the blind old man's view.

'I can't see anything,' he called helpfully and watched the old man wring his hands anxiously.

'They are there,' the old man croaked, 'they must be there. Please look harder before the ghost hour is over!'

Getting worried now, aren't you? The witch has kept folk away from here, but you can't leave so easily. Morghien thought.

'Aha!' he shouted and bent down to grab something from the river bed. He held it high, fist closed tight around it, and gave a triumphant cheer.

'And there's another!' he said and bending to retrieve the second. In his enthusiasm Morghien stood up and flung an arm out towards the old man, throwing a spray of water from his sleeve across the curtain of night-shrouded willow. The old man cringed back, almost falling.

'Sorry!' Morghien called with excessive cheerfulness as he waded back towards the bank. When he was a few paces away he tossed the fruits of his labours onto the grassy bank behind his pack.

The old man reached a hand up to the willow fronds, his fingers hovering in the act of pushing through the curtain. He went very still and then withdrew his hand back to the folds of his blanket.

'These are not coins,' the old man hissed.

'Really? You sure?'

'Of course. They are nothing more than stones,' the old man snapped.

Morghien made a show of peering forward. 'Oh, so it is.' He gave a disappointed sigh. 'It is a white stone,' he said in mitigation, 'it looked silver in the river.'

'It has a hole in!'

'So it does. Ah well, better try again I suppose.'

Morghien waded back to the middle of the river and started to walk in slow circles, staring intently down through the water. Three more times he gave a small cheer and reached down to grab something, frowning at the contents of his hand each time when he straightened up.

'They're just stones,' he called out for the old man's benefit, holding one up. 'Look this one's got a hole in too!'

'I do not care for stones,' came the old man's susurrus voice from the gloom of the willows. 'Fetch me my coins!'

'Temper, temper,' Morghien replied, ignoring the angry sound that provoked. He resumed his search and three more times went to grab at something in the water. After the third he waded part of the way back to the bank and tossed up six more stones onto the bank.

'More stones, I'm afraid.'

The old man screeched in fury. 'The coins are there, I can sense them. You are a fool if you cannot find them – my patience for stones is at an end!'

'Well, there's no need to be rude,' Morghien said in a hurt voice. 'I'm working on a song; do you want to hear it while I search?' he asked suddenly. 'It's very good.'

'Enough of your stupidity!' the old man howled. 'Find me the coins or I swear by the gates of Jaishen I shall tear the flesh from your bones and suck the marrow from your bones.'

Morghien took a step back. 'Fair enough, point taken – more looking, less talking,' he said, looking back down at the water. 'Found one!'

He threw forward something that glittered in the dying light, a silver coin. Morghien watched the old man's head rise and fall, following the arc as it fell with the stones he'd previously thrown. At last the old man hopped out from within the willow's boundary and reached out to grab the coin. His bent back gave the blanket a lumpy, broken look and the effort seemed to make him snuffle and gasp.

'I once knew a man who lived under a willow,' Morghien sang

out without warning, causing the old man to jerk his head up. 'That's how the song starts.'

'This is not one of the coins I seek,' the old man snarled.

He opened his eyes and they shone yellow in the fading light. The blanket covering him fell away and revealed wide scales that tapered to a point covering his head. When he opened his mouth again it revealed rows of sharp pointed teeth and a long bifurcated tongue.

Morghien made a dismissive gesture with his hand and continued. 'I once knew a man who lived under a willow, his eyes were empty and his teeth broke low.'

The old man gave a feral bark and his jaw distended, jerking forward once, then twice, until it resembled the muzzle of a dog. Pale, lifeless hands became even more clawed and turned in, but now looked stubby and reptilian.

'You could have saved yourself, but you bargained and then played the fool,' the daemon declared in a low snarl. 'For that I will eat your soul!'

'Coins he wanted, help he prayed for,' Morghien continued with a theatrical flourish, oblivious to what was happening on the river bank. 'I took his coins and him a fool for. A circle of stones I made, the trap sprung was not one he laid.'

The daemon hissed in fury and flexed his talons.

'Oh quiet, you scaly old wretch!' Morghien said irritably, 'you can't cross water so you can stay there hissing all damn night for all I care.'

'You cannot stay in the water, mortal. You will not deny me my prize, not now a bargain has been made.'

'Really? You should learn to listen, my friend.'

Morghien waded towards the daemon, jingling a handful of tarnished coins and offering them forward for the daemon to see. The act enraged the daemon further, but as much as it slashed and scraped wildly at the air they both knew it couldn't enter the river.

Reaching the bank, Morghien held the fistful of coins up and waved them just out of the daemon's reach.

'Dead man's coins, aren't they?' he demanded. 'Coins put in the lips of dead sinners while they're laid out. Some part o' the soul is tied to the coin, staying cool in the water to ease whatever torment awaits them.'

'They will not escape their fate,' spat the daemon, 'no witch's charm can deny it.'

Morghien smiled. 'Their last judgement ain't mine to pronounce, but I see no reason to let the lowest of Ghenna's creatures hold these souls as currency.'

'All souls are currency,' the daemon snarled, 'and yours will join them as soon as you leave this water.'

'Sorry, ugly, but I'm not the fool I look,' Morghien said with a smile. He pointed down at the daemon's feet. 'That's a circle of stones you're standing in. My magic may not be up to much, but it's enough to seal one of those for the night.'

The daemon screamed and raged at the barrier containing it, but to no avail. As hard as it thrashed it could do nothing to break free. Morghien smiled and reached one hand out over the water. A ghostly white arm rose up from the surface and deposited a handful more coins in his palm before contentedly drifting back down.

'One of the useful things about being possessed by an Aspect of Vasle,' Morghien continued, 'is it's not hard finding stuff in water. These'll be coming with me – I can always make a home for another few spirits. I don't think the witches of these parts'll be leaving coins in this stretch of river ever again.'

He stowed the coins in a pocket and dragged his pack from the bank, resting it on one shoulder to keep it well clear of the water he stood in. In the advancing dark he could make out little detail of the daemon beyond its glowing yellow eyes, but it was enough to see it knew when it was beaten.

'As for the stones binding you, the witch'll fetch them in the morning; once the dawn's light has made that scabby little body of yours melt like mist.' He gave the daemon a cheery wave and started making his way towards the opposite bank.

'Come dusk tomorrow,' Morghien called over his shoulder, 'those stones'll be strung on a chain and hung from a bridge. Since your kind can't cross water and the witch has got all the folk round here properly under her thumb, you'll have to wait for the bridge to collapse or the river to run dry before you're released. Either way, enjoy your time in the sun.'

He reached the other side and hauled himself out of the water with a groan. Once on the bank Morghien shook himself like a dog to get the worst of the water off before giving the daemon a mocking bow. Along the far bank he walked, heading for the village for a beer well-earned, whistling merrily all the way. The daemon could only howl.

A MAN FROM THISTLEDELL

Marshal Calath leaned forward in his seat and idly scratched his outstretched leg. It was a hindrance at the best of the times, but when the wind rushed down the chimney and rain thrashed at the window, the malformed limb caused him even greater discomfort. His host, Magistrate Derran, noticed the movement and raised an eyebrow. Calath waved the unspoken question away, brushing the trouser down and returning his hand to his lap.

A goblet of brandy nestled there while wisps of cigar smoke drifted past his face. Calath resumed his previous position, head titled to rest slightly against the high side of his armchair, half-looking into the blazing fire but focused on nothing. There was a sprawl of rugs underfoot, expensive weaves that covered the wood-tiled floor and looked bright and warm in the light of the room's three candelabras.

This snug was considerably less impressive than the formal elegance of the rest of the manor, but a welcome place to while away the last hours of the evening. After a cold day and a fine meal, Calath had even partaken in a small cigar himself as suitable accompaniment to the brandy, much to his friend's approval.

'I thought we might make to join the hunt over at Alscap Hall tomorrow,' said Magistrate Derran, every syllable rounded with hearty vigour.

Calath looked up through fragile eyes, his nervous features cautiously approaching a laugh until he realised the man was serious. 'Derran, somehow I think my leg will scarcely have healed by then.'

The plump magistrate stared down at Calath's leg through the warm confusion of brandy, then realisation caught hold and he threw back his head in laughter.

'Hah! Too true my friend, but I hardly would have suggested riding with the hunt. What a fine pair we'd make; yourself with that leg caught in the stirrups and me fretting about breaking the back of the poor beast I was riding!'

The marshal smiled weakly at the idea. For all the humour Ves Derran found in it, Calath could only imagine the prickling horror of being once more the comical centrepiece. He reached absently down to stroke the wolfhound dozing between their two chairs. The rough mess of grey fur shifted slightly at his touch, but the attention soon proved welcome and the dog leaned into Calath's thin fingers as he gently scratched the creature's flank.

'No, my friend, I meant that we attend in a vastly more civilised capacity. Count Alscap is well known for his hospitality; truly I believe he will take offence if I do not present such an excellent guest for his pleasure.'

'Now Derran, you know how I am not that sort of man ...' Calath began before a flurry of gestures and friendly heckles drowned out his soft protestations.

'Bah! None of that, quiet you old woman! Alscap is a fine man, perfectly without the pretensions you work so hard to avoid. I tell you, you will more than enjoy yourself there. I know what you city folk think of us – simple and insular to name a few of the words I've heard used – but some out here are the very best of humanity. And that brings me to my principal reason for taking you there. There is a certain young lady—'

'Derran, please! I had thought better of you,' exclaimed Calath, stiffening his spine to stare down his portly companion. 'I hoped to spend my time here in blissful absence of such harpings.'

'Ah my dear Calath, how could I attempt to imitate such a fine tyrant as your mother? My hands tremble to even contemplate the prospect.'

The magistrate who made such great levity of threats and curses bestowed from the dock, held up his meaty paws and shook them with great pantomime, but it failed to raise a smile. 'I demand nothing, nor will I suggest solitary walks and the like as I've heard done in the past. I claim no knowledge or ability in arranging the annals of romance. Surely my wife must have regaled you half-a-dozen times with my bungling attempts to woe her!'

Calath regarded his friend coldly as the magistrate chuckled at the memory, but was soon won over by the infectious noise. Once more the shy, bookish marshal felt great pangs of envy for his extravagant, expansive friend. The man took such magnificent delight in life and the Land around him, it was impossible to dislike him or remain angry in his presence for long.

Indeed, Ves Derran was renowned as a man incapable of retaining mere acquaintances. The regular traffic of callers and invitations testified to the fact that if you didn't consider the magistrate a friend, you couldn't have met him outside court. There were more than a few who bore him a grudge, for he was a terror for truth and protocol in his own domain, but five minutes at some gathering or another was easily enough time to secure an invitation to dinner, and reason to accept.

By consequence, it had always mystified the reticent Calath quite why Derran possessed such a fondness for him – but possess it he did, like a blazing torch of goodness that quite shamed those who looked down on the crippled academic. It was for this buoying reason Calath had accepted the open invitation when his health took a turn for the worse. His physician had prescribed country air, rest and companionship, and the timing had proved fortuitous. Derran had been delighted at the prospect, having been facing a month alone as his wife went to assist the wedding preparations of an orphaned niece.

'As I was about to say,' continued Derran, wagging a finger in mock admonishment, 'I feel sure there will be a lady there who will make the onerous task bearable. She is the daughter of a knight whose brother is no doubt known to you from Narkang—'

Calath raised a hand. 'Please, save me the credentials. You know I'd rather keep my distance from political families.'

Oh, I know what you're after,' replied his friend with a twinkling eye, ignoring the outraged look he received, 'but I was merely stating that any exacting parent would approve. Your mother could hardly object to the niece of the king's first minister, Count Antern, whether or not you like the man your-self. The woman herself is a delightful creature, both in looks and demeanour—'

'And I have heard that said before,' Calath broke in. 'I know well enough that a lady's demeanour is a measure of her docile stupidity.'

'And I swear I shall rap you about the ears with my stick if you interrupt again!' bellowed Derran in exasperation, his ears turning a curious purple by the force of his cry. Calath shrank back in his chair; too well acquainted with his friend to fear the man, but now able to believe the reports of how he ruled his court.

'Is that the end of your interruptions?' Derran barked imperiously. 'Yes? Excellent. As I was saying, she is a delightful creature; generous in spirit and deed, in addition to the intellect the Gods have granted her.'

The magistrate's face softened, his gentle smile returning. 'Calath, you forget I'm not your mother – for all I lament a lack of attributes that would have brought me to the post of High Inquisitor – but a friend who knows you as well as any, I fancy. I tell you this lady will enchant you. She is polite and well presented in all ways, but her parents consider her intelligence a curse to marriage for she has seen off several suitors with the power of argument.'

Derran's eyes twinkled. 'Aha! I thought a mind to complement your own would strike some vein of masculine interest. See how I know your mind better than yourself? Now, I shall say nothing more on the subject to protect you from any harping, trumpeting or even fluting. I am confident enough in my judgement as it is – a fortunate thing in my profession. Even drunk as a judge as I may be right now, I know you will be bewitched on the morrow.'

Derran scratched at the thick stubble on his face, pausing to peer curiously at his hand. He waved the stubby paw back and forth, then lowered it and set his goblet on a side table.

'And now I realise the need to retire. I bid you good night and dreams of the Lady Meranna.'

The magistrate heaved himself to his feet, tree-trunk legs as steady as ever despite the quantities of wine he'd managed since the sun neared the horizon. With a theatrical bow he left the fireside and stamped to the door, clicking his fingers to the hound that was already at his heel. Derran dragged open the ancient oak door and discovered his servant poised on the other side, arriving to refill their glasses.

'Aha, good man, I was wondering where you'd disappeared off to. I'm to bed, as that reprobate by the fire should also do. But fetch him some warmed milk first, and then retire yourself. Must have you bright and alert for tomorrow, eh Calath?'

Not waiting for an answer, Derran ploughed on past his faithful servant and off to his room. Milk was brought and sipped idly as Calath stared into the fire, a curious anxiety building over the possibilities of the next day. The flames danced carelessly in a manner he'd often dreamed of – unaware and free, ever graceful and mysterious.

With a malformed leg, Calath had found his entire life a struggle to maintain some form of dignity. A childhood indoors, away from the activity most noble-born boys engaged in, had left him with a face more thin and pale than handsome. He was painfully glad that there were men who admired his intellect, more every year as Narkang's prosperity bred a more genteel nobility, but few men envied a cripple.

Though that admiration and recognition were scant comfort, he reminded himself the flattered dandies and brainless soldiers – all so quick to mock in public and private – would all find their charms waning as the years passed. By contrast his skills and reputation would only increase in the coming decades. Glory might never be his, but the king was building a nation that might one day celebrate academics and Calath hoped he might leave a legacy that went beyond battles or petty court intrigues.

The candles burned low and a few eventually extinguished, but since Derran had dismissed the butler for the night Calath found himself amid shadows that grew steadily darker and sharper. The tall oak bookcases and cabinets, formerly so welcomed by a learned man, grew mysterious and watching. The marshal huddled up against the gloom, suddenly looking about at some perceived noise. Up behind the chair, into the corners, at the ground beneath the curtains; only once the room was fully inspected did he mutter chastisements for his drunken foolishness.

The dark was no friend of his, however and once unsettled the marshal found himself restless. Calath sighed and realised he should also be abed rather than linger with the embers of the fire. The room had chilled with the waning light; though still snug enough for a few minutes longer, Calath was glad to stir from the armchair. He hoisted himself upright, leaning heavily on his walking stick and dragged the guard before the fire. That done he made his way upstairs, all the while listening for dark noises about him though none ever came.

'Calath, is this not a wonderful morning?' Derran bellowed with infuriating cheer.

Calath winced as he glanced out the window on his right, which afforded him a fine view of the magistrate's neat gardens. The terrace and lawn were both covered in a generous sprinkling of snow, while the outspread yew glinted and sparkled in the morning sunshine. Faint tracks left by some small bird led across the ground away from an iced birdbath that stood proudly atop the terrace wall.

Calath could see the impressions of his friend's broad boots leading down the snow-concealed stone path. Derran's trail skirted the bushes on the left-hand side and led to a wrought-iron gate at the far end which opened onto the orchard. Alongside those prints were the tracks of his wolfhound, spread impossibly long from the dog's great stride.

'It looks cold,' Calath replied after taking in the winter scene.

'Ah, foolishness! I tell you there's nothing quite so wonderful as the scent of fresh snow on the air. It's not even cold once you're wearing a jacket; no wind to speak of, just glorious sun.'

'Surely the hunt will be cancelled now?' asked Calath as he took his place at the table.

He had dressed in the stiff, heavy woollens preferred for country walking in such weather, though he doubted he'd be venturing much beyond a cultivated garden. It was the uniform for social events of this kind and the expense was certainly preferable to standing out among the boisterous, bluff noblemen he'd meet.

'Cancelled? But of course not.' Derran chuckled, freshly shaved cheeks rosy with humour and the chill of without. 'They've been praying for weeks that the snow will come in time. It's a poor winter hunt without it and more dangerous, unless the ground freezes of course. The wolves get a fighting chance since their coats will have turned weeks back, and riders will be more able to see brichen boars before one's upon them. Caught unawares, they could be unseated and killed by the fearsome brutes.'

'It sounds an awful way to spend the morning,' muttered Calath.

Though he was approaching thirty-five winters, the marshal felt unaccountably nervous at the coming day. He picked idly at the food placed before him, but could stomach nothing more that some honeyed porridge and weak tea. A sudden shiver passed through his body, as if an ominous cloud had unexpectedly covered the sun, and his skin prickled up into an army of goosebumps.

'My dear man, are you quite well?' Derran asked with concern. 'You look as though someone has walked over your grave.'

'I rather think they have,' answered Calath without thinking, then shook his head at his own words. 'Forgive me, I'm talking nonsense now. I do feel rather curious, but no doubt it was the wine from last night.'

'Is that all? You look like you've had a fright. Unpleasant dreams?'

'I, I don't believe so. I just have the sense today will not be entirely agreeable, that there is some turn for the worst in the air.'

'Ah,' exclaimed the magistrate, 'you're beginning to sound like the old men from the village! Never happier than when they're predicting disaster, those old boys, but I'd always imagined it to be a country trait. Still, I suppose your work must bring you into contact with such superstitions all the time, it was bound to rub off sooner or later.'

His words had the desired reaction. Calath's colour returned somewhat and he spluttered his indignation at Derran's suggestion.

'How can you compare my research to the chatterings of the ignorant? And as for dismissing it as superstition, that's an impious insinuation as well as insulting. Much of my work concerns ...'

Derran held up a hand, holding back the laughter at his friend's sudden passion. 'I apologise, Calath! I know perfectly well the validity of your work. Was it not you who introduced me to the king when I last visited Narkang? If that great man endorses and supports your research then I hold it as true as commandments from the Gods themselves. I merely intended to demonstrate to you that the best method to shake an ill feeling is to stir the blood – and don't you feel the better for it?'

Calath opened his mouth to speak, then thought for a moment. He smiled, embarrassment lurking at the corners of his mouth.

'I suppose so,' he mumbled.

'Exactly,' declared the magistrate in a satisfied tone. 'I'm a fat fool only when it suits me, remember?'

With a snap of the fingers, Derran attracted the attention of his wolfhound. By the time he'd picked up a thick bacon rind from his plate the dog was sat at his side, expectantly licking its lips. The rind went down in one snap, but Derran ignored the hound's hopeful stare as it licked its chops.

'Right, I think we should be off.'

The magistrate stood and rapped the table with a professional assurance to draw breakfast to a close. Calath dabbed a napkin to his lips and rose to follow. At the door he hesitated for a second, glancing back out through the window nervously as if expecting some wild boar to be waiting for him out there. Nothing returned his gaze, only the idyllic scene of before, but still he couldn't fully erase the apprehension crawling over his skin. He jumped as the wolfhound scrambled down the wooden passageway after its master, the clatter of its claws echoing loudly in the enclosed space.

Only once the dog was out of view could he bring himself to follow, pushing heavily down on his stick as his leg felt heavier and more unwieldy as ever. The smell of beeswax polish accompanied him as Calath headed to the front porch, carefully stepping around the ageing bearskin rug in the centre of the hall. Its snarling, open maw seemed to follow him as he struggled down the stone steps; Calath could feel the smooth press of teeth upon his neck even as he walked away. Only the slam of the coach door relieved the pressure, and then at last he could see the morning for the beautiful day it was.

A sentinel line of straight-backed ash trees stood on each side of the driveway, kissed by the low, crisp golden light. The fields were fragments of a childhood memory; too perfect for the here and now and yet they endured for the entire journey. By the time their driver announced sight of their destination, Calath was as cheery as his hearty friend. Through the coach window he watched the country house grow large against the horizon and, as they drew nearer, was struck by the sprawling bulk of the hall.

Alscap Hall was a house far larger than his own; a mansion without fortification and cultivated grounds stretching far off in all directions. Despite its traditional architecture, Calath realised it had to be a recent construction. Only with the peace and prosperity of King Emin's reign could someone build in these parts with so little regard for defensive measures.

Made of reddish sandstone that seemed to glow in the sunlight and laced with snow, Alscap Hall was built in a square with thin towers reaching up from each corner. High arched windows were spaced down each flank, the near-side looking over frosted flowerbeds and statues to a large yew maze that stood in the midst of cropped lawns.

'An attractive pile, isn't it?' Derran commented. 'The count is new money so a little ostentatious – those towers for example, my goodness – but an excellent sort all the same.'

'Where did his money come from? It must have cost a fortune to build,' breathed Calath, mentally estimating the number of rooms the hall must contain.

'And it did by all accounts, but Alscap worked hard for the money. He started as a merchant's apprentice so he claims, but by the age of forty held a near monopoly on the coastal trade route. It's said he was instrumental in the submission of Denei to the king.'

'And was rewarded accordingly?' mused Calath, tearing his eyes away from the building. The magistrate nodded.

'And the rest; trade routes, preferential taxation, royal

commissions, even swifter justice if you believe rumour. But perhaps you'd know more about that than I, being a confidant of the king.' Derran was mocking him now, but the serious look on Calath's face stopped Derran's amusement short.

'Hardly a confidant, but the king is a master when it comes to recognising ability and using it to his own gain. The man would be a tyrant of the most monstrous order if his goals were meaner.'

'How do you mean?'

Derran's questioning face reminded Calath that few men were blessed with their king's luminous presence. Few outside his enclosed circle knew much at all about the man who wore the crown. King Emin, for all his political genius, was a secretive individual who disdained the social scene his queen deftly ruled.

'Well now, I suppose the best way to describe it is that though I feel I know King Emin only slightly, he remembers everything he's ever been told about me. The man is so intelligent he can quite capably debate with me on my own field of study – though he holds no particular interest in the subject. As men become your firm friends after five minutes of conversation, so they become Emin's awe-struck acolytes. But as much as I respect him, I fear him more so. There is nothing beyond him if he feels it necessary.'

'But still you align yourself to him?' asked Derran, his voice tinged with ghastly wonder.

Calath looked deep into his friend's large, red-veined eyes and nodded sadly. 'Oh yes, though sometimes I wonder. But if you spoke to him about such matters – with a spirit bolder than mine – I have no doubt you would fail to dispute a word he says. What sets him aside from a despot is that this nation is his life, his reputation and his legacy. No, perhaps that does not set him sufficiently apart – in addition, the strength of the nation at every level of society is his concern and the man assesses his work with an unbiased eye.'

'So you would not be surprised by the rewards he bestowed upon Alscap?'

'Not at all, Emin is a man you can trust. His enemies can trust that he will destroy them entirely, whether through ingenuity or force. His friends can trust that he will not forget a bargain, however unforgiving he may be to those who fail him.'

Derran stared at his friend for a moment before he shivered at the bleak world of politics. 'Then I'm glad that's isn't my life. The law may have its faults, but at least it follows rules I can fathom. The boundaries are set and written down for men to read and conform to. In your world it seems a man can die without even knowing what he did was wrong.'

'My world?' exclaimed Calath suddenly, as if waking from dream. 'Please don't think that I have any interest in that life at all. You've seen how I live; I'm hardly Count Antern. The king only maintains a relationship with me because there are few academics within the civil service. He seems to enjoy exercising his brain more than he has need of my knowledge.'

'How very modest of you,' beamed Derran unexpectedly, 'I shall introduce you to Alscap as special intellectual to the king!'

'If you do so I shall get right back in this coach and you can walk yourself home. I'm sure that bag of fur there will enjoy it more than you,' Calath snapped back, waving a hand at the wolf-hound curled peacefully under the seat.

Derran barked a laugh, at which the dog pricked up its ears but made no effort to move.

'I'm serious, Derran. I despise the men that any association to the king tends to attract. Please don't mention I know him, even as modestly as I do.'

The magistrate's merriment was hushed immediately by the earnest, near desperate expression on Calath's face and he nodded in acquiescence. Calath's mood softened at his friend's immediate acceptance, but before any more could be said the coach came to a halt.

Calath stepped down to see a fair range of coaches standing idle in the wide driveway, a handful of footmen gathered around the gaudiest, hunched into greatcoats against the chilly air and puffing away on thin clay pipes with their peers. An immaculately liveried footman opened the door and stepped back to reveal the mansion in all its glory. Only the skeletons of creeper around its wide domed porch seemed the slightest shade out of place and in the low winter sun even those sparkled magnificently with frost.

On the first step of the porch was a second servant, a silver tray of steaming goblets perched on the fingers of his right hand. As Calath approached, the man noted his struggle on the gravel and gave a click of his free fingers. The footman smoothly slid around Derran's portly form to arrive with an assisting arm, one that was gratefully accepted by Calath as he contended with the high steps.

He reached the top, noting with pleasure that they held no treacherous sheen of frost, took a goblet of the spiced wine and turned with his spirits restored to the great double doors before him. At that moment they opened and a tall, burly man marched through, stopping short when he saw Calath standing there. Noticing Derran following, the man's face split into a huge grin and he strode forward to grasp the magistrate's hand.

'Magistrate Derran! How good of you to come,' he exclaimed loudly. A slight coarseness to his accent affirmed Calath's assumption that this was Count Alscap. A working man come good in both voice and appearance; possessing the sort of hearty assurance and purpose that Calath, with his deformed leg and bookish mind, had never managed to cultivate as much as he admired it.

'My dear Alscap, you have the finest wine cellar in the county. More than enough reason to endure the strain of your company,' replied Derran, laughing and pumping hard on the Count's hand. 'May I present the most magnificent of my friends? Count Alscap, this is the Marshal Calath of Narkang.'

Calath found his slender hand engulfed to the wrist in a muscular grip.

'A pleasure, Marshal Calath,' Count Alscap declared. 'I've heard Derran speak of you often; he tells me you're the foremost scholar of our age.'

'Derran flatters me,' replied Calath, well aware how timid his soft voice must sound in such hale company. 'Such a claim I might only assert in my tiny field of study, and mostly because my contemporaries are of a rather less scientific nature. Also, I do not herald from such noble lands as Narkang; that is simply where I prefer to live and work. My family is from the rather more modest parts – Inchets, to the south-east of Narkang.'

The count nodded encouragingly. 'Not been there, but I know the name from my travels. They're said to brew some good beers in those parts, the Gods only know why I never managed to visit! Nonetheless, you're more than welcome to my home, I'd never have forgiven Derran had he denied me such rare company.'

Alscap's manner was so disarmingly honest and welcoming Calath found himself going against his nature and warming to the man immediately. They were the words of court flattery perhaps, but the count's deportment could not be further from that condition. He looked a man unafraid to be exactly who he wished to be, and Calath envied him that.

'Exactly as I predicted,' declared Derran with satisfaction. He opened his mouth to speak again but noticed a sternly dressed man hovering behind Alscap, wringing his hands anxiously. The count followed Derran's gaze and his face became stormy.

'Ah yes. Derran, Marshal Calath, please excuse me. My man here has some catastrophe he needs to show me,' said Alscap, adding in an irritated tone. 'Quite what, he's yet to bloody tell me, but apparently it's disastrous enough to drag me away from my guests.'

The count glared at his man, who wilted visibly but kept his lips firmly pursed as he shot a nervous glance at the newcomers.

Derran stared at the servant in puzzlement, but then shrugged and his cheer returned. 'Well we shall have to find our own way; I hope your mystery is worthwhile. If it is, come and fetch us!'

With that he stepped aside and bowed to the pair to let them past. Calath shuffled back as much as he could, for form's sake rather than any lack of space on the enormous porch, and received a cordial nod of acknowledgement from the count. His path clear, Alscap took up a furious pace with the servant scurrying alongside and Calath realised they were heading toward the stable-block, where three men stood with pitchforks before an open door.

Now,' announced Derran, dismissing the curious scene. He took his friend's arm and began to manoeuvre him inside. 'Let us join the others. They are on the east terrace?' The question was directed toward the servant who had been staring out after his master. The man jerked back to the present and nodded hurriedly.

Once inside the magnificent hallway Derran had to urge his friend on yet again as Calath hesitated to admire the room. A great staircase rose ahead, branching out both left and right and curling back to a landing above. A magnificent chandelier hung above them, while tall lacquered cabinets and a pair of stag-heads adorned the wall. The magistrate led Calath around the staircase to a passageway directly behind it.

This took them to a serene courtyard where a pair of orange trees overlooked an ornamental pond. Alscap Hall rose on each side of this square haven, while a single path meandered through the gravel to a second door up ahead. As they entered, the sound of casual chatter met their ears and they quickly found themselves entering a crowd all dressed for either hunting or walking; most also sporting badges of rank and title.

Calath hesitated in Derran's wake at the open doorway, surprised at the numbers gathered. The large reception room was full, as was the terrace beyond its three open doors. Children ran through the forest of bodies, young men posed and competed in their army uniforms or the latest fashion, while ladies did likewise or admired the colours and trappings of honoured soldiers.

A few knights wore their full colours over hunting leathers, and one scarred veteran even displayed the green-and-gold of the Kingsguard, to the admiration of all. Calath could see a formidable woman of about fifty keeping close to the veteran's side, basking in the esteem her husband was being shown. Though the man bore several scars to the face and one eye was concealed by a patch, this did not seem to hinder the confidence with which he addressed the fluttering young lady before him.

Derran stopped when he had advanced half a dozen steps into the room, matching the gaze of those who had turned to stare, nodding to others and staring through a handful until he saw his quarry. He turned, surprised to find Calath not at his heel, and gestured for the marshal to accompany him.

Calath did so, discomfort accentuating the weight he put on his faithful stick, but he managed to keep his head up as he made his way onto the terrace behind the widely welcomed magistrate.

It quickly became apparent their destination was a handsome family of three men and two women. Ruling the conversation was a knight in full colours whose fiercely earnest expression melted to a smile when he saw the newcomers.

'Magistrate Derran, so good to see you again.'

Derran beamed to all and pumped the outstretched hands of all three men with his usual fervour, before graciously kissing the hands of both ladies in tailored riding dresses.

'Sir Pardel, may I introduce a dear friend of mine? Marshal Calath, not of Narkang as he has already corrected me today, but of Inchets.'

Calath felt himself redden, but the smiles were friendly and he managed to join them rather than shrink back.

'Marshal Calath, it is an honour to meet you,' said Sir Pardel, bowing and then raising one hand to introduce the others. 'My son, Adim,' he supplied, indicating a broad youth dressed in regimental colours of white and blue. Father and son had more than a similarity between them, both men tall with deep chests and twinkling green eyes.

'My younger brother, Unmen Corl.'

Calath had reached out to grasp the hand of the unmen, but swiftly moved to kiss his onyx ring at the knight's words. The unmen wore no other sign of his position as parish priest and had dressed as any man of property might. He was still tall, with a pale complexion and smooth hands, as well as the vague generous smile Calath had noted on the faces of many priests.

Sir Pardel directed Calath's attention next to his wife, a plump and rosy woman, before finally introducing his daughter Meranna. She held out a spotlessly white gloved hand for the marshal to kiss, keeping it high so he hardly needed to stoop, and bestowed a dazzling smile.

Calath's tongue caught for an instant, but then managed to murmur 'My Lady,' to which he received a nod and slight curtsey. Meranna looked up to Derran suddenly, her face coming alight.

'Magistrate Derran, Marshal Calath must be the academic you spoke of over dinner a few weeks past.'

Calath felt a sudden heat rise from under his collar, but

Meranna's face betrayed no mocking. As Derran beamed and nodded Calath realised she was simply interested to meet a man of learning; something he considered fortunate in the company of dashing young knights and soldiers.

'I know Derran's sarcasm too well to take that as any great compliment, but I do admit to being an academic,' said Calath with as wide a smile as he could.

'Nonsense, ah, sir,' Meranna countered, belatedly remembering she addressed a titled man. 'The magistrate was good enough to lend me some of your works; I confess to more mathematical interests myself, but what I did understand I found truly impressive. Your descriptions and analysis of the Age of Darkness were truly illuminating.'

Calath managed not to blush, but his eyes dropped to inspect the floor of a moment. 'One of my more respectable works. Unfortunately my recent research has been of a rather less salubrious nature and several of my peers do not seem to agree with its validity.'

Sir Pardel gave a bark of laughter and clapped a gloved hand on his son's shoulder. 'He's got her going now, Adim. Let's see to our horses before growing something intellectual ourselves! By your leave Marshal Calath, Magistrate ...'

Both men nodded and Sir Pardel touched his wife on the arm, before giving Meranna an amused smile. The two soldiers and unmen marched down the steps to the garden where a gaggle of grooms loitered. One jumped up as they approached and gestured for them to following him to their horses, the three men sharing a joke that sent laughter echoing around the garden.

'I'm afraid my father's interests differ somewhat from my own,' explained Meranna, though not in apology.

'I'm sorry ...'

'No, not at all. He doesn't mind academic talk; it's simply that he doesn't understand it. He's actually been very encouraging to my studies, for all that my uncle disapproves.'

There was an edge to her voice then, not bitter for her expression was too proud for that, but noticeable enough to draw a reproachful glance from her mother. Before the conversation could continue though, Alscap's servant appeared at the back of the room to announce in a loud and clear voice that the hunt was about to commence. Those who were riding, mainly men but one or two young ladies among them, went with calls of wager down onto the lawns and followed the grooms away.

Calath didn't move, letting the flow of people stream past to either claim their horse or find a good vantage of the fields to the rear. Clearly the hunt was going to start off in the woods to the right, with the intention to drive any quarry out into the miles of fields behind and make any kill in view of the Hall. The terrace afforded a good vista and Calath's companions moved slightly away from the terrace wall as others vied for the best view.

As a group they edged towards the open doorway, lingering outside as the room beyond emptied also. From there he saw the scarred man of the Kingsguard have his sleeve tugged by Alscap's servant, back from the stables. He turned an ear in that direction to catch the man's words, realising from the man's face that the calamity was not yet resolved.

'Sir Chatos, Count Alscap requests that you lead the hunt,' said the servant in a hushed voice. The last few nobles to leave paid them no attention, but still the servant leaned towards the knight in a conspiratorial manner. Sir Chatos gave him a questioning look, but seeing his anxiety declined to pursue it.

'Of course. Will the count be joining us later?'

'He fears not, but hopes that his business will be concluded before you return.' The knight nodded, shrugged and straightened up to take in the people milling about the terrace.

'Very good, I shall of course do as the count requests. If he requires anything else of me, he need but ask.'

The servant bowed and Sir Chatos strode off to make his way down to his horse. For a moment the servant stared after the veteran and then he hurried over to Calath, avoiding the marshal's gaze as he did so. The servant cleared his throat audibly and Calath realised that it was Derran he sought, but Calath's interest was no less diminished, perhaps increased now that the magistrate's attention was required.

'Magistrate Derran, my lord requests that you come with me to deal with a rather delicate matter.'

Derran stared down at the man, irritation clouding his face. 'Matter? What matter?'

The servant looked uneasily at Derran's three companions, his hands clasped tightly as they had been on the doorstep. Lady Pardel immediately took hold of her daughter's resisting hand, giving Meranna a sharp look before excusing them both from the marshal's presence.

Meranna stood her ground for a second, as intrigued as Calath, before a tug on the arm overcame her resolution. Calath stared after her, enchanted by the beautiful young lady who had actually read his work for pleasure. Even with her mother dragging her backwards, Meranna had a grace that distinguished her from the crowd of nobility. He was too old to believe in love at first sight, but he felt that he knew his own mind well enough to recognise a kindred spirit. The servant gave Calath an unhappy look.

'It is, ah, a matter of an extremely unusual nature, and not something the count wishes to be discussed in company,' he suggested with pleading eyes.

Derran dismissed his fears with a wave of the hand and adopted his inquisitorial tone of voice. 'Nonsense! If it's truly that unusual then I insist on Calath's presence, his expertise in the unusual outstrips my own.'

The servant opened his mouth to argue, but caught Derran's expression and thought the better of it.

'Very well sir, please follow me.'

Leaving the cheerful spirits behind, Calath and Derran retraced their steps through the Hall and out the front door again. The servant could hardly stand the pace imposed by the marshal's malformed leg. He darted forward to open doors, rushed through then scampered back to silently hurry his charges. If it hadn't been for the plain distress upon his face the man would have resembled a spaniel running back and forth, leaping up to catch their attention then off scouting the path ahead.

If anything, Derran took exception to this anxiety and forced even his friend Calath to wait for him. While his nature was wonderfully calm in a social capacity, the magistrate was known for his 'impatience with impatience', as Derran laughingly termed it. The man believed matters happened in their own time and haste for haste's sake was unnatural. One of his favourite sayings was that no man hurries the tide, a reversal of the common phrase that was so typical of the large magistrate.

Their goal, unsurprisingly, was the stable block where Count Alscap had disappeared toward. The building was large, even for a mansion the size of Alscap Hall, and Calath guessed the count was a man who bred, presumably for racing since he wasn't from a military family.

It had two wings, the nearer of which seemed to house the grooms and stablehands from the upper story windows. One man remained outside, a pitchfork clasped threateningly in both hands until he recognised the servant. Still he eyed the newcomers with suspicion, but it was fear that dominated the youth's face. Nervously pushing back a sandy mop of hair, the boy shifted from one foot to the other and stole glances at the door he stood beside even as he watched the newcomers. Whatever lay within, it had obviously proved too unsettling and he had been ordered to remain without; a command he seemed more than happy to obey from the way his eyes widened as the servant reached for the door.

The clouds had gathered somewhat since their arrival. The sun no longer gave the thin layer of snow a sparkle and the temperature had remained low. Though it was only a hundred yards to the stable block, Calath's slow progress meant he was a little chilled by the time they arrived there.

Alscap's servant laid a hand on the door, thumb hovering over the crude latch while he steeled himself. Calath could only wonder what sort of horror lay within that men were afraid to even look at it. With a deep breath the servant pushed on and in. The scrape of a chair greeted him, but no words as Derran and Calath watched the gloomy space before them. The pair exchanged a glance, Calath noting the terror on the face of the young stablehand while Derran merely shrugged and marched on in. With a last glance up to the sun struggling vainly through the clouds, Calath followed suit.

The room was unremarkable, clearly used for storing harnesses, saddles and feed. The entire building was of young wood and Calath immediately noticed the pungent odour of unfinished ash mingling with leather polish, but it was the poise of every man there that really struck him. They had joined five men. Count Alscap was the only one seated, feigning a relaxed pose though his hand was kept on his sword hilt, three grooms stood with pitchforks tightly gripped, all of which were levelled toward the fifth man who sat curled in a ball in the far corner. The three grooms and their employer looked as ready to kill as to flee for their lives. For what reason Calath could not say, but clearly there was more to the dirty bundle of a man he could see.

As he inspected the room more closely Calath realised there were traces of blood on the floor and, as the prisoner raised his head to see the arrivals, the marshal could see his nose and lip were badly swollen and cut.

'Marshal Calath, I'm sorry but you cannot remain. This is a matter of the utmost secrecy, by order of the king,' protested Alscap as soon as he saw Calath, his voice wavering uncertainly.

'In that case,' replied Derran before his friend could speak, 'Calath is better suited to this gathering than I. The king has no need of a magistrate.'

This is a matter of the law, but I cannot have all and sundry knowing what has come to pass here. The king would be furious.'

'Then again I say this is Calath's affair also,' continued Derran. 'He is known to the king and his word trusted by him.'

Calath almost corrected his friend, who was not fully aware of his relationship to the king, before realising that Derran had, in his exaggeration, hit upon the truth. Whatever was going on here it reeked of the sort of dangerous mystery that King Emin so delighted in. When four armed men showed such fear of another, Calath felt sure the king would want to hear events from a known perspective.

While Calath was ignorant of the king's motives, he knew the man encouraged a variety of clandestine activities and pursuits within his private gentleman's club in Narkang. There he brought together a variety of men and women of disparate and rare skills. Mages, artificers and artisans rubbed shoulders with the men of trade who could fund and utilise their work, while others were pure academics as Calath was, but his explorations of theology and daemonology were not unusual in the debates they sparked there.

'Trusted by the king?' Alscap looked doubtful, being a man whose associations with King Emin were long and well-known. He studied the academic through narrowed eyes, but then suddenly his face brightened as an idea came to him.

'Then perhaps sir, if I'd taken Emin up on his offer of a gentleman's club membership, we would have met.'

The count's face was sharp with suspicion as he studied Calath's reaction to his words. Derran looked on, bemused but ignored.

'I fear not. The king is not a member of my club, nor any that I'm aware, and I'm sure that a man of your wealth and standing would suit grander surroundings than the Di Senego Club.'

Calath's voice was soft and assured as he presented what he knew would be the correct answer. Derran's confusion was increased when Alscap nodded in response.

'Well, that's unfortunate, but if you're a personal friend of the king you may of course remain. Kote, bring up those chairs for my guests.'

The servant glanced nervously at the ignored man in the corner, creeping around the table to retrieve the chairs, but never letting his gaze leave the curled-up figure.

Once the pair had eased themselves into a seat, carefully facing the prisoner as the mood in the room affected both, Alscap pinched the bridge of his large nose and began.

'The reason I brought you here, Magistrate, was to make this official and legal. The secrecy I think is justified. Certainly we don't want this man brought before your court, but he admits his guilt so I do not believe that will prove necessary.'

'But what crime is he charged with?' demanded Derran, his legal persona taking charge.

'Well, in short; he comes from Thistledell.'

Calath sat and stared; numb with shock as that simple, innocent word echoed around the room. The grooms flinched and stared fixedly at the ground, knuckles white around the pitchforks.

Derran half rose from his seat, mouth flopped open as the thick wattle of flesh beneath his chin shook. Of all the crimes Calath had imagined, this was furthest from his mind. His eyes darted to the motionless figure on the floor as he fought the urge to jump to his feet and flee.

Thistledell.

The name wasn't spoken these days. The ideas it conjured were too horrific and most tried to forget about it. The fear was propagated by the fact that no one knew what had happened there. The few former inhabitants Calath had heard of had been totally insane when they had been caught, but their rantings had confirmed that something terrible had taken place.

All the rest of the Land knew was that the tax collector for the local suzerain had travelled there as part of his annual rounds – to find the village gone. Signs pointing the way there had been destroyed; the buildings torn down and burned, the crops left in fields returning to the wild. Every remaining vestige of life had been erased; even the charred timbers had been buried.

There had been simply nothing left, barely a trace that a village ever stood in that place and it had been clear it was a deliberate effort. The tax collector had sent a messenger back to the nearest town after ordering his guards to investigate the freshly turned earth. It was then they had found the blackened bones.

'W ... who is he?' stammered Derran, rapidly collecting his thoughts while Calath still floundered.

'His name, well the name he gave us, is Fynn. He's been working here as a groom for almost six months now.'

'You've been employing him?' asked the magistrate in horror.

'I know, but he kept himself to himself and worked hard. The head groom had no reason to complain.'

Alscap said the words through a daze, as if repeating by rote something he could hardly believe. The tales had painted those who left Thistledell alive as monsters; capable only of violence and profane destruction. To have one in your employ, no doubt sometimes under the same roof as your children ... Alscap looked nauseous, small beads of sweat appearing on his ashen brow.

'Why the secrecy?' asked Calath, at last finding his voice

though it trembled through every word. 'Why not bring him before the court?'

Alscap gaped at the marshal, a flush of red returning to his cheeks. 'And have to tell my daughter that this man has been allowed into the same house as her newborn? That aside, I breed some of the finest stallion hunters in the country? Who would buy them now? Who would want their horses to be stud from one tended by a man of Thistledell? Half my staff would leave my service overnight! How many of my guests would return after today?'

Derran raised a hand to calm the count whose face had flushed red with rage. 'I understand. You're right, of course. This can be a very simple matter if he admits his guilt.'

Calath made a puzzled sound at that so Derran leaned towards him to explain, his eyes never leaving Fynn.

'No one knows what actually happened there, other than it was of the basest level. The king decided it was best to simply issue a private decree to all magistrates that coming from Thistledell was a capital offence. Technically he should be brought before me in the morning, but if he admits his guilt we can hang him and dispose of the body without allowing this to taint Alscap's household.'

'Hang him? Now? Here? Do you plan to just bury the body in the woods like a murderer? This cannot be the king's intention!' protested Calath.

Derran turned to face his friend, his expression sober and deadly serious. 'It is mere expediency, and as for the legality or intention, you yourself know the king. The law is his will, nothing more for all that he has codified it. You can't tell me he would deal with this openly?'

Calath stared in fearful wonder at his friend's tone, before realising he was right. The king would have no qualms about a swift and silent death; no doubt the Brotherhood had done exactly that many times, in the public interest of course.

It was the way of the world – a world Calath was part of for all his remote life, and a world he owed his privileged position to. The order brought to their nation was due to the careful, and at time merciless, hand of their king. Without that deft touch they would still be living in feuding principalities and his peaceful academic life would be nothing more than a dream.

'I ... you're right, I apologise.'

Derran kept his gaze for another moment, but then lowered his eyes, slightly embarrassed at his own actions.

'As do I, but I hope you will forgive my tone under these circumstances. Now Count Alscap, for this to be as it should I must hear the man's own admission.'

The count nodded and gestured to one of his grooms. The man, keeping a safe distance, reached out with the blunt handle of his pitchfork and carefully nudged the prone figure. The man calling himself Fynn jerked at the unexpected touch, but when ordered to rise, didn't move. A second prod encouraged the man, groaning and wheezing softly, to push himself up and sit up against the wall.

He was younger than Calath had expected. The marshal guessed at no more than twenty-five winters, but it was hard to estimate after such a battering. He'd have hardly been a man when whatever madness it was fell upon Thistledell. Calath felt a stab of pity for the boy, until he remembered the tax collector's report he'd read back at his club in Narkang. Limbs had been sawn off, bones gnawed. They had reason to fear him.

'When was he beaten?' asked Derran suddenly.

'When they realised who he was, he tried to escape. He'd been sleeping in the dormitory and apparently had some sort of nightmare. Vorte there can tell you more specifically.'

Alscap pointed to a hard-faced man with a bulbous nose and a thick beard that half-obscured a permanent scowl. He was older than the others, nearing fifty winters, but as nervous as the boys as he began to speak in a deep gravely drawl.

'He woke us up early, shoutin' all sorts in his dream. Started screamin' on about blood and buryin' the village. We thought it was just a bad dream; he's always been a quiet one, moody like. But then he started on about Thistledell and we realised what he was on about.

'Then he woke and saw us, but I don't think he was all the way awake. When Mijok here asked why he'd said "Thistledell", he said it was his home. He realised what he'd said pretty quick and made a jump for the window, but I caught hold of him. Bastard put up one hell of a fight, but there was three of us. Mijok slammed his head against the wall and he went down. We dragged him here to lock him in and fetched Master Kote.'

The man stopped, looking nervous under Derran's unblinking gaze and Calath couldn't help but wonder whether they had met in a professional capacity before.

'Thank you,' said the magistrate after a time. He drew a handkerchief from his pocket and attended his nose before continuing. Calath knew it to be a nervous habit, but the other men there marvelled at his cool demeanour, that Derran could be calmly taking his time before returning his attention to the monster. Eventually he did look back to Fynn.

'So, you've heard the charge and had time to gather your thoughts. What say you?'

The man looked up, his face a battleground of fear and shame. Looking from one face to another he found disgust in that of the count, the grooms could not bear the sight of their former friend and Derran's was the stony mask of a man passing sentence. His eyes lingered on Calath, who could not drive all sympathy from his heart at that plaintive face. Fynn said nothing to him, he made no appeal but betrayed a flicker of wonder before returning to the magistrate.

'It's true,' he said at last.

The words were no more than a whisper, but only Derran did not start at the sound.

'You understand what your admission entails? The law demands that you be taken and hung by the neck until you are dead, without delay.'

'I understand. It's time to stop running.'

With that the wretched figure buried his head in his arms. Derran looked from the count to Calath, a strain of relief at last visible.

'Well then, we should not delay if we are to keep this between us. I hope your grooms understand that this matter is not to be discussed ever again?'

Alscap nodded. 'They worked together for six months, they

were his friends. To protect my stock I'll keep them on, to protect themselves they'll stay and be silent.'

Fervent nods greeted those words and so Derran eased himself up with the help of his walking stick.

'Then we will need a noose.' It sounded as if he hardly believed the words himself but had to press on before his nerve failed him.

'Wait,' said Calath suddenly. 'I should take his account.'

'What?' cried Alscap in horror. 'What possible reason could you have for that?'

'Several, in fact.' Calath could hardly believe his own words, but the look in Fynn's eyes had stirred something within him and he knew the king would also want to know more.

'First of all, we don't know what happened in Thistledell. There are very few things the king detests, but a lack of knowledge is chief among those. We may never have another chance to understand what happened there, what evil walked our lands and perhaps might again. Secondly, for my research, be this madness or the work of daemons.'

The others looked horrified at the notion, but Alscap's protests had stopped short at the mention of the king. If the marshal was truly known to the king, then he must have a function of sorts no matter how feeble and protected he appeared. The king had no time for people he could not use.

'Very well, but at your own risk.' Alscap looked like he was trying to read Calath's expression, but the marshal was so confused in himself his face betrayed little.

'Could you please leave us? And fetch me some paper and ink?'

Derran arched an eyebrow, but the count raised a hand to silence him. His face betrayed new-found respect, but in case Calath was speaking out of bravado he laid a caveat in his agreement.

'If you're sure, but we leave the door open and Mijok will be watching. You keep enough of a distance that Fynn'll get a fork through the ribs before he can harm you.'

Neither Calath, nor the burly young groom looked entirely happy with the suggestion, but they made no comment and the others retreated out into the light. The call of hunting horns in the distance reminded Calath that life was continuing oblivious and sparked an ache in his heart. He didn't know whether it was good or bad, that so much went unnoticed, or that the world could continue so easily.

Calath didn't move until Kote had returned with several sheets of parchment, a quill and a small inkwell. The marshal kept his eyes on the motionless man ahead, part of him comparing distances to see whether he was truly safe. Once Kote had retreated, Calath used his good leg to kick a chair towards the condemned man. It skidded for a yard before the packed earth floor upended it at Fynn's feet. The man cautiously raised his head and risked a look at Calath.

'Sit.'

Fynn looked suspicious for a while, glancing warily at Mijok and the long steel prongs his former friend held ready. With a grimace, Fynn lifted himself up, gingerly touching fingers to his temple and lip, before righting the chair.

'You'll be dead within the hour, probably well before that. All I offer you now is the chance to put history straight – whether you choose to tell the truth is up to you. Don't think this will ever clear your name, if the king believes you, and I'll tell you now I've never seen him misled, then perhaps a handful of men will see it.'

Fynn nodded, wincing. 'I understand. What do you want to know?'

'I want you to tell me what happened in Thistledell, what you did and why. Tell me in your own words, we have a little time.'

When Fynn had finished speaking, Calath sat in silence, staring down at the page he had not even touched with ink. Whether he could ever bring himself to write those words, Calath was unsure. Perhaps it would be better if they were never given form. At the silence, Count Alscap poked his head around the door, then motioned for Mijok to fetch the prisoner and bind his hands. The others didn't enter and Fynn had time to meet Calath's eyes.

'Thank you.'

Calath nodded, unable to speak. Fynn's eyes were brimming

with tears, but strangely he didn't look afraid now. Calath took in his bearing and saw him as a changed man. It was as if a weight had been lifted from his shoulders, or perhaps a curse.

The marshal sat there even as they all left. He had intended to go with Fynn and be with him to the last, but now he realised he didn't have the strength, and in some way it was unnecessary. He had given the man a final gift and the prisoner walked calmly to his death. For his last few minutes Fynn would be himself. He had thrown off the taint that had followed him for years and there was nothing more he could be given beyond peace.

Calath hadn't offered the man empty forgiveness, hadn't said he understood. The crippled marshal had simply heard the tale of Thistledell and not hated the man before him. He had still seen a human being sitting there instead, something he realised Fynn had not considered himself in years.

When Calath heard a faint snap from the adjoining stable, a solitary tear rolled down his face. Alscap and Derran returned with stony faces, both staring down at the blank page before the marshal.

'Come, my friend,' said the magistrate, helping Calath to his feet. 'Let us get inside. It's a grim day's work but nothing brandy won't cure I hope, and the company of Lady Meranna might restore some faith in the world to you.'

'Meranna? A fine woman,' joined Alscap, clapping a hand on Calath's shoulder. He shook his head. 'I'd have thought her too spirited for you before, but not now. His was a tale I never want to hear, whatever use the king might find for it.' He sighed. 'I'll thank the Gods if some happiness comes out of today, if you want me to speak to Sir Pardel for you I'll gladly do so. But brandy first, I think.'

Fynn's Testimony

It's been years since I could admit where I'm from. It feels good to be able to say the name again. After those years of running, I don't fear it no more. Since I helped destroy the memory of Thistledell, I've lied every day o' my life. Before I die I want to have one last day of truth. It won't save me from the Dark Place, I know I'm damned but I— But you want to know what happened. Well, I'll try.

From a village of near two hundred souls, sixteen lived to pull down the houses, tear up walls and paths, salt the fields and burn the bodies. We hoped we could erase the memory of what'd happened, make the world forget Thistledell had existed. How many of us remain I couldn't tell you, I ran the one time I saw another, but I hope some have found peace. We can't all be to blame. We were no different to the neighbouring villages.

It was the Coronation Festival. He was a minstrel. We didn't think to ask why he was so far from a town for festival week, we were just glad to have him. Thistledell had a good reputation for merriment in the area. In the whole district no other village would claim to put on better entertainment, to have a grander spirit during feast days and festivals. We were proud o' that. Not boastful, but we worked hard on our preparations, harder than any other village. Perhaps we thought his presence to be our just dues. I don't remember now.

I was working in my father's inn when he arrived at the door. He knew my name already, said he'd been told our village was a joyous place to spend festival. And it was. Thistledell was such a happy village, not wicked as some have said; not deserving of such a curse, just a happy place to grow up where people didn't work too hard to enjoy life a little. Anyway, we were all so excited; it was going to be such a fine week. There were all manner of games, a different feast planned for each night, the king's colours hung from every tree and building. Yes, the king's colours. We might've been far from Narkang, but we were as loyal as you'll find anywhere between the Three Cities. If I had a life to stake on it I'd not hesitate.

He wasn't from around the shire, nor any Narkang suzerainty I've visited since. Whether he was from anywhere I don't know. For years I thought he was Farlan, but I met a wagoneer from Perlir and I realised he couldn't have been. His skin wasn't so fair, and the accent like none I've ever heard. But we didn't wonder too hard about that at the time, only about the tales he could tell us, the songs he'd know.

There was something about him that made us all like him. Straight away I mean, and not just the girls who thought he was the prettiest man they ever met. You took one look into those eyes, so black you almost thought they were just holes, and you couldn't say no to him. You didn't want to say no.

108

I . . . I don't remember much o' that time, only feelings. When I try to think about it, all I can remember is dread, and awfulness at what happened. I couldn't remember what had gone on, who had done what, but I could taste the terrible things even if I couldn't see what they were. The last thing I remember was standing at my father's bar watching the minstrel sleep. There was a smile on his lips and he was snoring softly, but it sounded like music to me. And he was beautiful; did I tell you that? Not like a woman is, not enticing, just . . . beautiful. You could stand there all day and just stare at him; it made you feel that the world was a better place.

After that, I don't know. Sometimes I dream of sitting down to eat or playing one of the games we had laid out, it almost seems normal them. But most are too terrible to say, just images – disgusting images. I get them when I'm awake sometimes, bad enough to make me sick when I'm working. I just have to squat down and hope no one is watching, mostly I blame it on the dogs bringing up something they've eaten.

I don't think there's anything more I can tell you about him. I spent three years asking wherever I went and I never heard a word. He wasn't a man people could forget, but it was as if he hadn't even existed. I even checked every way he could have got to our village as best I could, asking children away from the village. I got chased off a few times, but not once met anyone who knew his name or saw his face. All I can tell you is when I think of his face, I see him standing on the village square, laughing and eating peaches. I'm sorry. The next thing I remember was when he had gone.

We woke up with a cold mist hanging over the whole village, but not thick enough to hide what I've dreamed about ever since. The unmen – hung from the big oak on the green with an apple in his mouth and his legs roasted underneath. The rooms of my father's inn – each with a girl collared and leashed to the wall, blue tongues sticking out of their mouths and so much pain on their faces.

The wrestling pen – covered in bodies and limbs from the duels the foresters had played with their axes. The oxen, dead and stinking, cut and strung open and left to rot in the road.

And the children, oh the children . . . What happened to the children? The worst dreams are always of the children. Of the creatures that came from the forest. Of the feasts we shared with ghosts and daemons. In others we sold them to spirits and ghouls, I can see them licking their lips as they paid us in leaves. When I was working a few months back I had a sudden memory o' four little girls out skipping, hand in hand, off into the forest – leaving a trail of blood while hungry eyes watched from the forest. We didn't find a trace of most o' the children. Those we did, I think they'd been fed to the dogs by their parents.

None of us could say what really happened, only that we needed to hide it, that we needed to make the world think we'd never existed. We all suspected; we all suspected what we did, but no one knew anything. We just sat there for hours before we could move. All I remembered was the sound of a flute; a song with no words and the stars looking down and laughing at us.

But whatever blame we bear, whatever evil came from within us, it was still the minstrel who brought it out. I can still hear his voice; can still see his face. They're burned into my soul.

Oh, I forget nothing of Rojak.

VELERE'S FELL

My learned friend,

Knowing you as I do, I feel sure that the report I have copied below will be of great interest to yourself and certain fellows. I have no safe way to confirm any facts, but if it proves to be nothing more than a macabre tale I hope you will appreciate it on that standing.

This report bore seals of the highest secrecy; seals that bound the messenger, one Sir Daraz Tergev, to deliver it intact to the hand of the Menin lord himself, upon forfeit of his life.

— My Lord,

My life is forever yours, my words ever unworthy,

When this finds the favour of your hand I feel sure Numarik shall be conquered and Daraban within your sight. If Lady Fate is benevolent, she will see this to you before you see the pyres of our victory. What follows is the product of translated reports and witness accounts. They provide, at best, unsatisfactory conclusions, but it is beyond my power to exhume any more of the tale from the ruins of this place. Battle raged before we had even sighted Daraban's walls – though perhaps madness and anarchy are more suitable terms. Much of the city was destroyed or aflame when we arrived and only a handful of regiments resisted our entry into the city.

Needless to say we hold the city and your foolish Krann leads the revels and debauchery. While I lack your tribe's noble blood, my heart is Menin; it revolts me to witness such abandon with impotent commands on my lips. Your Reavers pursue their orders with a feral lust, but currently they are the only regiment other than my own Huntsmen with a semblance of discipline. As we sighted the city I smelled something other than death on the breeze and my gathering of documents, as ordered, has borne out my instincts.

Commissioned report of Prefect Iliole following alleged occurrences in the border region known as Velere's Fell

Having investigated the disappearances fully, I must conclude that the village of Three Stones has been taken by surprisingly bold Elven slavers. There is little more to do than send the remaining militia of Riverdam to deal with the situation. It is a disturbing tale but the impending threat to our borders overshadows all, the myth of the Menin Lord has given many over to madness and fantastic speculation.

The inquiry into this mystery was initiated by a pair of hunters who arrived at the gate of an outpost two weeks past. One has since died, unscathed but determined to deny himself both water and food. The other lives but his mind is damaged beyond hope. He is confined to a cell for his own safety after trying to scale the walls and walk to Numarik. The hunters spoke only in a fleeting, incoherent manner of what had happened in the Velere's Fell region; of unholy screams in the night, of an army of ghosts, and 'a plague that walked' — all encountered as the pair travelled home to the village of Three Stones.

I am told it is a vile backwater at the best of times, or so the landowner would have me believe. For my part I have never heard of the place and was hardly aware that people lived in Velere's Fell. I am advised that Three Stones is a recent settlement, the closest of a series of villages to that unremarkable hillock that lends its name to the region. I leave the significance of the name to more sober minds than the superstitious cretins surrounding me. What bearing such ancient history could have I do not know, but evidently it is enough to excite and terrify some.

A party led to the village by said landowner and my sheriff, a good and Gods-fearing man whose word I value, found little remaining. The inhabitants were gone, the cattle slaughtered and in an advanced state of decay. No trace is to be found of the villagers but the buildings were intact and no goods of value taken, an unusual departure to the conduct of past raiding parties but not one I shall complain about. In the interests of civic morale here I have instructed an accomplished officer to stay at the neighbouring village and report as necessary. This I hope will placate the population enough for the issue to be ignored in favour of real problems such as impending invasion.

— This is the earliest reference I have uncovered in the chaos of Governor Corren's offices, the administrator given rule of this region. The hunters' reports themselves are unhinged and of little value; however, the horrors they mentioned he placed at your feet, unsurprisingly I suppose. He seemed to believe that a 'gale of annihilation' preceded your armies, but I believe this horror beyond even your supreme mortal skills.

Report of Vantan Dey, Officer of Riverdam, to Prefect Iliole

Having spent two nights in this Gods-forsaken region I am ready to leave. There is an air to the lands all around here that fills me with dread. Some strange horror has suffused every stone and branch, creeping further into my soul with every breath I take. The people tell me nothing, they hardly speak to each other and the children do not play but sit silently in small groups.

The first night I heard strange noises, inhuman I believed, coming from the direction of Three Stones – although if that was the origin, the sound would have had to carry for almost five miles. Whatever the implications of that observation one draws, the conclusions remain dismal.

When I broached the matter with the innkeeper here he refused to listen to me, feigning business as an excuse to ignore it, though I saw in his eyes I had not been dreaming. His aid was required however, and willingly enough given, when I began to question others in the village – many of whom starting drinking as I broke my fast, if they had ever stopped. Of his assistance I remain glad; the mood of men and women here varies from sullen to aggressive and unhinged. I suspect there would have been violence had the landlord not been at my side. One man spoke of daemons that rode the land thereabouts riding down the damned, but his fellows quickly, and with threatening words to the both of us, hushed him.

For my own safety I retired early that evening to my quarters, from whence I heard the distant disturbance recommence and continue for half a bell – too faintly to discern the source and too disquieting to investigate in the dark. I had taken a room overlooking the village square and from there I could see the main road and houses, most of which were dingy and squat places.

From my window I observed how the strains on the wind seemed to sap the sanity and reason of the locals. They became more animated and vocal than they had been by daylight, albeit still aggressive and their words were mostly nonsensical. Fights flared from nothing; children viciously beaten for no reason and directly below my window I saw a woman stabbed through the heart. Despite my oath and shame I dared not venture out to her aid; having experienced their hostility earlier I knew I would be in the gravest of danger.

Later, once the village had quietened and the crazed sound faded to leave an ominous still silence, I watched a man run naked down the street and out past the boundary. The man screamed and moaned all the way, shockingly loud in the unnatural quiet night air and continuing until well after he had left the village – only to stop abruptly in a manner that chilled my blood.

Unable to sleep, I found myself pacing and gnawing nervously on my knuckle until the blood ran freely. A few swallows of the local moonshine did little to calm my fears; half-a-dozen barely impacted upon them but did at least allow me to settle. Attempting sleep I lay abed and listened to the abrupt, unnatural peace and drifted in and out of an uneasy sleep until, against the absence of cicadas or any nocturnal creature, some slight movement broke the silence.

This must have been several hours before dawn and I doubt that any other was awake – that or all were awake and similarly lying in the dark, staring fearfully at the walls. My curiosity overcame a tremulous spirit and I observed again from the darkened security of my window.

To my horror I saw a mountain lion walk unperturbed past the inn and take station by the well at the centre of the small square. Its hide shone so brightly in the moonlight I initially thought it to be a phantom or the conjuring of a frightened mind, but then a cloud dimmed Alterr's eye and I knew it was not so. There and then the creature whelped a pair of cubs, licking each clean with a tender touch before deliberately crushing their helpless bodies in its jaws. The corpses it left where they fell and sloped back up the street before disappearing from my field of vision. Nothing would have induced me to leave my lodgings and follow had it been a mere house cat.

The next morning I told this tale to the innkeeper. Initially he made attempts at humour, describing it as the sort of fever-dream induced by the local drink, but when I insisted he flew into an abrupt rage and threw my breakfast to the floor with a string of curses.

Eventually I calmed the man and persuaded him out into the street to look at the spot, which I had fixed quite carefully in my mind. Before we reached it I heard hooves or running feet and was struck on the head. I remember little of the incident and awoke to find myself in the common room of the inn, bleeding but fortunate in most other respects.

The villagers were quick to assure me the only blood to be seen in the street was my own, but their inexpert joking only added to my conviction. As for my accident, they claimed a horseman had knocked me down – a man swathed in black and hooded, unknown to them all so each insisted. I scarcely know where to begin my disbelief at the whole tale, but such was my dizziness and confusion I was unable to press the point.

Around noon I recovered enough to persuade two men to take me to Three Stones. Being large and uncomplicated men of disrepute, they seemed uninterested in anything but money so I promised them all I had on my safe return. Upon cresting the rise that preceded the village, a stench of corruption assailed us to such a degree that we all emptied our stomachs on the spot. When recovered, we were obliged to continue on foot as the horses refused to go further, shying at the sight of the village boundary and the unholy stink. What we found I can hardly describe in an adequate fashion.

Corpses littered the ground; many torn so horribly I can hardly believe it was the work of living beasts – surely only a horde of daemons could have enacted such horror, but how they could have been summoned I do not know. The closest to an incantation or charm that I could see, beyond those protective wards inscribed on the boundary stones, was a cross bound within a circle on the door of one house. It had been scratched into the wood by claws I would guess, and fairly recent too, but it was just one symbol rather than anything that could be a spell.

Some of the dead looked to be almost fresh, others had putrefied beneath the sun for weeks, but astonishingly there were neither flies nor vultures to be seen. Closer inspection of one corpse revealed smaller corpses within the wounds, where flies themselves had fallen victim to this corruption.

The buildings themselves showed significant signs of age and decay – though Three Stones has existed but a handful of years I saw fungus and rot everywhere. It was clear we could not stay long around such signs of plague and ruin without risking our lives. No amount of money would have persuaded my guides to remain until evening, had I lost my intellect so completely that I contemplated it myself. As it was the horses suffered the whip for most of the journey back, though more of a comfort to us than necessary inducement.

This letter I send with a trader whom I have persuaded to remain until it is finished. He is abandoning his interests here and will not stay another night before fleeing to Riverdam. I shall certainly follow him when my work is complete, but I fear it will take another night at this place as there is an ancient resident of these parts I have yet to meet. It is said he knows the folklore and spirits of the region as well as any witch might, but his home is apart from the village and must wait for morning.

No compulsion or reward could induce me to return to Three Stones. Once my questioning here is complete and documented I shall return to the city, on foot if necessary. Currently I can only be sure of the fear-stricken innocence of these villagers, whose lives are tied to this land and can scarcely comprehend escape from their serfdom. Their terror is genuine; born of a rural superstition I begin to share, and the root of their obstruction to my investigation rather than malice or complicity. None could account for the sudden presence of corpses in Three Stones and thus far I can gain no evidence that anyone has, or would, venture in that direction.

My memory of that awful visit grows ever more vague and hurtful with each passing hour, but there remains that one feature I remember with clarity. The symbol carved into the door of the inn, the most central of the buildings of Three Stones. I did not recognise it, nor could decide whether tool, weapon or claw had been employed to fashion it, but it now haunts my dreams.

Such is the strength of disquiet I feel whenever I recall that scratched image, I have found myself unable to recreate it for the locals, but they claim not to recognise the description. My fearful guides refused to admit its existence at all when questioned though they had seen it as plainly as I. As yet I find no worthy explanation (nor even fanciful account) that *seeks to explain these events, but there is a greater force here at work than one man can manage.*

— This was the only report to originate from that officer. Perhaps others were lost, but I found a statement signed by the trader that confirmed the madness of that village. In response the prefect secured an entire regiment of Vartin Guards, brothers of whom distinguished themselves on the field against us, to investigate further. This I conclude to be a sign that he considered this a serious threat; the Vartin Guard held to the last man when we attacked and bloodied the Reavers well.

The symbol of the cross within a circle is one I do not understand, but the device was echoed to a degree on the streets of Daraban. There, the central crossroad was aflame, with a multitude of precise grooves cut into the packed earth. Even when that unholy fire was extinguished it afeared all and our lesser beasts refused to traverse it. The devotee of Larat who accompanied our force denied all knowledge of it, though his reaction was one of great anxiety. Subsequently he made furtive gestures that put me in mind of warding against a daemon's presence, but rarely do Larat's followers fear any daemon so the meaning remains a mystery to me.

Letter to Governor Corren, an urgent request from Prefect Iliole concerning the disappearance of the 4th Regiment of Vartin Horse Guards

Most honoured Governor Corren,

I understand how inopportune the timing of this call is, but my district of Riverdam is on the brink of utter chaos and no level of threats will induce the population to denounce the call for surrender to the Menin. I appreciate your likely response, but events in the hill region of Velere's Fell have become a banner of hysterical discord with refugees actually fleeing towards the Menin armies.

The 4th Regiment of Vartin Guards had been preparing to march to Daraban and join the defence, but I managed to persuade its captain to first impose his sense and honour to the Fell region; a task he willingly undertook having observed the broken spirits of those he hoped to bring to war.

Entire villages have been stripped of life; sightings of daemons and monsters widely reported while madmen are driven to murder by the whispers they hear as night falls. One of my most trusted officers sent to the area has reported similar madness before also disappearing. I suspected slavers, but the 4th Guardmen have not returned or sent word either and I fear that accursed place has taken them.

I am at a loss. Every day brings rumours more outlandish than the last. There is a darkness stalking this place and those mages as once did live here have fled. The ancient myths of Aryn Bwr cursing the ground where his son was felled appear to have come true, though how any foul magics done by that long-dead king could still be in effect I do not understand.

All living creatures have abandoned the area of Velere's Fell; I myself have seen wolves and antelope flee north, side by side and disregarding the presence of the other. A wild dread envelops the population as the shadows grow ever stronger and the clamours of night dig their claws into our minds. Your attention is most urgent, the next riot will require military force but my militia joins the people in terror.

— I must assume the Governor sent word by some means to Numarik. Whether the situation grew worse I cannot tell but a response came from one Primarch Getalt:

Governor Corren,

Your request is refused with ridicule and wonder. Were these simpler times I would petition the forum for your removal. Need I remind you that Numarik will be under assault within the week? I only write this to you because your messenger hinders my every step for a response. I shall not even waste the Protector's time with such nonsense. Without Verliq our city will certainly fall and your situation resolved in the harshest of ways. The greatest army in the Land marches on our people. This unique and beautiful creation of our civilisation stands in greater danger from the War God's chosen emissary than your 'plague that walks'. If the Gods preserve us, remain in no doubt there will be consequences for your womanish fears. In the meantime I suggest you attend the defence of your own city.

— The personal diary of the Governor was damaged by fire and I only have scraps relating to his last days. Our intelligence led me to believe him a stoical soldier, but he hung himself before the assault and set fire to his chambers while his family slept. We were fortunate that anything remained. Such as I do have I record here:

The fires of night grow stronger, can it be true? ... Iliole sends no word, what has become of him ... the enemy lies to our south, only ... the Menin come, deliverance is at hand, the Gods forgive us for daring ...

Dark forms fill the sky, each night I fear ... so shall I submit to judgement of my soul ... I have seen the face of death ... but a creature of the Land. Hateful and warped beasts baying for the blood of the living ... what have we done to ...

... gone forever, they go and return, but who disturbed ...

... ancient folly ... Velere is dead ... cursed forever, we follow the path set by his kind and the Fell shall be that of our children ...

The shadow speaks to me. I can hear its voice like a knife in the wind.

— As is obvious, the man was lost to madness, but the sickness of this place goes beyond the insanity of its natives. I fear for us all and believe some have gone missing this past night. Daraz Tergev you know and knighted for his bravery, but his eagerness to depart cuts my letter short and it is not your shining presence he covets.

Your Krann ignores all guidance and amuses himself with the population. All order has disintegrated and the men fight amongst themselves in earnest. I shall make one final effort to persuade Krann Visel to withdraw; whether or not I succeed I shall abandon this place with my personal troops and the army standard you entrusted me with. I shall embrace whatever consequences you consider appropriate for this desertion.

I know little of Velere Nostil, who the region is named after, other than his assassination and his father's legendary grief. It appears this grief became manifest, or some terrible bargain was struck and endures to this day. Whatever the truth of millennia past, it drove refugees onto our spears and a thousand battles to be fought before our assault.

It is true about the absence of living creatures, your soldiers are the only living entities here. No bird or beast remains and it is lack of feasting that may yet cause Visel to save his men. If I fail to return, I pray to Gods I rejected long ago that I can prevent a similar fate for you, my master. The years have been blessed by your intervention and favour, I endeavour to be worthy and shall remain your servant beyond death.

General Gaur, Third Army of the Menin.

My friend,

It is believed in these parts that the Menin lord had intended to secure his own place in history by marching on Darbodus, stronghold of the cursed Elves. After his celebrated duel with the 'heretic' Verliq, the Menin lord pushed on to join the third army at Daraban. They were met on the road by Sir Daraz who was received in private by the Menin lord. Immediately after the meeting the Menin lord ordered the return home and all plunder save for Verliq's library to be abandoned.

A remarkable decision for the greatest warrior of the age, I feel, but less remarkable than the fact that while running for home they were caught on the road by General Gaur and a legion of his personal troops. Krann Visel's army numbered fifteen thousand when they marched from the Ring of Fire. Though they fought no real battles their fate remains a mystery, as does the engine of the long-dead Aryn Bwr's curse.

That the denizens of Ghenna walked the night in Velere's Fell cannot be doubted, no other force bar the Gods has that power. What evil facilitated it I shall not speculate, but I hear whispers that fatal accidents have befallen many suspected of necromancy.

I remain etc,

DAWN

From the hollows and slopes of the valley, tendrils of mist reached out over the Land before the sun rose to banish them for another day. Kastan could already see the blushes of dawn on the horizon. He'd waited half an hour already, watching the darkness of night recede and become the morning gloom; the colours of the day painted on a shadowy canvas as the sky steadily lightened.

Perched downslope, nestled about the meeting rivers, was the village he called home. They would be up and about soon, tramping out into the fields and seeing to the livestock. Wisps of smoke already rose from a few houses, up and away with a vitality the morning mist lacked. A faint breath of breeze brought the scent of the flowers up to his nostrils. That was another thing he intended to fix in his memory before the proud eye of Tsatach appeared in the sky; the clean flavours of the air inextricably bound to the glorious sight of dawn in his mind.

The morning chill didn't bother him. Kastan had settled into a natural dent in the steep earth, wrapped in a bearskin and cradled by the mountain where he'd spent his whole life. The valley below spread out to the south where the lower ground became lush woodlands fed by the mountain rivers; receding into the distance as dark smears on the horizon. Always open to attack these parts were, but this village was rarely bothered. In Kastan's life there had been only three raids on the village, the last being just a band of beastmen too pitiful to be captured for the fighting-pits.

That day the men of the village had looked to him for leadership when the alarm was sounded, even the veterans. Only fifteen summers old, Kastan had already possessed an air of authority that made battle-scarred ex-sergeants follow his commands. The immediate obedience had felt both natural and intoxicating.

That day he'd seen the sadness in his father's eyes as the man saw it was time for Kastan to leave. They both knew it had been coming; he'd bested every man in the village before the end of puberty, but the widower had been able to ignore the day not yet upon them until then. Seeing Kastan lead the counter-charge and cut down the largest of the attackers with ease, it had been clear to all that it was time.

As the sky brightened, Kastan wondered why he felt no regret at leaving. Perhaps because he'd always expected it; that from his youngest memories the old soldiers had told him he would leave to fight – perhaps because this village was always going to be too small for a Menin white-eye, the largest of all men in the entire Land.

Or is it because I'm a white-eye and have no use for regrets?

White-eyes didn't become farmers, or even blacksmiths or hunters. It had been more than a year since he could safely wrestle or spar with anyone from the village. Since then he'd only laid hands on another when a drunken fight had broken out, his prodigious energy channelled into hard labour and the study of any books he could trade or borrow.

The dawn chorus had ebbed and flowed over the undulating ground even as he'd left the house and walked up here in the pre-dawn dark. The sweet liquid voice of a thrush rang out between indignant outbursts from a blackbird. A choir of starlings chittered merrily from the village surrounds, but the call he had been hoping for came strong and clear over their gossip.

The red merlin wasn't one to participate in the greeting of the sun but, as most birds, they had chicks in the nest and were out hunting early. Native only to these parts, it was a rare sight to those who didn't know where to look and a beloved talisman to locals. The merlin's shrill 'kek, kek' sprang out from the stony slopes and brought a smile to Kastan's face. It would be years before he heard that sound again.

He didn't bother looking for the bird. It would be well hidden in the rusty-green undergrowth; three or four bronze tarnished eggs nestled peacefully on the ground. No one knew why the small hunter nested on the ground, often where the slope was little challenge to predators. The snakes that would happily feast of their eggs rarely did so, preferring to keep clear when they themselves could be the meal.

Kastan loved them for that. To make a home where they wished was to invite danger, but the swift birds would fight like demons rather than abandon their eggs. Perhaps that was why they were so fondly regarded by villagers who lived outside the Ring of Fire, vulnerable to the predations of the warped tribes of the Elven Waste.

At last, through the thin lines of cloud that bordered the horizon, the burning lances of dawn pierced the blue above. The dew-kissed pastures before him were bathed in warm, comforting light. Alone on his mountainside, Kastan breathed in the earthy odours of home as the blessings of the Gods blazed up and over him. This was the time of peace that he would store deep inside his heart, the shining core of his soul to sustain him through dark times to come.

He had no illusions about his future. The Reavers were the finest single unit ever to do battle in the history of the Land. As implacable as the Farlan Ghosts were, as furious as the Chetse Lion Guard might prove, the Reavers were greater still. Even the tales of the Elven Dragonguard, Aryn Bwr's elite, made them out only to be heroes one and all, but the Reavers were not interested in heroism.

Their training was comparable to torture, their ferocity unmatched. An average man wouldn't survive and few normals ever even tried to join; only the finest of Ascetites whose latent magic had driven them beyond natural limits. But in the main, there was only one sort of man welcome in the Reavers – white-eyes. Exalted and feared equally by their people, the savage sub-breed of humanity were the finest of all warriors and the very name of their regiment struck fear in the hearts of all.

'A last sunrise?'

Kastan leapt to his feet at the unexpected voice, every instinct suddenly alive. In one movement he was up and spinning to face the newcomer, blade sweeping up from his hip.

'I hardly think that's necessary.'

Kastan felt his grip inexplicably weaken. He tried to force his fingers closed again, but couldn't prevent the longsword falling from his hand and dropping to the ground. His struggle to keep his hand raised faded when he took in the figure before him. Slowly, Kastan stopped fighting and stared in astonishment.

The Menin were a tall, swarthy people with weathered skin and coarse black hair, their women were rarely so fine-featured or slender. A warrior people respected the qualities of strength and honour first and it was said beauty begat weakness.

The woman stood before him was quite unlike any he had met before and dressed equally as fantastically. Long tresses of coppery hair glowed bright in the first rays of dawn; her milky skin looked soft and fragile against the harsh lines of the mountain. A pale blue cape hung from her shoulders, fastened at the neck by an ornate gold brooch. Kastan couldn't make out the design; the pattern seemed to shift under his keen eyesight, which instead drifted down to the curve of her breasts above a rich green dress.

Her figure was slim and graceful, but the warrior in him could see the power still for all her slender charms. It was her face that really surprised him. A thin jaw, high, chiselled cheekbones and pouting lips curled into a faint smile – arresting and bewitching yet overshadowed by the unnaturally brilliant emerald of her eyes.

'You picked a fine spot to watch it from, but surely the top of the mountain would be finer still?'

Kastan could hear the goading in her voice. Quite apart from the treacherous ice in spring the mountaintop was full of dangers, but a white-eye was supposed to fear nothing. The prickle of anger deep inside collided with trepidation as he recognised her from the temple wall. For an instant there was a balance between the two in his heart, but he fought them and both receded before the sheer force of will. Surprise, anxiety, recalled knowledge – they all clashed behind those eyes but he refused to allow any such emotion to escape.

'I've seen it before,' he replied, keeping his voice level and his stance wary. 'I'm saying goodbye to my home, not to the Land.'

'I know that. Perhaps better than you might think,' came her strange reply. She half-turned away, then paused and looked back at him through long lashes.

'Walk with me a while.'

Kastan stared after the striding figure for an instant, stunned by the impact of her gaze, before he shook himself awake and bent to retrieve his sword. He returned the weapon to its sheath and shook out his cloak before he slipped it over his shoulders.

When he looked up, Kastan gave a start, his mouth falling open in surprise. The mysterious woman had inexplicably covered a hundred yards and stood waiting for him, hands on her hips in exaggerated impatience. Kastan breathed a soft oath as he realised this was all a test of some ineffable design. His lips tightened as a greater resolve came over him. If this were a test then so be it – she would see what sort of man he was.

The woman's irritation was genuine by the time he had sauntered over, taking time to enjoy the view and even pausing to savour the scent of a wildflower. Her smile vanished when at last he met those flashing eyes, but he managed to betray no consternation at her glower.

'Do you know who I am, boy?' she snapped, the honey tones of her voice suddenly supplanted by venom.

'I do, Lady. You honour me with your presence.'

'Hah, at least you know when to curb your insolence. Surely you know I am not renowned for my patience?'

'But of course I dismissed it as the prattling of priests.'

'You do not believe you should listen to your elders?'

Now he did allow himself to smile, hearing in her voice she was looking for something more than subservience.

'I'm too young to believe that. Since white-eyes live longer than most humans, I may be persuaded in time.'

She regarded him coldly for a moment. Then a smile broke over her face and the warmth of the sun suddenly returned.

'In the case of priests, I agree with you. I'm happy to have temples and shrines in my name, but I have little use for the pious. They tend to be deficient in worldly areas and useless to me.'

Kastan nodded, that was well known. The Lady – Fate herself – was unconventional among the Gods, perhaps unique.

She wielded little power and commanded few servants, yet was respected as if she were a member of the Upper Circle of the Pantheon. Kastan was burning with curiosity. He had attended his studies well enough to know she gave no straight answers. He would have to earn anything he learned. She was here to tell him something, but Gods were capricious at the best of times.

The Lady stopped, looking north past a copse of gnarled olive trees and into the vast golden rapeseed fields. Kastan took up position slightly down-slope of her, noticing for the first time that she was not much shorter than he. That was rare for any man, but she didn't appear to be oversized in any way. She merely met him on his own level. Tearing himself away from the burnished curls that spilled down her back, Kastan followed her eyes to focus on a kite hovering ahead.

'We will sit,' said the Lady suddenly.

Her words came unnaturally loud to Kastan's ears, and the compulsion to obey was terrifyingly strong. Turning, he saw two tree stumps where he would have sworn there had been none before. And yet there they were, weathered by sun and rain and perfectly placed behind the Lady and himself. He sank down gratefully, her command having drained his will to stand. She followed suit with perfect elegance and never once losing sight of the fields ahead.

Once seated, Kastan recovered his wits and wondered what this would mean for his future. He was leaving home today to establish his place in the Land, to seek the fame and glory that was all a white-eye could hope for. That Fate herself had come to speak to him was enough to set a worm of unease in his gut.

All the priests said she was a harsh mistress to those she chose for her designs, and what future could he have serving a God other than the Patron of the Menin? The hand of Fate was as likely a curse as a blessing. But how do you refuse a God when you cannot even remain standing in her presence?

'What do you hope for in life?'

The question was as abrupt as it was strange and Kastan replied with a blank face. He had been expecting many things, but not such a seemingly idle question.

'Well, boy? You must have some reason for leaving home.'

'I ... my reason for leaving home? I'm a white-eye; I wasn't born to stand behind oxen all day. Why does any man want to leave home?'

Kastan looked at the perfect features of the Lady and his mind went disconcertingly blank. Her ethereal skin seemed to glow with an inner light rather than the bright rays of dawn.

'Are you as unthinking as that?' she replied scornfully.

'Well ... I ... no.' He gestured to the cultivated fields surrounding the village. 'I want more from life than this.' Kastan felt as if a weight had suddenly been lifted from his shoulders. If it hadn't been ridiculous, he'd have sworn from the expression before him that she had seen it go.

'Then tell me.'

'My family's poor. We're farmers and nothing more. But I can make up for the death of my mother in some measure by winning a title or lands – no dynasty of my own but cousins aplenty and a father who'll soon be too old for ploughing.'

'You think your mother's death was your fault?'

'More mine than anyone else's!' he snapped. 'It was my birth that killed her, my birth that killed my twin.'

The Lady showed no anger at his sudden outburst. Instead her face became softer, her voice gentle rather than commanding.

'But that's just what you are. That's how your kind are born. There's no fault to atone for.'

'I've seen my father's face when he sees his nephews – when his brothers cradle their grandsons. Not once has he blamed me, but everyone knows it was because I'm a white-eye. By making something of myself, I can build a future for those who can appreciate it.'

She looked thoughtful for a moment. 'It's a hard thing to blame yourself for being born. Whatever the benefits for the tribe, it's a cruel way to bring a child into the Land. But put that aside for the moment, we must speak of the future. The past is who you are; the future is who you will become.'

'And who will I become?' Kastan asked brusquely.

She laughed and looked up at the sky. 'Indeed; that, my boy, is the question.'

He followed her gaze. White bursts of cloud hung motionless

above them, strangely shaped as though almost something he could recognise.

'Whoever you want to be,' the Goddess said at last. 'I think that best describes your future. Do you know why I'm here?' She looked back, but Kastan merely shook his head and her smile glittered.

'I wanted to meet you. I couldn't wait any longer.'

She smiled as confusion flashed across Kastan's face. This was not how Gods spoke in the tales. They commanded and nations tumbled. They reached out their hands and mountains split asunder.

'I shall explain. My goal is destiny. My tools are people, the great and the lucky. I can fashion a man's life as I see fit, beat him into whatever shape I require. His whole existence dedicated to one deed, to one swing of a sword or misplaced word. This is what I am and when I saw you I found a servant without equal. Your future is bright, young Kastan, so very bright it burns my eyes. And yet ... and yet I cannot touch you.'

Kastan looked up in surprise. Embarrassment and pride mingled in the Lady's voice. Her eyes were blazing now, shining so hard he could feel the light in the deepest recesses of his head.

'I have little use for priests – that has always been true. But for those who possess greatness ...' She tailed off for a moment and shook her head, a sad smile on her face. 'And yet even at your tender age I can hardly compel you. When I forced you to sit I could feel your resistance. You almost overcame it and the years to come will see your power flourish.'

Kastan didn't know what to do now, hang his head in shame or look up with pride. He found both strangely absent under the green lustre of her eyes. Slowly he allowed himself to sink into that light. Her voice continued and Kastan felt the rest of the Land recede.

'Within you is greatness, pure and unsullied. Within you lies the power to choose your own fate – to bend my machinations for yourself and become truly who you dream to be.

'I come to you today to present you with your future. Two paths branching out – yours alone to determine. Both will end unrealised if you don't become all that you can be, but if you succeed where you choose your deeds will blaze a trail through history, and whatever you do I cannot interfere. There is a purpose woven into the fabric of the Land that even I must obey. Some rules transcend all.'

She stood and looked down at Kastan, her face unreadable. 'I have been granted one boon, to speak to you now and tell you of your choice. I cannot affect who you will be, but what I am gives me the right to be present at that choice.'

Kastan stared back at her, unable to form words as a tumult of confusion swallowed him. He swayed slightly, rocking back on his seat at the weight of her words. His legs would not have been able to hold his weight had he been standing and even seated his body almost betrayed him. The weight of years was suddenly upon him; lifetimes flashing before his eyes, possibilities and horrors screaming through his soul. The sun flashed overhead, cloud and rain swirling around and fading to nothing in the same instant. The landscape changed. Kastan felt the Land age beneath his feet – an echo of the future that coursed through his veins.

And then it was gone. The sun was still climbing, the morning mist still slinking home. Kastan shook his head, gasping for breath that escaped him. He leaned forward and rested his elbows on his thighs, forcing his lungs to work again. Slowly he found his way back to normality. It felt as if he'd not breathed for years, that he had almost forgotten how. The cool clean mountain air scorched at his parched throat but gradually his heart slowed and the Land returned around him.

When he looked up again the Lady had not moved. She stood with her hands demurely clasped, a regal calm set into those smooth, full lips. She made no movement towards him, simply watching in a remarkably inhuman manner.

'Wha ... what happened?' Kastan asked, massaging his aching throat with his hand.

'A taste of the future. I'm going to show you who you could be, but for you to make your choice the feelings must come from within,' the Lady answered.

'I don't understand.'

'The paths before you are not static. They will change as you make choices in your life, as they would for anyone. To simply show you an image of one possible future is not enough. You must feel what you could become – understand what it means in your soul, else the choice is a false one.'

Kastan took a few more deep breaths, readying himself for what might come, and then nodded.

'Very well; do what you came to do,' he said, with an instinctual boldness that wasn't echoed in his heart.

The Lady nodded and raised one upturned palm to her lips. Her hand appeared empty, but when she blew him a kiss something rushed towards him. Sparkling threads of emptiness surged up and around Kastan's body, tenderly wrapping him in the inky oblivion of the night sky. The cocoon of dark contracted around his body and Kastan felt himself moving, soaring through the air and across the years.

A moment later the surge slowed and held. Kastan felt himself settle somewhere else; almost disembodied until he realised it was his own form, but utterly different also. He looked up and saw a storm on the horizon, recognised the Menin standard beating at the harsh wind. The sun was a wounded and dying creature impaled upon distant mountains, the clouds dark and malevolent as they swept over the Land. Before him was a huge host, dark armoured knights swarming in their thousands over a defeated foe. Lines of archers were spread out west, still and watching, while a division that could only have been the Reavers bellowed their wordless triumph amid a swath of torn corpses.

The whole scene looked like a dream, but Kastan could taste the blood on the air and hear the echo of steel still ringing in his ears. And no dream ever felt this free. Kastan didn't need to move his arms to feel the astounding power within them, to know how easily he had ripped men in two just moments ago when his sword slipped from his grasp. The tang of magic hung thickly in his throat, intoxicating and addictive but now under his control in a way Kastan had never dreamed of, let alone experienced. So much control; so simple to wield these tools and craft the Land to any shape he desired.

Great furrows had been driven into the earth, the rampant energies so hungry for ruin they had gorged on rock and earth once no man was left alive. The devastation was horrific and

Kastan fled within himself to discover what he had become. He had no wish to become a ravening monster. To his relief he found greatness there, not madness. A warrior and conqueror, but not the despoiling fiend he had feared. There lurked the burning red of pride alongside the sparkle of genius, but with such power how could pride be faulted? His achievements were his own, hard won and deserved, while his failures fuelled endeavour and been turned right in time.

'This is greatness,' came a whisper at his ear, 'heroism personified – matchless ability and limitless ambition. The greatest mortal ever to be born. The destiny of the Land is an unknown entity, any path encompasses us all and even I can only tell that it exists, nothing more. If this is where you choose to be, this destiny will be your companion. You shall be the driving force, the relentless energy behind history. Your place will be that of first among men.'

'At what price?' asked Kastan huskily, near overwhelmed by his sudden strength.

'The price? What change could come without a terrible price? You'll destroy nations, tear down temples and slaughter tens of thousands. Suffering follows any war, and your hand will touch the furthest corners of the Land. This destiny will be what is necessary; your part will be what must be done and you will be feared above no other. As a Menin you should understand the Long March that took your people to the Ring of Fire was never kind, but always necessary.'

Kastan nodded, his thoughts lost in the tale every child in his tribe knew. The Long March had left less than a third of the tribe alive, but brought the strong and the faithful to this fertile ground and made them great once more. The man who had brought it about was both lauded and reviled by his own people, both monster and saviour, but his place in history was assured.

'To be the engine of change is not to be a hero. Upon this path you will cause enormous pain to the very Land itself. Your life will be won alone, without the hand of your patron or any God. Your position you must fight for, your abilities you must teach yourself, your son you must desecrate for ...'

'My son?' Kastan could hardly believe the words as he said them. White-eyes could only have children with their own kind, and the females were so rarely born they were almost myth. He'd grown up in the belief that his father's line ended with him; that the Styrax name would survive only through his two cousins.

'Oh yes, a son and heir. A child who will grow loving you and jealous of you – who will never betray you but always resent the shadow he stands in, not realising your shadow lies also upon the entire Land. But your bride will have no love for you. Upon this path, you must take everything you want, sacrifice any principles and risk your very soul to strive for all your ambition demands. No mortal shall ever defeat you in combat, you shall be matchless throughout the entirety of history, and when the Land has need of such strength you will find a legacy like no other.'

Kastan felt the older form he inhabited call out to him, crying to be joined as one. Only the Lady's presence held him back and with a sudden blaze he was torn from the body and returned to the enveloping night. The memories ran deep, permeating his soul with enticing promises but the cool emerald light reminded him of who and when he was.

'And now the other path,' declared the Lady.

'What could possibly compare with that?' wondered Kastan aloud, reeling from all he had seen and the gnaw of hunger in his heart. The desire for power was the very fibre of a white-eye's being, each one born to love their brute strength and the intoxicating fury of magic in their veins.

'Peace – the joy and contentment lacking from the soul of every white-eye. There is more to life than what you have seen, more to you.'

Kastan relaxed into the swirl of thoughts and starry cloud, dropping down to find himself on a hillside very close to where he stood with Fate. There was an awareness of age, but little had changed other that the house he had built for himself looking down on the village from the north. There were children playing on the slopes before him. They all waved and then continued, happy under his watchful sight.

Kastan sensed he was older; not as advanced in years as before but following a more human path. Then he had felt near divine, a vitality far beyond human constraints, while now he was merely strong and healthy. Something told him many years had passed. The trees were so much taller, new ones had sprouted and matured while the comfortable assurance of middle age was all he felt in himself. He himself was taller and broader, but far from the failings of grey hair and shaking limbs. The biggest change now was in his soul.

As he looked inwardly, Kastan was struck by what he found there. Ambition and energy had been supplanted by wisdom and understanding. When his companion had said peace it had sounded such a small thing. Now calm infused his being, a sense of place in the Land without that belligerent spark of the white-eye part. Gently flowing through every fibre was a knowledge of himself and the Land that defied belief.

Kastan could feel the land beneath his feet; the huge heavy breaths of the trees, the rush of the wind and the smile of flowers as they looked up to the afternoon sun. The delighted flash of swallows darting up above and the muzzy warmth of a badger slumbering in the bosom of the earth – these things he knew as well as his own hands. They were part of him; they completed him as much as the restless ocean a thousand miles away drove his heart to beat. The earth belonged to him and he to it. He could sense his place in the Land, the fragile patterns of nature weaved about him and holding him tenderly close.

'This is where you could return. Never to have the son, but to be a father of sorts to generations and loved by each. To be teacher and guide to philosophers and heroes. To be the inspiration that drove them and the hand that ensured their fulfilment. To not worry when they look so curiously at you and wonder why you never became all you could have been. To live in an age of peace by foregoing the turmoil of another life, by turning your back on what might be. To inspire happiness in those you watch over, to know the effect of your teachings will ripple far beyond the horizon.'

Kastan smiled, basking in the tranquillity of his soul, allowing the Lady to draw him back to the hillside where they sat. He kept his eyes closed for a few moments, feeling the afterglow diminish until he was back to himself and remembered his own life as it was. He stood and stretched, feeling warmth spread down his spine and absorb the stiffness. Looking down the hillside he saw his father labouring up the slope. The man's head was down, looking at the earth he trudged on.

'Remember that nothing is for certain. What you saw were possibilities – ideas that are close to where you could take yourself, but as the paths are yours to choose, the shape they take is ever more open.'

Kastan nodded. 'I understand.'

'And have you chosen?'

Kastan took a deep breath, drawing in the scents of pine and earth, of dung faint on the breeze and the fresh oil on his sword. He could feel the blood pumping through his body, the skin close around his thick muscles and the smooth flow of breath in his nostrils. The weight of his cloak around his shoulders and the sword-belt drifted away with the breeze. He felt naked and refreshed, the strength of the mountain beneath him.

'I have.'

THE DARK OF THE MOOR

A Beginning

Before I begin this account I feel I must first confess its inadequacies to the reader. Being familiar with the conventions of the macabre tale, I fear this may prove unsatisfactory in comparison. This is the case because these pages contain the truth and I am forced to be reticent even with that. The how and why are questions that have consumed my hours since these terrible events began, but no measure of enlightenment has brought peace to my troubled spirit.

I have withheld details so that at least some measure of account be permitted to survive. The truth brought to light by my late mother was a secret born from the murky depths of unrecorded history. What accompanied it was death and darkness, and the Land cannot yet profit from such knowledge. It is my hope that one day some scholarly mind be permitted to draw these threads into a whole, but that day has not yet come and this remains overshadowed by a greater tale.

To the more inquisitive reader I say this – the whole truth has been omitted to protect those I love from a terrible spectre. I gained nothing from my understanding and my hand trembles at what I will now lose. I urge you to be content solely with what I lay before you, or you may well suffer the fate my mother unwittingly invited upon us all. I write this as a warning to those who follow as much as in the hope that one day the truth may out. I pray that this curse is one day lifted and these vague passages may yet provide a degree of understanding.

Coran Derenin, 6th Suzerain of Moorview, this 21st year of the reign of King Sebetin Thonal

The cold light of autumn was the first change to meet me when

I set eyes upon Moorview again. An ill pallor had taken hold of the countryside. It came as a grim shock to one whose recent visits had been conducted in glorious summer. The abandon of leaves and chill wind further muddied my already dismal mood. That I had been notified of my mother's death by a hurried and sparse note did nothing to ease the heart of a man whose very nature was to be seen in the detail and clarity of his work. To be denied knowledge of what illness had claimed my mother seemed a calculated iniquity, but at such unhappy times much does.

As we journeyed the last few miles to Moorview, already within what were now my lands, we entered familiar and beloved terrain. I knew within minutes the track would start to climb under our wheels and then I would truly have come home. Once that rise had begun, Moorview would be visible through the trees. For the first time in my life I dreaded it.

The sudden caw of a crow broke from the great forest of beech and scarred ash to disturb my brooding. I parted the curtains of the carriage window and my youngest daughter, Sana, forced her way onto my lap to secure the best view. Together we stared out into the tangled woodland that wore the colours of rust and fatigue. A mouldy odour rose up from the chaotic undergrowth to greet us and sickened yellow leaves waved a feeble welcome at my return. It was a familiar sight, but years of absence and city life had rendered the fascination of youth down to a base anxiety. For a moment I felt myself falling, drawn horribly into the snarl of skeletal branches and ancient cobwebs. Only the resplendent sight of my eldest son trotting alongside kept the malign labyrinth at bay.

Dever saw us looking out of the window and gave us both a fatherly smile. It was a warming sight. Dressed in the famous green-and-gold of the Kingsguard, Dever brought a proud piece of civilisation to a corner of the realm where myth and mystery ruled. Sana took hold of my finger in her small fist and pointed out past her brother to the invisible creature of the wood.

'Bird.'

I couldn't help but smile at the delight that accompanied her every new experience. She was four winters old and had learnt to speak earlier than the others, but for the main preferred uttering only solitary words. This habit had the peculiar effect of making the other party interpret their own meaning into Sana's words. My wife nobly attributed this tendency to Sana inheriting my love of poetry, but I knew well enough that her intellect would quickly outshine my own. Despite her tender years and heartening innocence, there lurks an understanding of others I feel sure will see her right.

Bird. What echoed in my head as we travelled to take ownership of my family estate was *Carrion Bird.* Whether the creature was a portent too I could not say. I lack the religious fervour of my parents' generation, but it was a fitting welcome to my former and future home – one I had been reluctant to visit while my mother was alive.

It was not long until Sana had tired of trees and we returned our attention to within the carriage. My wife half-dozed with the hint of a smile on her lips, while the other two girls were bent over some game of pebbles on a board of twelve wells that I had never fully grasped. Shifting Sana to the seat beside me, her eyes already on the game in hand, I squeezed myself into what room remained beside my wife and took the hand that was immediately offered. Touching it to my lips I drank in the heady scent that lingered on the lace of her gloves, before kissing her fingers fondly.

She was again dressed in city fashion, her more comfortable travelling clothes abandoned to impress her status upon the housekeeper of Moorview. The high-necked dress of a married woman had been expensively tailored in fox fur and black velvet, but what caught my eye was the collar of gold and jade that was set about her neck. It had been a wedding gift; a piece of family jewellery presented to my mother by the previous king that she had passed on in a rare fit of grace.

The housekeeper had never approved of my wife, Cebana, whose Canar Thrit origins were the only reason I could imagine for this distaste. Her family was of good name and her conduct impeccable, both with hapless servants and those abhorrent politicians I required her to charm at dinner. Madam Haparl,

Moorview's most devoted servant, would be more than reluctant to give up her rule of the household, but she could not argue with royal approval.

With a lurch up to the left, the carriage set itself onto the gentle slope I knew could only mean one thing. To confirm this, my sons cried 'Moorview!' with the same breath. In the next instant all three girls were at the right-hand window, straining to see the famous castle, though they had all been there many times before. As they matured, my children had each begun to realise the effect Moorview had on our fellow citizens of Narkang. Dever, as the eldest, had been most profoundly struck by the weight of what he would inherit.

As a recent recruit to the Kingsguard – which it hardly needs to be noted as bearing a special bond to the name of Moorview – we had kept back Dever's family name for fear of an ill air in the barracks. With the death of his grandmother, Dever then took the title that I had found little use for in my chosen path, Scion of Moorview. He had been determined not to avoid his heritage and made a point of wearing his badges of title on his uniform before we left.

He later confided to Forel that his courage had drained away when the barracks fell silent and Colonel Atam himself recalled aloud what family bore that crest. His brotherly confessor had told me that Dever near fainted in relief when cheers suddenly erupted from the entire company. I have heard from other sources that men wept with pride that the heir of Moorview wore the green-and-gold. Several went further still and said Dever is to be groomed as next Sunbee; champion of the Kingsguard legions and, by consequence, all the armies of Narkang and the Four Cities.

Ushering the girls back from the carriage window I took in the sight of my childhood home; the castle that abutted a moor soaked in the blood of perhaps a hundred thousand men. Built in three distinct stages, it was made a fortress after a century of overlooking Tairen Moor. While the most famous action it witnessed never reached its walls, more blood has been spilled within Moorview's grounds than most castles. The history I have never taken much interest in, but several volumes in the library concerned the sometimes less-than-noble history of my home.

To an adult eye it was not hard to see why local legend had always held Moorview in wary regard; cold and unyielding stone walls, the arrow-slits looking like suspicious eyes, the musty corridors and labyrinthine collection of cellars cut into the rock. With the wild beauty of the moor stretching so far into the distance, this region had inspired more than its fair share of tales even before the battle. I wondered how I had never felt anything but peace there until I noticed that there were no figures in the grounds before us. Devoid of life in attendance my home took the air of a mausoleum to past glorious dead. By contrast, my early years had been attended by scores of servants tending the castle and grounds. The lonely presence of the moors beyond had not encroached onto the grounds as I felt now.

The nearer we got to the castle the more noticeable was the disorder of the place, one I had never seen here before. Autumn is never the neatest of seasons, but now the feral reach of the moor encroached on this bastion's walls. In my heavy heart I could not help but wonder what else had come with it.

'Where is everyone?' muttered Cebana, shivering slightly under the same sensation as myself. She shot me an anxious glance before returning to the bleak scene, lips pursed.

I didn't answer, but she knew my moods well enough for that to be unnecessary. Instead of expecting a response, she distracted the girls by fussing over the ribbons threaded through their hair. Daen had successfully argued against being forced into a bonnet at her age, and fifteen-winters-old Carana had demanded to follow suit. The pair of them wore nine white ribbons threaded through their hair instead, fixed by tiny silver and ruby clips that were the height of fashion and the bane of my pocket.

'Ponies?' piped Sana suddenly.

This would be her first visit to Moorview as anything more than a baby and Carana had spent hours regaling her young sister with tales of the ponies that lived on the moor. For generations, Moorview's groundsmen had ensured there was a small herd kept half-tame here.

'Yes little one,' replied Daen, 'but not today, it'll be dark soon.

We'll explore the house instead. We might find some of those secret passages father's always telling us about.'

Sana's enthusiasm was deflected admirably and her smile lit up the dark looks that marked her so closely to her brother, Forel, and their maternal grandparents.

Leaning out of the window I knocked on the wooden frame of the coach and the driver reined in. Cebana threw me a questioning look as I took my wide-brimmed hat and long coat from the rack above the seat.

'I have as much a need to arrive in the right fashion as you, my dear,' I said in reply.

She smiled, the delicious curl of her lips drawing a kiss from me as I sat back down. Several times I had confided in Cebana that I had never felt suited to the role of Lord of Moorview. Only the cruelties of chance had thrust it upon me. Now, with its great grey stones in view, I seemed more of a pretender than ever.

'Moorview will not adapt to me. It has seen too many great men within those walls. I must become what it expects.'

'You're talking about Moorview as though it were alive again,' interjected Daen with an irritated tone. The image of her mother, she had always been a most practical child and saw no reason to change when she entered adulthood.

'There's more life within those walls than you might think,' answered her mother, reaching out to touch her eldest daughter on the cheek. 'I remember when your father brought me here to be married. I had eighteen winters – barely a few months older than you are now – and was suddenly presented with this place that would one day be my own. Your uncle had died six months beforehand so there was a queer mood anyway, but I was struck by a powerful impression that I had to prove myself worthy to Moorview as much as its inhabitants.'

'Mother, that's ridiculous,' snorted her daughter, unimpressed but still attentive.

'Perhaps so, but I took myself off after dinner and wandered the long gallery with a lamp; just myself and Moorview.'

'The one with that ugly stone at the far end?' interrupted Carana.

'That "ugly stone" is a memorial to the dead,' I snapped. 'You know very well what they died for so give them a little more respect, young lady.'

The long gallery of Moorview took up the entire end of the north wing. The roof of the gallery always reminded me of the peaked temples of Nartis, overlapping wooden beams of oak rising sharply toward the sky, while four tall windows occupied each end to illuminate the faces of those who had lived here. At the moor end was a massive chunk of stone, removed from the hillside on the order of the previous king, Emin the Great. A team of masons had worked day and night to smooth the surfaces until it was ready to be carved with the names of men and regiments slain on the moorland visible from that chilly vantage.

In anger I thrust the door to the carriage open and stepped out into the early evening light. Under the gaze of Moorview my anger waned and I reached back to touch Carana on the arm. Peace was gladly restored. Forel had already collected my horse from the second carriage and waited with exaggerated patience as I struggled my way into the thick folds of my long coat.

'Can I help, Father?'

I stopped my ineffective flapping and looked up at him with a needlessly sharp expression. He took no offence and, instead, slid from his horse to turn me around with an amused cluck of the tongue before extracting my elbow from its predicament. He then took my hat from my hands so that I might work at the problem more effectively.

'Thank you, and yes, I'll manage to mount a horse alone.'

Forel chuckled softly and jumped back up into the saddle of his beloved Farlan stock pony. I had offered to buy him a hunter like his brother's, but each time he had hushed me down and declared himself content with the nimble creature.

'Right then, do I look more like a suzerain now?' I asked once I had mounted, albeit less dramatically than Forel.

'No; the only suzerains I've met have been fat, stupid and rude. You're closer to the king than any of those fools,' was the laughing reply.

'Never fear, my brother,' Dever called as he rounded the carriage to join us. 'We'll feed him up on sweet meats and honey, take away his horse and get a pretty young maid to rub his feet soft. Then he'll be as venerable as the rest.'

'If you two have both quite finished,' I said with a rare smile, 'I would remind you, Dever, that you'll be a suzerain too one day!'

'Aye, my Lord, and I'll be the best of them all – fatter, stupider and with an ever ready supply of hot air to either speak in council or expel in polite company!'

I couldn't help but join in their foolishness and our laugher brought the girls to the carriage window.

'Well my Lord Suzerain, Lord Scion, do you think we could continue the merriment within perhaps?' asked my wife in her sweet tones. I gave a flourish of my hat in response.

'Of course, dear Lady Countess. Scion Derenin, while you remain able of body and mind, please lead the way.'

The brief respite from my mood had stiffened my resolve and I was suddenly anxious to be over the little bridge and through the creeper-wreathed walls that shielded Moorview from the world.

The First Evening

The gravel crunching and grating underhoof was the only sound to herald our arrival. The absence of greeting figures had never happened before in my lifetime. My idea of arriving with dignity fell by the wayside and I stumbled off my horse at a firmly closed door. It was a tall slab of heavy oak, sat at the top of five crescent steps and studded with iron pegs. I could clearly imagine the massive bolts driven home at top and bottom. Somewhere in the distance the crow saw my dismay and cawed its derision.

Dever and Forel slid from their mounts, running their eyes over the gloomy autumn appearance of Moorview. They were both grim now, contrasting the memory of a summer two years ago with this cold image. It truly looked as though the soul of this fine place had died. Our coachman, Berin, dropped from his seat and glanced over the horses before turning back to the coach, only to be waved back to the horses by Forel.

The main house, the oldest part of the castle flanked by newer wings and the single tower, was a monument to fading grandeur.

Sly trails of ivy stole across the gravel paths while the creeper dug its claws into the stonework, marching upwards to tear into the slate roof. Dark-leafed weeds had sprouted through the hard-packed drive and those cultivated plants in view stared disconsolately at the ground, cowering from the insidious creep of the moor. The wet smell of autumn and stone mixed with pungent moor heather, an achingly familiar odour that brought me back to reality as surely as the deep clunk of bolts from behind the door.

Dever straightened his uniform and stepped up beside me, feathered hat under one arm and pride brimming. Forel clicked the carriage door open and offered his arm to his mother, who stepped down with stately grace.

With a serene face, Cebana took in her surroundings while the girls bustled out behind her. Raising her hand to touch the brim of her slanted hat, my wife absorbed all those details of my home that assailed my spirits and dismissed them with a shake of her fingers. Reaching left she placed a calming hand on Sana's shoulder, glanced over her elder daughters with approval, and then stepped forward to take my arm as the door swung back.

A gust of stale air rushed out to greet us, withered and gloomy. The house smelled old and dead; as damp and musty as a sepulchre, and Sana gave a squeak of fright at the figure that appeared to greet us. My words of admonishment at our lack of greeting died when I saw how cruel the years and my mother's death had been. The stooped figure of the housekeeper forced her head up and through the dirty wisps of greyed hair she squinted at my face until a jolt of recognition shook her body.

'My ... my Lord,' she slurred through a ravaged and cracked voice.

As one I believe, Cebana and I gasped in shock, but the sound was drowned out by Sana's scream as she saw the woman's face. The little girl darted behind Daen who clutched both of her sisters tightly, her face pale and rigid.

'Madam Haparl,' I exclaimed, at a loss what further to say. The woman had obviously suffered a stroke since I last saw her; the left-hand side of her face sagged while her left arm seemed to be tucked and bound tight into her waist. In my shock I only vaguely registered Cebana marshalling the boys into action through my dumb gaping.

'Dever, Forel, help Madam Haparl inside. Coran, what's happened to the servants that she had to greet us herself, and alone? Daen, can you remember the way to the kitchens?'

Daen nodded rather apprehensively, but she wasted no time in stepping through the breach once Madam Haparl had been seated in the hallway. I heard my daughter stamping down the corridor and the echoes brought me to my senses as I imagined her considerable temper being vented on anyone she found there.

'Madam Haparl,' continued Cebana. Crouching down to be on a level with the withered woman she gently took her hand. 'Where is everyone?'

'They ...' The old lady paused to catch her breath, worn out by the exertion of her surprise. 'Most have gone, they won't stay here.' Her voice could not reach beyond a whisper but though her words were badly formed, I was relieved to see her mind had not been so affected.

'They won't stay here? In the name of the Gods why not?'

I spoke rather more harshly than I intended, but my remorse was assuaged when some of her old fire reasserted and I heard the scorn in her reply.

'They're scared. Only two stay in the house now; one don't know better and the other's a greedy little thief.'

'But what are they scared of?'

'Of what got to your mother,' came the soft reply. It sent me rocking on my heels as though struck physically. I opened my mouth to ask more, but a tap on my thigh from Cebana halted my demands.

'Not now, she needs to rest. Here, touch her hand, she's freezing.'

There was a vengeful fire in Cebana's eyes that I had rarely seen. For all of her conflict with Madam Haparl she had clearly been touched by the old woman's loyalty to remain in the house when those fit and healthy had fled.

'Forel, you go after Daen and find those maids. Whichever one seems like the thief, drag her to her room and see what's there. If you find anything then lock her in and we'll deal with her later. Here, take the house keys,'

Forel nodded and took the heavy iron ring. He disappeared after his elder sister, the jangle of keys setting an angry tune for her distant raised voice.

'Dever, go to the family room and get a fire going there, it'll warm up soon enough. Carana, go with him and find your grand-mother's wheeled chair. Can I assume it's still there, Madam Haparl?'

The frail woman before her nodded through a tear of thanks and Cebana nodded to her daughter who also darted off. 'Sana dear?'

The little girl looked up nervously from the doorstep, perhaps fearing being sent off into the black depths of the house, and hugged her cloth doll to her chin.

'Sana, go out to Berin, help him with the horses.'

The girl bobbed her head and darted back out to her devoted friend Berin. The coachman was teased by our other servants as a simpleton, but to us he was a trustworthy fellow who would die before seeing his beloved little mistress harmed.

Carana returned in a matter of seconds. Mother had found stairs difficult for years now, ever since a fall damaged her hip and pride. She had insisted on still using her jumble room at the top of the main house, but the ascent tired her and excursions around the garden had been conducted in her chair, assisted by a stablehand.

The wheeled chair was a crude and comical affair – a large wicker basket fixed to a wheeled frame by the local blacksmith. My mother's embroidered blanket lay neatly folded in the seat there. Cebana took it and shook it out, a musty echo of my mother rising up in the air about us. When I looked at my wife, her mouth was set in a familiarly determined manner and it struck me that Moorview would at least have one personality up to its rule.

'Please, I couldn't ...' began Madam Haparl but she was shushed immediately.

The old lady stared at Cebana's tone, and, sensing the same as I, ducked her head in compliance. She allowed herself to be helped slowly to the chair while I held it steady, and gave a satisfied sigh once she was settled there. Her good hand, if I can call that faded and cracked paw 'good', stroked the needlework of the blanket fondly, tracing the shape of flowers and birds in flight as Carana pushed her toward the family room.

I stared after them with a simmering anger in my belly, unsettling and vague. It was not like the staff to run home. The villagers were a superstitious lot, understandably so for people who live on the edge of an empty moor suffused with the blood of tens of thousands. Their stories were wild and deliciously horrific, but it was an unspoken rule within those tales that the restless spirits and other horrors were confined to the moor. Many of those who died there had been monsters in life. Each man and woman with a mind for tales understood that life would be too unsettling if the boundaries of civilisation could be breached.

As Moorview had stood firm against the tide of darkness that threatened to envelop our nation, so the tide of malevolence from the moors broke upon these dour walls and encroached no further into civilisation. I wondered what had changed that the villagers now felt Moorview's power was insufficient. The house seemed a shadow of its former potency, even to a learned and practical man such as myself. I could well appreciate the fears of the servants even if the reason was yet unknown.

I stood there for a minute or so, listening to the quiet of my home and the weight of years that beleaguered it. The familiar scents were there but overlaid by the spice of dust. The deserted corridors gave off a weary heartbeat of sorrowful creaks, giving up the ghost after so many years.

I was about to follow the voices of my family when a faint shadow darted at me from my right. I gave quite a start at the movement but it was only Berin's anxious face trying to catch my attention. Though he almost had to stoop to squeeze the tousled mop of hazel hair under the door beam, Berin hesitated to pass through it and contented himself with filling the doorway with his large frame.

'Your Lordship, sir,' he began, the words tripping and stumbling over each other. 'I went to the stable sir, to find feed for the horses. They're in a right state there, what should I do, sir?' Berin was near to tears, his wide honest face turning red with upset.

'Who are? What has happened?'

'The ponies sir, and a pair of horses too. They're in a poor state, been left there. Please sir, can you spare me to see to them?'

'Gods, it didn't occur to me!' I cried in dismay.

My mother had only required a pair of horses for her carriage since there was no one to hunt here these days, but the small herd of ponies was her constant delight. Her walks used to take her out beyond the ha-ha, to where the creatures spent most of the day roaming. The dwarf horses, the height of a man's waist, would cluster about her as she fed them. It had put me in mind of the parties held here when my brother and I were children; I think it did so for her too. It was one of the few times I saw her truly smile since my brother died.

'Of course, Berin, do all that you can for them; you remember where the well is? Get fresh food and water out for them, we can fetch more from the stream later. I'm going to send Dever to the village to round up the servants and bring them back. When they return, the stablehands are under your charge, understand?'

He nodded and then disappeared back to the stables. I knew him to be mild and gentle for all his obvious strength, but from his expression I suspected the stablehands would return to a nasty shock. I believe much of his devotion to Sana was the fact that she was a slender and delicate little thing, and Berin's huge compassion was moved by anything defenceless and weak. Though the ponies were not any less capable than their wilder relations, shut in a stable they would have been helpless.

The family room was a picture of lifeless order when I at last followed my family in – everything neat and tidy but arranged in such a way I could tell the room had not been in use recently. Dever had succeeded in catching a spark and was nursing an infant flame in the grate. Our aging housekeeper sat on his left, her eyes closed as though lulled to sleep by the sound of activity in her beloved house. I was loath to disturb her and decided my questions could wait. Kneeling beside my son, I took over his menial duty while Carana and my wife flung back the faded heavy curtains that shrouded the room in darkness.

The familiar screech of protesting brass filled the room as they did so, the thick, weighted drapes hung by tarnished hoops from the rail. Soon, shadow was supplanted by weak and reluctant daylight. It nosed suspiciously at the high armchairs, pushed into the corners and held up the dust accumulated in its absence with a reproachful glare. That display was enough to prompt Cebana to wrestle with the bolts and latches that held the terrace doors closed. With a gust of relief they opened and the cool evening air rushed in to reclaim its domiciled cousin.

'Dever, I need you to go to the village, there's still a little light left. I want a staff tending the house by tonight and your uniform will be the best incentive to overcome their fears. If that is not enough, and by the Gods your command as scion should be all they need, tell them their wages will be paid uninterrupted if they come back with you. For those who refuse, remind them who owns the village.'

Dever looked a little startled by that, for I am not a hard master and it would be an evil thing to evict people as autumn encroached. I hoped the fear of that evil would prove enough, but my blood had also been stirred by the pitiful state of house, housekeeper and ponies. In a rash temper I was ready to do as I implied. After a glance to gauge my mood, he turned and departed, his mouth set in a grim line.

I was left standing at the fireplace, my little fire struggling onward and upward, adrift in the energetic swirl of my wife and daughter as they fought to revive the house from its slumber. I'm afraid I could not bring myself to join them, not quite yet.

Unable to bear the oppressive atmosphere that ruled Moorview, I slumped into a chair, facing out through the terrace doors to the loneliness beyond. The light was fading fast, the gloom rushing out from under rock and heather towards us. It felt a vain effort to light the lamps, throw open the windows and set the fires blazing, but my family did just that.

Never mind the creeping chill of the air, my wife forced Moorview to breathe it in, to stir from its decaying slumber and return to the world of the living. By the time the servants returned, trailing disconsolately behind Dever's horse, Moorview had begun its rise back from the otherworldly grasp of the moor. Though darkness surrounded us, we shone our light as defiantly as we had before that great battle almost forty years ago.

It was late before we at last found ourselves back in the family room, resting a few precious minutes before retiring to bed. Supper was a meagre affair, a fatty broth and hard lumps of bread that was nevertheless hot and sustaining. I looked over my little flock with pride. Even little Sana now dozing in her mother's arms had helped. Though all five children appeared worn out, there was at least a satisfied smile on each face.

The rooms of the house had been tidied and cleaned as best we could, the stables would see no deaths, fires were lit in our bedrooms and fresh linen put on the beds. For all the work still to come on the morrow it was enough for tonight.

I took a moment at the window, staring out into the void made impenetrable by the flickering lamps behind me. From the dark of the moor came the sounds of night, the sudden crack of a falling branch, the hoots and howls of the wild. A soft shower of rain began to patter through the leaves of the trees that flanked the castle.

The rain did nothing to calm the creatures of the moor; if anything they seemed incensed by its failure to dim our lights. A discordant concert of insects, the click of bats and the bark of distant hunters assailed me as I stood resting against the shutter frame, but at my side I felt the uncaring strength of stone. When Cebana came to fetch me back, I felt a curious victory as I closed and secured those shutters.

Whatever worries I had could not penetrate that heartening sense. The thieving maid, the damaged roof, the broken cistern, and the chaos my mother had left behind; all only a few of the tasks I had to come. At least I felt at home again. That the servants crept about with fearful stares, jumping at the slightest noise and finding all manner of excuses not to be alone, I dismissed as the least of my concerns.

The Cold Light of Day

The next day came all too soon. After a light breakfast, we took a turn about the grounds to survey our home in the light of day. Berin delighted us all by bringing a pony to the lower gate, as

Sana had requested as soon as she opened her eyes. As most of them were, it was a gentle and affectionate creature – thin but with a shaggy coat hiding that from Sana. My daughter wasted no time in proclaiming the little mare her property, hugging it fiercely while her eyes dared me to deny her it. Needless to say, I could not. I had done the same many years ago.

There was a slight ground frost that morning, nothing severe but it added a sparkle that managed to redeem the muddy and overgrown features of Moorview. The sky was grey and unhappy, holding more than a promise of tears from heaven, but our turn about the grounds saw none and we were in as good a cheer as could be expected. Only the nag of my mother's interment spoiled the mood at all. She had of course been sealed in a coffin after her death, but family tradition stated that no one went to the final rest without a family member at their side.

My mother's unexpected death had made that impossible, but at least I could be there when we took her to the crypt. By some peculiarity, the family crypt was located more than fifty yards outside the walls, nestled at the foot of a rocky outcrop and overlooking the moor. The crypt itself drove a fair way into the rock, exploiting a natural fissure that had originally been used as a temple. Some ancestor of mine had built a shrine within the house itself and thus the temple had proved unnecessary since, during my childhood at least, our weekly worship was conducted in the village temple. Since it was consecrated ground, and secure, it had become a family tomb and served very well in that respect for many generations.

Seeing Madam Haparl being slowly helped out to the rampart terrace, I left my family and made my way up through the lower gate and up the stone stair that led up there. The main tower was set against the perimeter wall, at the near-side of which was a large terrace at rampart height that afforded an uninterrupted view of the moor. My intention was to chide her obstinate refusal to rest, but the gleam in her eye defeated such intentions. Despite the footman supporting her weight, her face was determined enough and she gave me no time to speak.

'My Lord, forgive the intrusion, but the sheriff is here as you requested.'

'Thank you, Madam Haparl.' I went to the battlements and leaned over to call out to the new scion. 'Dever, the sheriff is here, could you deal with him please?'

Dever nodded and, giving Sana a brotherly poke on the way past that produced a sudden burst of giggles, walked back with all the carefree confidence of youth. Returning to our housekeeper I dismissed the servant supporting her and directed Madam Haparl to a bench. It provided a fine view of the moor, but the slight camber of the ground was such that my eye drifted again and again off to the right. I could feel the presence of the family crypt lurking heavy and dark there, just beyond the trees.

'The priest will be here in an hour or so. He'll have morning rituals before he can come to see over the interment.'

A slight inclination of the head acknowledged my words, but it seemed I would have to be more direct.

'Your words yesterday – afraid of what got my mother – what did you mean by that?'

She flinched and pulled her shawl close about her, fixing her eyes as low as possible, now fearful rather than evasive. I took hold of her arm, then withdrew hurriedly as I remembered her stroke. She flinched at the touch but made no sound.

'I'm sorry ...' I began. As I did she gave a weak cough to clear her throat and I kept quiet to let her speak.

'Did the doctor not tell you, sir?'

Our voices were a remarkable contrast – mine loud and urgent, hers weak and incapable of haste. 'His letter was short and not very helpful. He said her heart gave out, nothing more. This house isn't the one I left; there's a stink of fear in everything now. Just what happened?'

'Her heart gave out, there's no doubt of that.'

'But what more?' I exclaimed impatiently. 'Had she been ill? Yesterday you near made out that she had been murdered!'

She made no reply at first, just stared out over the desolate moor. I followed her gaze, but instead of losing myself in the gentle curve of the ground my eyes came to rest on a small bird, a speckled wren if I remember my childhood accurately. It hopped a yard or so in our direction, cocked its head slightly and then kept still. For a few seconds I was sure the wren was watching us, its quizzical stance directed toward Madam Haparl as if the creatures of the moor also required an explanation.

With no apparent warning, the bird stabbed downward then took flight, a writhing worm in its beak. The unexpected movement made me flinch, only very slightly but enough to wake Madam Haparl from her reverie. Slowly, and with more than a little difficulty, she turned herself enough to look me straight in the eye. It was a cold face that regarded me, wary eyes made malevolent by the change of the stroke.

'I wouldn't know about that, sir, but the look on her face – it was like nothing I've ever seen, nor care to again. Your mother had no weakness of the heart, none that I knew. I was fetched when she was found. I stood by while the priest was called and I wrapped the body with her maid. I'll not forget the look upon her face, not if I live another sixty-four winters. The countess died of fright, terror that stopped her heart cold. What she faced there I don't know, but ...'

'But it was enough to kill her?' I breathed, the icy hands of dread clutching at my heart.

She inclined her head again.

'And no one saw anything? The dogs didn't ... The dogs! Where are they?' How I had failed to noticed before I could scarcely believe. One reason the house struck me as so empty was the lack of dogs underfoot, something that had escaped me entirely. My mood had been so affected, their absence had just been marked as yet another aspect of Moorview's gloom.

'The dogs are gone, sent away a few months back.'

'But why? What possible reason was there?' There had always been dogs at home; they were part of every estate and manor in the country. To send them away seemed absurd.

'They would have been no help. Didn't guard no more, just hid indoors and kept to the kitchen for the main part. They howled all night every night. None of us could sleep, so the countess sent them away. Only Cook's little rat-terrier was interested in going out, forever after a scent as the others yammered all night. Whatever afeared them all, Scraps was after. Chased trails all day around the house he did, till he got out one night.'

'And then?'

'Then we heard him scream. Never heard a dog scream before. They'll yelp when you tread on them, howl when they're lost, but Scraps, he screamed. It set the others off worse than before. That's when the countess said to take them away, give them to the villagers or the Winsan family.'

'And Scraps? What about him?' Gruesome visions swam before my eyes, of a torn little body being tossed through the air, of Cook's shrieks as a trail of blood led her around the house next morning.

'We don't know sir. Never saw hair nor hide again. No trace, no blood or anything. He was just gone. Fearless that dog was, would have chased a lion without thought. Till he screamed.'

I sat back, imagining the eager little terrier as I remembered him, a white bundle of energy and enthusiasm. Pictured him pushing his way out a half closed door, the moons half hidden behind black clouds as they illuminated his quest and he followed a scent that had consumed his days and nights. Racing down the terrace, perhaps following the paths or cutting off into the inky depths of the forest beyond, chasing his prey down.

Until he screamed.

'But what could have happened?'

'I don't know sir, but I've no wish to meet whatever your mother saw. Though I'll not leave here I've no wish to die.'

'Where did you find her?'

'The countess? On the second-floor landing, the corridor toward your father's old study. There'd been a storm that night, probably she'd heard the shutter there come loose and couldn't sleep for the banging.'

'The window was open?' I said sharply, but she just shook her head sadly, as if to say that I wasn't the first to wonder at that.

'One had slipped its bolt. The sheriff said it couldn't have been forced from the outside. Anyway, what man could climb that wall?' She jerked her head that way and I followed the movement. It was enough to remind me that my father's old study had been in the tower side, the wall sheer and free of creeper.

'Could someone have entered another way?'

'Of course sir, we've no need for guards in these times. I always locked the house, or someone did if my strength shamed me, but such a large house is impossible to secure completely. The sheriff said he could find half-a-dozen ways to break in, and then there's the downed tree that broke the window in the long gallery.'

'Ah yes, I saw that. What happened there? I didn't see any disease in the stump. It was a good silver birch, was it not?'

'It was, and none of the groundsmen could say why the storm blew it down.'

'Could it have been the work of man?'

'No sir, there was no sign of axe-work, only scratches made by some animal and that must have been seven feet off the ground.'

'So what has happened here? Tell me straight, I beg of you. Tell me what curse has fallen on my family and home.'

I must have sounded as desperate as I felt, for her sharp gaze softened as I spoke. She loved this place as much as I, perhaps more so, and I knew whatever distress I felt would be shared.

'I cannot, not for fear but I just don't know. I know only as much as the others; that some horror walks the moors at night, and the woods and the grounds and the very house too perhaps. I know to be afraid of the shadows. I know not to be alone. I know the spirits of the moor are restless for something. Dogs can feel the unnatural and hounds that wouldn't hesitate to make for a Brichen boar were so terrified they'd mess their own beds before going outside.'

The honesty in her rasping voice chilled me and I found myself unable to reply. It was Cebana who came to my aid, a comforting hand appearing on my shoulder though I recoiled from the unexpected touch.

'My dear, are you well?' she asked, alarmed by my reaction. I managed a weak smile that hardly convinced her, but she understood enough not to press the matter. 'The sheriff would like to speak to you, to pay his respects.'

My mind was blank for a moment before I returned to reality and struggled to my feet. Cebana ushered me toward the house, saying as she did so, 'Go on, he's in the library with Dever. I'll help Madam Haparl back inside.'

I did as I was told, the murmur of Cebana's voice receding into the background as I returned to my duties.

The sheriff was a solid, thoughtful man of thirty-odd winters. His bushy, sandy-coloured eyebrows jutted out to cast a shadow over his face, their wild excesses a strange contrast to his neatly trimmed beard. While his face appeared guarded, his manner could not have been more open. Though he was a landowner in his own small right and not my tenant, he was courteous and accommodating in every available aspect.

The maid had admitted stealing some minor trinkets, nothing grand that we would have missed unadvised. Dever had already decided that she simply be released from service and ordered to leave the district. This, the sheriff asked me to confirm – a suzerain has nearly as much legal power as a magistrate and it would save the man a trip if I agreed. I would have preferred her to feel a few stripes on her back but the decision, perhaps rightly, had been taken out of my hands and we moved on to other matters.

The details he gave me of my mother's death were as Madam Haparl had, lacking the atmosphere perhaps but congruent none the less. When summoned, he had inspected the scene and entire house as best he could. There were several ways a man could enter the house with no hurscals manning the walls, squeezing himself through easily tackled windows and the like, but no evidence that it had been done. Other than the look of fear on my mother's face, there was no sign of foul play to be found.

Forel and I watched the sheriff leave with the dejected maid trailing on the heels of his mount, then returned to the house to set our minds to the task of assessing my mother's belongings. Her jumble room had in former times been a painting studio. In summer it was a delightful place to spend the afternoons, light and airy with a bank of shutters on either side of the window to enhance the vista. Unfortunately, these days it lived up to its new title.

From that very room a whole host of paintings had been produced to hang in pride of place wherever they were gifted. Indeed, one great landscape painted there is hung in the great hall of Narkang's Silver Palace. Secretly, we have always felt it inferior to its sister piece here, but both kings have taken great pleasure in it and the scene is much copied for the nation's taverns.

Forel pushed open the door and we regarded the mess with a dispirited eye. Antique dressers, an ornate writing desk, stacked and forgotten pictures, all of these merely added surfaces for trinkets, papers of all sorts and ages, hats, scarves, ornaments and much more. For a full thirty seconds we stood there and contemplated how to even enter the room.

'It looks as if she was looking for something,' commented my son as he overturned a ribbon-bound packet of papers with his toe. It did indeed, for all the drawers were open and in places, letters had been placed with the individual pages side by side.

'But what could have persuaded her to create such chaos?'

Forel had no answer to that. He shrugged the question away and stepped carefully through the room. Picking up an official-looking document he brandished it in my direction.

'A deed. Perhaps she needed to raise some money?'

'I'd have heard of it surely?' I replied.

'Perhaps not. She was a proud woman, and independent. She was happy to live here all alone as the dowager countess rather than give up the estate to you. If she had needed money, would she have asked?'

I nodded at the truth in his words, though I felt for sure our nearest neighbours, the Winsans would have heard of any sale and informed me. Our families had always been close and to not offer any property to some part of the Winsans first would have been extremely strange.

As Forel picked his way about the room, lifting odd things and 'hmm'ing at what was revealed, I decided that we first needed to collect all the papers together, then they could be sorted and we could investigate what other treasures were here. I suspected that I would find one of the writing boxes on the floor would contain my mother's favourite jewellery. No doubt an evening would be spent trying to remember the tricks to open the various compartments.

I decided to investigate the box room at the end of the corridor, hoping to find some convenient container there to collect all those papers and then spend a relaxed evening investigating the past. This part of the house had been hardly attended by the servants. Their quarters were all on the other side, in the south wing, and it was the least important area for day-to-day use. Dust lay undisturbed on the long, worn rugs that ran down the centre of the passageway. Only the occasional draught or passing human had disturbed its rest since long before my mother's passing.

The sight caused me to wonder whether the maids had been forbidden to come up here. This isolated section of the upper floor seemed to have been hardly inhabited from the desiccated remains of some flowers in a dry vase on the landing. I made a mental note to ask Madam Haparl about this as I made for the handle of the box room. Just as I touched one finger to the speckled brass handle, a sudden shout of alarm broke the musty peace.

I ran back to the jumble room, reaching the doorway only to collide with my son as he stormed out, bellowing at the top of his lungs. Forel swung himself sideways to avoid me, but succeeded only in hitting the jamb and rebounding off to slam his shoulder squarely into my chest. As a tangle of generations we flew back across the thin passageway to hit the wall behind. I had no time to collect my thoughts, nor chastise his recklessness and discover the source of the excitement, before he took hold of my arm and dragged me with him.

'On the moor! Come on, we've got to get the horses!'

Forel wouldn't let go, or pay any heed to my protestations, so on we went in a madcap descent. We clattered down the wooden staircase that led from the attic level, then Moorview echoed with the deep clump of boots on stone as we descended the central stair. Servants scattered before us, panic on their faces at Forel's incoherent cries. Skidding to negotiate a corner, I caught sight of his face. The youth was flushed with excitement and a manic grin on his lips.

'Forel! Who's out there?' I called as our eyes met momentarily. The boy didn't stop to speak, but shouted his answer as he darted off into the main hallway.

'Who knows? But they're out on the moor!'

As I rounded the corner I saw the ashen face of a maid and it came home to me why he was so excited. Growing up here, I found nothing surprising about a figure on the moor, but who would venture out there now? The road, such as it was, turned north directly after it passed the castle so there was no short-cut to be taken and only a madman travels off the road. I pursued Forel into the hall and caught sight of him taking a small corridor to the right. He was heading for the stables. When I got there, his stock pony was already out of the stable with Forel astride.

Dever came running around the north wing as Forel took the reins in one hand and raised his cavalry bow to me in mock salute. The horse was unsaddled, but Forel was a light cavalryman and they all learned to ride and fight bareback in the Farlan style.

'Dever, go with him! He's off onto the moor!' I shouted to my eldest as Forel spurred past his brother. Dever ran up with a questioning expression, either through incomprehension or having missed my words.

'What's going on?'

'Follow your brother, he's seen someone on the moor and is chasing them.'

'Right, get Toramin saddled while I fetch my sword,' he replied in an infuriatingly level voice.

'There's no time for that!' I protested, only to have my son take me by the shoulders and look me calmly in the eye as one would an excitable child.

'Father, I can't catch him anyway. A stock pony over a wet moor will outpace any hunter; I can't sprint Toramin out there for fear of breaking his ankle. If I can't stop Forel then the least I can do is have a blade ready when I catch him.'

Eventually I realised the sense of Dever's words and nodded, wasting no time for chat before going to the stable. I entered to see three startled grooms standing stock still, but behind them was Berin with Dever's saddle already lofted on one shoulder. The man might have been simple, but he knew Forel's wild streak well enough to realise Dever would be sent out after him, wherever the boy was headed.

I ran around Toramin and pulled the halter over the powerful hunter's head, the superbly trained warhorse unfazed by the commotion and remaining quite still while he was attended. As we led the creature out, Dever emerged, fixing his swordbelt around his waist while slung over his shoulder was Forel's cavalry sabre. He nodded to me and lifted himself easily up into the high saddle. With a gentle kick of the heels the hunter eagerly leapt forward, reaching out into that effortless long stride the breed is noted for. I went on foot, my horsemanship rusty enough that I decided not to follow. Moorland in autumn can be treacherous even for an experienced rider and my own horse was a fine image of myself; grown portly and whiskery for all his enthusiasm.

By the time I had made my way around the northern extremity of the house and out the lower gate, Toramin had already crossed the wooden bridge over the ha-ha and was flying through the meadow beyond. They disappeared down the slope at the far left-hand corner, trees concealing their passage down to the moor until at last I saw them emerge at a significantly slower pace. Forel was already out and making his way across the moor, seeming to making little progress covering the miles of land that stretched into the distance.

As for his prey, it was nowhere to be seen. The only quarry was a single grouse, rising up in alarm at Forel's passage and winging east out over the moor. The game would have been welcome in the house, but Forel's mind was not on the practicalities of country life and he ignored it. Even when the bird wheeled suddenly in the air and almost retraced its path toward us it was ignored and headed undisturbed for the forest to the north of the castle.

Moorview, as one would expect, was built at the edge of the rise that separated the wilds from our inhabited section of this part of the Land. With nothing higher than gorse bushes to obscure the eastern vista, it was possible to see many miles into the distance, though there's little enough to see. Indeed my mother had often told me those celebrated victors, King Emin and the scarred pretender who fought alongside him, had stood in her very studio to plan the battle.

It didn't take Forel long to slow and permit his brother to catch up. By that time a fair audience had appeared on the terrace. The grooms had been first to arrive of course, followed by the maids we had passed on our descent. Then my wife and daughters appeared, Sana uninterested in the lack of spectacle and preferring to swing herself through the air between her anxious sisters.

'What are they doing?' muttered Cebana in my ear, not taking her eyes off her beloved boys for a moment.

'Forel thought he saw someone on the moor. Ah! If I'd stayed upstairs instead of letting him drag me down, I'd have seen where they went.'

She scanned the empty miles of open ground on either side. 'But how could anyone hide out there? Even on a horse it would have taken them too long to get to cover. The nearest is directly towards us.'

She was right and the idea set a prickle of trepidation down my spine. Forel was not prone to fancy for all the excitability of youth. If there had been someone there I could see only two conclusions. Either the traveller had hidden somehow, though cover was low and horseback affords a good view, or they required no mortal means to disappear. Whatever the truth, I felt sure that this incident would contribute to the air of ghostly visitation that enveloped Moorview and its occupants.

I was still a sceptic, but the queer mood had spread from the servants to myself. There was a chill in the air that bore no relation to our current season. I looked up to the sky and saw ugly clouds forming. Rolling in over the heads of my sons were dark and threatening shapes, promising a storm to come and soon. I heard Cebana shoo everyone back to work, but I stood a long while and watched Forel's disconsolate return, shivering slightly at the change in the heavens as I remembered the burial still to come today.

The Storm Begins to Break

I remained out on the terrace until my sons returned, staring over their heads at the empty moor as they trotted glumly home. As the pair crossed the ha-ha, I noticed Dever nudge his horse over to his brother's and reach out to grasp Forel's arm. Though the younger of the two hardly lifted his eyes, I knew that the gesture was the best consolation he could get. Rarely were words required between them. Dever knew his brother's moods better than his own. Forel's breezy calm was sometimes eclipsed by fierce passion, and at such times any failure was taken most gravely, however it came about.

They walked the horses past me and around the north wing, the sleek flanks of Toramin glistening slightly with sweat though it was Forel's steed that had been through the greatest effort. The stock pony – the excellently named Mihn for he was perfectly quiet and loyal – looked as fresh and willing as ever, his thicker coat hiding any evidence of exertion.

As for Forel, his eyes remained downcast as he passed, though I was sure his shame was unjustified. Dever nodded to me as they passed, having dropped slightly behind his brother, and I saw no real concern on his face so I left the matter. If Dever felt the melancholy would pass soon enough, then I could busy myself with other matters.

The cloud over the moors continued to mass. It was clear that a storm was imminent. All I could hope for was that it held off until after the interment and the running repairs to the roof held. The work had been rough and ready since we had no craftsmen employed here, but the castle had endured worse and I feared no storm.

Returning inside I made for the kitchens, a pang of hunger catching me unawares. It was such a short walk to the kitchen I decided waiting for a maid to answer the bell would be pointless. I still found a childish delight in raiding my own kitchen and made my way down the dim panelled corridor towards it. I paused to take in the atmosphere of the house – the servants seemed to have melted silently into the woodwork. Enclosed in silence I could not detect a single presence, as though I were alone in the entire castle. Only the occasional beat of a hammer somewhere high above, a distant pulse running through the body of the house, reassured me that it was not so. At least one person remained hard at work repairing the roof in anticipation of the impending assault.

I walked into the upper kitchen and stopped to take in the unfamiliar sight. A long pine table stretched out before me, bare and scrubbed clean, while a great fireplace crackled off to the right and steps on the left led down to the stores. A kitchen is a grim place to be; weak light, a cacophony of smells that often are less than pleasant, grease and blackened fat caking pans and implements. Hardly somewhere a gentleman spends any more time than he can help.

Quickly I realised that I didn't know where anything was and in the dirty light I couldn't see anything that looked appetising. A cat prowled in the far corner, silent and alert for the slightest of noises. The high sloping windows afforded little luxury of detail, but with the fire crackling away angrily the shadows could not entirely swallow the dirty grey hunter. Cats in these parts are only partly domesticated; it is best to call them encouraged.

Our rat-catcher paused as I watched, holding my breath for fear of disturbing its quest. The cat crouched slightly, dipping and cocking its head to one side as it waited for its prey to venture out. The shoulders tensed, its entire body freezing into readiness. I felt my hands tighten, imagining the spring, the reaching claws and teeth puncturing like hot needles. Suddenly a burst of noise from below ground startled the cat into life once more. I also jumped at the flurry of whispers from below and it was I the cat fixed with a contemptuous glance before disappearing behind some casks.

I held a hand to my chest to feel the sudden pounding of my heart, but as I did so, words floated up to me from the stores below and I crept forward like a thief to discover what was being said. As I neared the open stairway I saw faint lamp light spread over the rough stone. Moving around the stair I closed as far as I dared, for some reason suddenly obsessed with a hunt of my own.

'I 'eard the suzerain say it, they saw a man on the moor.'

'In daytime? It can't be!'

'There's a storm comin', s'all I know. My cousin said the ragged man brought a storm with him.' A man's voice now, clearly this was not just the idle, foolish gossiping of the younger kitchen maids.

'But Madam Haparl said he wouldn't come, not with a Kingsguard here!'

'I told you, the old bitch's mad, she's scared t'be here alone. We should leave, 'fore tonight.'

'We can't. I heard 'im say to the sheriff to turn out our relatives if we ran away again. What do we do?'

I guessed from the voices that they numbered only three, but it was clear that something had still been kept from me by the servants, whether fact or random fear.

'Can we stay? Surely they can't turn us all out?'

'You 'eard the scion; bastard'll do it. Asked their man Berin I did, 'e said the suzerain's some man of the Narkang council an' you know what they're about.'

'So what do we do?'

I thought I could tell which voice belonged to whom now. There was a tall, surly faced house-servant who would fit the thick accent of the man's voice; a sickly kitchen maid of no more than fifteen winters was the one who had overheard everything, while a round-faced upstairs maid came to mind at the softer, less abrasive accent of the second girl.

'What can we do, but keep our 'eads down and out the way.'

'That's all?' gasped the upstairs maid.

'All I know of. We can't get out of 'ere, but when it got the mistr'ss, none of us saw nothin'. Reckon it'll be after the suzerain and 'is family, but we done nothin'. Jes keep to your room and don't leave each other, understand?'

As the two girls murmured assent, I heard heavy footsteps in the corridor outside and the meaty tones of cook.

'Abela, Nyan, where are the pair of you?'

I hurriedly rose, pulled my tunic straight and strode out with what I hoped was an imperious expression. As I reached the door, I met cook on the way in, fairly terrifying her when she saw me. She was not a large woman, solidly built perhaps but with less fat than muscle on those arms. I managed to stalk past her without stopping while she stood with one hand to her mouth to stifle a cry of alarm. Behind, I heard the skitter of footsteps up the stone steps, but the image of their faces was not enough to bring a smile to my face. That remained troubled as I went to the family room and slumped down into one of the high armchairs.

It was time I put my brain to use in this matter, but where to start I just could not imagine. The fear that saturated the house, my mother's death, the man on the moor, this 'ragged man' – these were pieces in a puzzle I could not quite grasp. Glimpses flashed before my eyes but I had no way of knowing truth from rumour and superstition. My head began to ache at the intangibility of the situation and so I resolved to find a way to remedy that. Much of my position in the City Council deals with the bureaucracy of city life. I am at my best when distilling information from a pile of papers and thus my mind turned to the chaos of my mother's room.

I stood with renewed purpose, my eyes meeting the portrait that hung above the fire as I did so. It was a powerful image – my father in his prime as youth met experience in his middle years. He had died while I was still only young and this was as I remembered him, the steely gaze that I knew could soften into the same heartfelt laughter my brother had also possessed. The artist, an odious weasel of a man but one of undoubted talent, had depicted father as local legend told after the battle of Moorview.

The sitting had been only three months before my father died in battle – at least, I prefer to think of it that way rather than the ridiculous little skirmish it was – and a full fifteen since the battle of Moorview, but the strength had remained. He wore a weary but triumphant expression, a shining broadsword lowered to the ground as his foes lay slain. Father had laughed, then scowled, when he saw the painting. He had declared it fitting for the Lord of Moorview and the pages of history, but willing to admit the truth. I can still remember the waver to his voice as I sat on his knee and he told me a closer reality.

The shining sword that gleamed so perfectly had been presented to him well after the battle, after he'd returned from the Waste with the battered remains of the army. His weapon that day had been a plain blade, the end of which was lost out there on the moor. It had broken during the desperate last defence where father had fought side-by-side with King Emin, the ferocious last assault that had made a name for both him and all those few Kingsguard who survived.

By the end of the day his sword had been nicked and blunt,

only fit for beating a man to death. Mud and gore covered father's face – his helm also rusted out there somewhere – and he claimed to have been so tired he hardly cared to ask how the day had been won. He did not witness the death of the Menin conqueror – none near enough to witness it survived Cetarn the Saviour's storm of magic, whatever anyone claims – but he was one of the heroic few to survive the fort. The old king and he saved each other's life several times as the grief-mad Menin heavy infantry fought to the death, and even now their legend is one of the greatest of the nation.

As I stood there, lost in my childhood, a maid scuttled up and nervously informed me that the priest had arrived. Since we had no butler, and the housekeeper no longer strode about her domain watching all, the servants were in the unusual position of having to address us directly. I hardly minded myself, for our home in the city is an informal place, but the maids here had lived under the savage tongue and traditional mind of my mother. This girl fairly trembled as she spoke, her words blurting out chaotically before she bobbed a curtsey and fled. With a sigh, I straightened my jacket and went to meet the man.

'Unmen, welcome to Moorview,' I said as I entered the formal reception room.

The room was not in the best of states, faded rather than opulent, but that had not prevented the priest from perching delicately on the edge of a chair, as though trying to touch it as little as possible.

As I entered the room, he was sitting with his hands folded neatly in his lap. It put me in mind of a child, left by its mother somewhere with instructions to behave and disturb nothing. As soon as he saw me, the unmen leapt to his feet with a guilty expression though he had been doing nothing more than admire a painting from afar.

'Thank you, my Lord Suzerain, I'm honoured to be asked, though I wish it could be under happier circumstances.'

I faltered somewhat, wondering what rumours had reached him until I saw he meant nothing more than the passing of my mother. 'Did you see the countess often? I don't believe you were unmen here when I last visited.'

'That's correct, my Lord ...'

'Please,' I interrupted, 'I never became used to the title of scion and "My Lord Suzerain" sits even more uncomfortably. Minister Derenin is how I'm known in the city, that's the only title I've earned.'

The unmen bobbed his head rather awkwardly. I suspected he had been careful to memorise the protocol for addressing my family. As a country pastor he would have little experience of the ruling class, but could hardly afford to offend a suzerain and I commended the respect he offered, even if I did not require it.

'Thank you, Minister Derenin. I, um, I was only made unmen a few months after your last visit, but at the beginning I saw your mother quite frequently.'

'I'm sure you did!' I said with a smile. Loving my mother dearly as I did, I would be the first to admit that she would have found this timid and humble young man an irresistible opportunity to bully someone. 'But that changed, did it?'

'Well, yes, it did. About six months ago, after her trip, she became withdrawn.'

'Her trip? Where did she go?'

'You did not hear?' The unmen looked suddenly terrified that he might be guilty of gossip. 'She ah, well she ...'

The man looked up at me with such a pathetically helpless expression I almost laughed. Instead, I managed to keep quiet and wave him to continue.

'Your mother, the countess, went to visit some knight who lives sixty or so miles north of here, along the moor's border. I'm afraid I cannot remember his name but no doubt your mother will have corresponded with him. There, ah, there was a degree of talk in the villages as you can imagine, but by the groom's account the knight was extremely elderly and there could, well ...'

I smiled inwardly as the unmen turned slightly red and he floundered hopelessly. No doubt there was crude talk, a dowager countess paying visits in the autumn of life.

'I would not concern yourself with that. Tell me, did you see her at all after this visit?'

'Occasionally, of course. She rarely made the trip to the temple so I had grown accustomed to making the journey here once a fortnight and performing a service in Moorview's chapel. It was the least I could do for the woman who had paid for all of our recent repairs. At any rate, more often than not over the past six months the countess would send someone down to tell me that she could not spare the time. I only visited a handful of times during that period and each time she seemed more distracted.'

'Do you know what she was doing?'

'She hardly spoke to me, but I do know she wrote and received a number of letters. The boys in the village did well out of it, she paid a dozen copper pieces to ride and take letters for her.'

'Do you know who she was writing to?'

'I'm afraid not, I never saw any of the letters myself and they're commonly left at a local tavern for collection. I can ask if you would like; perhaps compile a list of where they went.'

'Thank you, that would be good of you.'

I stood in silence for a while, thinking of the piles upstairs. While this is a remote district, there are four or five towns within a week's ride. The king's peace was strong enough these days for a child to safely travel such a distance to deliver a letter and their parents would be glad of any extra money.

Before we could continue the discussion, I felt a tap on the shoulder and whirled about in surprise. Dever's broad smile greeted me. I believe he was beginning to look for opportunities to catch me unawares and lost in dismal thoughts, but before I could discern anything from his expression he kissed the lapis lazuli ring of the unmen and introduced himself. Only after the niceties had been concluded did he return to me.

'Father, Forel is removing grandmother's coffin from the sinkhole. We're just assembling the staff so you should go and change. I'll take the unmen out to the lawn and we'll wait for you there.'

I stood there for a moment, ready to delay the interment so

I could question the unmen further before realising that would be inexcusable. The rites of the dead must of course come first. Once that was over I could fully throw myself into my investigations, but until then I had a duty.

The effort of ascending the great stone staircase grew with each step. The strength drained from my legs, my leaden feet sluggishly rose and fell and I was forced to grasp the thick oak banister that ran up one side. With a firm grip on this I dragged my reluctant frame onward, urging my feet to make up the ground before I fell. Eventually I found myself at the top of the stair and on the second floor of the main house.

With one hand resting lightly on the tapestry that covered the wall here I slowly manoeuvred my way down the passage. After a few steps I paused to catch my breath and calm myself. The events of the past few days were taking a significant toll upon my mind and the prospect of the ceremony sapped almost my entire reserve of energy. In its place came a gnawing guilt that I had been too long absent, that I had parted with my mother on frosty terms after my last visit. My body cried out to be allowed to curl up and sleep, to hide away from the cloying loss that coursed down each echoing corridor and collected inside of me.

Taking deep gulps of air to clear my head, I found myself absently inspecting the fading material before me. The tapestry had been there for most of my life but, as much here, the colours had waned – the threads jutted out like the ribs of a starving man and the pungent odour of dust hung about it like the stench of death. Taking down the huge depictions took half-a-dozen pairs of hands so they had not yet been disturbed. I doubt anyone really paid much attention to them these days, but as I did so now I realised that there had been some damage done, and recently or so I guess.

The tapestry illustrated the Final Judgement of the Gods. There were two areas of damage, on either side of the Chief of the Gods but stopping short of touching His divine form. On His left was a blackened and burned patch that I eventually recalled had once shown the armoured figure of the War God.

The other side had been slashed or torn but by lifting the material back into place I could see the kneeling form of the last king, Aryn Bwr, the leader of the rebels as he heard the proclamation that cast him to the Dark Place. Such a deliberate defilement was obscure, but obviously not without meaning. The vandal had carefully singled out the two figures for his attack, but taken obvious care not to damage the central image.

What sort of a mind could have a grudge against opposing figures, one long dead, I could not fathom. It seemed as unlikely that any vengeful spirit could bear a grudge against those two as it was that one of our own servants might. I began to conjure all kinds of alternative hypotheses that jostled in my mind with the creeping pain of mourning. The pressure mounted and assailed my mind, sending the corridor swimming before my eyes. As I reeled, my questing hands found a doorframe to support me. The feel of unyielding wood beneath my hands gave me a rock to cling to, a reminder of the here and now. I felt my fingers digging into the grain of the wood, breathed in the ancient scent that faintly lingered and rested my brow against the merciful cool of my support.

With great gulping breaths I drove my way up to the surface, where Moorview was waiting in silent patience for its master. Though sweat streamed down my face to mingle with the tears of loss, I found the strength to stagger to my chamber. With each successful step, the load grew lighter and though I was near exhausted by the time I sat myself down on the corner of our bed, my strength and resolve had returned. I took a moment, perhaps a minute, to compose myself and then returned to the struggle of normal activities.

Dressing in the formal robes of a suzerain, draped for the first time in years in Moorview's colours, is an effort even with a manservant to help, but I was glad for the extra work if it gave me time alone. Though I felt terribly weak, sickened and in need of the moral support of a cane, I believe none of the assembled faces remarked anything particular about my appearance. Even my perceptive wife didn't see any more than the heavy grief of a son. It was an encouraging arm that she slipped under mine as I nodded for the procession to begin.

I shall not recount the interment. It provides nothing of note to this history other than to have intensified the air of oppression surrounding Moorview. The family tomb was as it has ever been; past an iron gate bolted into the stone of the hillside, just inside a bottleneck of rock, icy cold and eerily lit by candles – yet at the same time quite still and unnaturally peaceful. Ledges had been cut at intervals into the rock. As you move deeper within you pass through the generations of ancestors and advance toward your own grave. It is a disconcerting progression, but my mind was distracted and absent. I remembered my childhood and feeling a distinct pleasure in knowing where I would ultimately rest, one that later grew into a faint dread. Now I felt neither fear, nor interest – just a numb emptiness.

A slight strain of guilt ran through me as I felt myself muttering the words of the service by rote, not registering their meaning as the unmen prayed and offered fervent blessings. In what felt like a matter of minutes we were out again in the daylight, or what little managed to evade the marshalled legions of storm-cloud and illuminate our dreary scene. Cebana and I lagged behind the others to watch them as they went about their lives again. I held her close, her perfume wafting delicately past my nose, waxing and waning against the thick wet odour of pine and heather.

'Is it right to be so proud of one's children?' I asked suddenly.

Cebana gave me a quizzical look, but said nothing so condescending as to question my motives. 'I cannot see any reason against it,' she replied. 'To claim their successes as your own would go beyond pride, but to be glad of their abilities and potential? You're so devoted to your children it surprises me you even ask such a question.'

I shook my head to rid myself of the notion, but my eyes lifted to the happy figures striding on ahead. Dever walked tall and confidently, Carana nestled under his arm as the pair meandered down the edge of the ha-ha. Forel had made for higher ground, his little sister held tightly in his arms. For all his sharp wit, Forel was as helpless before Sana's innocence as Berin and spoiled our angel whenever she required. Sana herself was glad to be carried, that the whole world might better see her new pink frock and hair tied up in bows.

As I watched, one of those delicate hands shot out to point to the ponies up ahead and Forel let Sana slide to the floor, keeping hold of her hand as they trotted forward together. I heard Forel's easy laugh, and though I missed his words I knew he'd be soon taking the girl in to change her delicate clothes. Then Sana stopped dead, the sudden change in her manner drawing my eye. Forel turned back to ask what had happened but she ignored him, staring out north-east though I could see nothing there.

Forel crouched down beside her and she turned to look at him. I caught a glimpse of her face, now grave as she exchanged a few words with Forel. He cupped her tiny face in his hands, I could not make out what he said but she nodded in agreement or understanding. With a last glance in the direction of her concern, Sana permitted Forel to pick her up again and start off to the house. I would have caught them up but she saw me watching and gave a slight wave that eased my heart. Whatever she had heard, or sensed perhaps, had been dismissed with a few words so I made myself ignore it, aware of my own agitated state.

Daen had taken herself off down the little rabbit run that sloped gently down, past the family tomb and through a small copse of gnarled, stunted yew trees. The tomb was built into an outcrop of rock surrounded by such trees, glaring out through those ragged branches like the craggy scowl of a giant. The slope was steep, but the rabbit run took the safest path down to a slight clearing and it was there Daen had gone. I could see her back as she stared out toward the sky; I think perhaps she was fixing the image in her mind for when she found time to unearth mother's easel and paints.

'It just seems, impious, that's all,' I replied, recalling that I had left my wife's words unanswered.

'Impious?' That from anyone else might have sounded mocking, but Cebana was too good a person.

'That I should see so much potential in them. That I should hope and urge them to so much, when I feel I have not the capability myself. The Gods made me as I am, and I act dissatisfied with my lot. I expect more of them, of all of them – I felt it only natural that Dever would be celebrated within the Kingsguard, but why? My father was a warrior, but not I. Why then do I expect Dever to become champion of the Kingsguard? Have I turned some formless dissatisfaction into a drive to make my children more than they might themselves? To be more than the Gods perhaps intended?'

'Oh Coran,' cried my wife. Whether her tone was of frustration or affection I could not tell for at that moment, perhaps in answer to my question, the heavens opened. We had no choice but to run for the shelter of the castle amid monstrous crashes of thunder, laughter and shrieks, while fat raindrops burst like flowers flashing through spring in one dramatic instant.

Clattering through the lower gate and up the steps we bundled into the family room as one, stamping and shaking like our ponies out in the meadow. Even in such a short space of time, the force of the deluge had been enough to fairly soak us. The girls fussed over their hair, the boys their dress-uniforms. Cebana rushed off with Sana to dry her head before she caught a chill and I ... I stood back to watch with a slight smile. For all my forebodings, my fears and foolish doubts, this simple scene reminded me that life continues and no amount of brooding will change that.

There is still laughter in the world after death, no matter how dear the deceased. I had observed at the funeral of Cebana's cousin that laughter is all the more important when the dead will be sorely missed. There was grief all around that day, the loss of a smiling friend to all had cast such a deep shadow on the assembled family. With one idle comment breaking the gloomy hush, the man's sister had caused greater healing than the priest's kind words. The smile of memory was still fixed upon my face when the unmen opened the door, a letter in his hand.

'My Lord, I hope I'm not intruding ...'

'Of course not, please come in.'

He hurried around Daen and pattered up to me with a rather comical urgency, offering the letter up directly. 'A boy from the village brought this to the house. He said a wool merchant had left it at the inn and then it had been forgotten with your mother's passing – no one was willing to bring it here. It's addressed to the countess.'

I looked down at the letter and saw the careful calligraphy that indeed spelt out my mother's full name – and curiously, her full title too, something that seemed overly formal for a personal correspondent.

Forel offered a knife over. I took it and turned the grubby vellum over to see a blob of wax stamped with a seal I did not recognise. Sliding the dagger underneath the seal I freed the letter and opened it up to read what would again plunge my spirits.

Countess Derenin,

I write to ask you to plague us no longer with your letters, feminine fancies and dangerous talk. 'Why dangerous?' you may ask – and I feel sure you will, considering that you have demanded to know everything else from my neighbours and I. Be content that the elderly knight you infected with your talk of monsters and ghosts has been greatly damaged in the mind by such notions. Thus I have been forced to send him to an asylum, in spite of his advanced years and frail condition, because of the danger he now poses to others.

I only hope you are content with the hurt already done and do not pursue this matter any further. The common folk have been mightily disturbed by your agitation and you are certainly no longer welcome in this district. Whatever truths you feel you know about the myth of the ragged man, and be sure it is nothing more of a myth in the minds of sane and Gods-fearing men, I hope you will keep those to yourself lest they infect others with the madness one good and venerable man already bears.

Yours, etc.
*Count*_____

I read the letter with a trembling hand, then passed it to Cebana who had moved around the unmen. Angling the page to catch the best light, Cebana quickly read it through, her lips moving silently through the words.

'Such venom,' she muttered.

'Strangely so,' I replied. 'He states her full name and title; to be so rude to a woman who commands the respect of the king and his court indicates either he is the madman, or that she has frightened him terribly.'

'An old woman?'

'Not directly, but I wonder what she said to our good count here to get him so riled.'

Cebana passed the letter to Dever who scanned it hurriedly, leaning slightly to permit Forel to do the same. When he had finished, Forel looked up to me with a spark in his eyes.

'Well, we don't have the letters, but we must have a host of replies. We should be able to piece most of it together, surely?'

'It seems the only way to unravel this mystery. If only there was some order to her papers – you saw the chaos upstairs.'

I sighed. The mystery had taken a wider grip. Now madness followed in its footsteps and I feared what more I might learn. But what choice did I have? Could I forget the events surrounding my own mother's death? Live with this air of oppression and terror into winter and beyond?

'But perhaps there is,' said Cebana slowly. 'Your mother kept a day book for all the years we have been married. She must have written the most inconsequential things in it, so why not this great mystery that had consumed her days for half a year?'

She was of course right, and even in my delicate state I felt a surge of excitement rush through my body. I started towards the door when a wave of dizziness briefly surrounded me. I had to make a grab of Dever's solid shoulder to prevent a fall. He immediately dropped the letter and took a firm hold while Forel darted over. Together they urged me back while Cebana cried for a chair to be brought up. For a fraction of a second, stars burst darkly in my mind. The motion of being urged back stirred my wits to return and I struggled against the combined strength of my sons to stay upright.

The moment had passed, it was nothing more than the residue of the earlier episode they knew nothing of and I was sure it heralded no serious illness. The combination of stress and days of travelling to my childhood home had unsettled me to be sure, but I was determined not to be slowed by one brief spell of dizziness. My protests were met with considerable argument, but I would not be swayed and the compromise of my sons escorting me there secured my passage to the jumble room.

Outside, the rain had not abated and black clouds raced in over us, spurred on by a furious wind that grew with every minute. The day had been fresh enough, full of promise but lacking in much of a breeze. It was a strange contrast to the strength that had chased us inside and now whistled down chimneys, rattled our shutters and tore at the slates on the roof.

The cool protected calm of the main stairway muted the sounds of the breaking storm, until we ascended to the upper reaches of the house where ancient timber stood in place of stone. Here draughts pounced from every direction and the wood creaked and groaned under the assault. The boys looked at each other in slight alarm, fearful perhaps that the roof might give or be torn off, but I knew Moorview could stand this. By cautious steps we made our way to the jumble room, picking our way through the scattered shreds of my mother's recorded life.

Forel immediately went to the window and stared out over the moor, but there was little to see in the deluge that assailed us. He stood there for half a minute, his lip pinched white between his teeth. Dever only let go of my arm when he was convinced of my grip on a desk near the window. My balance and strength had returned as we ascended the stair, but Dever had accepted no word of protest. Only then did he set about lighting the lamps of the room, for the light outside was fading fast with the advancing weather.

Presently, we set about gathering handfuls of papers. These were collected up into a single pile and deposited into a box Forel had unearthed from the foot-well of a desk. As we tidied, assembled, investigated and rearranged, no trace of the day book was to be found. Her three writing boxes gave up more letters, some faded and cracked missives from my father, some recent, but not the book we sought. In a drawer I found its various incarnations ranging from last year to before my brother's death. Older ones yet were stacked in no order behind a pile of musty and moth-eaten material. Enough recorded thoughts to piece together much of my mother's life, but none of the past year, it seemed.

'Well, it's not here,' declared Forel in exasperation.

He looked up at us from the last drawer. Dust had settled on the hazel of his eyebrows and I exchanged a glance of wearied amusement with Dever. Forel saw it and ran a hand back over his head, sneezing violently at the cloud he disturbed. When that abated there was precious little humour in his face, his eyes were bloodshot and his voice muffled as if hampered by a cold.

'I've had enough of being up here. Let's get these to somewhere with air and see whether they were the effort.'

He gave his brother an irritable nudge and the burly youth stepped out of Forel's way before turning to pick up the meagre fruits of our labour.

We returned to find the family room in slightly more order than when we had left. The unmen rose nervously as I entered, but of my family only Sana did any more than raise eyebrows at our return. The little girl rushed over to demand attention and I gathered her up in my arms; not trusting my strength to throw her up in the air as she loved, but the affection still brought a sparkling smile to her doll's face. Her hair was still loose. As she ran to me, Sana shook the beginnings of a plait from her hair and I knew that I had been an excuse to avoid her sister's attentions.

'What is all that?' asked Cebana.

I let Sana back down to the floor, giving her a pat on the backside to send her back to Daen's reach, and then went to sit beside my wife.

'We couldn't find the book, but these are all her recent letters so they should tell us something at least.' I paused, and looked over to Forel who had yet to sit as he cleared his head at a window. 'Forel, could you ring for a servant please?'

He nodded and reached over to the bell-pull, which quickly brought the man I'd overheard in the kitchen. He looked more than a little apprehensive and sagged with relief when I just asked him to bring Madam Haparl. The housekeeper hobbled in, determination etched into her face as the servant hovered on her elbow. The unmen again jumped up at the arrival, this time to offer his seat, which, with a glance toward me, was accepted gratefully.

'My Lord Suzerain?' she whispered once settled, her voice hardly rising above the crackle of the fire.

'My mother's day book,' I replied. 'Do you know where it would be?'

'It isn't in her jumble room? I thought I'd took all her papers up and locked them in—'

'You locked the door?' Forel interjected. 'It was open when I went up the first time.'

'But it can't have been! I had the only key.'

'It was open, I'm sure of it. Did no one borrow the key at all?'

'No one, though Emila asked what I had put up there.'

'Emila?' said I, not recognising the name.

'She arrived just after your last visit here my Lord. She'd been in service as a lady's maid over in Coloch. She'd been put out after bearing the count's bastard daughter.' Madam Harpal paused to catch her breath, the trio of sentences enough to tire but not defeat her. 'She'd been staying with her uncle, Master Tinen of the inn, when your mother decided to take her on. Her baby had died of fever you see, your mother took pity. She said I was growing too weak to help her, and none of the girls here had the training or sense to be a lady's maid.'

'Where is she now?'

'Back at the village I suppose. She wasn't a house-servant so she left when your mother died. Awful upset she was, they were as close as I'd ever seen with your mother.'

The lamps flickered as a renewed burst of wind howled down the chimney and the shutters rattled and clacked on the window frames. I looked over to the doors that led out onto the terrace as bursts of lightning shone through the gaps in the shutters. The companion thunder roared so deep and loud that Moorview itself seemed to reel from the fury. Carana, whose back was to the window, gave a start of alarm at the furious crash. With the strengthened wind blowing in off the moor we could hear the drum of rain against the shutters themselves.

'So Emila must have stolen the book.' Daen paused from running a brush through Sana's hair, looking up first to Madam Haparl and then over at me.

'Why would she?' countered the housekeeper. 'Emila and the countess were as close as can be. If she had wanted some reminder, the whole staff could testify of her devotion. No one would deny she was deserving of some trifle to remember the countess by and a day book is hardly valuable.'

'I believe it was precisely her devotion that led her to steal the book,' I declared, rather boldly perhaps but I was sure it was near enough to the truth. 'I think what is recorded in that book led to my mother's death, collected from her letters.'

'Letters?' questioned Madam Haparl, but as I opened my mouth to answer her Forel jumped in.

'But what about the original letters? Did she take them too?'

'Damn the letters!' I bellowed. Jumping to my feet I felt a renewed vigour rush through my body. 'I want that day book and I'll find it in the village!'

As those words hung in the air, time hesitated; suspended in a fearful pose. Then the storm breached Moorview. With an infernal howl the wind tore open the shutters covering the terrace door. The heavy wooden shutters were flung against the stone walls and held fast by the wind, two furious heartbeats of lightning illuminating the paved terrace beyond.

Then with one great head-splitting crash they were slammed back in. The glass they had once protected shattered under the impact and hurled shards across the room as a shadow of darkness leapt into the house. The wind snarled the fire into submission, overturned or extinguished lamps and whipped around my terrified family. An inrush of darkness enveloped the room, flowing thick over the flames from the spilled lamps.

A momentary silence descended as all sound was sucked from the room. Bursts of blinding light seared through my eyelids as I cowered before the gale. A jolt of pain seemed to echo through the house and through my feet I felt it struck, once, twice – the hammer-blows of thunder detonating about my ears.

I crouched lower, then felt the page of a letter slap up into my face and all fear faded. Peering through the sudden gloom of the family room I saw my family similarly huddled. The doors to the terrace had been torn from their hinges and my mother's papers thrashed in the intruding squall.

I jumped to my feet, running the few paces to where Cebana and Daen had been sitting. My wife was now sprawled over her two daughters, Sana enveloped in a protective cocoon. At my touch Cebana recoiled as if stung, but then the wild look in her eye receded and she ran questing hands over her precious child. Stepping back, I looked for the others. Forel was at his other sister's side. I could see blood on Carana's face, a black stain in the weak moonlight. As he raised a hand to touch it she slapped him away. Looking back down, Cebana hugged Sana tight to her chest and I knew there had been no injury to the frailest of us.

As I checked, Dever was up and unhurt, I saw the ruin of the door as the long brass hinge swung in the continuing wind. With each gust, a pattern of raindrops spattered further into the room. I was suddenly struck by the notion that this was no natural occurrence, that some other agency had vented its rage upon us. My thoughts turned to whatever daemon had hunted my mother and the next image in my mind was that of the defenceless village a few miles away.

I ran for the door, unable to brook any delay though my daughter was bleeding and my family in chaos. I had been taken by some consuming mania: by the thought of that innocent girl, unaware of what monstrous visitation was surging through the night towards her. And perhaps she was not the only one in peril. Perhaps the rage of this unnatural storm would be vented upon them all and I had placed so many lives in danger with that one declaration of intent.

I ran through the house past the terrified faces of the servants and, amid shouts from all directions, barrelled my way to the stable-side door. Throwing back the bolts I tore it open to be greeted by the fullness of night's fury, a gust of wind driving me back while the sky itself cackled and spat.

As the drapes of the room came alive I readied myself to sally out. Even as I stood there I saw slates fly and smash on the cobbled yard. With painfully slow steps I managed to get a few yards out into the stable courtyard, before an unexpected change in the wind's direction launched me headlong at the stable. I fought my way inside the door to be greeted with terrified whinnies from the inhabitants. As I slammed it shut again I saw Berin emerge from a stall, as afraid as the horses but still doing his best to calm them.

'Berin, saddle my horse for me, I must get to the village!'

Berin stood stock still, shaking his head with wild eyes fixed upon me.

'Do it man! Have you gone deaf?' It was unfair of me to vent my anger upon him, but at least it seemed to return Berin to his senses.

'Can't sir!' he barked nervously in reply. 'He'll throw you.'

I stopped, curses jostling on my tongue but before any could escape I realised the truth in his words.

'Then saddle Toramin, he's battle-trained, he'll cope with the storm.'

Berin stared back at me for a moment but made no further argument. He hefted Dever's great saddle in one hand while the other gathered the reins from a peg opposite. Those he passed to me, his fear of the raging storm now forgotten as he studied the flaring nostrils of the hunter. Though Toramin was battle-trained, any sudden movement might still panic him as the wind howled overhead. As it was, the horse was perfectly placid while the saddle and reins were fitted and in a matter of minutes I was astride as Berin laboured open the stable door.

I nearly lost control as we left the stable. A great shard of lightning cleaved the sky and my steed reared in surprise. Instead of kicking and bucking to dislodge the weight, Toramin merely circled and backed away from the booming peals of thunder echoing around the landscape. It did not take me long to guide him round to the drive and then we were off, the horse more than willing to sprint away from the moor.

We ran with the spirit of the storm on our heels. Up above, the clouds raced to outstrip us and the night roared approval at our foolish abandon. The smaller flashes of lightning were what lit our path for us, beyond Moorview the land was a dark and forbidding place. Only the good condition of the road kept either of our necks whole and only once did I have to make the hunter leap to avoid a fallen branch lying in our path. Hunched and spiteful hawthorns whipped all about, I felt several times the talons of those trees scrape down my scalp and catch my tunic but nothing would deter me.

Then the road dipped and we charged down into the long sinister straight called Gallows Walk by the local people. The reason for such a name was forgotten even before the battle of Moorview, but never more apt as when I entered the eerie, sheltered avenue overhung by yews and pine. There was a curious calm on the needled floor, for all that the tops of these trees seethed and slashed at the air.

I kept my head down and concentrated on the road ahead, trickles of rain working their way down through my hair and into my eyes. My vision blurred with water and I had to flail at my face to clear it. My clothes were soaked by then and my efforts did nothing more than provide vague respite. I returned my attention to the gloom ahead as a new burst of lightning lit the way ahead, a fork arcing down to strike somewhere off to my right.

Through the fierce light I saw a fragment of what lay ahead. Framed by the trees that arched into a near-tunnel, was a figure. It was motionless, facing me but with no face I could see. All I made out was a gigantic form, clothes flying wildly in the storm though the figure itself was firmly rooted. The face must have been hooded for all I saw was the dancing edges of this spectral image, the centre of the storm as I charged on towards it.

I had no time to reach the storm-clad spirit, nor stop or even think past the terror that wrenched at my heart. As the light drained away into shadows, a blinding pain burst on the side of my head. Stars whirled as I felt myself tossed sideways, a blur of leaves and branches spinning past on eyes before I succumbed.

Blackness flared, then enveloped my mind as the Land receded and there was only silence.

A Grave Understanding

I awoke to Dever's worried face. I could not tell how long I had been lying there, but the storm had lessened from when my eyes closed.

'How are you feeling?'

I tried to sit up, planting my elbows underneath me before my strength gave way. I was lying at the foot of a pine. As Forel stood to one side holding our three steeds, Dever lifted me gently until my back was set against the tree trunk.

'I feel, ah, in pain,' I said eventually, raising shaky fingers to my head to probe for a bruise or blood.

I was glad to find a ripe lump under my fingers, but no vital fluids. The pain was an ache rather than the stab I expected if my skull had been cracked.

'Well perhaps that branch put some sense back into your head,' snapped Forel from behind his brother. 'If you'd been paying attention when you left, you might have noticed your ancestral home on fire.'

I looked up in alarm and tried to stand, but Dever placed a hand on my chest and I could not resist.

'Enough, Forel, that does no good. Calm yourself, Father, the fire's out and did little real damage. About as much harm as this branch has done to your thick head.' He raised a broken piece of wood with a cautious smile and held it out for me to see.

'A branch?'

'It was lying beside you.'

'But the man ...' I tried again to sit up, this time with greater success. Dever took my elbow to steady me as I blinked away the sharp bursts of light before my eyes.

'What man?'

'The ... Oh Gods, the book!' I struggled with my son until he let me rise, as unsteady as I was, keeping a firm grip on my shoulder when I tried to mount.

'No more galloping tonight, and certainly not on my bloody horse! The village isn't far, get on that overfed creature of your own and we'll walk you there.'

'No, there's no time ... the girl—'

My protests were cut short by a tone of voice that could have come from my own father, one deserving of the title Lord of Moorview. 'Quiet! You're not rushing off anywhere; I'm indulging you in even taking you there. If you insist in putting yourself in any more danger we'll truss you like a turkey and drag you home. When Mother takes one look at that lump on your head you'll not leave your bed for a month. Am I understood?'

I mumbled assent, resisting the urge to stare at my feet like a child. Whatever fervour demanded I get to the village, he was no doubt right that I had collapsed enough for one evening. In any case, I had lain on the road long enough for it not to matter. A few more minutes could not help the girl now. In my dazed state I felt cold and distant. I was certain that the maid would be dead, but the realisation could stir no emotion.

I mounted my horse and Dever took hold of the reins – watching carefully for any mad break for the horizon, though in truth my whole energy was spent on keeping in the saddle. Forel trotted alongside, with Toramin's reins in one hand, his eyes scanning all about but there was nothing to see. Even the trees had spent their energy and now only vaguely saluted our passing as the storm rumbled well off to the north.

When we reached the village a crowd was gathered on the green, standing before the stone shell of a building as flames lit the faces of those throwing buckets of water. The fire must have burned quick and fierce, consuming everything. A man detached himself from the group and ran over, his face and clothes stained with soot and mud.

'My Lord?'

'Was that the inn there? Was that the only one hit?'

'It was, my Lord. It's a doubly cursed night, my niece is missing too.'

'Then you must be Master Tinan,'

'That's me, my Lord. Have you seen Emila?' Whatever curiosity he had at my manner, it was overwhelmed with fear for the girl.

'I'm afraid not, but it was her I was coming to see.'

The conversation went no further as a shout from away to my left attracted our attention.

'Oh Gods,' moaned the innkeeper as two men came into view, one carrying a body. A woman's white sleeping shift trailed down from the still form to stick to the man's legs

'I'm sorry, Moren,' called the man with the body as he closed on us, his face grave. When they came closer I could see that he was nearly completely soaked. 'It were too late when we found her.'

'We went looking as soon as we heard her!' called the youth, unable to keep still at the man's side.

His eyes leapt from the body to us and back again while he chattered on. The girl's face was obscured by long strands of wet hair. I caught a glimpse of pale white teeth and what was either mud or a bruise on her neck. The innkeeper met them and took Emila's body in his own arms, holding her slender corpse as easily as he would a child.

'We heard her scream, but she weren't there when we looked.'

'Quiet boy,' snapped the older man with a scowl. 'I'm sorry. By the time we found her in the stream she were already gone.'

The innkeeper sank to his knees and began to weep loudly. A woman standing by the remains of the inn shrieked and ran to his side. By unspoken agreement we all stepped away to give them room for their sorrow, and I, drained of emotion as I felt, took the man who had brought the body to one side to speak to.

'You found her?' He nodded, realising who I was from my clothes and startled that I would be there to take an interest. 'The boy said you heard her scream?'

He nodded again, shooting a look to Master Tinan before replying.

'We did, I've never heard the like. Shrieked like a banshee she did, close past our house. When it stopped we went out to see who it were, but she must have fallen in the stream and been taken down by the current. We found her about thirty yards further. And oh Gods, the look on her face!'

I didn't need to ask. I remembered Madam Haparl's words about my mother's corpse. My heart ached for another lost to this mystery as Dever came to join us.

'There'll be nothing of the book left. Emila's ... was staying in the attic; it'll have been the first to go.'

'The poor girl, dead for the love of her mistress. If I'd been quicker perhaps ...' My voice trailed off. What use were words now? Emila was dead, killed for her loyalty. No words would change that.

'Perhaps we can still salvage something from this night.'

I looked back from the mourning aunt and uncle in surprise,

but had no strength to chastise Dever for his lack of respect as he continued.

'From what I remember of grandmother, she would not abide untidiness. That day book was pristine always, she'd even trim the edges if they started to look ragged. I can't believe she would have kept the letters loose inside. Surely she would have copied them down and put the originals away if the information was that important.'

'But we looked through her papers already,' I protested.

'The writing boxes. We took the papers out of them, but you always said they had hidden compartments. We didn't open any of those.'

'Gods, I forgot all about them! But that means ...' He matched my gaze and nodded, a spark of fear in his eye.

'That means we should be at home. Forel!'

We both ran for our horses and mounted directly. I was weak and light-headed, but the dignity of grace is an easier sacrifice than the safety of my family. Forel looked up from his conversation and by instinct leapt up into his saddle to follow us. There was no time to speak as we rode, no time to explain.

I couldn't force the image of that limp and soaked figure hanging dead in the man's arms, but this time it bore my wife's face. The image was too painful to bear and I kicked my heels hard into the flanks of my horse to escape the pain of such thoughts.

As we reached Moorview, Daen ran out to greet us. The storm had abated but it was no summer evening and she hugged herself to disguise her shivers. Worry was etched into her face, but it relieved me still to see nothing more.

'Father, at last.'

'Is everyone well?' I replied, slipping off my mount as fast as possible. The boys followed on my heels leaving the three horses untethered for Berin to collect.

'We're all fine, but about an hour ago the wind suddenly became as fierce as before. The shutters in the jumble room must have been loose, it ripped out the entire frame. The wind was so strong down here; the Gods only know what it was like up there.'

I stopped and took her by the shoulders. She looked tired,

drained by the course of today's events and unable to endure more.

'What about the writing boxes? Where are they?'

'The storm destroyed everything. When we managed to open the door the desks were overturned, the papers flung out over the grounds and sodden—'

She had no time to continue as I turned and smashed my fist against the uncaring stone wall behind me. A deep rage welled up inside me – this had all been for nothing. Shouting curses at the world, the spectre that plagued the moors and my own damned luck, I hardly noticed Daen shout at me until she took me by the shoulders and pulled me around to face her.

'She took the letters out! Listen to me! When you left to get the book, Mother went to take the letters out. She remembered grandmother showing her how to open the compartments so she went to look there and found some letters.'

I stared back like an idiot, wordlessly gaping while Dever and Forel gave a shout of victory and clapped each other on the shoulder. Of course Cebana would know how to open them. She would be the one to inherit a lady's writing box, why rely on a man's memory to work them? Some imitation of joy surged in my heart until as I pictured the limp sodden figure of Emila and wondered what danger Cebana had exposed herself to.

We ran to the family room where Cebana stood, a small packet of papers in her hand. She wore a faint smile on her lips, half hidden by the papers that were still bound in ribbon. Embracing her fiercely I pressed my lips against hers, murmuring words of love. When I could draw myself away, I took the packet from her hands and led her off to another room. Our children looked furious at the move to exclude them, but I ignored their faces and shut the door behind me.

We walked down the corridor to the library, taking two lamps off the wall as we passed and using them to light the fire there. I do not deny that I was taking my time through an apprehension of what we might discover. Any sense of victory had faded into nothing as I was reminded these letters had caused at least two deaths, that the truth within them might be horrific and terrifying.

At last I developed the courage to start. We settled down onto a small sofa near the fire, huddling together with the comforting presence of books around us. The tall window was still shuttered and the heavy drapes drawn so I felt secure and comfortable as I began to read. Cebana reached for another of the letters but I held on tight, selfishly perhaps but I wanted to know their contents before exposing my wife to it. There were nine letters in all; some from correspondents whose names I recognised but several I did not.

I cannot say what suspicions they provoked in me – only that they dealt with a single event in one form or another. Most seemed idle hearsay until combined with the others, while one was remarkable that it had ever been written and another quite shocking for the damage it could cause to so many, hinting as it did towards heresy, blasphemy— But I must say no more.

My mind returned to the despoiled tapestry upstairs, to the damaged figures of that most famous scene. My stomach tightened as I understood why it had been done. The eighth letter told of a glimpsed scene that seemed a fever-dream, but as I recalled those marred depictions I realised the horror in the author's mind had not been madness.

Cebana tried again to read what I had but this time I was sharp in my denial. I could see her anger and hurt, but my fear was manifest. She saw it in my eyes and it caused her to cry for me. There we sat for the best part of an hour I think, holding each other tight and weeping as only lovers can.

Three times did she demand to share my pain and each time I was more resolved to keep it from all of them. Dever flew into a fury that I refused him, Forel was prepared to force the packet from my breast pocket, but my calm silence eventually won through. All I could think about was enduring the night and returning to Narkang in the morning. Eventually they realised this and helped me, but Forel and Daen especially continued in their questions.

Firstly, we saw to the house. Doors were locked and windows barred, we kept weapons close to hand as though preparing for a siege and in truth that was how we now felt. The servants felt our mood and those who I asked to stay awake took to their assigned stations with knives and cleavers taken from the kitchen. It was a curious collection of sentries that stood guard that night, as the womenfolk kept to our bedchamber.

Sana had picked up on the fear of the house and our main concern other than to stay awake was to keep her calm. There was a wild look in the girl's face, as if she had guessed the truth though it would have meant nothing to one of her years. She spoke as little as normal, but without one of her family holding her she would draw herself into a ball and whimper.

The night drew on. I paced the corridors, sometimes alone, sometimes with my sons. Each of us carried a blade and a lamp, but we heard nothing. Only once did I open a window to mark the weather. The storm had ended. The air was still and I could make out the black outlines of clouds in the sky with the light of the uncovered moon. I tasted the fresh night air, the rising scents that follow the storm and almost smiled. The worst, it seemed, was over. There was a peace on the Land I had not detected since arriving. The moors seemed merely that, no more than empty miles of heather and peat soaked in rain. And then I noticed the quiet.

It was not the silence of night, for what night is ever silent? It was not calm, there was no peace out there but the empty noise of a dead place, of a noiseless brooding or lurking predator. It is hard to understand that utter quiet for one rarely hears it. The absence of disturbance falters before this weighty space – devoid of sound but clamouring with sharp thoughts and buzzing anger. I slammed the window as fast as I could and latched it well, locking the door of the room behind me and stamping my way downstairs to pierce the fog about me.

I awoke to a haunting flurry of notes that rang out through the house. I had no idea of the hour, but as I raised myself to my feet I felt leaden, as though it had been the sleep of the grave. My body protested each movement, cried out at each step and my head was so fogged I twice found myself pressed against the wall for support. Still the music played. The high unearthly notes of a virginal or harpsichord echoed in ancient tones through the wood and stone of this rock in history – a hypnotic song that caused my eyelids to droop. I had to fight to stop myself from sagging to my knees such was the weight I felt on my shoulders.

'Father,' came a voice from behind me, choked and wavering though whether it was my head or the voice I could not tell.

Contriving to turn around I fell onto one knee, but held my head up to see Dever and Daen clasping each other in their own efforts.

'The music ...' was all I could say, wondering which of my children was playing such a wonderful tune. I had no memory of any of them learning to such a proficiency.

'Sana's missing!' blurted Daen out as they reached me. Her voice was a tired slur, drunken with the music.

Behind them, I saw Forel and Cebana making a slow journey down the stair from upstairs, Carana close behind. Fear clarified my mind once more. Though my body was treacherously weak I lurched down the stone steps that led toward the discordant, beautiful sound. The ground slipped beneath my feet time and again – the music dragging at my heels so that each step safely gained was a victory won.

I reached the ground floor and turned left, towards the ballroom and long gallery that lay at the north end of Moorview. My destination was fixed firmly in my mind, the memory of a virginal propped in one corner of the ballroom, lit by the moonlight until I'd closed the tall drapes. Even as I crashed into a table on the corridor I did not take my eyes off the door ahead of me.

With a painful lack of speed I dragged myself to the door. With each step the musical strains grew to abominable levels. When I reached it and placed my hand on the tarnished brass handle, the melody was singing so violently at my ears I felt a wet touch of pain that felt like blood seeping from them.

I turned the handle, only to find it unyielding. In my weakened state it might have been carved from a single piece of stone for I could not move it even a fraction. And then suddenly the music stopped, so abruptly the last note seemed to vanish from the air rather than gradually fade away. As the ache of the music receded, my head began to clear and my strength started to return, even as the voices of my family behind me grew more insistent and real.

The door would not budge, but with the end to that awful, enchanting music I remembered another door off to my right. I turned to see it slightly open and ran with my last remaining strength. I threw the door open, hand on my sword but it remained in its sheath as I saw Sana before me, sitting placidly at the virginal which had been rolled out from the corner to stand before the ballroom's great windows. The drapes had been opened and clear moonlight shone through, bathing her delicate features with cool white light.

I could see no one else but still I walked cautiously, looking all about me with my blade slowly emerging. Only my daughter giggling at my actions broke that caution and suddenly I threw myself toward Sana to gather her up. Her arms felt cool and smooth as she wrapped them about my neck, unconcerned and unaffected. It was a complete departure to the whimpering and nervous child of earlier, but profoundly welcome.

The others burst in but I ignored them, instead placing Sana back down on the stool she'd been sitting on. The stool had a cushion placed on it to raise her up to the correct height, but she could not have been the musician.

'Sana, who was playing just now? Was it you?'

She gave me her best smile, innocent and knowing in one bright flash, and shook her head.

'Man.'

'What man? Where did he go?'

A flicker of confusion crossed her face and she looked to her left at the other half of the virginal stool beside her. Patently there was no one there so she looked back over her other shoulder to scan the room. The ballroom was almost entirely empty of furniture, certainly it contained no places to hide and she returned her attention to me with a shrug – that and a smile was the only response I received.

'What did he look like?' I urged.

'Big.'

'And his face?'

'No face.'

Perhaps any other parent would have slapped a child for being so foolish in conversation, but this was how Sana spoke. It was a curious habit, but one that made clear the anxiety of before was gone without trace.

'No face? What do you mean?' questioned Cebana as she appeared at my side.

I held up an arm to stop her going any further in case it distracted the girl's flighty mind, but Sana only waved a little greeting. 'Do you mean he had no nose perhaps? Or was an eye missing?'

'He had a nose. Silly! Had eyes, had a mouth, had a nose. No face.'

There was something about her speech that made me believe her. Whichever way she meant it, Sana was sure that the man had no face.

'How about his clothes? How was he dressed?'

It was a question I dreaded to ask, but knew I must. The child screwed up her face in thought for a moment, her button nose wrinkling before her smile shone again in the moonlight.

'Ragged.'

The warning was clear enough. Neither barred door nor proud walls of history could protect us. It was the final reminder of my inadequacies and of the rank and name and history I had never wished to inherit. Thus I have written these words, through night and day till dusk is now at hand. The cloud-wreathed moor has sullenly waited for my emergence and now the hour comes.

Though my hand trembles at the prospect of what I must do, I believe I can bring these events to a conclusion. Those letters I have read again and again. They linger at the edge of my sight as I write now. My eye has drifted to them constantly and though what they reveal is an awful truth, there remains a chord of hope in this dismal symphony. The letters are now collected with a variety of more innocent correspondences that might provide directions to the foolish. All will lie safe in my jacket pocket.

As you must know, I was named for one whose body lies somewhere out on the moor. He was hardly a celebrated figure. He received no hero's funeral and his death was recounted as a terrible one, however heroic, but he did what was necessary and was remembered warmly by those who owed him a debt. I go now to join him and the other lonely voices of the moor – to face the ghosts of the past and the fate I have chosen.

This statement I leave here. A man must be permitted to leave account of his life and last days. My king will require it and my family must be assured that it was love that took me from them; that it is love that demands they investigate no further and secure a similar promise from the king.

The dark of the moor will know from my resolve that its secrets remain safe, despite these feeble scraps of parchment. One cannot lie to the dark and I pledge with my life that this curse shall go no further. With the new day I can but pray the Gods bless me and walk with me now – and that in the morning the sun will again shine on Moorview.

AFRAID OF THE DARK

'Mother, why do you let him do that?' Cara snapped as she entered their small kitchen.

Her mother looked up with a tired expression, a tiny woman struggling under the platter of food.

'Do what, dear? Can you just ...' She nodded towards her shawl that was about to slip from her shoulders. Cara obliged and rearranged it, but the girl steadfastly remained in her way.

'Scare the children. Grandfather's telling stories again.'

At thirteen, Cara didn't think of herself as a child any more, rather a second mother to her younger siblings. She tossed her hair haughtily, as she had seen the older girls of the village do, and waited. 'Mother, are you listening? Why don't you stop him scaring them with his stories?'

'Yes Cara, I'm listening,' her mother said patiently, 'but your grandfather is head of this homestead and the stories are our heritage.'

'But he's telling them how bad we are, how we deserve our troubles by betraying the Gods. He's scaring them, telling them how we're lower than the other tribes.'

Her mother let out an exasperated sigh and handed Cara the platter to take in herself, hoping the weight of it would cut any argument short. The look in her eyes was so much like her father's had once been. These days he wore the same tired, defeated looked that they all bore in these lands. It was hard to retain the vigour of youth in a place where snow could fall for half the year and slavers prowled the highways. Their hardy crops were only just a match for the conditions and life was a constant strain.

'Take this in and get the others round the table. We've had this conversation before and there's nothing more to say. Keep that temper of yours or your father will put you over his knee.'

She gave Cara a look that made it clear the subject was closed and turned to retrieve the rest of supper. The girl stamped her foot as best she could and returned to the main room. It was by far the largest in the house, a great roaring fire on one side and an oak table large enough for the whole family on the other. Outside, the wind howled, flinging handfuls of snow and icy rain against the shutters. Despite the fire the room was chilly with a pervading smell of damp thatch in the air.

They were eleven in total; three generations of noise and bustle. All the children sat around the eldest member of the family, a stout, bearded man of sixty summers. His rough, calloused hands gripped his stick tightly as he leaned forward to stare into the eyes of the youngest.

'And now Nersa,' he said in his deep voice, 'why do we not leave the village lines at night?'

The girl stared back, a little fear drying her throat as she tried to reply. Grandfather's word was law in the homestead and there were few who'd argue with him in the village. Even the others of the Elder's Circle bowed to his judgement and his grandchildren respected rather than loved the stern man.

'Because of the Saljin Man,' whispered the child. She hardly dared to look up as she said it, so strong was her fear.

Cara snorted in the background and slammed the dish down onto the table, spilling a little food on the table in the process.

'Cara, that goes onto your plate and it's all you'll get tonight. I'll learn you respect for the food we eat, no matter how many hungry nights it takes.'

Cara turned to protest, but met her mother's gaze as she did and her eyes dropped. A slap on the behind sent her back into the kitchen to fetch a pitcher of water but it was her pride that was smarting. When she returned, everyone was sat at the table, bar her grandfather. He stood behind the largest chair they had; a solid wooden armchair stained black with age and smoke. Only grandfather was allowed to sit in it and to the children it seemed as laden with majesty as any golden throne. More than once Cara had felt the back of his hand when he found her in it, curled up and asleep with her head on the high polished back.

'Cara, perhaps you should be the one I ask about our history,' her grandfather said angrily. 'Are you now a mage? Are you so strong and brave you don't fear the Saljin Man?'

'Master Dorne says there is no Saljin Man,' she mumbled, trying to stay defiant as she stared down at the reed-strewn floor.

'Master Dorne?' he roared. 'Master Dorne's a fool and a snivelling coward. You ignore whatever rubbish comes out o' his mouth, the man has never marched even with the army! Master Dorne'd piss himself if you even suggested leaving the village boundary after dark.'

There was clear rage in his voice now and Cara's parents exchanged a worried look, but neither spoke. Cara kept still, the spark of defiance cowed by his sudden outburst. Her father took her arm and shoved her down onto the bench beside him.

'Cara, stop your nonsense now, it's time to eat. Father, please don't work yourself up, she knows not to take Dorne's word over yours.'

'Hah! You two are too easy on her. The child needs a firm hand or you'll find her under a tree one morning,' the old man growled.

He glared around the table, daring anyone to contest his words. No one dared to and at last he took his seat, opening his hands to issue prayer to the Gods. When he had finished they began to eat in uncomfortable silence, one broken by Cara's younger brother. He spoke hesitantly, in a tone so quiet it would have gone unheard on any other day.

'Grandfather, why do we pray to the Gods? You said they cursed us.'

The hush went beyond normal silence. It was a question rarely spoken, but the unusual mood and the foul weather had affected everyone. Now, though the boy was only five, it earned a smart clip round the ear.

'In the name of the Gods what is this? Have I been deaf and dumb all these years? How can such ignorance have come into this home?'

Cara's grandfather slammed his hand so hard down on the table that every cup jumped and spilt. As sad trails formed and ran to the floor the younger children began to cry under his furious gaze. Cara refused to buckle this time and met his stare, knowing what she risked but her stubborn streak waxed stronger than her fear.

'Well, girl, you wish to defy me? Are you so knowledgeable the lore should be given to your charge?'

She swallowed gently, determined not to be treated as a child. Before she opened her mouth to speak, however, her mother spoke up in her defence.

'Ozhin please, she's only a child, she ...'

'Quiet, woman, were you taught nothing? For seven thousand years our children have never been too young to learn about the Land. I don't think that'll change because of one stubborn child,' he growled, staring her down until she shrank back into her seat.

'Well, Cara? Speak.'

'I ... I don't think the Saljin Man exists. He's just a story grown-ups make up to keep the children quiet. There's no daemon in the woods, only wolves and bears. You're mean, scaring Nersa and Drel, it's not fair.'

He regarded her coldly, as if lost for words to express his fury. When he did speak it was in a way she had not heard before; quiet, slow and chilling.

'Then please, brave warrior, go and prove me wrong.'

At this her mother jumped up, crying out for this to stop but he silenced her with a hand. 'I'll not be called a liar by a child o' my own line. So arm yourself, Cara, and go to battle.'

He jabbed an accusing finger towards the drape-covered door. Naturally, Cara made no move, surprised that he'd even suggested it, but the flicker of defiance kept her back straight.

'Well, girl? Go I say, or sit and think of the strapping that comes,' he bellowed in a voice to shake the walls of the house.

When still she remained, Ozhin kicked back his chair with venom and stepped towards her to make good on his promise. A shriek escaped Cara's lips and she darted away, rushing to the flimsy safety of the kitchen and slamming the door behind her. Ozhin took one more step and stopped, at last securing the reaction he'd been looking for. He returned to his seat with a grunt and gave the rest of the family a hard look before returning to his food.

Cara held the door firmly shut and tried to smother her tears, both of fear and humiliation. When the flutter of panic in her stomach subsided she realised her grandfather wasn't coming to get her yet. He'd not let anyone get up until supper was all gone and there was nothing for Cara's mother to smuggle back to her daughter.

She crossed the room to be near the stove's warmth, sitting in a miserable pile beside it and hugging her knees to her chest. It was then that she noticed the door sitting ajar, a finger of cold creeping in to tickle at her toes and stubborn will.

'I'm not afraid of the dark,' she whispered as her courage returned. 'There's nothing dangerous out there – no wolf's stupid enough to be out in this cold. I'll cross round and bang on the front door, that'll show grandfather how stupid he is to frighten the others.'

She slipped on her mother's fur and wrapped it tight around her skinny body, then paused a moment at the door to remind herself there was no daemon waiting outside. She yanked it open and the icy air rushed in. It was savagely cold outside, bitter and biting now dusk had turned swiftly into night, and the ferocity made Cara gasp. Determined not to back out now, she carefully pulled the door closed behind her.

The darkness was almost complete; no moons that she could make out behind the brooding clouds, but enough scraps of light crept out from the house to show her the ground she knew so well around their home. Off to the left was the Kaszin household with their barn adjoining, and running from that house to her own was the fence that served as boundary line for the village.

The fence marked the limits of their Land after nightfall, a thin wooden frame that would keep out no hungry creatures but nevertheless was supposed to keep the village safe. She started off around the house, keeping to the middle-ground between the fence and house, but stopped dead after a few yards as the greater moon drifted out from behind a cloud.

Ahead of her stood a man – a man outside the fence! It was

impossible to make much out as he was wrapped from head to foot in a grey cloak, as any traveller would have to be to survive the cold, but she was certain he wasn't from the village. Aside from anything else, no man in the village would dare step outside the fence, even drunk they'd be too frightened. It wouldn't be suggested even in jest, but how did a traveller find their way through the forest at night?

Hooded and cloaked, she couldn't see his face but this was indeed a man, not the daemon said to haunt the wilds at night. He took a step towards her, fearlessly keeping beyond the fence, and she briefly saw his black boots against the grey of his cloak. The snow lessened a moment and she saw he was looking straight at her so she waved hesitantly, not sure what else to do.

'Do you guard this village at night?' called the stranger in a voice that cut through the wind without impairment.

Clear and crisp, he sounded foreign but a man none the less. She looked down to see that she had her eating knife gripped in one hand, having drawn it without thought. Returning it to her belt Cara approached the boundary line and stuttered out two questions.

'How are you out at night? Don't you fear the Saljin Man?'

A chuckle floated through the darkness to her muffled ears. 'I fear nothing of the night.'

Cara looked down at the boundary and smiled nervously, the expression hidden by the collar of her coat.

'I don't believe he exists either, he's just a tale my grandfather tells to scare the children. He's going to strap me for thinking different,' she added with an edge of misery.

'His fear is a prison.'

She nodded at the strange words, suddenly hating the blinkered fear they'd been taught all their lives. 'He'd never believe anyone would dare be past the fence at night, even he's too frightened to ever do such a thing. I'll call him, show him how wrong he is.'

The figure inclined his head, indicating the ground beside him. 'Join me out here, prove to him who's the braver.'

Cara giggled with fearful delight. 'He'd be so frightened, he'd scream and wet himself like a baby!'

Summoning her courage, Cara shouted her grandfather's name as loud as she could and hopped over the line to the stranger's side. Her voice carried well over the lessened wind and in moments the front door of their home jerked open. Cara felt a flicker of victory rush through her shivering limbs as her parents and grandfather all rushed out, pausing for a moment before spotting them beyond the fence.

With a scream, her mother rushed forward, shrieking Cara's name, only to be held back by her own husband. Grandfather Ozhin seemed rooted to the spot for a while, then staggered forward, crying out but the wind swallowed the sound.

Cara watched their horror with a fading sense of jubilation, the terror on their faces only increasing with every moment. The moment of shock had gone, now she saw her mother wailing and screaming in a heap, her father's arms wrapped tight around her chest in a desperate attempt to stop her coming any further.

She looked up to her new friend for explanation. Only then did she see his face, the ice and teeth. Sharp eyes and night's haunting music shrouded her from the distant cries, dulled by a descending veil.

And then there was only white and the sound faded to nothing. The Land turned perfectly still and silent as the cold wrapped its arms around her.

THE PICTURES OF DARAYEN CRIN

'Who's there? What do you want?'

'Oh it's just you – both of you is it? Goodness, you gave me a fright. Well don't just stand there silently, come and give your father a kiss. No, no; nothing's the matter. I was asleep, that's all – asleep and dreaming.'

'Of course I can see in my dreams, you little scamp, I wasn't always blind you know!'

'Oh, you didn't know? Well, all the same, I remember enough to love my dreams. I was just a child when I lost my sight. My fourth birthday if this old memory of mine can be trusted – a short time for certain, but I saw something of the Land at least.'

'Yes, it's hard sometimes, hard indeed. Makes my heart ache so bad it's fit to burst sometimes, but I've lost less than most and I thank the Gods for that. I remember only glimpses mostly; enough for me to know what a house looks like, or a person, but not so much I weep for the sunset over the valley or the view from the Bale Tower.'

'Well, yes; I do weep when I sing the ballad of Mistress Bale, but that's because it's a beautiful song. If folk choose to believe I'm weeping for any other reason, that doesn't bother me when it earns the coin to put food on your table! Hah, don't be so shocked, Ethia! Being blind doesn't mean I'm a fool. If the Gods wished me this way I'll not complain, but if fools choose to see some grand nobility in it that's not my fault either.'

'Yes, it's this house I've seen – your mother moved in here

when we married; your grandmother had taken Ethia's bedroom the year we started courting. She lived with us long enough to see one of you born and that helped her find peace. I like to think the house hasn't changed a scrap over the years. I'm sure it has, but even today I see it with the eyes of a child, one ten winters younger than you, Daken.'

'What took my sight? A fever, or so the doctors claimed.'

'Believe them? How am I to know, I was a little boy at the time. I remember the fever well enough and the failing of my sight. It took a few weeks I recall, no blowing out of the lamp there; more like a shadow gradually— Hmm. It's funny, I've been so careful not to say it that way for years. I wonder why it came to mind now?'

'Oh, your grandmother. Perhaps no one's asked me about my sight since she died, more than likely I suppose. Well, that's how it was, a shadow descending, darkening everything around me. It upset Mother to hear it described that way, don't ask why.'

'What part of "don't ask" was unclear, eh Daken? No, you're too young to hear about that, why don't I tell you a story of the man you were named after? No? Are you sure? He was a savage one in his earlier years, bloodthirsty and brutal; hardly the trusted general he ended up – isn't that the sort of story boys like to hear?'

'Ah, the pair of you! No, I don't think you're old enough. Oh enough of whining, you both should be getting ready for bed shouldn't you? Where's your mother?

'No, stories of the Mad Axe are different; bloodthirsty white-eye he might have been, a story's different when it's about your own family.'

'Yes they are – dammit, Daken, they are! Enough of this, to bed the pair of you! Shut up and go to your rooms or I swear by the Gods I'll cane you myself.'

'Children? Children, are you in here?'

'Ethia, please, shush. I know, I frightened you. I'm sorry. I didn't mean to, I just lost my temper. You have to understand, this is a subject I've not talked about for twenty years.'

'No, it's more than just my losing my sight; I wish it were only that. You don't remember her but my mother was always a lovely woman, so kind and caring, but before I was born she was also a happy woman. This is something my grandparents told me when I was about your age, they thought I should know. The only memory I have of her face is a smile like the sun, but when you lose your sight you have to get better at hearing things instead.

'My mother was, for much of my life, frightened – frightened and sad. When I was younger I thought it was my fault. I still remember the day I described losing my sight as a shadow falling over me. She wept for two whole days, all the grief for my father that she'd hidden from up until then.'

'You've no idea the effect your birth had, Daken. Yes, you too Ethia, my mother never saw you born but you were on the way and it was the final touch that allowed her to let go of the fear she'd carried half her life. I'd always wanted a family, a proper one that was more than just my mother and I – one full of happiness rather than loss. The two of you made us complete, but you did something else I didn't expect. You gave me my mother back, the one I remember smiling down at me in my early years. The woman who'd been full of joy, returned to me for that last year of her life. For that I can never thank you both enough.'

'My father? Yes, this is about him. You know he died when I was very young, don't you? I don't suppose anyone said anything more than that though.'

'They did? An accident in Narkang? Well, of a fashion, I suppose. I, ah – I probably shouldn't tell you this, not until you're a little older, but I think you deserve an explanation for my temper. Before I do, mind, both of you just remember this is all over – there's nothing to fear now. That's what brought back my mother's happiness, the sight of Daken alive, whole and happy. It's over and there's nothing more to fear.'

'Yes, I know I'm repeating myself. Thank you, Ethia, but it's important you understand. Very well, where to begin?'

'At the beginning, yes, Ethia. Something you will learn in class soon enough is that history is a complicated beast, and the beginning is often hard to discern. For a start, not everything they will teach you is quite the truth, sometimes there will be little details left out.'

'Sorry, I'll get to the point. My father was called Darayen Crin and he was a merchant. Two years before the Menin invasion – do you remember when that was? Good, well, two years before that a man and a woman died in mysterious circumstances in Narkang.'

'No, I don't know what those circumstances were, no one knew. That's why they were mysterious. You have to understand, this story was told to me by my grandparents when I was a boy. I'll tell you what I know, but I just don't know everything. All I can say is that the old king was involved; the man who died was a friend of his and one memory I do have is of a King's Man standing in the parlour talking to my father. He was the tallest man I ever saw, tall with blond hair and a long scar down his face. That man frightened me, enough that I had to be taken out of the room by Kolus while they spoke.'

'Kolus? He was the estate foreman; already an old man by the time I was born. I don't remember much about him, only that he was always very gentle and had a gravelly voice. He was a soldier once I believe, during King Emin's wars of conquest, but he never even raised his voice to me. Anyway, the King's Men – there were two, but I don't remember the other – they had come to tell my father to stop writing letters and asking questions about the deaths in Narkang.'

'They were called Marshal and Lady Calath, I believe. Marshal Calath was my father's cousin; I think the family still live up in Inchets, not too far from here. As for his wife, she was related to the king's first minister, a powerful man called Count Antern. I don't think we ever found out what happened, but once I spoke to a travelling minstrel from Narkang about it. He remembered the matter because the city had been aflame with rumour for a few days; all sorts of ghostly talk about them being murdered in a locked room, but then a common thief confessed and was executed for the crime.'

'He laughed about it at the time – said the whole instance had become a byword for the power of rumours. I don't know if it exists today, but at the time he said the phrase "a marshal's reflection" was used to describe something repeated so many times it became distorted beyond all recognition. Why the King's Men felt the need to travel here and warn my parents about such a distortion I've never understood, but in some ways I think my mother was as frightened of them as much as anything else in the Land!'

'Now, my father had been very close to the marshal despite being many years younger. He had, in fact, visited the couple mere weeks before their murder. He was on his way home when a rider caught up his wagon train and gave him the news, asking him to return to Narkang to answer some questions. On his way back a second rider cancelled the request and told him the culprit had been executed so he returned here, knowing he wouldn't arrive in time for the funeral and having a family of his own to attend to.'

'Stop interrupting, Daken. Now where was I? Ah yes, he returned home and life went on as normal. I assume my father was grieving, but I was too young to remember, I'm afraid. I do know that one day, a few weeks after he came home, a letter arrived from a distant aunt in the city he'd seen briefly during his stay – some gossipy old spinster, nothing like your aunt at all of course.'

'Hah, yes indeed, but don't tell your mother that! Anyway, after receiving her letter my father became very depressed, he refused to attend to the estate's affairs and spent most days locked away in his study. He wouldn't speak to my mother for long periods, I remember her being very upset and hugging me while she wept. What was said and what happened I don't remember, but he started writing to city officials and the Watch commander about the murder, which of course prompted the visit by the King's Men.

'After they came and warned him off, intentionally frightening Mother in the process I'm told, Father became even more withdrawn. He wouldn't eat, he refused to sleep or work. He became obsessed with this murder, quite forgetting his own family. Out of desperation my mother took me to visit a mage called Archelets who lived nearby. He owned Beller Hall, you know the one?'

'Yes, that's it. He was a rich mage who didn't have to work for the city guilds or anything, he was of a good local family and my parents knew him well. My mother went to Mage Archelets and begged his help. He agreed, naturally, and suggested my father come and help him with his experiments. My father was an educated man and, while he wasn't a mage of course, he was skilled with his hands and the mage needed some practical assistance.

'I'm told a mage is a difficult person to refuse – but all I remember of his visit was the tricks he performed for me, far in excess of anything some hedge wizard at a fair would be able to manage. Needless to say I was as delighted as I was terrified of the man, but I'm told my father took a lot more persuading. What transpired has been lost to history, but eventually my father agreed to work with the mage and the next morning travelled to Beller Hall to begin.'

'It seemed to work; he came back after sundown and hugged me for the first time in weeks apparently. Whether because of the activity, distraction, or a stern telling-off from Mage Archelets, my father remembered he had a family to take care of and did so. He had moments of melancholy and was frequently exhausted by the work he was doing for the mage – of all things, carpentry, glass-blowing and overseeing work by the blacksmith over in Garranist – but much of the man he had once been returned and life started heading back to normal.'

'No dear, it didn't turn out that way. The mage was conducting experiments with mirrors – the details I never heard, but somehow he was using magic to etch an image onto the silver-back of special mirrors.'

'No, not like the one your mother has, mirrors he and my father made especially for the process. I never saw it myself of course, but my mother for a time had kept one of their early successes – not very detailed but my grandparents said you could clearly make out the lines of my father's face in the mirror. He'd posed before the fireplace in the mage's study, grinning with joy at the shared success.'

'Somewhat like a painting, yes, but more accurate and only in the finest shades of grey. The process was to expose the mirror before whatever scene they wished to have etched and use some magical process to set that into the mirror. How exact it all was I don't know, but I do know they discovered something strange the more they experimented with the process. The greater amounts of magic they used, the worse the images turned out. The pictures were blurred in parts, on occasion some details hadn't been etched at all – it was as if they didn't exist.'

'No, not Father – a vase was the only one I can remember. The picture showed the line of the panelling on the wall behind, unbroken as though nothing was there. Another had a blur across most of the mirror, from one side all the way across to where my father stood at the fireplace. The image of him was poorly etched, as though he had been moving throughout the process, but he was very careful to be still. The process was not a quick one and neither of them had any desire to waste the mirrors they had to make themselves – it was a costly and time-consuming process.'

'What was the cause? Well they didn't know, they couldn't understand it. In desperation they tried to increase the magic used even further, at which point something very strange happened. The next image was of my father as usual, but there was another figure in the room. It was indistinct, but at the window there stood a woman where of course there had been none in real life.'

'Yes, so they realised. Mage Archelets recognised the figure at once, despite the lack of detail. It was his mother; a woman dead some thirty years by then, before the conquest. Both men were terrified, this hadn't been their intention at all. Mage Archelets realised the increasing levels of magic used was bringing out echoes of the past. The more they used the further back they could reach. The vase had stood there not long before they started work so it had left only a small impression on the Land – he described it as ripples on a pond, the biggest of which might last for years. His mother had often stood at that window, looking out over the gardens beyond, and some echo of her had remained.

'To my father this awakened only one thought, the obsession he had tried to bury those past weeks. For what could leave a greater impression on the Land than a murder? All this he kept from his friend, but his sullen nature returned and he left for home early that day.

'That night my father broke in to the mage's house and stole the apparatus and several plates they had already prepared. He never came home again, but travelled with all speed to Narkang – determined to discover the identity of his cousin's murderer.'

'Yes, Daken, I'm afraid he did. Mage Archelets was naturally distraught, but beyond sending a message on to a friend of his in Narkang there was little he could do. He was an elderly man, my father in the prime of his life. With a heavy heart he went on with his experiments with the remaining equipment he had, pursuing them further still.

'What he discovered prompted him to send a second message, this time by fast courier to the king's uncle with whom he was acquainted. They acted with all haste but it was too late, they didn't reach the former home of Marshal Calath in time. Watchmen broke in and discovered my father in the upstairs study – dead on the floor with some hedge wizard he'd hired in Narkang a few hours previously, both lying amid the smashed wreckage of the mage's equipment.

'They had to break down the study door as well; it had been barred from the inside. Mage Archelets told my mother the last pictures he'd created had used greater magic still and in them could be seen my father.'

'Yes, my father who was by then on the king's highway to Narkang. My father who was standing there in the same pose as he always adopted in the pictures, for ease of comparison. But he wasn't alone in the pictures – there were other figures. One was Archelets' mother, another a man he guessed from the stature to be the Hall's previous owner.

'Except now, each was facing my father – looking straight at him and reaching out. In the very last, the other figure had almost touched the image that was my father's echo. My mother never discovered what was etched in the pictures in Narkang, only that there were three of them. The last was still in the broken picture-box when my father's body was found. He never saw what was on it.

'Around that time I came down with a fever. For a week I

sweated and raved, close to death. When I recovered, my sight was already failing, but of that week I had only one memory. It was the dream of a room where the furniture was all covered by dust-sheets and a figure stood facing me – a shadow with claws, reaching for my eyes.'

SHADOWS IN THE LIBRARY

Gennay Thonal got up from her desk and stretched. Somewhere behind her, muffled by a heavy drape, a window shutter rattled its bolt under another gust of winter wind outside. On her desk the flame of her oil lamp leaned slightly away, as though under the breath of someone who'd been sat beside her, but Gennay was quite alone in the still library.

The fire nearby hissed lazily and for a moment the curtain of shadows around the walls drew back, before settling comfortably back into position. It was dark there with only two lamps and a fading fire to light the large, empty room, but neither the chilly breath of night nor the gloom on the ground floor were enough to disturb Gennay a shred.

She reached up towards the timbered ceiling with a slight moan of effort, but the stiffness in her back wasn't enough to stop a smile from stealing over her face. Young and supple, Gennay felt the ache fall away as she continued the movement around and down again until her fingers brushed the rug underfoot. The exercise was one she'd done most days for more than a decade and proved no difficulty even now.

As a little girl she'd nagged her father into allowing her professional training rather than the staid, formal version girls of breeding were normally permitted. It had instilled an athletic grace few of her peers possessed and even fewer of their mothers would approve of.

'Ah, Father, you dangerous progressive,' she said with a grin, looking over the balustrade beside her with a burgeoning sense of pride. 'First allowing such unwomanly behaviour, now bringing learning to the unwashed masses.'

On the floor below there was a mess of boxes and workmen's tools, but in Gennay's eyes it was a dream slowly taking shape. Shelves on the walls, drawers waiting to be filled – she could picture the finished product in her mind and had been able to for months now.

On the point of collapse less than a year ago, the old building had been derelict and damp. This winter might have seen it all fall inwards under the stinging ocean breeze and freezing temperatures, but the roof was now repaired and strong once more; the marauding cold of Narkang's streets tamed to a manageable chill.

'New life,' Gennay whispered to the hush of the empty building, 'we're breathing new life into this city, whatever they might say about us.'

The young woman pulled her shawl back up over her shoulders and stepped closer to the fireplace. The library was a massive building and from her desk Gennay could observe proceedings in the large central hall around which everything else had been built. Despite the repairs, Gennay still worked with a shawl over her head and fingerless woollen gloves. After nightfall the fire took an edge off the cold, nothing more, but that made all the difference to a woman forced to work later than her employees.

Once a guildhouse for shipping merchants, the building was in three distinct parts – not quite forming three sides of a square, while an eight-foot wall penned the remaining ground to form a cobbled courtyard. This part, the largest of the three, consisted of the oversized hallway over which Gennay now looked, to serve as a library in conjunction with what had once been a large meeting chamber just off the main room. Behind Gennay were another few rooms to be used for private study, while the newer north wing would house the three school rooms where the best and brightest of the city's children would be educated.

The oldest part of the building, the guildsmen offices, would house the scribes and copyists who would earn the money required to keep the library going, penmanship and learning always being in demand in a trading port. Gennay's father, Count Bastin Thonal, had bought the building and paid for its renovation, in addition to amassing the books and scrolls for the library, including copies of his entire personal collection.

It was to be his legacy, his gift to the city he'd found wealth in, but – ever the businessman – he'd decided against an annual drain on his income, preferring to force the library to be self-sufficient whether or not his eldest child was its administrator.

Gennay reached out to the fire and warmed her hands for a moment longer before returning to her desk to pack up. It could easily be left for the morning, the night watchman would not disturb anything, but still she tidied every night. She ordered and stacked her correspondence then arranged the books and papers so even the strictest of her childhood nannies could have found no cause for complaint, all ready for her return. One pile for each of the library's functions with a fourth for the building works, each consisting of half-a-dozen or more sheaves bound with coloured ribbon.

Before she stood again from the desk, Gennay's eyes lingered on one of the piles, the one concerning the school. The matter grew more complicated every time she considered what would be taught, how and by whom. Narkang was not presently a centre for learning and even finding capable secular teachers was proving a struggle.

'A shame my brother doesn't have patience for the efforts of others,' Gennay said to the library at large. 'He would make this so much easier.'

She spoke without rancour, loving Emin unreservedly, but the young man had always been irritated by people failing to grasp concepts as quickly as he did, let alone his few attempts to teach anyone. When Emin was young his father had been forced to beat him for throwing an apple at a cousin, because the man hadn't been able to keep up with an explanation given so rapidly it was barely intelligible.

'And that's typical of my brother,' Gennay said with a laugh as she lowered an iron cover over the fire's embers. 'How many beatings are given with a slight sense of pride? At the age of twelve Emin blackens a man's eye from over a dozen yards away – earning himself a new bow and the finest instructor the following week.'

She picked a lamp up from the desk and started off down the wide stair that curled around the north end of the hall, eyes on the new stone lintel above the main door to the south wing. Halfway down however she stopped, sensing a slight gust of wind run up the worn steps towards her. Gennay looked around and frowned. Up on the mezzanine the shutter rattled its bolts again like the gentlest of unquiet spirits, but that was the only sound.

'No, there can't be a window or door left open,' she surmised after a moment of silence. 'We opened few enough today and I bolted them all myself before Sarras left.'

To confirm her thought she twitched open one of the long drapes that covered the enormous windows on that side of the hall. Through the mullioned windows she saw a few fat flakes of snow fall at an angle. Clearly the breeze was strong enough to throw around any window that had been left open, not just make it tremble.

The young woman hesitated and returned in her mind to a few hours previously when the former lay brother, Sarras, had come up to her desk. Having been brought up in a monastery, the tall man was wary of any strong-willed woman and tended to creep up to her desk like a deer ready to take flight, even more bundled up against the cold than Gennay.

They had checked the rooms together as always, moving methodically through the library to check the bolts on each window and lock the remaining doors until at last, Gennay would unlock the main entrance and lock it again behind Sarras. It was a ritual that was less necessary now the main building work had been done, but one she felt a curious pleasure in its monastic formality – quite aside from reassuring the young woman that she was secure there when alone after nightfall. With so much work to do before the official opening of the library, she couldn't afford to only keep to the few daylight hours of winter. The night watchman had been instructed to arrive only when the Hunter's Moon was above the rooftops so for a few hours she was, unusually for a woman of noble birth, quite alone in the library.

At the bottom of the stair Gennay stopped again, setting the lamp on a nearby table and cocking her head to listen. After half a minute or more she let her breath out in one long puff, satisfied there was no breeze or movement coming from any of the open parts of the library. She wove her way around the workman's tables where shelving and desks were being constructed and opened the peep-hole set into the great main door. She had to stand on her tip-toes to look out and flinched when she did as a gust of icy wind rushed through the grille to catch her unawares.

A second try revealed the courtyard just as she had expected; empty of people, with an icy sheen on the cobbles and a little snow drifted up against the right-hand wall. Gennay could just about pick out the swirling descent of a few snowflakes in the faint starlight and felt surprised that not more had fallen. As yet it was only a scattering, but the temperature had dropped dramatically today and Narkang was readying itself for a sustained siege of white.

'My thick boots tomorrow, I think,' she said to herself, preferring to speak aloud and break the silence.

She snapped the peep-hole cover shut again, then whirled around. Somewhere behind her there had come a sound, barely audible over the closing hinge but distinct none the less.

'Or was it?' Gennay muttered. 'Am I just imagining things at long last?'

She took a step forward, arms wrapped around her body until she realised she was acting like a frightened little girl. 'Oh Gennay, if Emin was to see you now you'd never hear the end of it. It's a rat if anything at all – no bolts are going to stop them getting into a building of this size.'

She stamped her heel against the flagstone floor and listened to the echo race around the empty library. No scuttling sound followed it, no scrabble of a startled creature or anything else.

'Well, there you are, it was your imagination,' she declared loudly.

Despite her assurance, Gennay's fingers went to a pocket in her dress and closed around the comforting shape of a knife handle. It was something Emin had quietly insisted that she carry, despite the fact she was be escorted to and from the library each day by Pirn, her father's most trusted retainer.

As soon as he'd heard she would be alone in the library with Sarras, Emin had given her a small dagger to keep on her person. Gennay's protests that the timid scribe, Sarras, was terrified of her had drawn only a sardonic smile from her younger brother and she'd eventually agreed to keep Emin from worrying. Now, however, she felt glad he'd insisted, however sure she was about Sarras.

It was a strange little weapon; its blade no longer than the handle with a gently rippled edge that was sharp enough to shave with. With her thumb Gennay slipped off the toggle that kept it in its leather sheath and advanced a few steps, listening all the time.

Once she reached the centre of the hall she stopped, knife still in her pocket. There were three doors ahead of her, each flanked by an empty bookcase that protruded out from the wall. To the left was a thick door that led to the kitchens and store rooms behind, all currently unused. From where she stood, Gennay could see the bolts were closed, so she discounted that. It was thick enough to mask most sounds and any thief stood behind it was going to stay there. The rear rooms did have access to the other wings, but it only took Gennay a moment to confirm that the doors leading from each were just as securely fastened.

The sound came again, a slight scratching on the edge of hearing, no louder than the whisper of fingers brushing a page – except the reading rooms were empty. The shelves in two had been completed and the first scrolls set upon them, but she'd checked and shut the doors herself. No one could have got in without her hearing from her desk, almost directly above the door.

'Which means it's a rat,' she said with slight relief. She didn't like the creeping creatures of course, but they were unavoidable in a sea-port and Gennay had seen enough not to be frightened. Just to be sure, she went to fetch her lamp and moved it to a shelf where it would cast its light inside the room. Ever mindful, she checked it was secure and out of the way in case the rat ran out and startled her, then moved forward and gave the door a thump.

Nothing happened, there was no sound from within at all. Gennay pulled her knife from her pocket and held it ready while she unlocked the door and pushed it open. It swung easily enough to reveal a dark room four yards by six, containing a high shuttered window and a table in the middle. On the table was a small pile of books, one of which had half-slipped from the top and lay open at an angle down the side of the pile.

'A draught on the pages?' Gennay wondered as she took a cautious pace forward. The room was steadfastly empty of living creatures, the only movement was her shadow stealing over the shelves. 'Ah, it must have slipped and the pages slipped one by one, rustling as they did so.'

In a flash her courage returned and Gennay marched into the room, closing the book with a firm snap and setting the pile straight. They were the first works to have been delivered by her most unlikely resource, the Knights of the Temples.

In an effort to impose a high standard of literacy upon their young officers they required that each be taught something of a copyist's skill. The result was far from the beautiful work done by monks or a mage, but it served for business records and also Gennay's purposes. The Knights of the Temples had many accounts of travel in addition to their collections of myth and scripture, but were reluctant to release anything from their libraries that they had not gone to the expense of copying.

Just as she was finished a crash echoed through the hall and Gennay shrieked in alarm.

'Mistress Gennay?' called a concerned voice from behind the door, 'Mistress? Is all well with you?'

Gennay gasped with relief, then laughed at herself. It had come from the main door, a wooden staff knocking on it most likely.

'Yes Pirn,' she called, hurrying forward. She opened the peephole again and saw a whiskery face pressed up against the grill, peering forward. 'You gave me a fright, that's all. I'm perfectly fine.'

Quickly returning her knife to its sheath, Gennay unlocked the main door and pulled it open. Pirn marched on in, eyes scanning for danger and hand on his sword.

'Peace, Pirn,' Gennay said soothingly, 'I am fine. I thought I heard a noise and when I went to investigate you banged on the door.'

'A noise?'

'It's nothing, I've already checked. Just a book that slipped from a pile in one of the reading rooms.'

She pointed toward the open door behind her and Pirn nodded. He strode forward and poked his head inside. Satisfied there was no danger, the former soldier returned to the door and beckoned inside his companion.

'Come on then, Bewen,' he said gruffly, ushering forward the night watchman who'd been loitering outside. Bewen hopped forward out of the cold and whipped a grey woollen cap from his head before bowing to Gennay as best he could with a large fur coat in his arms.

'I brought your thick coat,' Pirn explained, 'it's got bitter since Lord Tsatach closed his eye.'

'That was very kind of you.' Gennay slipped on the coat and collected a thinner one from a hook behind the door, bundling it up in her arms. 'Have a good night, Master Bewen,' she said once she was done. 'Don't be so foolish as I was and start imagining strange noises in the night.'

'I shan't, Mistress,' the white-haired watchman said with a bob of the head.

She handed him the ring of keys he would need for the night, which he accepted with another bob and slipped them onto his belt with a practised movement.

'I'll set some traps, catch you a few rats by morning.'

Gennay laughed, a feigned grimace on her face. 'And a lovely present they'll be, I'm sure!' she said as Pirn led her back out the door. 'See you in the morning.'

The following day was a busy one, presided over by a pale winter sun that did little to warm the stones of the library. Gennay arrived not long after sun up, fairly dragging Pirn from his bed and hurrying him through the empty streets. A few inches of snow had settled on the roads, but it was the night breeze whipping in off the ocean that had made Narkang's streets treacherous. At every intersection the pair were been forced to shuffle over ground polished smooth by the icy wind, but it wasn't far from the Thonal household and they arrived there before anyone else.

'Master Bewen!' Gennay called as Pirn knocked ceremoniously on the library door. She felt a moment of anxiety when her call was not replied to immediately, but then she heard the thump of feet on the flagstones.

'Mistress Thonal,' Bewen said as he eased the door open. 'Good morning to you, and you Master Pirn.'

'No excitement in the night?' Gennay asked, noting the ageing man's face was crumpled into a frown.

He shook his head, eyes scrunched up in the day's light. 'None, my lady, quiet as the grave. I checked the rat-traps not long ago, didn't catch a thing.'

'Forgive me, Master Bewen, but you don't look like a man who's had a restful night.'

'Restful, Mistress? No, I suppose not, but bad dreams is all, nothing for you to worry about.'

'Been at the brandy on duty?' Pirn asked, a warning tone in his voice. Bewen was allowed to sleep once the library was locked up; he was a light sleeper and anyone breaking in would certainly wake him.

Bewen grimaced as he stepped back from the doorway to admit the pair. 'Now you know I don't do that no more, sir, not on duty. It was an old lump of cheese I brought as part of my supper, nothing more.'

'See that it stays so,' Pirn commanded sternly.

The night watchman bobbed his head in acknowledgement, aware that any man with a history of drinking would be watched carefully by his master's steward. He fumbled briefly at his belt before freeing the large ring of keys and returning them to Gennay.

'Thank you.' She put a hand on his arm as she took the ring. 'Bewen, what did you dream of? I've not seen you look so out of sorts before.'

'I, ah, I don't rightly remember, Mistress. I think I was trying to find my way through the city, I don't know where I was going. All I remember is shadows on the streets and me taking one wrong turning after another.'

Gennay hesitated and stared into the man's rich brown eyes. Her lips were pursed as though anxious but, before she could say anything, Bewen shook his head and gave a short laugh.

'Now don't you pay any regard to that, Mistress – my dreams

never made much sense my whole life, and for certain they never meant a thing about where I was or what preyed on my mind. Half-gone cheese has made me see boats flap their wings and lift off the water before, and a watchman's mind has time enough to wander far.'

Gennay smiled at the idea. 'You're right; too long by oneself leads to an over-active imagination. Do you read?'

Bewen's face fell a little. 'Never had much call to learn, Mistress, was born to a deckhand and a seamstress.'

'Then you shall have to join our first class,' she declared, shaking her head as Bewen opened his mouth to object. 'No, it will be good for both the teachers and you, quite aside from the fact that it would be a terrible waste to spend night after night in this place and not read any of the works we're collecting.'

Seeing her mind was set, Bewen bobbed his head again and smiled uneasily, retreating out of the library as fast as he could and back to his home in the south of the city.

'Are you sure about that, Mistress Gennay?' Pirn asked with careful politeness as he watched Bewen cross the courtyard. 'He's a shade too old for learning, I reckon.'

'Nonsense, no one is too old, and as much as anything he'll be a good challenge for the teachers we're employing. He can be my spy in the lessons too,' she added brightly.

Pirn was careful not to let any expression cross his face. 'I'm sure he'll be delighted to help.'

'Good.' She prodded him on the arm. 'Now get yourself back to the house, I'm sure father's got two dozen things you need to see to.'

She ushered him out and shut the door firmly behind Pirn before heading up to her desk on the mezzanine, pulling open the two largest pair of shutters on her way.

'There we are, a bit of light,' she announced to the empty library, glad her father had agreed to replace the glass in the tall, shutterless windows that provided the bulk of the hall's light. 'Now, let's see about reviving that fire before Sarras gets here.'

As night fell, the library again emptied with alacrity, the last of their half-dozen newly hired scribes hurrying out the door with an almost apologetic look on his face. As Gennay watched him shuffle gingerly across the snow-covered courtyard a slight movement caught her eye.

It had been too brief in the gloom to be sure of, but for a moment Gennay thought someone had poked their head around the open gate at the far end of the courtyard. The scribe himself made no sign of seeing anything as he neared the gate, head low against the light falling snow. When she looked again, the darkness there seemed empty so she sighed at her own foolishness.

'Mistress Gennay?' asked Sarras from behind her. 'Is everything okay?'

She turned and looked at the tall man's anxious face that was punctuated by his curiously straight eyebrows. 'Of course, I thought I saw something but it was just ... well, it was nothing, just a trick of the light.'

Relief flooded his face as Sarras nodded. 'Very good, should we perhaps look through the letters of application before I leave?'

Gennay agreed and shut the main door before leading him back up to her desk. The sound of their footsteps on the stairs sounded oddly loud now they were alone and Gennay felt a slight unease creep into her heart as they started leafing through the applications from townsfolk.

There were several hundred already, for children of all ages. It had already been decided that half would come from the families of merchants and traders – people who could pay for the tuition and contribute to the library's income, so the other half could be chosen from families without the money.

Gennay's most difficult task had been to devise a test for the illiterate children brought to their door by parents equally lacking in learning. She agreed with her father that educating the most intelligent of Narkang's poor would improve the fortunes of the city, but Gennay had found picking the lucky ones a difficult and heartbreaking exercise.

'What was that?' Gennay asked suddenly, looking up from her desk.

'What, Mistress?'

'That sound, didn't you hear it?'

Sarras smiled nervously. 'I heard nothing, only the fire.' He pointed behind him where the fire was crackling merrily still.

'No, not that,' Gennay said with a shake of the head. She looked out over the balustrade, down at the hall below. There was no one there, the main door shut as she'd left it. 'I thought I heard a scratching sound.'

'Rats, Mistress? It's so cold outside, they'll be seeking out the warmth.'

Gennay frowned at him and he wilted under the look. 'I don't think ... ah, you're right, I've just been spending too long in this draughty old place.'

She reached for the next piece of paper. 'Oh, I don't remember this one at all – Barra Entashai, son of a cook and a dockworker.'

'Master Koyn met that one, I believe,' Sarras said. 'A cocksure street-brat he said.'

Gennay nodded, reading the short summary written by the ageing man who'd been her tutor for several years. 'Master Koyn said the same about my brother,' she said with a smile. 'It might be a sign of intellect.'

'He's older than the rest.'

'Not by too much. He passed the test easily, as you'd expect of one older – maybe we should see him again and ask something a little more difficult of him.'

Sarras inclined his head in acquiescence, but before they could move on to the next Gennay slapped her palm down on the desk.

'There! That scratching sound, did you hear it?'

He shook his head but Gennay ignored him and rose, leaning on the stone balustrade as she looked down at the hall below. 'I heard something, I'm certain – and it wasn't a rat, it was a more regular sound.'

'I heard nothing, Mistress,' Sarras said, bewildered. 'Perhaps you are tired and we should stop for the day.'

She turned to face him, poised to speak, but then closed her mouth again and thought better of whatever was on her mind. 'Perhaps you're right, I've kept you here too long. Get home to your supper.'

Not waiting for a response, she ushered him towards the door, suddenly irritated by his meek manner. Sarras went without an argument, casting one curious look around him when he reached the bottom of the stairs, but not lingering. They completed their rounds of the library in record time, Gennay marching through the dark rooms of each wing with a brusqueness that seemed to cow Sarras further.

As soon as they had finished, he was scuttling for his cloak, head bowed like a contrite novice. He had barely got it around his body before he was fumbling for the door and his words of goodnight came out as a frightened whisper, but before she could do anything to apologise he had set off across the courtyard, heading for home.

Gennay watched him go, then gave a start as she saw a flicker of movement in the dark shadows of the gate, as though someone had just stepped away.

'Sarras,' she called hurriedly. He stopped like a dog yanked back by its leash. 'Did you see a movement there?' she said loudly. 'Through the gate?'

He glanced behind him, then shook his head. 'No Mistress, did you see someone?'

'I ... I thought I saw someone step away. Have a care when you leave, just in case.'

Sarras nodded and took a tentative step towards the gate. He was not a brave man, but large enough that most cutpurses would think twice about approaching him on a street patrolled by the City Watch. Walking cautiously, he peered forward before he reached the gate, but saw nothing. When he hopped a few paces through into the street beyond, he whirled around, arms up to ward off a club, but nothing came and he lowered them again, abashed.

'There's no one out here,' he called almost apologetically.

Gennay nodded in relief and waved goodbye. 'Then I apologise, it's just my imagination. Thank you, Sarras, have a good night.'

He returned the gesture and made to turn away from the gate before catching sight of something further down the street. Attracting her attention again, Sarras pointed at something in the distance.

'I see Masters Pirn and Bewen coming to collect you,' he called.

'Thank you!' she replied, reaching for her coat as Sarras waved goodnight and disappeared around the corner.

Gennay shut the door again and slipped her coat on before heading back up to her desk to order her papers before her escort arrived. Pirn was a busy man and she didn't want him to be waiting around while she got ready. While tying the papers up she stopped abruptly and cocked her head to listen. The library was quiet again, silent enough that she could hear two pairs of footsteps in the courtyard.

'Daft girl,' she muttered, covering the fire again. Then she heard it, a distant whispery sound from somewhere down below. Gennay ran to the balustrade and leaned out, but the hall was empty.

'I'm sure I heard that,' she declared with more certainty than she felt.

She checked her desk. The piles weren't quite as neat as they could be but it was good enough so she raced down the stairs, determined to look at the reading room below before Pirn reached the door. Once there, however, her boldness faltered and Gennay found herself staring at the closed door for a moment.

'No, I'll not start being timid now,' she declared and yanked the door open.

Inside, there was nothing but shadows and a handful of books. In the gloom within she could see they had been left carelessly spread over the table; one of the scribes must have been looking for something and not bothered to tidy after himself. Gennay walked in and picked up the books, stacking them into two neat piles just as a crisp knock rang out from the door behind her.

'Coming,' she called over her shoulder.

Gennay left the room and started toward the door when a tiny breath of wind seemed to carry across her back. She gasped and whirled around, heart hammering, but there was nothing there. Her hand went to her pocket and closed around the knife handle, but the library was again still and silent. The reading room was dark, only the lines of furniture and books really visible within. It had a small window at the back that led on to an inaccessible light-well, but that was solidly barred.

'A draught can still creep past,' she muttered, watching the room suspiciously.

After a while of staring, she felt her eyes begin to water with the effort. As they did, the twilight seemed to shift and move slightly, reaching towards her. Gennay gave a small gasp and took a few steps back, but then she blinked and the gloom in the small room returned to normal.

'Mistress Gennay?' called Pirn from behind the door.

'Coming,' she replied, suddenly desperate to be away. She fumbled a moment with the key, one eye on the room behind her but nothing seemed to move there now. Gennay wrenched the door open and stormed out, almost barging Master Bewen out of the way in the process.

'Mistress? What's happened?'

'Nothing.' Gennay gave the room one last, cautious look, then shook her head and handed over the ring of keys. 'No, just my imagination again, I'm afraid. Master Bewen, the keys are yours – no cheese for your supper, I hope?'

The night watchman smiled and shook his straggly white hair. 'No, Mistress, a nice warm pie tonight.'

'I'm glad to hear it,' she said brightly. 'Come on Pirn, it's cold out here!'

'Aye, Mistress,' the retainer said with a suspicious look. 'Good night Master Bewen.'

Gennay marched across the frosty courtyard as quickly as the ice and snow would permit. At the gate she glanced back to where Bewen stood watching them. He saw her looking and ducked his head, closing the door with a thump.

'All still fine, Mistress?' Pirn asked as he moved ahead of her, through the gate.

She followed him and looked at the near-empty street suspiciously. Off to the right she saw a figure at the far end, half in the shadow of a doorway and conspicuously still.

'Who's that?' she mused.

Pirn took a step forward and squinted, but she realised his eyes wouldn't be good enough to make much out in the dark.

'I don't know. Should I fetch a watchman?'

'Because he's standing out in the cold? They might want a little more reason than that. Foolishness is not a crime, despite my brother's opinion on the subject.'

Gennay squinted at the figure, trying to make anything out. She could tell from the clothes and stance that it was a man, perhaps broader than average with a tradesman's coat and hair that was either fair or greying. While this was a better part of the city, the man's clothing wasn't so out of place, but he did appear to be staring directly at them which was unusual.

'Doubt he's a thief,' Pirn said eventually. 'They'll not hang around so long once noticed.'

Gennay nodded and on cue the man turned and disappeared around the house he'd been standing by. 'Well, he's gone now.' She pulled her hood low over her face and brushed a flake of snow from its brim. 'Time we did so too.'

'Aye, Mistress, but keep an eye out for him again, mind.'

She nodded and stamped her feet, feeling the cold more deeply than ever. 'I will, now move yourself, that mention of a pie has made me hungry!'

Arms wrapped around her body, Gennay hurried down the dim corridor of the guildsmen offices towards the warmer main hall. It was dark and cold here, and near-silent with only three men working in one small office. They had a fire lit there, but the scribes jealously guarded its warmth and resented every second the door was open.

Here in the corridor it was as cold as the street outside, Gennay guessed; bare stone was ever cold and the ceiling high enough to draw all warmth away. Her head felt heavy and fogged, as though she'd been at her father's brandy, but she knew it was just a combination of the cold and sleeplessness.

From nowhere a grey shape appeared beside her. Gennay yelped and reeled away, crashing into a door on the other side of the corridor and falling through it as it yielded to her weight. The faceless spectre hissed and raised its billowing grey arms towards her, lurching forward as Gennay scrabbled on the floor of the empty room.

She screamed and kicked wildly, trying to flee but her boots found no purchase on the musty rush-strewn floor. At last her heel caught something and she pushed with all her strength, slamming the door on the creature as she drove herself back and half-upright.

The phantom shrieked and Gennay screamed again, fighting her way to her feet. She heard running footsteps in the corridor, but couldn't bring herself to move anywhere but back until her shoulders were against the barred shutters of the office window. There she stood, trembling in the darkness, until the door opened again. Her hand was on her knife-handle by the time she recognised who it was; Sarras, the chief scribe. He peered fearfully around the door, not seeing Gennay for a moment but when he did the man gasped and opened the door fully.

'Mistress Gennay? Are you hurt?' Sarras asked as he advanced towards her, but Gennay didn't hear him as she saw a grey figure on the ground behind the man.

Her mouth fell open as the figure moved. It wasn't a ghost at all but a young man, one of the scribes in her employ.

'Oh Gods,' Gennay gasped as Miriss sat up, one hand holding his shoulder. 'It was just Miriss.'

'What happened?' Sarras gave Miriss a puzzled look, clearly unsure who was the injured party.

'He startled me; I just saw a grey shape appear, thought ...'

Sarras reached out a tentative hand for Gennay to take and she did so gladly. 'He tried to grab you?'

'No, just appeared suddenly in his robe.' She gave a nervous laugh. 'It's a novice robe from the Temple of Death, isn't it? Fate's eyes, I hadn't realised he'd even taken a novice vow.'

'Yes, all orphans they take in become novices,' Sarras said, still too confused to join her laughter. 'He was wearing it against the cold.'

'I didn't, I didn't know ... Is he okay? Miriss, I'm sorry, you startled me.'

The scribe was only a winter or two younger than Gennay, but smaller than she and thin too. The door slamming onto his shoulder had knocked him flying and she could see from his face he was still too dazed to hear her.

As her heart calmed and her wits returned fully, Gennay

realised his face was contorted by pain. One of the other scribes touched his right arm and the young man gasped and recoiled. The shoulder itself looked strange and lumped.

'Oh no, it looks dislocated.' She advanced a step and the supine scribe's eyes widened with fear.

'Sarras, quickly – take him to the bonesetter near the old baths, tell them to send the bill to my father.'

The scribe nodded and helped Miriss to his feet while Gennay watched anxiously from a distance. It took both Sarras and the other scribe to help Miriss to the door and down the stairs to the main entrance. She followed them, cursing herself under her breath and ignoring the curious faces from the team of carpenters at work in the main hall. Sarras wasted no time in getting Miriss out the door and across the treacherous courtyard, the three men walking together like some fantastical beast.

Gennay followed them out and stood in the courtyard, realising her hands were still trembling. The shock had only intensified the ache behind her eyes and for a moment her eyes blurred until she screwed them up tightly and leaned back against the library's stone wall.

'I'm losing my mind,' she muttered, her moment of nervous laughter gone entirely.

The previous night she'd managed only an hour's sleep at most and when she'd arrived at the library it looked as though Master Bewen had done worse than she. When she'd questioned him about it, the night watchman had been evasive and uncomfortable – clearly keen to get away from the building despite his protests that the night had been entirely uneventful.

The sun was going down now. She could see the sky darkening and had found herself over the course of the day dreading nightfall. What little sleep she'd managed last night had been a collection of jumbled, disjointed dreams, ones that had reminded her of Bewen's own.

She'd been walking through the library's corridors just as she had when Miriss surprised her with the hood of his robe down low – except in her dreams they were strangely unfamiliar and threatening. The shadows had lain thick on the ground, sometimes obscuring walls or blocking her path. She'd been forced to turn down corridors that did not exist in the real library, but were interminable in her dreams.

All the time, Gennay had sensed someone watching her, or something. She heard footsteps echo through the courtyard, but when she opened a set of shutters she saw no one there. In an empty room she had sensed a constant presence, always just behind her shoulder, out of sight but as close as her own shadow.

After a moment of recollection, Gennay was chased back inside by the cold evening air. Not so biting as the previous day, it was still too chilly outside to be there with only a shawl around her. Back inside, she saw the workmen packing up for the day, also eager to be home before the pale daylight vanished. She ignored their anxious looks as she headed up the stairs, but at the top she realised they were all facing her way. She curtly bade them a good evening and headed for her desk, the look on her face enough to see them out as soon as they'd dropped tools and found their coats.

Within a minute, Gennay was alone, sat at her desk with her head in her hands. As she stared at the page below she found the words squirming under her gaze and the throb in her head increased until she closed her eyes again.

'Oh I'm so tired. I'm tired and stupid,' she muttered, vainly massaging at her temple.

She sighed and stopped, tentatively opening her eyes as though afraid of what she might see. There was nothing there, just a mess on her desk and the cold empty library all around her. The one lit lamp in the room was on her desk and the rest of the hall was becoming increasingly gloomy.

As she sat there, she felt the shadows intensify and grow threatening. A sudden sense of panic blossomed in her stomach. She glanced around and saw there were no looming grey figures now, just a disquieting emptiness, but that failed to help her spirits.

'Right, I'll go home before the light's gone,' she declared with flimsy resolve. 'I don't want to be here after dark and clearly I'll get nothing achieved in this frame of mind.'

She covered the fire and carried her lamp downstairs – moving with exaggerated briskness to make as much noise as possible, suddenly afraid she'd hear the rustling of pages again before she left. She collected her coat and extinguished the lamp, sparing a last glance for the twilit library. Nothing stirred.

'Master Bewen can check the library tonight; I'll send him back with the key.'

With that she left and locked the door behind her, hurrying across the courtyard until she was in the street and not so completely alone.

'Dangerous streets, these,' said a voice behind her. 'You might want to be careful as you go.'

Gennay jumped, her hand going to her mouth to cover a scream as she whirled around. There was a man behind her, stocky with greying hair and a commoner's clothes. She took a step back – it was hard to tell, but he looked like the man who'd been watching her in the street the previous day.

He was older than her; a few winters older than Pirn, Gennay guessed, with as many signs of a hard life etched into his face. His grey hair was not quite unkempt but, as with his clothes, some attention to it wouldn't have gone astray.

'What is that supposed to mean?' she asked, taking another step. He didn't attempt to make up the ground but stood beside the wall, a mocking smile on his grubby face.

'Well, you're out here now. That makes it dangerous to my mind.'

'This street's well patrolled by the Watch. If I scream they'll come running soon enough.'

The man just smiled in a vaguely patronising way, reminiscent of Gennay's brother in that it made her immediately want to slap him. 'I ain't the one who just popped a man's shoulder out.'

'What? How do you know about that?'

'I passed your gaggle of scribes, put it back in for 'im. I've seen it done a few times in the past, the longer you leave it the harder it is to get it back in. Good thing he's a scrawny little bugger that boy, not much muscle to get in the way.'

'And they told you I did it?'

'Well, said he'd fallen badly after you startled him. Sounded odd, but I ain't the sort o' man to rule out the curious.'

Gennay put her hand in her pocket, just in case. 'And what

sort of man waits to address his betters in the street after performing such a service?'

'One who wanted to talk to you anyway.'

He pushed off from the wall and took a step forward. She couldn't see a weapon on the man, but his coat was easily long enough to hide a dagger or short-sword and there was something in the gleam of his eye that made her feel even more vulnerable than she had in the library.

'Well, I must leave, and I suggest you don't follow me – my father's steward will be meeting me and he doesn't take kindly to your type.'

'Few men do,' the stranger agreed with a grin, 'but that's life for you. I'd appreciate it if you did spare me a little time however, Mistress Thonal.'

She froze. 'You know my name?'

'Aye, there's a lot of talk about this library you're building – learning for the common man and such.'

'You wish to be educated?'

The man chuckled at that and shook his head. 'I've got my letters and a whole lot more learning besides, but I've given up hoping I'll ever appear educated. No, it was the library I was interested in, was hoping I might find some information in these books of yours.'

'The library is not open to the public, the collection is barely starting to be assembled. The valuable works have not even been delivered, if that's what you're looking for.'

'So quick to judge,' he sighed. 'I'm not looking to steal, just to learn some odd bits of history, and about the Knights of the Temples. Someone said you were getting copies of their libraries.'

'Then come back in the morning,' Gennay snapped, making to move away. He stepped towards her, not quite barring her path but making it clear he could if he wished.

'I'm more of a man of the shadows myself, was hoping I could borrow your key and look at a few works before the steward and watchman arrived to lock up for the night.'

Gennay shivered. 'Even if I was willing to let you, I doubt you'd find the shadows in the library to your liking.'

'Eh?' He frowned. 'Not to my liking? There something wrong with the shadows in there?'

'What? No, it's just ...' She shook her head. 'It's nothing, just an idle comment from someone who's not slept as much as they need to. Sir, I don't know who you are, but I cannot allow you access to the library, not until it is officially opened and certainly not unattended.'

He regarded her without speaking, as though trying to puzzle something out. Before the stranger could say anything more however, a voice came from down the street and they both turned.

'Gennay!' called a young man, hurrying forward through the snow. He wore a long cloak but as he closed the man flicked it aside to make clear to the stranger he was carrying a sword.

'That appears to be my cue,' the stranger said. He gave her a small bow. 'Thank you for your time, Mistress Thonal – keep a weather eye on those shadows.'

Gennay gasped at that last comment, but he was off before she could overcome her surprise and reply. The stranger trotted away towards a side-street, not with undue haste but he covered the ground quickly and had disappeared around the corner by the time her brother reached at her side.

'Gennay? Are you well?' Emin asked, giving her a worried look. 'Who was that?'

She forced a smile and nodded, trying to ignore his piercing stare. Her brother's eyes were a lighter shade than hers, so pale a blue they were halfway to white and even she found them unsettling when he asked questions in earnest.

'Quite well, and the man didn't give his name – he was just interested in the library.'

'That's all? You look like you've seen a ghost – did he threaten you? I can catch him still.'

She raised a placating hand. 'Nothing like that, he just unnerved me.'

To emphasise her point she took hold of her younger brother's arm. Emin was hardly rash, but protective of his sister and sufficiently skilled with a sword that he'd easily outmatch the stranger.

'That's all?' Emin lifted her head to look his sister straight in the eye. 'That's not like you, to be so frightened by a stranger for no reason.'

'I've been taking fright at all sorts of things this week, jumping at shadows,' she said, managing a brief laugh. 'I'm over-tired, little brother, that's all. My mind's been playing tricks on me because I'm not getting enough sleep – if you'd spent any time at home this last week you'd have noticed that.'

The corners of his mouth twitched. 'Uncle Anversis has had me out by nightfall, watching shadows as it happens.'

'So you've not been drinking and whoring all night?'

'Not so much as you think.' His smile was a wicked gleam. 'And anyway, where's the fun in paying a woman? Far better to talk her into it.'

Gennay raised a hand to stop him. 'I don't want to know the details, just as long as none of my friends are involved.'

'Best you don't know then,' he said firmly.

She shook her head, trying not to laugh. 'Well, at least it won't be the virtuous ones, I know you well enough for that. Why has Uncle Anversis got you chasing shadows?'

'Ah now, it's for a better reason than you might think. We'd been discussing malign spirits for reasons, well, reasons of far too much wine to be frank ... however, it led us down an interesting path; that of drummer boys in these winter months.'

'Drummer boys? You mean those gangs of youths who walk through the streets making a racket and trying to extort money from people?'

As she spoke, Gennay shivered and Emin slipped an arm around her shoulders, setting them on the path home. 'They're the ones; Uncle claimed they were performing a service to the city whether they knew it or not. I thought they were nothing more than a bunch of common thieves. So of course, a little evidence was required and I've spent a few evenings on rooftops watching them come and go to see what nasty spirits were chased away by the commotion.'

Gennay laughed, the sound abrupt and startling in the evening quiet. 'Oh honestly, the two of you drink too much. So, once you watched the hordes of the Dark Place chased from Narkang's streets you thought it was time to escort me home?'

Emin just smiled his infuriating smile. 'Something like that, yes. Come on, enough shadows for the both of us today, I think.'

The next day came and went in a flurry of activity. Gennay started the morning late, her mother insisting that she rest rather than be heading to the library before dawn was fully established. It had the desired effect and when she did leave the family home it was with a renewed spirit and fervour for her work.

Engaged in practical details of the offices and cataloguing the largest crate of books thus far, Gennay had no time to even think about the strangeness of the previous days. By the time the light waned and the library was taken over by shadows, she was as ready as the others to head home, weary but undaunted.

By the next day, the scribes in the guildsmen offices were working on their first commissioned work and the library, for the first time, offered a glimpse of the place it would one day be. As the sun sank to the horizon and the craftsmen left, Gennay stood side by side with Sarras on the mezzanine, looking down at the hall below.

'We're getting there,' she said at last, the pair of them savouring the shared sense of achievement. 'It's been one of those days when I feel we got something proper done.'

'That we have, Mistress Gennay,' Sarras agreed, looking more at ease in her company than he ever had. 'Perhaps we should close up early today, in celebration?'

She turned, knowing he was not one for laziness. 'Are you trying to be gallant, Sarras?'

The tall scribe blushed and lowered his gaze. 'I apologise, Mistress, I hadn't intended it to sound that way.'

'But?'

He hesitated, then bobbed in agreement. 'But you need more than one good night's sleep, and you're not the only one. My imagination's been playing tricks on me too and some of the young clerks have starting taking fright at nothing. Today was a good day, Mistress Gennay; let's not allow our own foolishness to change that.'

She smiled, wanting to laugh and hug the man but knowing she could do neither. 'Very well, I do see your point. Go on then, chase your scribes from their offices and send them home. I'll tidy up here.'

Sarras went as instructed, taking the ring of keys with him to lock up that end of the building on the way. Gennay damped down the fire beside her desk and set about arranging the piles on her desk, piles that had only grown larger now more books had arrived and she was in the middle of preparing a card index. She stacked everything neatly and walked around the desk as the first pair entered the hall, two young copyists talking excitedly.

She smiled and wished the earnest young men a good evening, but as she did so her sleeve caught the pile of index cards and spilled them across the floor. To make it worse, a half-dozen or so kept going and scooted over the swept flagstones, ending up halfway down the stairs.

'Oh for pity's sake,' she muttered, surveying the mess.

'Do you need a hand, Mistress?' called one of the copyists, halting at the main door.

'No, you go on,' Gennay said, shaking her head at what she'd done. Her mood was good enough, however, that she was soon smiling at her carelessness and dismissed the pair with a wave. 'Get yourselves off home, I'll be done here in just a moment.'

Her smile became broader when, as she waved, she discovered one of the cards had managed to get stuck inside the voluminous sleeve of her green woollen dress. It fluttered out and before she could catch it, swooped down to join its fellows on the stair.

'Oh honestly, how did I manage that?'

The remaining scribes soon followed the first two, each calling goodbyes to Gennay, until there was only Sarras waiting for her by the main entrance.

'Start without me,' Gennay said in a slightly muffled voice as she bent low to pick up the cards. 'I've dropped a stack and will need a while to put them back in order.'

Sarras assented and went to lock the south wing door that led to the guildsmen offices before he started towards the kitchen and stores. Gennay fetched the last of the cards and carried them back to her chair, arranging the pack against her stomach until she had a single, ordered block again.

From downstairs came the click of latches and scrape of bolts and for a moment Gennay pictured Sarras as he went through the routine. They were both meticulous people and she could easily imagine each sound as it came; Sarras always followed the same routine every night. Eventually. there came the nearer scrape of the door into the hall and the oiled click of its lock, but then there was a few seconds of silence.

Gennay frowned at the cards in her hands, surprised at hearing absolutely nothing until a slight grunt of annoyance broke the quiet. She smiled; Sarras had spotted something out of place. No doubt one of the workmen would be receiving a telling-off in the morning.

There were footsteps and the creak of a hinge, then a gasp. She looked up. That wasn't the sound of a man irate. Gennay set the cards down just as Sarras emitted a strangled whimper. At the balustrade she leaned over and saw Sarras backing into view, his face white with terror. The scribe had his mouth open and arms raised as though about to ward off a blow.

The keys tumbled from his unresisting grip and clattered on the stone floor. His whimper grew into a fearful keening and his hands shook with fear; so terrified was he that Gennay watched him stagger a few steps away and then his knees simply gave from under him and he collapsed onto his behind.

That seemed to break the spell for both. Gennay raced down the stairs, but before she could reach Sarras he had scrambled to his feet and run for the door, shrieking. He slammed it behind him hard enough to rock it on its hinges and rebound, swinging back towards Gennay and crashing against a table behind before she could make up the ground.

Instinct made her falter, but then Gennay was out of the open door. The cold wrapped around her exposed face like a whip and she faltered, seeing Sarras slip on the frosty cobbles but fight his way up again and barrel onwards, crying out piteously all the while.

Gennay turned around, a sudden spark of fear in the pit of her stomach. Through the open door she could see the left-hand of the two reading rooms past a tall shelf stack, its door half-open. Inside, it was dark and she couldn't see much but she pulled out her knife before edging forward all the same. There was a stack of books on the table, one open upon it, but nothing else that she could see through the gloom. She blinked. The shadows behind the desk seemed to squirm as she peered hard enough for her eyes to water and blur. When she looked again all was still, but before she had a chance to investigate further an inhuman shriek came from beyond the courtyard, followed by a heavy thump.

Gennay turned, almost dropping the knife in her alarm. There were shouts and screams coming from the street. Without stopping to grab the keys to the library, she ran towards the commotion. More voices added to the clamour, horses and humans all panicked and fearful. She reached the gate and stopped dead, uncomprehending of the chaos in the street at first. There were people running towards her from all directions, men shouting and somewhere a young child howled. Torches bobbed through the evening mist, lending the scene an ethereal air.

A coach drawn by two bucking horses was hauled to a halt by its driver, dragged askew across the road, and a coachman had jumped from it before the wheels had even stopped turning. He ran to the back of the coach and Gennay saw a bundle of cloth there on the ground. The cold seemed to intensify around her, fear freezing her gut and numbing every sound and sight.

The coachman rolled the bundle of bloodied rags over and Gennay felt a scream well up through her body, but no sound escaped her paralysed lips. As the coachman turned away she caught a glimpse of the bundle's face and the terror in Sarras' dead eyes, his neck twisted unnaturally.

Gennay backed away from the sight, ignoring the shouts from somewhere further down the street. But then she stopped and, with dread, looked back across the courtyard at the library entrance. Through the open doorway, the lamp flickered and shadows danced on the wall behind.

'Something he saw? The room was empty, no?'

Gennay nodded, unable to stop herself glancing at the now-shut door to the reading room. It was late in the evening, but Gennay had insisted on returning to the library after supper and her brother had accompanied her.

'Are you certain it was empty?' Emin persisted. 'Did you look inside yourself or were you more intent on Sarras as he fled?'

'What are you suggesting?'

He shook his head. 'Nothing as yet, I'm merely wondering if there could have been someone in there to frighten Sarras. You watched him run from the building, it would be natural for your attention to be drawn to the movement of that and miss a small detail of someone staying still.'

'Emin, go and inspect the room yourself, there's nowhere to hide!'

'Not without help perhaps,' he countered, 'but there are ways and means to conceal one's presence – trickery in addition to magery.'

Gennay stood and prodded Emin in the chest. 'And what exactly was he doing in there, this mage? What horrors did he conjure to frighten Sarras so and for what purpose? This is a library, Emin! There's nothing of value or importance here.'

'Not true, there are books – information. Knowledge is power; this could be someone opposed to the education of the masses or aware of a secret hidden in the books you've had copied, unable to get at it without alerting the owner.'

'And risk their interest be declared to the Land at large as a death is investigated? Killings attract attention, Emin, surely you realise that? A man would have to be desperate to go so far – and if that was the case, why was I spared? I know more about the library and its contents than anyone else, why not approach or try to kill me first?'

Emin ignored his sister's blossoming anger and sat back on the corner of her desk. 'Murders that look like accidents aren't investigated much. Perhaps Sarras' death was a warning to you, a threat of what could happen. You told me a man approached you in the street a few days ago, asking about the library and wanting to get at its contents.'

'He was a vagrant,' Gennay interjected, 'more a ruffian than a mage!'

The smile turned indulgent. 'They don't all wear silks, dear sister; I've met mages who are dangerous and hard men.'

'Don't be such a braggart,' she snapped. 'Patronising a few

dockside taverns doesn't make you an expert on the darker side of the Land. You're a fool for any man who acts the rogue, worse than any simpering girl hoping to find a heart of gold. You've always been willing to swallow whatever guff any scarred veteran comes out with, and pay for his beer as you drink it in.'

Emin was silent a moment and remained sitting. For a moment Gennay saw a flash of anger in his pale blue eyes but then it was gone.

'And you, dear sister, have forgotten I'm not a little boy any longer. I may love a tale of adventure, but I can tell when a man's lying and – more importantly in the dockside taverns – when he's going to try and murder me for my purse. I know more about this city than you ever will because of what I hear between the lies – the criminal gangs and worse, whose city of Narkang is unlike yours in every way.'

He stood abruptly and walked away from the argument. Gennay watched him descend the stair like a cat, with neat, quiet steps. 'Time to inspect this room that so frightened poor Sarras.'

'Emin, please—' The words died in her throat as Gennay went to the balcony overlooking the hall.

Her brother paused mid-step and looked enquiringly up at her. It occurred to Gennay that her brother was dressed in a far more sober manner than usual – as he had been the night he'd frightened off the stranger too. The quality and cut of his clothes were fine, but without adornment beyond a tiny family crest embroidered in black on his grey collar. With his assured smile and a duellist's poise he looked far more the merchant adventurer he doubtlessly claimed to be in those dockside taverns, rather than the ferociously intelligent noble son he was.

'Please?' Emin echoed. When she said nothing more he gave her a small nod, acknowledging her unvoiced concerns. 'Trust me, Gennay, I don't frighten so easily as Sarras – I'll walk calmly away from whatever horror is lurking within.'

Without waiting for a response, Emin crossed the hall and yanked the door open. He took a half-step inside before stopping dead and gasping. Gennay felt her breath catch but in the next instance she saw the total lack of fear on her brother's face.

'Is that supposed to be funny?' she demanded.

Emin cocked his head in a non-committal way she recognised easily enough.

'Emin, a man died here, show a little more respect than you do the rest of the Land. When I do find out which of my friends you're chasing after, I'll be sure to tell them the story of when you got your head stuck in the banisters.'

'Feel free, it makes me seem loveable.' He smiled and stepped to one side so she could join him at the entrance to the reading room. 'Well, here we are, face to face with the horror of your untidiness.'

She looked inside. The room was as she'd left it, a small packing crate of books still on the floor under the desk and perhaps two dozen on the shelves on either side, with a handful more scattered over the table top.

Gennay took a tentative step forward before a surge of exasperation washed away the last of her fears. She marched in, Emin following close behind, and started to collect the books from the table.

'I don't know who keeps leaving them like this. It must be the foreman, or one of the workmen looking at the illustrations.'

Emin rounded the table, nudging one book so he could inspect the gilt lettering on the spine before reaching the far end where another had been left open. He inspected the page and turned it over to look at the leather cover.

'Then your workmen have strange tastes,' he announced, holding it up for Gennay to see. 'This is one of Father's – well, the copy he had made for the library.'

'Not so strange really. That page it's at, the plate's very striking. Most likely they were just leafing through and lingered on an image they liked.'

'Aryn Bwr's return to Keriabral?' Emin looked doubtful for a while as he inspected the page. 'Seems an odd one to linger on. If memory serves there are several of Zhia and Araia Vukotic that a labourer might find more interesting.'

Gennay raised an eyebrow. 'Oh really? And might those be the ones where the artist is said to have used local prostitutes as the models for the heretics? Honestly, Emin.'

He flicked past a dozen pages until alighting on one illustration. 'Ah, Zhia, my first love!'

'Don't be so disgusting!'

'Hah, well none of your friends could ever match up to her,' he said and raised the picture for Gennay to see. She looked away with a snort which only added to the young man's glee. 'Brilliant and beautiful – monster or not, I'd like to meet her before I died.' Emin laughed. 'At least – a decent length of time before I die, not just a few moments! Araia I just feel sorry for.'

'Sorry for her? She's a heretic, cursed to be an immortal vampire for her crimes against the Gods! How can you feel sorry for that?'

Emin returned the book to its original page, his face serious once more. 'A heretic yes, but not one whose share of the blame should have been equal. The five Vukotic children all received the same punishment for their crimes, but Araia and Feneyaz merely followed their brilliant siblings. They were the most remarkable family ever to have lived; the two lesser children would have had little option but to follow where the others led.'

'They still had a choice!' Gennay protested, her irritation as much with Emin perusing the pages while talking as much as what he was saying.

'Perhaps, but how much of one we'll never know. The pressure to follow their family and the orders of their king must have been immense.'

He hesitated and picked the book up to bring it closer. Gennay saw Emin's lips move slightly as he re-read some words, then looked up at her.

'Who copied these?'

'This one? It must have been the monks out at Dastern Monastery, they did all the copying of Father's religious works.' She frowned at his expression, aware Emin was rarely so intent and serious on any subject. 'Why, what's wrong?'

He didn't speak for a while but stared at the wall, obviously trawling his memory. At last he did speak, but when he did Emin sounded uncharacteristically hesitant. 'I may be mistaken; it's been a while since I read this ...'

'Emin what is it?' Gennay demanded. 'Stop being cagey, I've

never once seen you incorrectly recall anything you were interested in so tell me what's wrong.'

He nodded, still looking distant. 'Aryn Bwr's return to Keriabral – the page this was left opened at. "As the ghost hour began, the great heretic returned to his fortress of Keriabral to find it fallen to siege. What once were mortal men now feasted upon the dead and desecrated the gardens of his beautiful fastness; the children of Larat and Veren suckled upon the marrow of his queen's bones."'

'Those lines aren't in the original, I'm sure of it. The breaking of Keriabral was a celebrated victory – a heroic sacrifice by the Yeetatchen who knew Aryn Bwr would soon return and they needed to destroy his greatest castle before he wiped them out.'

Gennay took the book from him. 'And this isn't in Father's copy?'

'I'm certain of it, the lines have been inserted – but what monk would do so? The implications are, well, significant to the reader's impression, especially considering the crimes committed by Aryn Bwr's forces during the war.'

As Emin spoke, Gennay scanned the page and then turned to the next, looking those lines over as she did. She frowned and turned back, then switched between the two quickly.

'This page has more lines, the script is cramped. It looks like a new page with the adapted text inserted into the book.'

Emin began to look around the room rather more carefully than he had before, inspecting each shelf individually and even the table itself. 'Strange it was this book open at this page, when Sarras took such fright he ran out into the street and under a carriage. More than strange, that's a coincidence I don't care for.'

'What are you looking for?'

He bent to look at the underside and legs of the table. 'I don't know,' Emin said eventually, not appearing to have found anything of interest. 'Perhaps this is simply some monk angry at the Gods and inserting heresy into this text by way of revenge.'

'But you don't believe it.'

Gennay closed the book and tucked it under her arm, clearly intending to inspect it further and see if there were any other passages she would need to have removed.

'So what then? Some daemon creeping its way out of the Dark Place to irritate me? Frankly, they'd do a better job by rearranging my index system.'

As though defeated, Emin slumped down into one of the reading room's chairs. He looked puzzled and perturbed and, for perhaps the first time in her life, Gennay saw him properly confused about what was happening around him, but instead of cheering her up the sight just rekindled her own buried anxiety.

The worry of the past week caught up with her again and seemed to add gloom to the already dim room. Under the weight of it her limbs felt sluggish and weak; she joined Emin in sitting and the pair remained silent for a long while.

'If this was the work of some bitter monk, he's a petty man even by the standards of his profession,' Emin announced at last, 'and it still doesn't account for Sarras. If it was a complete coincidence, the two circumstances meeting like this, it means we know nearly nothing about either – yet if they are linked somehow, the link entirely eludes me.'

'Sarras saw,' Gennay said quietly, 'or thought he saw, a ghost. No, don't look at me like that, I've not gone mad. This past week has seen more than a few strange happenings, I've felt a presence on several occasions and heard what I've put down to rats more than once. Though he denies it, I'm sure Bewen has experienced something out of the ordinary—'

'Bewen experiences life through a bottle of whatever he can get his hands on,' Emin interrupted. 'He's hardly a reliable witness.'

'And how about me? Do I meet your standards of reliability or do you think me just some foolish, over-excitable girl?'

Emin bristled at the accusation. 'Don't put words in my mouth. Have I ever treated you that way? Ghosts are rare in the Land, far more so than most people believe, but rats are rather more common. Anyone working here late will hear strange noises, man or woman, so a drunk's confirmation is no confirmation at all.'

'What about a man so frightened he bolted from the building with no thought to his own safety, nor mine?'

Emin had no answer for that and his frown only deepened. He looked his sister up and down, then reached into his tunic and pulled a silver chain from underneath it. 'Here, take this.'

Gennay did so. The chain was nothing remarkable, strong and simple, but from it hung two very different charms. The first she recognised; a finely-worked charm with Death's bee symbol in the centre, made for a finer chain than the one Emin wore it on. The second was made of iron and simpler, consisting of three long horse-shoe nails bound together with wire, their points curled back on themselves to form hoops at the end.

'What's this second?'

'A witch's charm, for warding off malign spirits.'

She put it down. 'Are you mocking me?'

'Not at all,' Emin insisted, his face serious. 'If there's any mocking to be done, it would be of me. This is what I've worn whenever I've been following the drummer boys, trying to see spirits flee their path. Ghosts should fear Death's symbol and anything bolder should hesitate before a witch's blessing.'

'You expect me to wear it?'

He shrugged, the hint of a smile returning to his face. 'I expect you to be sensible. We don't know what's happened here, but it doesn't hurt to take precautions in case it *is* something supernatural. At the moment all I can think of is to rule out possibilities. If a ghost or spirit is on the table, so to speak, these charms should either ward it off or tell us answers lie elsewhere.'

'Why don't we have the library exorcised while we're about it?' Gennay said sharply.

Emin's smile widened. 'Exactly my thoughts – it can't hurt now, can it?'

To Gennay's astonishment her brother was true to his word. When they returned to the library in the grainy morning light, a tall, black-robed priest of Death was waiting for them at the courtyard gate. He cut an ominous figure, motionless with his hood up and not a scrap of flesh exposed to the pale sun. Against the clean new stone of the wall he echoed his forbidding God even more than usual.

'Unmen Karanei,' Emin said, greeting the man warmly after he bowed to kiss the large oval ring bearing Death's rune the unmen proffered.

Gennay did the same and received a nod in response, but it was to Emin that the priest finally spoke. 'Master Thonal, a pleasure as always.'

As Emin led them into the courtyard, the priest slipped his hood back and revealed a face quite incongruous with his soft, educated voice. Gennay suspected he wasn't a Penitent of Death by the man's robe – most penitents raised to the level of unmen retained a sign of their impious past – but Karanei had a soldier's face.

His grey-shot hair was trimmed and neat and his cheeks freshly shaven, so there was no disguising the two parallel scars that ran up from jaw to crown up the left side of his head. One cut crossed his ear and left a neat diagonal line on it, the other had sliced off the very top corner – Gennay had seen similar injuries before but never so neatly side-by-side.

'Karanei is an unusual sort of priest,' Emin explained, seeing Gennay's surprise. 'We're fortunate he is in the city, he really is the very best at what he does.'

'What he does?' she echoed, the fatigue of the last few days meaning she took a moment to understand. 'You're a daemon-hunter?'

'It certainly wasn't a bear that did this to me,' Karanei said sternly, indicating his scars.

Despite Emin's obvious amusement at the scene, Karanei looked impassive, either bored with continually explaining himself or just uncaring of what Gennay thought.

'Is that even sanctioned by the cult these days? Emin, this is ridiculous. If news of this gets out the library could be ruined by gossip before it's even opened!'

'You suspect there's a ghost or malign spirit in the building?' Karanei demanded. 'Yes? Well, then you want an exorcism. How do you think that's done? An ordained priest bears Death's touch and can pray and conduct rituals which may drive off whatever's there, but may do nothing whatsoever.

'If you want to be sure, find someone with a spark of magic – that way they know what they're dealing with, can add some force if necessary, and discover whether they were successful. There's always the possibility that you just piss the spirit off and it tries to claw your head off, so maybe being able to handle a more physical confrontation would be a good idea too.'

'And what are we paying you for these intangible services?' Gennay demanded, refusing to be cowed by some unsmiling renegade priest.

'You think I'm a fraud? Hah, you're more like your brother than I first thought.' At last Unmen Karanei did smile, but it was grudgingly done and fleeting. 'I'm here as a favour to Master Emin – this cock-sure little sod sticks his nose in more than he should, but he's helped me in the past. As for being sanctioned by the cults, of course I am – stipended too, so don't you worry about me demanding payment off anyone.'

He continued on to the main door and thumped on it for the night watchman, Bewen, to admit them. Gennay gave her brother a look but he pointedly ignored her as he sauntered past, his usual infuriating smile on his lips, and she found she didn't have the energy to upbraid him further. When Bewen pulled the heavy door open he gave a start at the sight of Karanei, but managed to compose himself well enough to bow as the priest of Death swept past.

Gennay watched the man do a quick scout of the great hall, assessing every room and exit in a glance, before reaching into his voluminous sleeve to fetch something from underneath. It was left to Emin to offer Bewen a half-explanation and relieve the man of the keys, firmly ushering the bemused watchman out and shutting the door on him.

'There, we're alone now. The other scribes won't be in today, I sent them all a message last night.'

'Good, scribes tend to be an excitable lot. The last thing I need right now is a load of them shrieking like eunuchs.'

Karanei extracted a slim bag from his robe and produced a misshapen stick of chalk from it. He went to the furthest door, which led to the north wing, and drew a large rune with swift, confident strokes, muttering under his breath as he did so. Out from this he drew four lines of script, more angular marks that looked like unfinished runes until he went back over them and overlaid them with a strange curving script.

'A charm of protection,' Emin explained as Karanei went to

do the same on the door behind them that led to the guildsmen offices, 'activated by magic imbued into the chalk.'

'Indeed,' Karanei commented, 'and merely a precaution, Mistress Thonal – I take my personal safety rather more seriously these days. Emin, do you remember your studies well enough to do the windows?'

Without waiting for an answer the priest reached into his bag again and tossed Emin a second shard of chalk. The young man did as he was told, pausing only for a moment when Karanei went to inspect his work.

'Godless wretch,' the priest muttered sourly at what Emin had drawn on the windowsill, a simpler symbol than Karanei's but still nothing Gennay recognised.

Whatever Emin had done, Karanei's expression soured but he made no effort to erase the image, only touching a finger to the runes and moving on to the next. Before long the room was finished and he produced a small lumpy candle which he proceeded to rub the wick of like a firestick until it sputtered alight. He set the candle on the floor and sat before it, palms angled towards its flame as though he was warming his hands.

Emin beckoned to Gennay and led her to the stairs, heading up until they were standing beside her desk and only able to see Karanei's head over the balustrade.

'He's going to be a while,' Emin whispered, perching on the corner of her desk. 'Rather than do some general exorcism he'll give the energies in the building a gentle nudge, see what's here and whether there's any point.'

'And if there is?'

'He'll slap it down pretty hard most likely – don't worry, it won't even notice us in the meantime.'

'I thought ghosts only came out at night?'

Emin shook his head. 'No; well, yes I suppose, but they're always there – it's just under dark they've got more power and people are more likely to be afraid at night, which makes them more susceptible.'

'So any ghost would be sleeping now?'

'Something like that.' Emin fell silent and returned his attention to Karanei.

It was clear he didn't want to talk any longer so Gennay busied herself with the index cards she had abandoned the previous evening, too tired to face the school's accounts just yet. No more than ten minutes later, the priest called up to them and made Gennay jump with surprise.

'Emin, is this one of your jokes?'

The young man hopped up and went to the balustrade. 'Jokes? What are you talking about?'

'That twisted sense of humour you believe you're famed for,' Karanei said with a note of irritation. 'If so, I don't get the joke and nor do I appreciate it.'

Emin glanced back at Gennay, then shook his head. 'No joke, I give you my word. Why? What have you found?'

'Nothing. Nothing at all.' Karanei eased himself upright, his face a picture of puzzlement. 'This is an old building and a man died in the street outside, but there's nothing here. No breath, echo, whisper or scent on the breeze.

'The building isn't just empty, it's been scoured clean. I've only ever seen this after an exorcism; the Library of Seasons itself is no more dead than this place.'

At Emin's request, Karanei performed an exorcism anyway, keeping his muttered complaints to a muted minimum. Emin had seen how Gennay had taken the priest's verdict and it worried him. Instead of being comforted by the reported lack of ghosts her shoulders had fallen and her attention pushed elsewhere. They had sat in silence until Karanei finished, Gennay shrugging off Emin's efforts at conversation and staring off towards nothing much.

Even once the priest had left she was not forthcoming, something that worried him further. Gennay made a show of busying herself with the many matters of the school that required her attention, but Emin could see that neither he, nor the project she was so devoted to, occupied her thoughts.

'Gennay, talk to me.'

'I am.'

Emin bit back a frustrated reply. 'No you're not, not really. Karanei's news upset you, didn't it?'

'Of course not. The library is not haunted by anything but my fancy; that's good news.'

'Is that it? Is that the problem—'

'Emin, enough!' Gennay snapped. 'Stop interrogating me, this is my business, not yours! Whatever the problems in this library they are mine to resolve and do not require the hand of some overly inquisitive fool who fancies himself as an adventurer.'

'Hey now, there's no call to lose your temper.'

'Isn't there? Look,' she said, pointing to the piles of paper on her desk. 'All this needs to be done and more will have appeared by the end of the week. You may have no cares in the Land, free to play whatever role you decide, but I don't have the luxury.

'I doubt you've bothered to think much about my future, but I assure you others have. Grandmother has more than one scheme on the go to marry me off before midsummer's day. I'm a noble-man's daughter, useful only to provide children to some brainless young fool of good breeding, who'll most likely get drunk one day and find himself spitted on the end of my brother's sword for some slight or idiocy.'

Emin took a step back. Gennay was an even-tempered woman and rarely flew into a rage, but once there she was not one to be talked down easily.

'Well, turning on me won't help a jot, I'm only here to try and help.'

'How exactly?' Gennay asked, slapping the desktop with her palm. 'Aside from wasting my time with your reprobate acquaint-ances, what have you done to help beyond sending my clerks home so another day's work is lost and the date for the library's opening a day closer?'

'Gennay, a man died here yesterday,' Emin said. 'You cannot expect his friends and colleagues to march to their desks the fol-lowing day.'

Gennay took a breath and looked down. 'I know,' she admit-ted, 'but nor can I afford to fail in this. Sarras was my friend too, but he knew how important this was to me – as it was to him. It's my only defence against an arranged marriage and he knew it – why do you think he worked so hard? It wasn't for the wage I paid him, nor just out of natural diligence.'

Emin hesitated. 'Are you saying ...?'

'Oh of course not! Don't be such a bloody child, not every-thing comes down to sex! He was my friend. Do you understand the concept? He didn't want anything from me except the chance to prove he could do a good job, but we were friends and he wanted to help me succeed.'

She rose and prodded Emin in the chest, anger inflamed once more. 'You've never really understood friendship, as contemptu-ous as you are of all those less intelligent than you, but one day you'll have to learn people have a worth that cannot be measured by intellect or strength.'

She stepped back, suddenly deflated and Emin saw her shoulders sag as she continued in a quieter voice. 'You're my brother and I love you, but your tendency to see folk as tools to be used, or problems to be tackled, will be your undoing – mark my words. Now, please Emin, go away. I need to be alone.'

He opened his mouth to protest, then closed it again. Nothing he could say would help matters. Gennay just needed her own space to grieve in whatever way she could.

'As you wish, but I don't want you to be alone here today.'

'Emin, I will be fine,' Gennay said, shaking her head. 'You heard your friend, there's no ghost haunting these halls. I ... I would prefer to be alone. Please?'

He nodded, unhappy but unwilling to press the matter. 'I'll return this evening to look in on you.'

'That won't be necessary,' Gennay said. 'You can tell Pirn to come as usual, but I don't need my brother babysitting me.'

Emin bit his tongue and acceded. As he left, Gennay didn't look up, but just when he closed the main door behind him Emin heard a small sound emanate from the mezzanine where his sister sat. Unable to tell whether it was the barest of sobs or a sigh of relief, Emin stood at the door for a dozen heartbeats caught in indecision.

Eventually he turned and headed back across the courtyard to the street beyond. The morning felt warmer than previous days, the wind off the ocean having lessened, but still the young man pulled his coat tight about him as he walked. Out in the street he looked around at every person in view.

None seemed to pay him any mind, everyone busy about their day when the short winter days curtailed so much, but just as he was about to move off he noticed a shape that could have been a man in the shadow of a building. He squinted but could make out nothing at that distance. The house was the best part of a hundred yards down the street and it was hard to be sure, but the longer he looked the more he sensed it was more than just his imagination.

'Unless my sister's malaise is catching,' Emin muttered as he started out towards the building.

Well before he reached it a carriage trundled down the street and obscured his view. It was mere seconds before he could see his destination again and nothing appeared to have changed, but something told Emin his prey was gone. He walked without haste, crossing the street after the carriage had passed, but once he reached the overhang where a water butt stood the area was certainly empty.

Emin went as far past the water butt as he could without trespassing, to a small wooden gate a few yards behind. Pushing up onto his toes Emin could just about see over the gate, but there was only a child in the yard beyond, playing with a long length of rope until she saw him and stopped to stare back.

Satisfied no one had gone that way Emin returned to the water butt, feeling rather foolish now.

'Clearly it *is* catching,' he muttered as he stood at the water butt, 'but this would be a good vantage point. Far enough to remain unobtrusive, but with a direct line of sight to the courtyard gate.'

His eyes alighted on the water butt itself, an old wooden cask roughly lined with pitch. Its upturned lid was pushed askew and a leaf hovered precariously at the exposed gap. Emin plucked it away and was about to straighten the battered covering when he noticed a cross had been roughly scratched into the wood. He ran his fingers over the wood; the scratches were light but had been done by something stronger than a fingernail.

'As someone might do if they were standing here, watching and waiting.' Emin smiled and shook his head. 'But perhaps that's something of a stretch.'

He chuckled and flipped the lid over so it was the right way up, then straightened it so it sat snug on the butt. On the other side someone had scratched a circle in approximately the same position.

'Now that's curious.'

He ran his fingers over the mark. It hadn't been made with any great care or skill, nor was it a single, unbroken circle. Instead it had been done in a number of curved strokes, overlapping and of varying lengths.

'Which makes it even less likely to be anything significant,' Emin pronounced at last. He raised the lid and flipped it over quickly. The two symbols did correspond to each other, but most likely it was just they naturally occupied the same place each time some bored labourer had played with his knife while he waited.

'For pity's sake, now I'm looking for a mystery in everything. A cross and a circle mean nothing by themselves. Even combined they're just a rune without context so why am I wasting my time?'

Emin slapped the lid back into place and headed back into the street. Gennay clearly didn't want him at the library, but his interest had been pricked and he wasn't going to let go of the matter yet.

'There are more possibilities to rule out now malign spirits have been,' he mused.

He took the next turning off the street and started towards the old town district of the city, where many of the city's mages lived in relative isolation from the chaos of everyday life. Perhaps one of them would be able to provide the answer.

After a frustrating day, Emin returned to the library just after sunset, to find a pair of men in heavy coats loitering outside the door, arguing quietly. In the dark he didn't recognise them immediately and when he called out it was with his hand on his sword handle.

'Master Emin?' one replied. It turned out to be Pirn, his father's retainer, with Bewen the night watchman peering out from under his battered cap. 'I'm glad you're here sir, perhaps you can help.'

'What's going on?'

'Mistress Gennay won't let us in, she's locked herself inside.'

Emin scowled and pushed past them to thump heavily on the door. 'Gennay, it's me – open the door!'

'Emin, go away – leave me alone.'

'Don't be so bloody stupid, when have I ever done that?'

There was no response. 'What brought this about?' he asked Pirn.

'I don't know,' Pirn said. 'When we got here she said she was staying for the night and refused to open the door.'

'She didn't open the door at all?'

Both men shook their head. 'Couldn't hear anyone with her, sir,' Pirn continued, 'but something's not right, this ain't like her.'

'No, no it isn't.' Emin thumped again on the door. 'Gennay, open the door, I'm not going away.'

'And I'm not leaving the library tonight,' she called from behind it. 'Whether it's my own fears or something else, I've had enough of jumping at shadows and dreaming of ghosts. I've barely slept in days and I'm going to stay here until I work this out.'

'As you wish,' Emin replied, 'but to get rid of me you have to open the door and prove to me you're alone in there.'

'What are you talking about?'

'Indulge me.'

'Oh for goodness' sake,' Gennay said. At last she turned the key in the lock, giving the door an exasperated kick as it stuck briefly, then opening up and stepping aside for Emin to see in while still holding the door.

'Satisfied yet?'

'No.' Emin walked into the library, pushing her arm out of the way without comment as he inspected the room. Pirn and Bewen took one look at Gennay's expression and stayed where they were, but short of grabbing Emin by the ear there was nothing she could do to stop him.

'You've fetched yourself some supper,' he noted aloud as he paused over a small parcel of wrapped cloth on one of the desks. The door to the reading room where they'd discovered the altered book was propped open and a lamp burned steadily on the far wall within.

'Are you facing your fears, or those of Sarras?' Emin wondered as he stared into the room, but when he turned to Gennay for an answer she just stared determinedly back.

'Finished your inspection?' she said at last.

Realising his sister was indeed alone, Emin agreed that he was finished. His initial fear had been someone inside preventing her from unlocking the door, but since that was clearly not the case he didn't have much way to interfere without sparking another argument.

'I've finished. Pirn, Bewen, you can both go home for the night. I'll watch over my sister.'

'You'll get out is what you'll do, little brother!' Gennay pointed out the door. 'Go on; leave me as you said you would.'

Emin inclined his head. 'I did say that, but I'll not go far. There's a pleasant enough tavern just down the street. I'll spend the evening there and keep one eye on this place, I think.'

'Well, I'll be here until morning, by which time I suspect you'll be dead-drunk and rolled into the street without your purse.'

'I'm sure I'll be able to take a room there, don't you worry about me.'

'Hah, so it's a whorehouse too? What trials you endure, dear Emin, to see me safe through the night.' She gestured again to the door. 'Well, go on then, go and play with your clap-raddled sluts and leave me to my work.'

Emin did as he was told, sending Bewen back with a message for their mother. Pirn refused to leave, claiming an obligation to their father for her safety. Emin didn't even bother arguing and instead invited the man to drink with him and share a few war stories at the nearest tavern – an upscale place where the occupant of the best table at the window was more than willing to give his place up to a richer man.

By the time a second jug of wine had arrived and they'd ordered the day's stew, Pirn started to relax in the company of his master's heir. They'd known each other for years, of course, but the strictures of society were a constant limitation.

'What about the Bales campaign?' Emin asked, pouring them both some more wine. It was weak stuff as they had a long night ahead of them, but slipping down very nicely in the warm corner they'd found.

'Aye, went on that one too. More've the same really; Baron Heshen never thought tactics were worth the effort.'

'I'm amazed you managed to survive any battle,' Emin laughed, 'with incompetents in charge at every step.'

Pirn nodded and scratched his whiskery cheeks reflectively. 'Guess you tried not to think too hard about that, you take their coin, you do what they say. Anyone who suggests a nobleman couldn't find his arse with both hands ... well, most ain't like yourself, Master Emin. We'd have been strung up quick as you like, so no one dared say such a thing.'

'What a fucking waste – Heshen only cared about having his way with every virgin he could find, so I've heard. His father before him liked to fight and liked to conquer, but didn't care much for much that didn't involve killing, and our present lord ...' At Pirn's expression Emin tailed off, but was unable to stop himself from grinning.

'Now Master Emin, I know you like a joke but I'm a loyal man o' Narkang.'

'Calm yourself, Pirn, I've no complaints about the duke – indeed, the way he manages his court is masterly, you'll see no defter a touch or tease in the best-reputed houses throughout the Land.'

Pirn frowned, but knew he couldn't say any more. A soldier of Narkang and firm in his view of the Land, Pirn's mood had soured at Emin's description – even more so for the strains of truth it contained. The Duke of Narkang was a man adept at flirting between factions and keeping them all breathlessly guessing which way he'd go. With powerful neighbours on three sides, political acumen was a requirement for any ruler of the Freeport of Narkang. For more than one reason was Narkang described as a whore of a city.

'No, what I find saddening is the lack of ambition from most rulers,' Emin continued after a pause. 'The years of gathering wealth and power, but not bothering to do something with it. I can't see how I'd be quite so attached to an heir to devote my life to consolidating his position.'

'You're young – and unmarried – Master Emin. Things look different on the other side of a marriage bed.'

Emin shrugged. 'I suppose, but why not leave something rather more lasting? I could name you a dozen rulers who fought for decades just to attain and keep power – but it's not as if you can take it with you. The priests of Death are rather specific on that detail.'

'Power's no small thing, sir, an' just keeping hold o' it's no small task. There's always someone hungry for more. If I might speak frankly?' Pirn said.

Emin nodded, one eye still on the dark environs of the library.

'Well, it's yer father's household, but there's not much restricted to his heir. If you'd grown dependent on the goodwill o' others, you might see it different.'

Without warning, Emin sat bolt upright, one hand reaching for his sword as he stared out the window.

'What is it?'

The young nobleman didn't respond immediately, frozen on the point of rushing for the door. 'Someone loitering by the library gate,' he said eventually. 'Not doing much, just waiting like a thief's lookout.'

In the darkness it was hard to see any more than the fact there was someone there. That there was a man was all Emin could make out, one in a coat and hat as would be expected on a cold winter's night. There was precious little light in the street, but Emin had paid the gateman of the house opposite to keep a lamp burning at his door and it shone enough to pick out shapes and movement across the street.

The man kept still, not pacing or swinging his arms to keep warm – he just lounged against the side of the gate with his back to the courtyard wall. Emin blinked and in the same moment thought he caught sight of some small movement – some dark shape flitting around the corner to the shadowed gate itself – but whatever it was, the gate remained closed.

'What happened?' Pirn asked, seeing Emin blink hard, then frown and squint harder.

'I don't know,' Emin said, 'thought I saw movement, a second man but ...'

Pirn eased himself around their table so he could look out too. The veteran's face hardened and his hand went to the dagger on his belt. 'Too close to be innocently standing out in the street at night.'

'Unless he's a decoy,' Emin pointed out, 'looking to draw out anyone keeping watch over the library.'

'Master Emin, this ain't the duke's treasury.'

Emin grinned briefly. 'A little too devious for my own good perhaps.' He rose and dropped a few coins on their table beside the half-drunk wine. 'Let's go have a talk with our friend out there, see what he's up to.'

The pair headed out into the chilly night and started down the opposite side of the street. Before they were out the door Emin was talking inconsequentially about some fictitious racehorse, knowing any conversation or lack thereof would carry over the crisp night air. It served no purpose however. Almost as soon as they had turned in his direction, the stranger started off from his post – not hurrying, but moving briskly away.

Emin gave Pirn a look. As one, they broke into a run and their quarry scampered around the corner of the adjoining building. In a heartbeat he was out of sight so Emin sprinted away from his companion and ran with all speed to the corner. When he got there the side-street was empty so he pelted on down it, keeping to the centre of the street to avoid anyone looming suddenly from the shadows.

At the next corner he checked around, but saw no one and he realised the futility of pursuit. There were a dozen hiding places for a man in the dark, some already behind him. Off to his left was the high rear wall of the library's grounds, difficult to scale and precious little within, but as likely as any other possibility.

Behind him, Pirn's heavy footfalls heralded the retainer's arrival, puffing hard at the unwelcome exercise. Pirn was fit and strong for his age, but anyone with that much white in their hair knew their running days were behind them. His cheeks were flushed and chest heaving for breath as he also inspected the street.

'He might have scaled the wall,' Emin said, pointing.

'Bloody acrobat if he did,' Pirn replied after a pause. 'I'm not getting over that.'

'If he did, he's not getting into the library easily,' Emin decided, 'so there's little point in following on the off-chance. Better to be near the front, Gennay will hear anyone breaking in – it's not impossible but every window's bolted so they won't be doing it quietly.'

With one last look around the seemingly empty street, Emin and Pirn retraced their steps to the courtyard gate. As the echoes of their footsteps were swallowed by the night, Emin noticed just how quiet it was, this far past nightfall. But for the few lights, he could have easily imagined them alone in a deserted city.

What sounds of life there were from other parts of the city were faint and unidentifiable. The strange sense of isolation made Emin feel unaccountably vulnerable in the patch of light he'd arranged to cover that section of street, as though he could sense invisible, hostile eyes watching him from the darkness.

'What was he doing here?' he wondered, trying to shake off his nervous mood.

He scanned the stonework of the wall, for a moment expecting to see crosses and circles scratched somewhere there. Finding nothing he entered the courtyard and looked around, taking a while to see into the lines of shadow along the far wall but eventually giving up his search.

'If he was acting lookout, then lookout for whom?'

'Probably just scouting; checking the coast's clear.'

Emin wasn't convinced. 'This is no housebreaker,' he said. 'There's nothing valuable enough to justify these efforts, so what's the purpose in all this?'

He stared up at the library as though expecting an answer from the building itself, but it remained quiet and dark aside from the trace of light from Gennay's lamp that shone through the library's high windows. Then an answer came and startled him into movement – a woman's scream tearing through the hush of night.

Emin ran for the door as Gennay cried out again, Pirn close on his shoulder. The door wouldn't budge, it was stuck fast and all Emin could do was smash his shoulder uselessly into the thick oak.

'Gennay!' he yelled at the top of his voice.

From within came a crash of something falling, then more

screams. He redoubled his effort, battering at the solid wood while his sister shrieked in mortal terror within.

'Mistress Gennay!' Pirn bellowed in his ear, more than willing to lend his own shoulder to the work but still it had no effect. 'There must be another way to get in!'

Emin stopped and frantically ran his hands over his clothing. 'Metal, what metal do you have on you?' He grabbed Pirn and shook the larger man like a rat. 'Metal! A brooch, anything!'

He ripped his cloak from his shoulders, bursting the brooch pin that fastened it and fumbling a moment with the remains. Pirn watched him with astonishment, but then Gennay screamed again and he was searching his clothes too.

'Ah damn,' Emin shouted suddenly, drawing his sword and holding it up. It was a slim weapon, made for speed on a city street rather than the battlefield, with thin curved metal bars forming the guard. Using a knife he scraped frantically at the leather grip until he'd stripped a piece away, then worked away at it until he could draw out a pin from the handle itself.

That done, he worked at the guard until it loosened and he could slide it over the blade, discarding everything but the guard. He dropped it on the ground and pushed it into the corner between wall and flagstones, stamping at an angle until it was bent out of shape. With the damaged guard and the brooch pin Emin set to work on the lock, working at it frantically while sounds of breaking glass came from within.

'Old man over in Arwood taught me,' he called as he worked, in answer to Pirn's unspoken question. 'Only learned it to sneak out of the house.'

It seemed to take an eternity, but at last Emin caught the pin he was looking for and felt something give way in the lock. He turned it all the way and jumped to his feet, pausing only to grab the stripped down sword he'd discarded. Inside, the library was a chaotic mess of books and dancing flames.

Emin looked around in desperation, but couldn't see his sister – the desk she'd set up to watch the reading room was overturned and the room itself aflame. The bookcases on either side of it were similarly burning, broken lamps spilling oil at their base.

'My cloak,' he yelled to Pirn who ran to fetch it, but before the man returned Gennay screamed again and Emin saw movement up on the mezzanine.

He ran to the stairs without waiting, keeping well clear of the burning bookcases that had each been set alight. Halfway up the stairs he faltered, not because of the flames that Pirn was already attacking, but at the sight of his sister. Gennay stood past her desk, turning wildly, one way then the next with her burning coat wrapped around a broken stick of wood.

'The shadows,' she shrieked, whether to him or the Land at large he couldn't tell, 'it's in the shadows!'

Emin looked around as he advanced up the stairs. He couldn't see anything unusual except for the speed with which the flames were spreading around the library. Downstairs, Pirn was beating furiously at the flames with Emin's cloak but seemed to be getting nowhere and already the haze of smoke filled the room.

'Gennay, come here!'

His sister whirled around, makeshift-torch held out like a weapon. 'I can't,' she sobbed, 'the shadows are out there!'

Emin hurried forward but Gennay took fright at his approach and backed off towards the straw-packed boxes of books she'd just set alight.

'Gennay!' he yelled, 'we have to get out! The shadows can't hurt you; I won't let them hurt you! But we need to get out of the library.'

She shook her head, moving constantly as though not daring to keep her attention fixed on him. Torch held out before her, Gennay turned left then right, fearfully looking all around as though there was a viper in the room.

'Gennay, stop!' Emin shouted as she set fire to the papers on her desk, but before he could do anything more she screamed again and lunged for him.

'No! I won't let you hurt him!'

Emin staggered back, slipping down a few steps before recovering his balance. His sister, oblivious, attacked the chimney's flank with a mad fury, beating at the stone with her torch until the coat dislodged entirely and dropped in a burning heap on the step.

At the loss of her weapon against the shadows, Gennay seemed to deflate. She fell to her knees, weeping with uncontrollable terror. Emin tried to pull her up but she was a dead weight in his arms and before he had dragged her down a few steps there came a sound that chilled his heart. The door to the library crashed shut.

He looked up to see Pirn run at the door, frantically yanking on the handle to try and pull it open again. It wouldn't budge and Emin saw him start to panic, running for the nearest exit to the hall but finding that locked too.

'Pirn!' Emin called. He ripped Gennay's keys from her belt and threw them to the man, then ducked his head under Gennay's arm and hoisted her up.

The flames seemed to deepen now, the air rapidly filling with choking smoke. Emin glanced back and saw most of the mezzanine was aflame. A gust of smoke rolled over them, causing Emin to heave and cough for a moment before he could get Gennay down to the ground floor.

'It's jammed!' Pirn wailed from the front door.

Emin ran over as best he could and grabbed the keys off him. In the smoky half-light of flames it was hard to see, but he realised the man had been using the right key. He shoved it in the lock and felt the key collide with something halfway – the lock had been blocked up.

'What's going on? The lock was clear!' Emin cried, working away with the key but getting nowhere. 'Someone's done this, someone's trapped us inside!'

He turned and tried one of the other doors, the nearest leading to the offices. As he tried keys, none of them seemed to work. There were only six in total and he tried them all, but none would turn the lock no matter how hard he worked at them.

'Piss and daemons, I can't move it!'

He glanced back; Pirn was holding his sister up and watching him anxiously. Behind him, shadows danced down the stairs as the flames rose steadily behind the balustrade. The rear way, past the reading rooms, was also blocked by a burning bookcase which had been pulled down across the corridor. Half the books had fallen out and they blazed bright underneath, but the new wood was also starting to burn already.

'Gennay! What have you done?' Emin wondered aloud,

realising it was she who'd fired the building out of some mad desperation to fight off the shadows. He turned back to the door to give it another try before he went for the one on the other side of the room.

A wordless howl from Pirn stopped him before he could even find which key had fitted best and in the next moment a strange whisper raced around the room with the crackle of flames. Emin turned and the keys fell from his hands as he gaped. There was a figure on the far side of the room. Difficult to make out through the smoke-filled air, it stood in the lee of the staircase, just before the door Emin had intended to try.

His hand went to his belt but Emin found he'd discarded his sword on the staircase and the figure seemed to know it, turning to the stairs briefly before the whispers came again, like distant chants and laughter mingled. It took a step towards them and Emin realised it wasn't the smoke that made it indistinct, the figure was no more than a shadow in the place of a man.

'What in Karkarn's name ...' Emin gasped before smoke filled his lungs and he began to cough and retch.

Gennay seemed to wake up at the sound of whispers and raised her head. Seeing the figure she started to scream uncontrollably, and so violently her body convulsed with the effort. It was all Emin could do to prevent her from smashing her head on the door behind them, while his head started to swim at the smoke in the air. Panic set in. He couldn't see any way out and the shadow-daemon slowly advanced towards them through the library's uncertain twilight.

Something on the mezzanine fell with a crash and a sheet of yellow flame rose briefly. Emin saw the daemon falter at that, becoming more translucent in the briefly waxing light. Pirn saw it too and began to howl about the flames as Gennay had been.

'The flames, the light keeps it back!'

Pirn didn't wait for a response and jumped up to run to the nearest burning bookcase. One arm raised to shield his face from the heat, he dragged a burning book from the pile there and tossed it towards the daemon.

The book clattered over the stone floor, missing the daemon but making it falter once more. Buoyed by his modest success,

Pirn grabbed a second and a third, crying out as he burned his hands but refusing to stop. Each one briefly diminished the shadow, but even those that passed straight through its body didn't stop it entirely.

'Pirn!' Emin spluttered through the smoke filling his lungs, 'it's not enough! We need a way out!'

Whether the man heard him or not Emin couldn't tell, but he didn't stop and now the daemon concentrated solely on him. Walking with predatory, staccato steps, the shadow peered at Pirn as he scrabbled around for more books. Emin struggled to stay standing as his head began to spin, a painful wooziness filling his mind as Gennay continued to wail. She lay helpless in his arms, taking deep breaths to scream and increasingly her cries were interspersed with coughs and wheezing.

He felt himself sink to one knee and didn't have the strength to stand again – he could only watch as the shadow suddenly darted towards Pirn with unnatural speed. It crossed the stone floor in one step, gliding as much as anything, to surge right up to the retainer's face just as the man turned with another burning book in hand.

Pirn shrieked in fear and fell back; collapsing onto the pile of flames he'd been dragging books from. In a moment his clothes caught and he began to flail wildly while the shadow stared down at him with malicious interest. The more he thrashed the more he became enveloped in fire and Emin barely found himself able to remain on his knees, let alone go to help the man. A dark pall seemed to cross his vision and Emin felt himself sink back as the effects of smoke took their toll, as the shadow at last bored of the burning man and turned its attention his way.

Through the darkness he saw a sudden light emanate from the main door. Emin lurched drunkenly around to see wisps of glowing white play around the jammed lock. The distant whispers in the air turned suddenly angry and sharp. In the next moment the door burst open and a man stormed through, light playing about his body like tendrils of mist raging at the dark.

A gust of cool wind accompanied him and Emin fell towards it, gasping for clean air even as he retched at the smoke inside him.

The flames in the room surged up to meet the fresh air and the shadow-daemon faded in the renewed light. The stranger looked around the room and stepped towards Emin, who blinked and heaved on the floor nearby. Through his blurred, confused vision it seemed to Emin that the man's outline remained where he'd stood for a heartbeat, a figure in white light standing in opposition to the daemon, but then it was gone and he felt strong hands under his arms.

With what strength Emin had left he pushed up, dragging his limp sister with him as the man hauled him toward the door. A scream of rage crashed around the library hall then was eclipsed by the roar of flames, but Emin had only one thought in his mind – escape.

They charged for the door even as it started to close of its own accord, the newcomer dipping his shoulder and riding the blow as he dragged Emin out—

And then they were outside, the cold of night rushing forward to meet them. They staggered across the courtyard and to the street beyond, Gennay loose in Emin's arms. As soon as they were out of the courtyard Emin crashed to the ground, his sister falling on top of him. The stranger pushed Emin's clutching hands away and tendrils of light again started to play around his body. Behind them there came another crash from the library, some large beam falling and taking part of the roof with it. The roar and crackle seemed to intensify after that, the fire renewing its efforts to consume the building entirely.

'I'm sorry, she's gone,' the stranger said, his voice hoarse with effort.

'What?' Emin coughed, 'No! She can't ...'

He turned Gennay's face towards him and saw the emptiness in her eyes, and the words died in his throat. He stared down in disbelief but the stranger didn't give him time to grieve. He grabbed the weakened Emin by the armpit and placed one hand on his chest as Emin began to cough again. He felt a warmth in his chest, a tingle of magic rushing through his body that seemed to fizz through his veins and burn hot and sour on his tongue. Emin's eyes widened with astonishment as his bones seemed to hum and resonate with the energy being driven through him, then a great surge forced its way down his throat and another coughing fit took him.

He bent and retched as he coughed, feeling the surge of magic race from his lungs with the force of a punch. To his astonishment a mist-wrapped cloud of smoke was expelled, to dissipate on the evening breeze as he gaped at the stranger. Whatever the man had done it restored Emin's wits and he looked at his saviour with a flicker of recognition.

'You, you were in the street?' he said, panting desperately. 'A few days back, you frightened my sister.'

The man nodded. 'I spoke to her,' he corrected, 'what frightened her was somethin' else entirely.'

He was a man past his middle years, dishevelled and dressed like a wandering tinker. But for the magic he'd displayed, there was nothing remarkable about this ragged stranger at all, but Emin found himself able to do little but stare in wonderment at the man.

'Who are you?'

The man twitched his nose and glanced back at the library. The flames continued to rise from its roof and shouts for water began to echo across the street.

'Name's Morghien. Guess you could say I'm the enemy of your enemy.'